MA

BABIES

"The Dark Before the Dawn"

by Jennie Moench

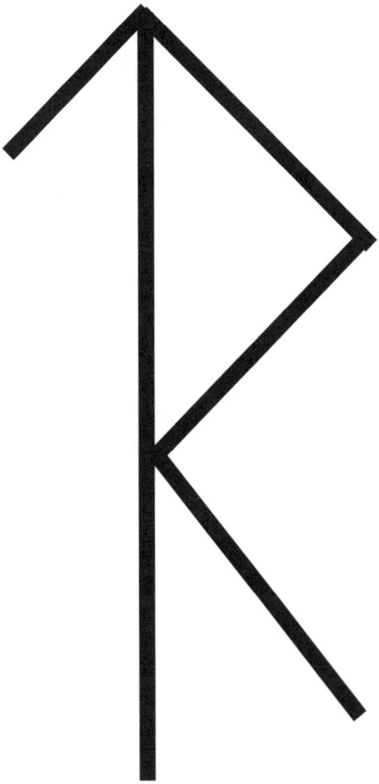

WARRIOR
Publications, Inc.

First Edition
A work of Fiction
Published by Warrior Publications Inc., Flint, Michigan
ISBN: 0-9722196-0-9

For my brother David,

I'll never forget riding in the car while you drove and taught me to read about the shy mole who broke away from the ordinary and had an adventure. You were the first to take me to an art gallery, first historical museum, first professional live theater performance, first drag show. I only wish that you could read this, my first novel.

PREFACE

August, 1873.

Silence. Unnatural silence. No chirping of birds, or rustling of the wind, not a sound. There, the sweltering heat baked a one room shanty, a festering blemish on the brown dust. There were no trees for shelter, and no grass to cushion the ground. The shack was depressed and desolate, like the dirt surrounding it.

Inside, a tall, pale young woman in agonizing pain lay silently on the floor in a corner. She suffered in silence, not wanting to call out as sweat ran off her thin body. Screaming would not change her ordeal, and she felt that she had no right to complain. She knew she wasn't worth the trouble. No one would help anyway.

Several yards from the house, a small wooden door sealed the entrance to a hole in the ground. The jagged pieces of rough lumber covered a room as large as the shack above. Burrowed under the cool earth, a long, thin man with white, snarled hair was busy stirring the contents of a cast iron pot with a long willow branch. A low flame under the hanging pot licked the sides and sizzled when the slop inside spilled over the edge. His wild blue eyes flickered occasionally as he stood mesmerized by the contents of the pot. His left hand trembled slightly with the inevitable weakness that comes with age. He rocked himself back and forth, gripping the top of the brace that held the pot that swung back and forth. Mumbling, he stared into the pot, waiting and waiting until a thick skin of brown slime slowly rose and popped. This made him smile.

"Almost," he exhaled slowly, softly, with reverence. He

gazed into the thick liquid. Bubbles formed around the sides of the pot. Then, in the center, a bubble formed. In it, he saw the young girl in the shack. She still lay in the dirt, dampened by her own sweat. Helpless and panting, she tore at the dirty cotton dress that bound her. Ian leaned into the pot, peering at the girl with interest. "Almost," he repeated in a whisper.

He stirred the liquid again, scraping the sides with the crude kind of whisk. Stepping back, he threw his head back and began humming to himself, gently rocking back and forth. Then he stopped and listened to her scream.

"Almost," he whispered once more. He looked into the liquid again, stirring thoughtfully. Another bubble formed. This time, she was propped up on her elbows with her knees bent and her legs spread wide—another scream. She pulled at her dress with one hand. She bore down with fists clenched with an agonizing wench on her face. "Almost," he hissed.

With eyes closed, he threw his head back again and hummed to himself. As he rocked back and forth, concentrating, he said "The baby will live. The mother will live to nurse the child and make it healthy." The old man concentrated on the baby. He wanted to be inside its mind, to be inside its little body. It was struggling. The man's heart began pounding harder and each breath became more difficult.

Finally, there was no more humming or rocking—just a quaking, tight feeling, like the pressure of being held underwater. With his eyes closed tightly, he squeezed his body together and pushed. He was oblivious to the black smoke gathering around him that was replacing the air with something else— a fuel for the fire.

Inside the house, the young girl's mother moved beside her on the ground. She had a sour, disgusted look on her face as she watched a dark mass emerge from between the girl's legs. She shook her head silently while the girl bared down. Unable to stifle her screams, no longer trying.

The baby's head slowly pushed out. A cloudy but transparent sac contained it— a witch's veil. Inside, it struggled, but made no sound. Lucy, the girl's mother, watched the whole thing anxiously, knowing that the newborn couldn't breath.

Maybe it won't live, she thought to herself. Maybe it will die. She continued to sit motionless, watching the pitiful little thing struggle in its airtight bag. She looked at its small, blue body lying on the dirt floor as its mother gasped and fell backward, breathing hard. Then another push, and the afterbirth came.

Still, the baby laid there, struggling a little less all the time. The young girl sat up and stared in disbelief at the baby enclosed in the bag.

Underground Ian lay on the floor, his eyes shut tightly, unable to take a breath. He was unaware of the black, hot smoke filling the underground laboratory. His body was hard with tension, his face was white and twisted, and his heart felt like it was about to explode. Then he felt total release as the young woman held her new born close to her chest. Tears rolled silently down her cheeks as her first born cried loudly. All the pain was forgotten.

Lucy looked on, indifferent. "You know, you should've let it die. Babies begot by their own grandpas usually turn out to be idiots."

The young woman just looked at her mother soberly, assessing the wiggling bundle in her arms. The infant made a soft cooing noise, looking up sweetly into its mother's face with intelligent blue eyes. The proud mother smiled. This child is no idiot, she thought to herself.

As Lucy stood up and walked to the open doorway, her expression turned to one of alarm. "Looks like Ian's started some kind of fire down there." The young mother and child were so absorbed in getting to know one another that they almost didn't hear, but then the earth shook violently with an explosion. Lucy screamed, "Now he's done it! He's going to kill us all!" She grabbed the sides of the doorway, holding tightly as the outside support for the overhanging roof fell to the ground. The young mother held her baby tightly, leaning over it to protect it from falling debris. When the rumbling quieted, a loud cracking and another boom proceeded the fall of the overhang as it collapsed and blocked the open doorway. Lucy jumped inside, lost her balance, and fell to the dirt floor.

Inside, the house was dark. The open doorway was all that had lit the interior. Unable to see, both women slowly moved to their feet. Dirt and sod from the ceiling showered from their hair and bodies. The baby let out a reassuring cry as its mother painfully stood and rocked it back and forth. The motion soothed the child into a quiet sleep. Lucy felt her way toward the blocked entrance. A jagged light shone through the left side of the door frame. Lucy carefully pushed her fingers through. She could hear a crackling noise outside. Slowly, she tried pushing the fallen roof out and away from the opening. It barely budged. With her foot, she pressed harder until the opening was large enough for her small frame to fit through.

Outside, a fire raged high above the wooden door to the cellar. Lucy shook her head and stood with her hands on her hips. "Looks like that hole will be his tomb," she muttered to herself.

The young mother squatted down on her knees, held her baby, and peered through the opening Lucy had made. She wanted to see, but wasn't sure she could safely manage crawling through the hole while holding her child. She knelt near the blocked entrance.

Outside, Lucy continued to stare at the red hot flames shooting up from the cellar where the fire was contained. There was no sign of life, and no noise except the crackling and roar of the fire. Then, a heavy black cloud of soot crawled up and over the flames. Slowly, it rolled into the sky and snaked toward her. As she watched, it curled around and embraced the house where the newborn suckled in its mothers arms.

CHAPTER 1

AUGUST 1973

Anastasia looked around herself. The sidewalks were busy for a Sunday morning. It was her day off, and she really didn't have anything to do. She was planning to visit her brother, but if something more interesting distracted her on the way, all the better. She was feeling light on her feet, not having any immediate concerns. She had that carefree feeling you have when you're only nineteen and have no one to answer to. It was often lonely living by herself, but the freedom from her dominating mother and the pride of being able to support herself, were worth the trade off.

Luckily, she lived close enough to her mother's house that she could walk there and visit with her older brother, sister, and father, as often as she dared. Granted, sneaking past her mother was treacherous. Sometimes she ended up walking back to her apartment without getting in. Worse yet, sometimes she would be chased back out, dodging various objects that were being heaved at her. She never could understand her mother's craziness. No one knew why her mother acted the way she did.

Away from the house, Anastasia was able to think about Marilyn, her mother, more rationally. She could detach herself and see things clearer after taking a step away from the situation. Now her mother's behavior seemed even more bizarre. Marilyn just wasn't like other people. Her obsession to dominate went beyond the limits of a sane person. As Anastasia grew up, there were so many things she assumed were normal that she slowly realized were forms of abuse.

The first time Anastasia snuck out her window was to spend the night at a pajama party. She was nine. By the time she made it to the party, it was almost ten at night. From outside, she could hear several girls laughing with a radio playing. The house was all lit up, and she could see her friend Cathy through a downstairs window. She was so excited to walk up the stairs to the front door. She rang the bell and the girl's father answered the door. Anastasia smiled up at him and explained that she had received an invitation, and she was an expected guest. The man looked behind her perplexed. Then her friend's mother stepped up from behind. "How did you get here honey?" she asked.

Anastasia frowned. "I-I walked", she stammered.

"It's nearly eleven o'clock. Your mother let you walk here by yourself at this hour?"

Anastasia's eyes darted down then from side to side. She wanted to get in so desperately. "Yes, she's working and couldn't drive me." The parents looked at each other. Then Cathy's father opened the door and let her in. Anastasia could tell they weren't convinced.

"Let's call your mother, just in case." Cathy's mother bent down and looked at Anastasia.

"But, she's at work," Anastasia insisted.

"Well, what time does she get home?"

"Not until tomorrow morning. She works third shift." Anastasia looked straight into the lady's eyes with the determination of a nine-year-old who wanted more than anything to be giggling with the little girls in the next room.

"What about your father?"

"Oh, he's dead." It was another lie.

The lady looked a little defeated. "Okay, but you better let me know if you don't have permission to be here."

"It's okay, I asked her before she went to work," Anastasia assured her. Then she turned toward the door that surely held the room of giggling girls.

It was wonderful, and Cathy's parents never complained about the noise. They gave the girls popcorn and soda. After hours of games and telling stories, the girls finally started to dose off, but the door was never locked. In fact, Anastasia noticed that there where no locks on the outside of Cathy's door. Anastasia was free to go to the toilet as many time as she needed to. She was even given permission from Cathy's mom to go into the refrigerator and get more soda. Was this the way other people's parents were? Anastasia was curious. After all the girls were asleep, Cathy and Anastasia talked quietly, lying on their stomachs with pillows rolled up under their chins.

Cathy laughed. "Oh, your mother doesn't really lock you up in your room at night, does she?"

Anastasia could still see the look Cathy gave her that night. She felt like an alien. How could her world be so much different?

Taking in a deep breath, Anastasia shook her blond tresses, tossing the memories from her head. "Today is my day off", she reminded herself.

She strolled closer to the river and noticed an abnormally large number of people. There was music. It was a festival. Anastasia smiled with anticipation. What kind of festival it was didn't matter. What mattered was that there would be new things to look at, and there was music. As of late, the only opportunity she'd had for music had been in the bars. She was still saving for a television, and would never dream of spending anything for a radio until she had her TV.

As jazz played in the background, some of the merchants on the other side of the street were having a sidewalk sale. Children grasped balloons and various things to eat as they were being led by the hand. Oh, this is perfect, she thought. Her mood was light again, and there was a little skip in her step.

As she approached the next intersection, she could see a

group of people gathering around something. A thin, grey haired lady with a small suitcase for a purse, an overweight man in a sleeveless t-shirt, and nine or ten others made up the crowd that was laughing and pointing. Anastasia pushed her way into the circle of people to see what was going on. In the center was the object of their attention, a mime. He was dressed in traditional black with a top hat and white makeup. His eyes were circled with black, as were his lips. His long, thin body and his smooth skin made him look youthful, although it would have been impossible to recognize him. Interesting, she thought.

She slowly circled around the crowd, peeking through the cluster of people. He was pulling the traditional mime rope and seemed to be preparing to hang himself. There- she caught his eye. She saw his dark brown eyes following her through the crowd. Then he stood on his toes, pulling the imaginary noose tight around his neck. He pointed to his hat, which was now laying at his feet. No one admitted to understanding the gesture. They just darted their eyes back to the imaginary noose.

Anastasia smiled. She could hear his angry thoughts. At that moment, he looked directly at her. Did he know she was listening? She ducked again between the people and continued her slow circle around the crowd. She stopped again behind a clean cut man, who was holding his young son's hand while comforting an even younger child who was strapped to his back. The older child, like many of the adults, was fascinated by the clown. Still, no one tossed a coin.

Anastasia noticed the mime slip something very quickly into his mouth. She might not have noticed if she hadn't been standing so close. Again, the mime looked directly at her, then glanced away. He was stumbling on his toes, making surprised and anxious faces at the crowd, tilting back and forth, back and forth. Quite suddenly, he jumped, and then jerked backward sharply. His head and body convulsed. Blood oozed out between his lips. The young boy screamed and grabbed his father's leg. The mime rolled his eyes back into his head in the most hideous way. The young boy's father, along with the rest of the crowd, stared in quiet horror. Another smaller scream broke the silence as the mime slowly spiraled to the sidewalk. Anastasia was the only one still smiling at the bloodied limp body. Amid the little boy's crying, she heard a female voice shout, "Call an ambulance!"

Then a bolder young man bent down and touched the mime's shoulder. To his shock, the mime quickly jumped to his feet, embracing the young man and kissed him squarely on the mouth, blood and all. Another hush fell on the crowd. Then slowly, as the mime began to gather up his belongings, the audience took on a hostile face.

The little boy was still clinging to his father. But now his father's lost look began to grow dark and angry. "You scared my son! What kind of a clown are you? You're supposed to be entertaining us, not scaring the pants off little kids!"

Others began to echo the same sentiments, and the violated young man with bloody lips stared dangerously at the mime. Anastasia stood quietly, taking note of the individuals who made up the angry crowd around her. Then she eyed the mime, who now faced the mob. Tipping his hat then bowing deeply, he picked an imaginary flower out of the air and presented it to Anastasia. She giggled and looked at him flirtatiously.

Making one last obscene gesture to his audience the mime turned and ran south down the sidewalk. The young man who had been kissed broke into pursuit. The rest of the crowd grumbled and watched with interest, as the two disappeared down an alley.

Anastasia looked down at her pretend flower, which she held carefully by its pretend stem. She stood there alone after the crowd had walked away. She was listening. Did he make it? She couldn't hear him, but she also couldn't sense any pain. Yes, he must be okay, she decided. She turned and walked north again, gently carrying her rose.

The festival was centered around a stage that was set up in a small park. People where lying in the grass, listening to a jazz band. Anastasia noticed that the group of people was really a collection of many smaller groups, little subsets, often made up of a mommy, daddy, and kids. She shrugged with a twinge of resentment. Then took her lone self to an empty spot and sat in the grass, holding her knees.

The music was gentle. A heavy black man on stage seemed to be singing a type of lullaby with his horn. She closed her eyes and took it all in. It was wonderful. For an hour, Anastasia sat there listening to one band after another, wishing her brother were there, too. Then the announcer told everyone to drive safely and to be sure to enjoy an evening of shopping and international food.

Slowly Anastasia stood up and walked back to the side-walk. She gave one more glance south before she turned again toward her mother's house. He's okay, she reassured herself.

Her mother lived in one of the older, small homes just off the main city streets. The house's wooden siding was in need of a new coat of paint, and the roof was beginning to sag in the middle. It wasn't in as poor of shape as many of the old and abandoned homes on this block, but it wasn't especially impres-sive either. It reminded Anastasia of her father— small, incon-spicuous, and tired.

She stopped two houses short of her mother's and darted between, then behind the row of houses. She walked through the yards, keeping an eye out for familiar faces. She cut the corner of the neighbor's yard and snuck up to her mother's back door. She stood beside it awhile, listening. There were no sounds.

Carefully she squeezed the handle to the screen door and opened it. She tried to keep the squeaking as soft as possible by pulling the door handle down. Luckily, the entry door was open. She peered in. Quietly, she stepped inside and closed the screen door. Then, on tip toe, she moved past the laundry room door, and past the closed doors of her old room on the right and her mother's on the left. The next room on her left was the kitchen, and on her right was the front room. She peered cautiously into the front room. There was her father, sitting in an old easy chair and looking back at her over his newspaper. He moved his eyes to the left to let her know that her mother was sitting on the couch, facing the TV. Luckily it was tuned to a noisy action flick that helped to cover the noise of Anastasia opening the closet in front of her and stepping inside. She held her breath a moment and listened. Her mother didn't notice, or she didn't care this time.

She grabbed a loop of rope hanging from the ceiling and pulled gently. A folded stairway slid out a little too quickly. Anastasia caught it, then gently lowered it to the floor. Crowded by a rack of clothing on one side and shelves on the other two, she still managed to squeeze onto the stairway and ascend.

The attic was dark and stuffy. A window fan hummed from a distant window. Pin holes of light escaped through the ceiling. As Anastasia reached the top of the stairs she turned to her left. Her brother was looking up at her from the edge of his bed, where he was reading. He reminded her so much of her father downstairs. He had the same beaten expression, the same dull brown eyes, and thick mousy hair that was cut in the most traditional medium length haircut ever invented. He was over six feet in height and stocky. He used to be thin and wiry, a few years ago. He waited for her to reach his bed before they whispered their hellos.

Anastasia could relax now. Their mother never came up here. Even if she'd heard them talking, chances were she'd ignore it. It would be too much trouble to run Anastasia out of her house at this point. She sat down on a cushion that was on the floor across from her brother. This was her spot. She was the only one who visited him anymore. Their sister, Stella, never came up.

"There was a festival downtown today," Anastasia announced to her brother.

"Yeah, I heard they were going to be having some kind of International Festival this weekend. Did you go?"

Anastasia looked up into her brother's face. She loved him so much. He was such a nice person, so concerned and giving. Why didn't other people see how great he was? He had few school friends and none as an adult. How old was he now? Almost thirty and still living at home. He was the oldest, and he always took care of his sisters as best he could. Anastasia wondered what he would do if anything happened to her and Stella. What would he do? He would have absolutely no reason to live. He only stuck around because they needed him. That was why Anastasia took great care to assure him of her dependence because she never wanted to be without him.

"The music was great! I wish you could have been there. Why didn't you tell me about it? We could have planned to meet there?"

Her brother's face brightened a little. "Next time."

"So, what are you reading?" Anastasia pulled the book's cover toward her to look at it.

"Oh, just an old book of poetry. Its copyright date is 1865. I found it in a batch of old books that came into the store Friday." He tossed the book to her and grabbed another from a stack next to his bed. "Now, look at this one. Its called *The Book of Enoch*. It was supposedly written by the grandson of Methuselah."

Anastasia's interest piqued as she carefully handled the second book he passed to her. The binding was old and dirty. The pages were brittle.

"I haven't finished it yet, but it's very interesting. It's just as old as several of the books in the old testament, but when the books of the Bible were being bound together, for some reason this one wasn't included." Anastasia glanced up at her brother and then returned her gaze to the sacred book in her hands.

"I know you'll be interested in reading it. It goes into detail about the time before the great flood, and even names the 'sons of God' who came down from heaven and corrupted us with their knowledge."

Anastasia straightened her back. "What are their names?"

He looked at her blankly for a moment Then he took the book back and studied it for the correct passage. "The first 200 angels came down to take wives and have children. Their leader was Samyaza. The other chiefs were..." He flipped a few pages and stopped, studying the text, then leaned toward his sister and pointed toward the unpronounceable names. "Urakabarameel, Akebeel, Tamiel, Ramuel, Danel, Azkeel, Saraknyal, Asael, Armers, Batraal, Anane, Zabebe, Samsaveel, Ertael, Turel, Yomyael, and Arazyal. We were taught sorcery, incantations, and the dividing of roots and trees. It also says that the women conceiving brought forth giants." He looked up at his sister thoughtfully before continuing. "And that Arazyal, he was the one who taught us to fight, to make swords, knives, shields, breastplates, and mirrors. You ought to read it when I'm finished." He handed the book back to Anastasia.

She leafed through the book. "Yes, I would like to." Looking back to her brother as she set the book on top of the stack of old books she continued, "let me know when you're finished." She intended to use the rest of the day with her brother, not reading to herself.

"So, what's Stella been up to?" Anastasia changed the subject.

"Same old thing." Her brother shrugged. "I think she's gotten worst since you left, but she's quieter about it. I keep seeing her in new clothes. I'm not sure if she's stealing them or stealing for them. I hope it's the first one." Then he looked down at her with a serious scowl. "You know what she does."

Anastasia just nodded. She knew. "I don't see her as much since she got fired from the print shop." For the last couple of years, they had worked together. In fact, Stella had helped get Anastasia her job. "Has she found another job yet?"

Her brother shook his head. "But I haven't heard Mom yelling about rent, so I figure she must be keeping up. I bet she's expecting to live on unemployment for as long as possible. We haven't been talking much lately. That's why I suspect she's doing it again. She knows I'd get mad at her, so she just doesn't talk to me."

Anastasia looked thoughtful. "I think maybe she came up to my apartment. Someone was banging on my door a few nights ago last week, but I was so tired that by the time I got to the door, no one was there. I've been working twelve hours a day, six days a week, for the last couple of weeks."

"Wow! You should be raking in the bucks."

"I hope so. I won't see it on my check until Friday. I think within a month I might finally have enough for a TV."

"That's great. It would be company for you." Anastasia's brother stopped and stared for a moment.

No, Anastasia thought, don't worry, I'll still be here visiting you. Her brother just looked at her for a brief moment to acknowledge that she had heard his thoughts correctly, then he went on with the conversation.

They laughed and talked for several hours. It was getting late. She had anticipated staying until her mother went to bed so that she could sneak back out. Her brother had made himself a rope ladder that she could hang out his window, but she decided against the inconvenience.

Besides, the rope ladder was really for emergencies. The reason he made it was because of an incident several years ago when their mother, during one of her rages, nailed the attic door shut while he was still up there. It was three days before Anastasia was able to get past her mother to pry it open. Stella and their father were too afraid of Marilyn to help him escape, although Stella did act as a lookout.

Carefully, Anastasia descended the stairs. Then she stood in the closet listening. She listened for thoughts, but also noises. Her mother had a way of deceiving her. There had been times when Anastasia knew that her mother was sleeping, yet when she came around a corner, there would stand Marilyn, wide awake with a wooden spoon in her hand. Anastasia had many a lump and bruise from such encounters.

Slowly, she opened the door and peeked out, careful not to poke her head out. Better to look and step out quickly, than to get your head slammed in the door jam. When she felt satisfied that it was safe, she stepped out and shut the door. Her brother would take care of the ladder. She paused a moment in front of the living room. Her father smiled at her again over the same newspaper and nodded good-bye.

Such a kind person, Anastasia thought. She often wondered if he was afraid her mother might kill him if he stepped out of line. Anastasia was inclined to believe she would. He quietly went to work every day, then sat silently in that old chair, never saying a word. He gave Marilyn his paycheck every week. In return, she paid the bills, cooked, and kept the house clean. They appeared to be the typical husband and wife who had grown up in the '50's, but the appearance was so deceiving.

After exiting the back door she jogged toward the street that would take her back downtown. The evening was perfect. The temperature was comfortable. She could even see a few stars, and the moon was a large yellow crescent. She tilted her head back and closed her eyes, letting the moon shine full on her face.

Marilyn sat with her back against the headboard of her bed. She was trying not to watch Anastasia's happy gait as she moved quickly over the sidewalk. There was almost a feeling of longing. What was it? Did she miss holding her child? Marilyn tried to cancel the thought, tried to push those maternal feelings away. They were a sign of weakness, that other women entertained, but weak was how other women allowed themselves to be. Marilyn didn't understand these other women, and didn't want to understand them. In fact, she hated them. She despised their cheerful acceptance of subservience. She despised men for creating and dominating the society that tricked her into wasting her life as a maid and nanny.

Her interest in her children had always been the knowledge that one of them would be her means of escape. She knew there was a sickness in her. Now she needed to hurry the process of Anastasia's flight to full independence. It was obvious that Stella and her brother would never make proper parents.

No, it was Anastasia. She was the best choice.

Anastasia reached her block sooner than she would've liked. It was such a nice evening on the empty moon-lit streets. She was tossing her head, letting the light breeze pick up fine strands of her hair and tickle her cheeks and neck. It was delightful, almost sexual.

Then, with a little start, Anastasia became aware of something. She looked around. Had she been too careless? Even though this was a familiar sidewalk that she tread every day, it was still downtown Center City. It could be dangerous.

She nervously looked around and behind her. No one. She sped up her uneasy pace and kept an eye out for shadows behind her. She tried to calm herself and concentrate on what she had heard. Someone was definitely watching her, almost like a predator watching his prey. Where was he? She kept looking around, increasing her pace. She took a key ring out of her pocket and arranged the keys so they stuck out between the knuckles of her clenched fist. She was almost to her door. Then, with a quick turn of a key in a lock, she swung her door open and backed into the opening. She took one last look both ways down the sidewalks from the security of her doorway, hiding behind the big metal door. Still, she saw no one.

She carefully closed the door and locked it. Then she sighed, feeling safe and secure once again. She turned toward the stairs. Moonlight from a window above the doorway lit the double wide staircase. Anastasia grabbed onto the railing. When she looked up, she froze.

At the top of the stairway was a landing that allowed two choices— to turn to the left, into Anastasia's apartment, or to the right, into Mrs. Brown's apartment. Mrs. Brown was a childless elderly lady who lived alone. Yet, inside her doorway, peeking out at Anastasia, was a man. He was tall and thin with wild piercing eyes. His shoulder length yellow hair was tangled and dirty. He stared at Anastasia for probably a full minute before he slowly pulled back inside and closed the door.

Anastasia felt very uneasy as she crept up the staircase. Who was that man? She listened hard, but couldn't hear anything. Mrs. Brown did talk occasionally of a niece. Could this be her niece's son? That feeling she had of someone watching her, it wasn't the yellow-haired man. He had been just as surprised to see her as she was to see him.

She unlocked her door and flipped on the light before she entered. Then she locked and bolted the door behind her. Too bad she didn't have a phone. Maybe she should knock on Mrs. Brown's door. She turned the corner to check her kitchen nook and then looked into the bathroom before she sat on her bed. Her apartment was one large room with a bed in the center. She had crates stacked up on top of each other with planks between them. This served as a shelf for her clothes and a few things. Her kitchen was really just a sink, cabinets, and a stove. The refrigerator was missing.

Anastasia was still preoccupied with worry about Mrs. Brown. She couldn't hear or feel anything. In fact, that was part of the problem. Why couldn't she tune into some kind of feelings from Mrs. Brown? Was she asleep? She and Mrs. Brown hadn't been on friendly ground since Mrs. Brown noticed Anastasia bringing a man into her apartment late one Saturday night. Anastasia could still see the blatant disapproval in Mrs. Brown's glare as she opened and then slammed her door. At the time, Anastasia had just shrugged it off— no great loss. Now she felt a little ashamed of herself. It was a dangerous thing to do, letting a stranger know where you lived and even inviting him in. She wouldn't have done it if she hadn't been drinking. But, she survived. Life goes on. Fuck her if she can't take a joke.

Anastasia got up and took off her shoes, brushed her teeth, peeled off her clothes and got into bed. Well, whatever the deal was with Mrs. Brown, she wasn't sending out any bad vibes.

Anastasia went to sleep.

CHAPTER 2

Breakfast was the usual bread with peanut butter and a large glass of water. Anastasia enjoyed looking out her window as she ate. It was part of her morning ritual. After showering and dressing, she started out the door for work, completely forgetting about Mrs. Brown's visitor.

Her eyes glanced passed her neighbor's doorway to the stairs. Then, what was that? Anastasia looked back quickly to Mrs. Brown's door. She could have sworn she saw a dark liquid running out from under her door. She stopped and squinted at the wooden floor boards. No, nothing. Uneasiness haunted her as she descended the stairs. She looked up one last time before she opened the door at the bottom of the steps and walked out.

Outside was the cool dampness of early morning. She was glad to have a destination, but sad at the prospect of spending her day inside working. Work was at the print shop, where she had been a full-time employee for over two years, starting when she was only seventeen. High school had gotten in the way of work, so she'd quit just before beginning her senior year.

School never taught her the things she needed to know anyway, or so she thought. She needed to know practical stuff, like how to run a printing press so that she could make a living. How would diagraming sentences help her make a living? Real people were never writers or artists. These were just make-believe people on TV. Real people had jobs they didn't like, to make money to pay their bills. And professional people, like doctors and lawyers, those people came from other neighborhoods and families that had nothing in common with hers. If she could just afford to have her own house and family some day, that would be— well, it was too much to dream about. She didn't want to disappoint herself by dwelling on such an ambitious dream. Just work hard and be happy where you are. That was always her philosophy.

The print shop she worked at was one of the larger ones in town. It occupied a large warehouse six blocks from her apartment. All but a small area in the front was used for the large presses, paper cutters, and temporary storage. She had learned to use every piece of equipment involved with printing, except the light up tables and tools that were used for layout and design. She had no desire to be trained on that equipment. That was where the creative people worked like Kevin and Brian. The owner, Mr. Lowe, was getting old. Every year, he promised to retire, but never did. He had an office where he spent most of his time. His son, Jack, was a husky middle-aged man who usually worked at the front counter when he wasn't running back and forth, checking orders and handling problems. Anastasia liked both Mr. Lowe and Jack. They were two of a kind, fair, but all business. They worked long hours and expected everyone else to do the same. That was why Stella had been fired.

She was coming in with a hangover too often and had started sleeping during her breaks. One day, Jack let her sleep and wouldn't allow anyone to wake her. When she finally woke up, he fired her. Anastasia felt bad that it happened, but she couldn't blame her boss for doing it. She knew she would've done the same.

Oliver was an older black man who had been with the company the longest. He ran the presses and was also a good worker, never late or absent. He kept to himself, but on occasion, when Anastasia had gotten too close to him in conversation, she noticed the smell whiskey on his breath. She suspected that he regularly drank his lunch.

Jim was almost short with a slight build. He was in his mid-twenties and drove the fork lift. He loaded finished orders into delivery trucks. He had been working there for seven years. He was good at repetitive work, but he had a hard time dealing with problems or changes from the standard procedures. He was slow, but a good worker, and was never late or absent. Anastasia loved Jim for his good nature, but also felt a special bond with him. They were raised by completely different standards, by completely different people. But fate had bound Jim with Anastasia and her siblings together. Jim was their brother. It was one of those secrets that everyone knew about. Jim was born second, four years after Anastasia's oldest brother. During a difficult delivery forceps were used. Marilyn suspected right away that the newborn had sustained an injury to its brain, but at first she thought it might heal. The baby was home from the hospital a full month before he began convulsing. Marilyn would have let it die, but her husband took him to the hospital. When it was discovered the baby had slight brain damage, Marilyn was quick to sign adoption papers. She wanted no part of a baby that was damaged.

There were three salespeople, two of them were pretty ordinary men, Jeff and Stan. The other salesman, Skip Morris, worked the front counter. He was always trying to be funny at someone else's expense. All too often, Jim was the one who got the bad end of his jokes. Anastasia didn't care for Skip, but she had to admit he was as nice to look at as he was obnoxious. Now that Stella was gone, Anastasia was the only female employee, and she liked it that way. Everyone treated her special, and she really preferred the company of men.

Today she was at the paper cutter, cutting business cards. They came off the press in large sheets. She was carefully cutting them into 3.5 by two inch squares. It was boring work, but she was nearly finished. She was making a game of it by timing herself, trying to increase her speed. A big ugly clock hung high up on the wall in front of her. She needed to cut one more stack of twenty-five sheets before first break.

"You're going to lose a finger," Jim said from behind her.

Anastasia looked over her shoulder. "Only if you startle

me!"

Jim's expression took on a serious note. "Anastasia, uh, what does 'oral' mean?" Jim stared at her waiting for an answer.

"Well, what do you mean, Jim? Like an oral book report?"

"Huh, well, Skip was asking me questions, you know, kidding around again. I'm not sure what he was talking about," Jim admitted in a hushed voice.

"Jim, just ignore him. He's a jerk." She shook her head.

"Okay, but still, what does 'oral' mean?"

Anastasia sighed. She knew this was trouble, but she answered, "Oral usually means spoken."

"Oh!" Jim smiled and walked off, looking as though he just caught the meaning of the joke.

A few minutes later, Anastasia was in the break room, which was really just a corner of the warehouse. It consisted of a vinyl-covered sofa, three chairs, two vending machines, and a coffee pot. Anastasia loved the free coffee with all the cream and sugar she wanted. It was heaven to be able to indulge herself without the remorse of spending money. She prepared herself a large, sweet cup of coffee, then sat back in one of the cushioned chairs. Skip and Oliver were already sitting near each other, involved in a discussion when Jim walked in with his biggest, most arrogant smile. He looked at Skip, then continued on to the coffee pot. Jeff, Stan, Kevin, and Brian all filed in behind him. Jim got himself a candy bar, then pompously settled into the sofa across from Skip.

"So, Skip," Jim interrupted loudly. "Just what kind of sex topic did you want me to speak about?" Everyone looked at Jim blankly, especially Skip.

"Or maybe you just want me to tell a sex story or joke?" The corners of Skip's mouth were beginning to curl, but he still stared at Jim with a confused look.

No one spoke. Then Jim piped up again. "Anastasia told me what 'oral' means, and I know what 'sex' means, so Mr. Smarty Pants, yes, I do like oral sex. Now I'm wait'n for you to tell me what kind of sex you want me to talk about."

Now everyone was staring at Anastasia, who was coughing up her coffee.

Stella rolled her long, lean body over in bed. She was finally starting to feel better. It was Monday afternoon, and she was still sick from Saturday night. She slowly sat up, swinging her feet over the side with her eyes still shut. Sitting on the edge of her bed, she groped the top of her night stand for a package of plain soda crackers. She had set them there early Sunday morning, when she'd first gotten into bed. Finally, her finger tips wandered across a lone cracker. It was stale and a little dusty. She crammed it into her mouth anyway and chewed slowly. Aspirin, she needed aspirin, but she didn't want to risk running into her mother in the hallway. What was that combination of vitamins her brother used to set out at night for her and Anastasia? It had always made her feel so much better the next day. Too bad the old stick-in-the-mud wasn't speaking to her. Where did he get his morals anyway? She sat there several more minutes, listening for movements outside her door.

She felt achy all over. Looking down at her long, thin fingers, she could see that she had lost a couple more of her plastic nails. Now she was down to five. She needed Anastasia to glue her nails back on and paint them, and to cut her pale yellow hair again. She just needed Anastasia. If I can just get up and around, that's what I'll do today, she thought. Maybe her sister would know what those hangover pills were, too.

Standing up slowly, then bending down at the knees to retrieve her jeans, she carefully emptied the pockets. There was a man's wallet. She pulled out a thickness of bills and began counting— still over $100. She didn't bother counting any higher. Inside the wallet, she also found a driver's license for a Daniel Montgomery. The picture showed a chubby man with a short haircut and dark eyes. Then she read the part that made her groan— his address. He lived in Center City, New York. He had lied. He said he was from Detroit! "God damn it," Stella swore aloud. All she needed was to run into the little toad some night.

What Stella did wasn't prostitution, it was robbery, and her last date hadn't been as drunk as she'd thought. He came to while she was stealing his wallet. That was when she hit him with an empty bottle. That was why she tried to only "date" men from out of town. Run-ins with prior dates were always ugly.

Anastasia was glad to be on her way home. She planned to fix herself something to eat, then read, or maybe play solitaire. But as she got within a block of her apartment, suddenly there he was again. He had spotted her. She could feel it, the same as last night. Someone was watching her. She slowed down and looked around. The streets were fairly busy, but no one seemed to be paying her any attention. She scanned the sidewalks. A skinny black man with ragged clothes gave her a toothless smile. She nodded, but quickly walked past. It wasn't him. It was coming from somewhere else, across the street maybe. She was glad for the daylight, but still uneasy.

Finally, she reached her apartment. To her surprise, stuck in the crack of the door was a flower, a red carnation. She pulled it out and looked around, but no one was near. She opened the outside door, and then she looked up the stairs.

Feeling childish, she realized that she was scared to go up and afraid to stay down. Why, all of the sudden did she feel so frightened and vulnerable? She'd been living alone for over a year. Why was it just now starting to make her paranoid? She decided that the best thing to do was climb the stairs as quickly as possible.

She had bound halfway up when Mrs. Brown's door popped part way open, revealing the same rag tag blond man. Anastasia stopped abruptly and grabbed the banister to avoid loosing balance. She was breathing hard as the two locked eyes. They just stood there at a standoff for several seconds, maybe a minute. Finally, Anastasia began feeling angry. Why was she afraid? This was her apartment! The anger began to set into her jaw, across her forehead, and into her brows.

She was just about to ask the man who he was when he pulled himself back and shut the door. She let out a sigh, and then finished her climb and unlocked the inside door. Glancing over her shoulder before she entered her apartment, she was sure she saw Mrs. Brown's door close again. He had been watching her through a crack in the doorway. She stepped in quickly, then closed and bolted her door.

Was he the one who left the flower? She held it in her hand a moment and concentrated. No, it was left by someone else. Well, it was still a nice flower, she decided, filling a glass with water and setting it in the window. She was pleased with the way it brightened the little room.

Before long, concern for Mrs. Brown began creeping into her head again. She tried to relax by convincing herself that the man across the hall was probably just some long lost nephew of Mrs. Brown's. He was odd, but not the psycho killer she was letting her imagination make him.

Dinner was a lettuce and bologna sandwich. She indulged in a chocolate toaster pastry for dessert, while reading a book her brother had lent her, a Gnostic text, *The Gospel of Saint Thomas.* It was a hobby that Anastasia and her brother enjoyed, reading ancient books. To her, anything that had survived so many centuries had to be important. Otherwise, its survival would be too accidental.

She was absorbed in her reading when she heard a shuffling sound. Looking up at her door, she realized that someone was on the stairway. She froze in mid-bite of her pastry. It was a shuffle, shuffle, bump noise, and it was getting louder. Whoever it was, they were getting closer to the landing, nearer to her door. Anastasia couldn't concentrate on the source of the noise. She was too frightened. A shiver went up her when she realized that whoever it was, was now making a shadow under her door. They were standing in her doorway. She sat up straight, gripping her pastry so hard that it popped in the middle and crumbled onto the floor. Then came a knock. She was too afraid to get up. Maybe if she sat still, they would think she wasn't home and leave. But the knocking persisted, louder, with more strength.

"Anastasia? Are you in there?" Anastasia let out a deep breath. It was Stella.

"Yeah, just a minute." She stood up, brushed the crumbs off her lap, and looked down grumpily at the chocolate pastry on the floor. Then she unlocked and unbolted the door for Stella.

"What took you so long?"

"What were you doing out there to make so much noise?"

Stella looked at her sister, plainly offended. "Wow, I'm glad you're so happy to see me."

"Sorry, I've just been having some strange feelings lately, and they're making me really jumpy." Anastasia was trembling, and her voice was getting shaky. She folded her arms and sat on the floor at the foot of her bed. "I'm glad you stopped by. We haven't seen each other in awhile. I just haven't had a good day." Anastasia looked at her sister, then took a few deep breaths, trying to regain control.

"So, what's been going on?" Stella set her big, noisy purse on the floor before having a seat beside her sister. Reluctant at first, Anastasia explained the events of the last couple of days.

"So, why don't you go knock on the old bat's door?" Stella picked at the broken pastry on the floor beside her.

"Well, now that you're here, maybe that's just what I should do," Anastasia declared. She already felt better, much more confident. Stella had a way of making even the most precarious situation seem normal. Everything was matter-of-fact with Stella, and for someone who had made a profession of solicitation, robbery, and assault, she was very honest.

Anastasia was on her feet and had taken a step forward. She hesitated. "So, Stella, are you going to go with me?"

"Sure." Stella was examining the last large hunk of toaster pastry for any foreign matter before she popped it into her mouth. Then she stood up and followed her sister to the door.

"So, what did you say this guy looked like? Think the old lady might have landed herself a young beau?"

Anastasia turned to look at Stella impatiently. "I'm sure Mrs. Brown would never choose to have a weirdo like him hanging around. He's got to be a relative," she declared.

Now she was feeling more than confident. Righteous would almost describe her feeling as she marched across the hall with Stella in tow. She knocked on the door. No one answered, so she knocked again. This time, she could hear some movement. She pushed her ear closer to the door. Someone was standing close to the other side, but didn't open it. Anastasia looked over her shoulder at Stella with a serious look, then pounded on the door harder. Despite the silence she knew that someone was standing close to the other side of the door. She pressed her ear to it again. She could almost hear breathing.

"Mrs. Brown!" she called, pounding on the door again. "It's me, Anastasia." After another fruitless pause for a response Anastasia spun around and looked at Stella.

"Maybe there's no one home." Stella shrugged.

Anastasia shook her head. "There's someone in there. He's just not opening the door." Anastasia's fear had turned to anger again. "I don't know who that is in there, but I'm going to find out next time he pops his goofy head out the door!" The duo retreated back into Anastasia's apartment.

"Why do you even care? I thought you didn't like that old battle axe anyway."

"Well, what if he did do something to her? I mean what if he's got her stuffed in the freezer or something? I just don't like the looks of him. I'm going to tell Mrs. Brown that too. In fact, the next time I mail in my rent, I'm going to write a letter and let my landlord know that she's got some man living with her. I think it's against the rules, or something!"

"Oooh! Ya'mean your going to tattle on her?" Stella was on the floor again with her bag in her lap.

"Well, I wouldn't care, but you should see this guy. He really gives me the creeps." Anastasia was watching her sister pull a bottle of 151 rum out of her purse. "I thought it was strange, you carrying a purse. Is that what was making the bumping noise in the hall?"

Stella nodded as she broke the seal on the bottle. She took a drink, then handed the bottle to Anastasia. "I really need ice for this," she complained, taking the bottle. "You didn't bring any ice, did you?" Stella shook her head no. Anastasia sighed, then tipped the bottle and made a face. The burn hit the back of her throat and settled in her stomach.

"So, what's up with you?" Anastasia settled back against the foot board of her bed.

Stella proceeded to pull a few more packages out of her hand bag. A small box of false nails, two bottles of nail polish and a pair of hair scissors. "I was hoping that you could do me a couple favors. In return—" Stella hesitated as she pulled the wad of bills out of her purse. "I'll take you out tonight." She smiled at Anastasia as she fanned herself with a handful of twenties.

"Sure." Anastasia shrugged. "But we have to be home early. I have to go to work tomorrow."

"I know." Stella barked, obviously annoyed. The subject of her dismissal was still taboo.

After fetching a couple glasses, Anastasia went to work on Stella's nails. She secretly got a little giggle from her sister's obsessions. Stella dearly loved having long red nails and having her hair look nice. At the same time, she was in a constant struggle with her femininity. She always wore jeans, because that was what she felt comfortable in. She tried every once in a while to experiment with colored eye shadows and liners, but she only made a mess of herself. She scoffed at other people's weaknesses, especially other women. Most women, the smart ones, were afraid of her. An innocent glance in her direction could be a painful mistake. But, secretly, Stella watched other women with a longing. She wanted to be the princess just once, although she would never say this out loud.

The two sisters had always acted as each other's beautician, but not because either of them were interested in cosmetology. It was just that paying someone to do these things would just be too extravagant. Besides, it gave them a chance to talk and be intimate. There was something about physically touching. It was the closest thing to hugging that ever happened in their family.

"So, have you met any interesting men lately?" Anastasia asked. This was the only safe thing she could think of to talk about. She had entertained the notion of asking about the money, but decided that she'd rather not know the details.

"No, but I did stop by Charley's last weekend and talked to Nick for awhile, before it got too busy." Stella had a crush on a bouncer at one of her favorite hangouts.

"Hey, if he's working tonight, why not ask him out for breakfast?" Anastasia offered.

"Oh, I don't know. I don't want him to think that I'm one of his groupies. We can go there last and see if there are any other girls hanging around, if I see that bleached blond out there prancing around him again I think I'll beat the shit out of her. The only reason I didn't last time was because she was glued to Nick all night. I couldn't even catch her going to the bathroom." Stella spat the words out in a rage. Lucky for the bleached blond that she had a good bladder. Following an unsuspecting woman to the bathroom and then pushing her out a back door or into a broom closet was Stella's favorite trick. She was definitely dangerous. So far, Anastasia didn't know of any confirmed deaths connected with her sister. Although, there was one questionable incident that involved a young woman who died of a brain aneurysm a couple months after Stella kicked her repeatedly in the head. This was another 'taboo' subject.

Anastasia finished gluing on Stella's nails and was applying the red polish. The glass of rum at her folded knee was beginning to taste better. She enjoyed the familiar warm feeling it gave her.

"How about you?" Stella asked, interrupting the quiet. "Have you met anyone lately?"

Anastasia made a face, then told Stella the story of the

mime. It made for an interesting conversation. Anastasia even added a little insight into her own feelings. She thought that he would be good in bed, and the fact that she didn't really know what he looked like made it all the more erotic. Stella hummed in appreciation.

Stella was instructed to be still, as her sister began the process of trimming her hair. First her rounded bangs, then the back. Stella was admittedly bad at styling her hair. Instead, she kept it in short layers with horseshoe bangs. It was easy to take care of, but it was the same style that she'd had, since she was sixteen. She felt trying for a new look was hopeless. Instead she settled for her familiar, comfortable look.

As Anastasia was finishing Stella's hair, they both froze when they heard a sound from Mrs. Brown's apartment. They were silent as they listened to a few more stomping noises. It sounded like someone climbing stairs. They were both absently following the sound up Anastasia's wall with their eyes. It stopped, then came back down.

"What on earth?" Anastasia whispered.

"Sounds like he's crawling up the wall," Stella replied.

"Shh!" there it was again, more movement. Now it was a scraping sound, coming closer. Then the familiar stomp, stomp, but this time it was intermixed with a thumping noise, only a few feet from where they sat on the floor. The wall was all that separated them from the source of the sounds. Again, their eyes watched the sound travel up the wall. It paused, and then went down again. Finally, a loud bang made both of them jump.

"What is he doing?" Anastasia whispered in a panic. "Do you think I should tell the police?"

Stella turned her head slowly and looked her sister straight in the eye. "What you need to do is get a hobby. You're spending too much time listening to the neighbors. The old witch was just putting something in the attic. Get a grip!"

Anastasia took a deep breath. She didn't realize how tensed up she had made herself. "Okay, that must be it. She's probably got an entrance to the attic on her side." She let out another big breath. "You know, maybe I really need to get out. It's been a few weeks since I've been out at night. All I ever do is work."

Stella turned back around. Anastasia finished cutting her hair. She was still shaky, but the rum seemed to help.

They were on the street just after the sunset. Anastasia was feeling relaxed and confident now. The rum had worked it's magic. The evening was cooler than yesterday, but to Anastasia it was perfect. She threw her head back, closed her eyes, and breathed in as much of the evening as she could. When she opened her eyes again, the first thing she noticed was the moon. It was large and round. She nudged Stella and pointed up.

Stella was wearing a denim jacket, a t-shirt, and jeans. With her short, tapered haircut, she could've been a hood from the 50's. She followed Anastasia's finger to the sky. "Yeah, looks like a full moon."

"No." Anastasia nodded. "But almost."

Stella took the information as fact. She had long known of Anastasia's intimate relationship with the moon. When they were very young, they noticed that her menstrual cycle was in sync with it. Whenever the moon was full, she started her period. If she was outside in the moonlight at that time of the month, she would double over with cramps.

"So, where do you go on a Monday night?" Anastasia asked.

"I don't know." Stella pondered for a moment. "They have female dancers at Dixie's."

"Why would you want to see female dancers?"

"Because, there are tons of guys there!" Stella looked at Anastasia as though she were a total idiot. "You really haven't been out in a while, have you?"

Anastasia blinked. "Not on a Monday."

They walked several blocks. The sidewalks were deserted. Most of the people they did see, they tried to pass without making eye contact. They were walking through some pretty rough areas of the city, but there was a lifetime of familiarity to all of it. They weren't seeing anything they hadn't seen before.

Dixie's was next to a set of railroad tracks in an old building that might have been a depot at one time. There was music, and people were milling around the door and in the parking lot in small groups. The asphalt all around the place was in desperate need of repair, with weeds popping through the cracks. The shabby brown brick building didn't look any better. The windows were covered with painted plywood that needed a new coat. But, Stella was right. There were tons of men, and they were all looking at the two sisters as they walked to the entrance.

"You two dancin' tonight?" someone shouted.

Stella made a hump noise. "Not in this dump, but I'd be willing to give you a private performance later on."

There were several snickers. Anastasia looked the crowd over, but didn't recognize a soul. They all looked alike to her—long hair, unshaven, t-shirts, jeans, and well on their way to inebriation. She could smell pot, and at least one of the little groups looked to be snorting cocaine. They pushed past everyone to the open door. The bouncer was a tough looking man in his early thirties. He was a big guy with a full beard and ponytail. Both arms were covered in tattoos.

Stella eyed him then pinched his arm lightly. "Nice tattoo," she purred. Anastasia just stumbled in behind her, feeling a little light-headed. The bouncer gave Stella a half smile and made a snarling sound. He didn't check either of their IDs.

It looked as though a low hanging cloud had snuck in past the bouncer, as well. Anastasia stood still, squinting into the smoky haze and tried to orient herself. In the foreground were crowds of people talking or staring straight ahead. Anastasia followed their gazes and made out the figure of a woman in her underwear flaying her arms, high above everyone. At first, Anastasia thought she looked like she was drowning. Slowly she began to realize that the woman was dancing on a table.

"She must be really drunk," Anastasia said aloud, tilting her head, watching.

"She's one of the dancers." Stella looked at her sister

suspiciously. "Are you high or what?"

Anastasia just glanced away and didn't answer. She was feeling a little confused. Stella grabbed her arm. "Common, let's get a drink. You need a shot to perk you up." Such was Stella's logic.

They walked past a couple of tables with dancers on top. Anastasia moved closer and peered up. Yeah, they're defiantly in their underwear, she thought. She was contemplating that they should at least have on costumes, when she felt Stella roughly pull on her arm again. She was half-dragged to a bar stool.

"Two shots of whiskey!" Stella was holding two fingers up at the bartender. He slopped two shot glasses full of the yellow liquid and set them in front of the two sisters. Stella had a twenty on the counter. The bartender made change, but Stella just glanced at it and left it sitting there in front of her.

"Here, drink this," she pushed one of the glasses to Anastasia. "This will sober you up."

Anastasia looked down at the little shot glass. Then, with the fingers of her right hand securely gripped around it, she obediently brought it to her lips. She took a sip and shook her head. God, it burned. Then she downed the whole glass. Sitting in silence she felt the liquid warm her whole body and settle in her stomach. This must be what it would feel like to swallow fire, she thought.

"Wanna' beer?" Stella was in her face again.

"Yeah," she answered.

They started talking again, this time about their family, and about more personal, emotional things. Anastasia was feeling more sure of herself. Either Stella's theory of whisky- induced sobriety had some merit or, more likely, Anastasia had become so drunk that she thought she was sober. They spoke of their child-hood and openly admitted their devotion to their brother, talking frankly about important things in a way that only blood can—especially when it's mixed with alcohol.

After sipping on a couple beers, Anastasia started looking around for the bathroom. She stood up, then had to grab onto the bar to steady herself. Stella pointed her in the right direction. Anastasia carefully pushed through the crowed aisles toward the back of the saloon. It was a slow process with all the men jeering and talking to her. She and Stella were two of the very small number of women in the place who weren't working.

The bathroom was dirty, with two doorless stalls and a rusty sink. But, it was empty and served its purpose.

When she stepped out, she noticed a dark, curly haired man standing near the bathroom door. It was as if he were waiting for her. She stopped and looked up into his eyes. They seemed so familiar. She smiled, then turned back toward the bar. He was a tall, nice looking guy, but she was too drunk.

She was slowly making her way back, talking to this guy and that one, when someone reached through the crowd and grabbed her arm. It was Stella. She had a look of urgency in her face.

"Anastasia, we need to go, now!"

She nearly pulled Anastasia off her feet. They were at a trot by the time they got to the door. Stella was ignoring her sister's questions and demands to know what was going on. She gave a look over her shoulder as they passed the bouncer. Anastasia looked toward the bar and noticed a short, stocky man with dark, thinning hair looking back at them. He charged as fast as he could in their direction, looking like a little bull with steam coming out of both nostrils and a dangerous glare in his eyes. Anastasia didn't know who the man was or why he was chasing them, but it was obvious that Stella was moving fast to get away from him. Anastasia quickly decided she didn't want to shake hands with him, either.

They ran out the door and into the street, dodging a few cars, while crossing in the middle of the block. They were running at full speed along the railroad tracks, in the general direction of their mother's house. The little man was still following.

"You're going to die, bitch!" he shouted.

Anastasia noticed that he had a friend. Both of them were shouting obscenities. They were running madly past old buildings that were closed or abandoned. They were getting into an area where the street lights were so far away that they were now in total darkness. All Anastasia was aware of was the moon and starlight, and two crazed men running after them. The ground was uneven, with large pieces of debris here and there. Both of them stumbled several times. Anastasia was worried that they needed to find a place with people, but Stella was now holding her hand, pulling her as fast as they both could run. Finally, they came to a small residential street. Most of the houses had been torn down, but there was a paved road.

"We're going to kill you! Dirty bitches," the men screamed.

The voices were getting closer. They scrambled down the road. Anastasia noticed a pain in her right ankle. Stella was also limping. Their breathing was labored, but they realized that they were running for their lives. They had to find people, a lighted street, or somewhere to hide. The next block did contain more houses, but all appeared to be abandoned.

"Give it up! We'll kill you fast if you just give us back the money. You want to die slow?" Anastasia could gage by their voices that they were getting closer.

They were coming to another cross street when they heard the most heavenly sound— sirens. A new rush of adrenaline helped them run head long into the path of the police car. Stella began waving her arms. The women were screaming. Stella reached the car first, running up to the driver's side window. Anastasia collapsed onto the hood of the car. She was gasping for breath and trembling so badly that her legs gave out and she slid onto the ground. The second officer ran to her side and helped her to the back seat of the police car. Both officers were very kind and patiently waited for them to catch their breath before they began questioning. Another car had been called to chase the two men who were perusing them.

"Boy, we sure were lucky to see you. Those two guys were going to kill us." Stella gasped. She was now sitting in the back of the car with Anastasia.

"Actually, someone called in a report that two women were being chased along the railroad tracks, then down Huckleberry. They even described the assailants."

The surprise was obvious on Stella's face. Anastasia was still so out of it, she wasn't even aware of the conversation.

The police began gathering information. Stella claimed she had no idea who the men were. She explained that they had began bothering them when they were in the bar, so they left, not knowing that the duo would pursue them home. When asked for a description of the men, Stella was very general and acted unsure of herself. Anastasia just lay huddled sideways, with her head against the back of the seat and her feet on the pavement outside the door.

After a few more minutes, one of the officers became aware of someone outside the police car. He jumped out. Stella strained to look out Anastasia's window to see what the commotion was about. Anastasia raised her head, and then jumped out of the car and into her brother's arms. She began crying uncontrollably, gasping for breaths between sobs. He patiently held her, rubbing her back.

"Did someone call you?" asked Stella, getting out of the Anastasia's open door. "How did you get here so fast?"

"Mom sent me." He was giving Stella a hateful look. It was obvious he would like to say more to her, but restrained himself because of the police officers. Stella recoiled and didn't ask any more questions.

"So, is it all right if I walk my sister home?" he asked the officer. The two officers huddled together for a few minutes, then asked Stella if she could stay for more questioning and to sign the complaint. Stella seemed to shrink when the officer mentioned the part about signing a complaint, but the look her brother gave her made her nod her head in agreement.

"Go ahead and take her home, but she needs to come into the station tomorrow to give her statement."

Anastasia was gaining a bit of control. Her brother managed to turn her around and lead her off into the direction of her apartment. "Thank you," he said, still holding his sister by the shoulders. He gave Stella one more angry look, and then led Anastasia away.

They walked together silently until Anastasia slowly began to catch her breath. She wiped her nose on the back of her hand. Her brother offered her his jacket sleeve. Anastasia laughed softly.

"That's okay," she smiled. Stopping, she bent over far enough to pull the hem of her shirt up to wipe her face.

"You know, it's not safe running with Stella," he said softly.

"Yeah, I know, now. I guess I never thought about it before. It never occurred to me that one of her guys would go after both of us like that." She stopped and looked her brother in the eyes. "I know that they were going to kill us when they caught us. I know they were serious."

Her brother just nodded at her gravely.

They had started walking again when Anastasia looked back at him thoughtfully. "How did you know where we were, anyway?"

"Mom. She pulled the stairs down and screamed at me to get up. She told me to get my ass down and run at fast as I could to the train tracks, that you were in trouble. She even gave me this." He opened his jacket and showed Anastasia a gun tucked in his pants. "I didn't even know she had a gun."

Anastasia was shaking her head. "Neither did I."

"When I was going out the door, she yelled for me to use Huckleberry. She was holding both sides of her head and staring straight ahead at nothing. You know how she does when she sees things."

Anastasia nodded.

"You know, Mom loves you the most." Her brother said it without any animosity, as though he was just stating a fact.

Anastasia shook her head no, furiously. "No, not love. It's something different, like she has some kind of special interest in me, but it's for her own purpose. I don't know how else to describe it, but I can feel it."

They walked further in silence. "Well, whatever it is, you're lucky to have her on your side." He gave her a nervous look. They both knew better than to criticize her. Anastasia giggled. It was sad, but over the years they had learned to laugh at these observations. It was a matter of survival, because if you didn't laugh, the alternative was perpetual fear and depression.

They were getting near her apartment, within a couple of blocks, when Anastasia realized that she was sober. The combination of fear and exertion had jolted her back to her full senses. She was walking, unaided now, and the crying had ceased. She was starting to think clearly about what had happened, and what she needed to do the next day.

"What should I tell the police tomorrow?"

"Well, I wouldn't tell them any more than you have to. Mom said that the men chasing you knew Stella, that Stella had dragged you into one of her messes. Is that true? Did you ever talk to those guys?"

"Never, they just chased us out of the bar and down the street, screaming at us. I heard them mention money. Maybe Stella stole some money." She looked at her brother. They knew that this was a typical Stella thing, robbing drunks. "I'll just tell the police that, except for the part about Stella knowing them. I won't see Stella beforehand, so I really won't know anything more. It won't be a lie."

Her brother nodded in agreement. "What about a description?"

"I'll just describe them. There are lots of men who could fit their description. They'll never find them anyway."

"I hope not, and even more, I hope they don't ever recognize you. I think you should just keep to yourself for awhile. No more bars, especially with Stella."

Anastasia didn't need to be told that. She had already told herself.

When they finally came to her door, she reached into her pocket and produced the key. She stopped to take a look around.

No funny feelings this evening. She let her brother in. He was prepared to stay with her until he was sure she felt safe and secure. Together, they climbed the stairs. Again, the blond, disheveled man popped his head out the door. Then he shut it again just as quickly.

Anastasia's brother looked alarmed. "What was that?"

"Oh, just one more annoyance. I'll explain when we get inside. I wonder if there's any of Stella's rum left. I could use a drink." Anastasia wearily changed subjects, but her brother couldn't keep his eyes from Mrs. Brown's door.

Anastasia unlocked her apartment door and led him inside. She was disappointed when she located the empty rum bottle. They both sat down on her only piece of furniture, the bed. She explained the whole story of the strange man next door. Her brother looked concerned, but Anastasia brushed it off. She explained that she wasn't experiencing any bad feelings from Mrs. Brown, so the whole thing was probably nothing to be worried about. Actually, she was still afraid of this man, but she didn't want her brother to worry.

They fell into small talk, and then a discussion on books. Slowly, Anastasia began to feel drowsy, and it was getting late. Her brother reluctantly agreed to go home. After he left, she did fall asleep quickly, but her dreams where violent and startled her into wakefulness twice. First she dreamed that she was being chased, and then that she was tied up and smothered with a plastic bag. She was relieved when she woke up a third time to see that the sun was newly risen. Time for work.

CHAPTER 3

Stella looked at her clock from bed. It was 2:30 PM. She couldn't put it off any longer. She had to get up. Last night, had been a disaster. If only Anastasia hadn't been with her. She was afraid to face her mother. Last night she had gone on to another bar and stayed until closing. Then she had gone to an after hours joint. She was relieved beyond words when she came home and found everyone asleep. But now she had to face her, and no one else was home.

Stella stood up and put on an old, threadbare robe. She pulled on a pair of socks to keep her feet warm, and then bravely stepped outside her room.

Everything was quiet as she silently slipped into the bathroom. She checked herself in the mirror and smoothed her hair. Then she washed the mascara from under her eyes. No more stalling, she told herself. She pushed through the hallway and rounded the corner into the kitchen.

There was her mother, sitting with perfect posture at the table and drinking coffee. She was wearing a pressed cotton dress, and her hair was pinned up and saturated with hair spray. Every hair was carefully positioned and secured in its appropriate place. She reminded Stella of a character on the Donna Reed show. Even the gold watch fastened around her left wrist was just right for the perfect suburban housewife. How appropriate, thought Stella, seeing the irony in it. The watch never worked. It was a just a prop for the world's best housewife.

The room was immaculate, the way she kept the whole

house. She was just sitting with her eyes fixed on Stella, quietly sipping out of her coffee cup, carefully setting it back into its saucer. Stella had never known another person who religiously used a saucer, even when she was alone. Only her mother.

"How are you feeling?" Her voice pierced the air, jabbing Stella in the stomach.

"Fine." Stella walked to the sink and poured herself a glass of water. She stared out the kitchen window as she drank the water down. Turning toward the doorway, she made a futile attempt to retreat without the verbal whipping that she knew in her heart was inevitable.

"Just a minute." Stella froze at her mother's words. "I want you to sit down, right here." Stella obediently turned with her eyes cast down. She walked over to the table, took a coaster from the center of the table for her glass, and gently sat down across from her mother.

Marilyn continued the torture by remaining silent. She slowly sipped her coffee and stared out another window behind Stella. The minutes passed slowly as Stella sat granite still, hands on her lap, eyes cast down at the table in front of her. Only her mother could make her cower like this.

"You nearly got your sister killed last night." Marilyn started the speech in a normal, even tone.

Even though Stella was terrified, it was a relief to hear the silence broken. "I'm sorry."

"You are an adult. Whatever you do outside this house is no concern of mine, unless it puts your sister in danger." Her voice was beginning to rise. "I understand that as a healthy young woman, Anastasia needs companionship, someone with whom to confide and talk." She said this softer; and then she fixed her gaze at Stella and held it until Stella was looking back. "But, you are not a good companion. You are a lazy, drunken, dangerous, dirty whore. You are so disgustingly vile, I can't stand to use my own toilet after you've been in there, but you're all I've got to work with. You and that mousy brother of yours."

She was now standing. Slowly, she leaned across the

table toward Stella, bracing herself with one hand. "But you listen to me. If you cause Anastasia to get hurt or killed, you might as well lie down dead beside her, because suicide would be better than what I'll have in store for you. And don't think I don't know all that goes on. Just like last night, I always know, and you would never, never, be able to get away from me."

Stella was looking fearfully at her mother, afraid to move at all. Marilyn stood up, took in a breath, and then turned and walked out of the house through a back door, off the kitchen. Stella continued to sit until she could no longer hear the click of her mother's heels on the sidewalk. She was trembling as she stood up. Then she ran to the bathroom and vomited.

Anastasia woke up feeling well, but tired. Work went by quickly that day, and all week. She wasn't plagued with the feeling of someone watching her, but the stranger next door regularly popped his head out the door when he heard her coming up the stairs. Anastasia tried to ignore him. She didn't hear from any of her family members, either. All week, she just came home from work and read. She was lonely. Even food was loosing its appeal. Everything smelled bad to her. In fact, by Thursday, she went through her cupboards and threw out anything that gave her the least bit of suspicion of being spoiled. Then she scrubbed down her entire apartment.

Friday was payday. Anastasia was excited. She planned to pay her rent in advance. Then, in two weeks, she intended to buy herself a brand new TV with her next paycheck. She stopped at a couple of stores on the way home to compare prices again. The price on the TV she had long ago decided to buy was still the same, $107.00. It was a black and white model with a twelve inch screen. Color would have been nice, but it would have cost twice as much. Black and white would be heaven.

She stopped at a local grocery store for a few things. She noticed that the cheap wine was on sale, two bottles for $3.00. Why not? she asked herself. She was going to splurge. Peaches and cream, and wild berry berry. Anastasia smiled and threw them into her shopping cart. She thought about how some of her schoolmates had been so excited when they turned eighteen, because they could legally buy alcohol. The part that made Anastasia smile was that she was still using the fake I.D. she had bought by mail order when she was only fifteen, since she didn't have a drivers license. The grocer cashed her check and sold her the money order she needed to mail her rent. That reminded her. Should she attach a note and tattle on her neighbor? She decided that she'd think about it later.

Half skipping with her two grocery bags, she decided it would be best to stay at home, since she had to work the next day. She could feast on potato chips and bologna sandwiches with peaches and cream wine. It would be lovely, she thought.

She rounded the corner near her apartment, when there it was again— that feeling that someone was watching her. She sighed and looked around. It was beginning to get dark, but she could make out a figure standing flat against the wall near her door. She slowed, but continued on. Then she saw him take a giant leap, like a cartoon character, placing one foot down and then another. He swept the hat off his head and gave a long low bow. It was the mime, dressed in the same costume and in full makeup, just as before.

She gave a little giggle and nodded her head at him. He took a few steps toward her and offered to carry her groceries with a gesture. She handed him the bags without hesitation, then pulled keys out of her pocket. As she was unlocking the door, the thought did occur to her that she was about to allow a stranger access to her home. She turned to look at the man again. He was wearing the biggest grin, and his deep brown eyes sparkled. There was not the slightest hint of danger behind his face. She held the door open for him. They walked silently up the stairs. Every time she looked back at him, he gave her that heart warming smile.

She was so giddy she barely noticed the man next door popping his head out. The mime did, and cocked his head in a puzzled way. Anastasia just burst into laughter and hurried up the rest of the stairs. It was an unusual situation. Then she wondered if the man next door was thinking she was the strange one, with her painted friend.

It was as she was holding her apartment door open for him that she realized that neither of them had spoken a word to each other, ever. She decided this was a fun game, and to play along.

Once inside, the mime, for the first time, looked a little awkward. His confidence seemed to be wavering as he looked around. He was not quite sure what to do next. Anastasia was leaning on the closed door, looking him over. She could see it was making him uncomfortable. So, she did it awhile longer. Slowly, he became aware that she was enjoying his predicament. He glanced nervously around, one of his strong arms hugging each bag. He was taller than Anastasia and had a slim build. The makeup made it difficult to judge his age. Anastasia felt he was young, but old for his years. She could also feel his heat. Sexuality seemed to seethe from him. Yet, he was becoming afraid of her, and this was just what she wanted. It quickly became apparent to both of them that she was in charge now, regardless of who had originally initiated the meeting.

She slowly stood up and motioned for him to follow her into the kitchen, without taking her eyes off his face. He gave a little nod of understanding, and then shyly looked away. Setting the bags on the counter, he glanced at her for more directions. She stepped around him so closely they almost touched. He stiffened, then innocently watched her empty the contents of the first bag. She set out the bread, cheese, bologna, and chips. Expertly, she put her fingers into the creases of the bag and poked them together gently. His eyes were focused intently on her hands as she gently recoiled the tips, pressed the folded sides against the bottom and folded the bag over. Now, she leaned her body against the cupboard, her breasts blocking the view of her hands. She was looking at him boldly, watching him, as he was watching her. He looked up at her like a little mouse at a circling hawk. She smiled.

Pulling a bottle of wine out of the second bag, she held it up to him. He nodded his head yes. Setting the bottle next to him, she turned and walked to the cupboard that contained the glasses, slowly and deliberately. She knew he was watching her.

The one thing that she was not lacking was glasses. Inside her cupboard was a complete set— beer glasses, shot glasses, wine glasses, even a few fancy goblets. She chose two large matching goblets with giant bowls and long stems. She smiled, thinking about the night when she and Stella had hidden them inside their jackets when they left the bar.

The mime was still watching her from the other side of the room. Their lines of vision connected and embraced as she turned to walk back toward him. Reluctantly, she shifted her focus to the wine, breaking its seal by twisting the cap. The pink fizzy liquid popped and sprinkled them lightly, as it hit the bottom of the goblet and sprang back up. Foam gathered thickly at the rim of the goblet. It covered the liquid and filled the bowl, like a warm, pink cloud.

Anastasia precariously dipped her index finger into the foam and drew it toward her mouth. That was when the mime reached out, grabbed her hand and thrust her fingers between his warm, moist lips. Their eyes locked as their bodies closed together.

He wrapped his free arm around her, gently sucking on her fingers. She instinctively began kneading his shoulder. Her breathing was getting heavier. She rubbed her breasts against his chest, straddling his right leg. She was grinding herself into him, as he pressed her hard with his hand in the small of her back. Now he let go of her hand. He replaced her fingers with her lips, pulling at them with his own. They locked in a passionate kiss, while his hands moved to embrace her. His right knee was now bent as she was riding his thigh. He moved his hands down her, sliding his fingers into her seat. She reached up and held his neck as he lifted her. He carried her out of the kitchen and slowly lowered her onto the bed.

He crushed her, moving his mouth down her body. She tangled her fingers through his dark curls, arching her back, and closing her eyes. He slid both hands up her T shirt, driving his fingertips into the cups of her bras, squeezing her as he pushed up her shirt to expose her breasts. Anastasia sighed as he locked his thick passionate lips onto one nipple and then the other. His hair tickled her sensitive, bare skin. She was rubbing his shoulders. Her mind focused on her pleasure. He held her spellbound for an eternity, until she could bear it no longer. Then she pulled at his clothes, undressing him. He pulled away, grabbing onto the buttons of her blue jeans. She struggled to bend forward and managed to pull off his shirt, but he grabbed her trousers. Jumping to his feet he yanked them off with one mighty pull. He leaped back to the bed, kneeling beside it. Anastasia held his shoulders, trying to move him on top of her, but he stubbornly grabbed a hold of her waist and buried his face between her thighs.

They made love late into the night, each fighting for dominance. Elated when triumphant, delighted with defeat. He was all she thought he'd be. Yet, he never spoke a coherent word through it all.

A loud ringing woke her up, alone, with the sheets sticking to her. Somehow, she had remembered to set her alarm the night before. She reached up and pushed the button that stopped the ringing. Looking around her, she realized that part of the source of the stickiness was still smeared on her chest, white and black grease paint. If he had stayed the night, she would've been able to see what he looked like, as well as cuss him out for the mess.

She lay back down, savoring the details of the night before. It was like a wet dream. Who was that man? She smiled, even though she knew she would probably never see him again. Then reality set in. Work, Saturday, overtime. She jumped up, showered, and was out the door in record time.

CHAPTER 4

Jim walked slowly down the sidewalk, trying to kill time. It was okay to be an hour early for work, but Mr. Lowe wasn't there to unlock the door if he arrived any sooner. He enjoyed being around people, having someone to talk to. Work was all he had to look forward to since his mother had died the year before. Since her death, he'd been living alone in the only home he had ever known. He tried to keep things neat, the way she did, but the wallpaper was faded. The kitchen walls were so dingy from smoke and thirty years of living that he couldn't remember what color they used to be. The furniture was worn. Even before her death, she had long ago thrown blankets over it to avoid getting poked by a stray spring.

The refrigerator didn't stay cold anymore. In the summer, milk would spoil if it wasn't drunk within a couple days. The handle broke off long ago. That was why Jim kept a table knife handy up on top. All he had to do was push the knife carefully into the side and pull, so in Jim's mind, it still worked just fine. Besides, it never occurred to Jim to replace anything. Most importantly, he didn't want anything in the house to change. He desperately missed his mother and still cried at night. The loneliness was painful.

He had always known that the parents he loved weren't his biological parents. Mr. and Mrs. Ireland were Christians of strong faith. They prayed everyday of their marriage for children that sadly never arrived until Jim. They took Jim in with open eyes, dedicated to love him no matter his handicap. There was never a time when they lied about his birth. His father especially believed in openness about the subject and was clearly disappointed with Marilyn's lack of interest. It was Jim's biological brother who never forgot his younger sibling. He kept the lines of communication open, the children would even sneak over to play with him occasionally. So, the four children grew up together, but separately. Jim was the lucky one.

"Morn' Mr. Lowe," Jim called out when he turned the corner. Mr. Lowe was standing in front of the door with his key in the lock. He had a waxed paper bag and a newspaper under his arm.

"Good morning to you, too, Jim. I brought us our usual couple of donuts this morning. Nutty, right?"

Jim nodded.

Mr. Lowe pushed the door open and let Jim step inside. Jim walked in and flipped on the lights. "I'll go start the coffee, Mr. Lowe." Jim had worked for Mr. Lowe since he was eighteen. Now he was twenty-five. Jim's mother had known Mr. Lowe from church, and that was how he got the job. They still went to the same church. Every Sunday, Jim would search the pews until he spotted him. Then he'd wait outside, just so he could wave to him when he and his wife came out. Then he'd wish them both a good morning. He always admired Mr. Lowe. Secretly, he wished Mr. Lowe had been his father. His own had died when he was young.

Mr. Lowe and Jim had a leisurely breakfast together in the break area. They sipped coffee and ate donuts while Mr. Lowe read the highlights from the newspaper out loud to Jim. This was their regular routine. Mr. Lowe had started it to help Jim adjust to working, years ago. Now it was just a habit. Jim needed to have a routine. Mr. Lowe liked helping Jim, so it made for a gentle start for their day.

At about a quarter to nine, the other workers started coming in. Anastasia punched in at just a couple of minutes to nine. Skip was the last to arrive at a quarter after nine. The day was starting out to be pretty typical. By nine thirty, everyone was in place, starting off where they had stopped the day before.

Anastasia was still preoccupied with memories of the

night before. Trying to concentrate on work was difficult. She was still at a cutting machine, separating business cards. Just as she was about to start a new sheet, something caught her attention out of the corner of her eye. When she glanced back at the pile of uncut stock, there was a vision of her mother. The image vanished in seconds. Anastasia shook her head and blinked. She stopped working and tried to clear her head. Why would she be thinking of her mother, and why would her mother be smiling at her?

She spent lunch alone in a corner drinking coffee, but couldn't help noticing Jim was excitedly discussing something with Skip. This could only mean trouble. Soon after lunch, Anastasia found out what the discussion was about. Jim ran excitedly to her and explained that Skip had promised to help him out by introducing him to this really hot chick he knew. Anastasia knew this was going to be trouble and gently warned Jim, but his painful ignorance of women and the exciting opportunity Skip offered were just too much to refuse.

CHAPTER 5

Grey smoke streamed out of a small cone of incense that was sitting on a plate on Anastasia's radiator. She was reclined on her bed, reading beside an open window when she slowly became aware of someone coming up the stairs. Then there was a knock at her door. It was her brother.

"Hi there! I knew if I held out long enough, you'd come visit me." Anastasia hugged his neck. They exchanged a few greetings and then had a seat on the edge of her bed. He looked around curiously.

"Anastasia, why are you burning incense with the window open?"

"That smell!" She cringed. "Can't you smell it? It's driving me crazy."

He took a deep breath, and shook his head. "No, I only smell sandalwood."

"Well, I can smell it. I think it's a dead mouse, but, I've cleaned everywhere and I can't find it. Do you think it could be in the wall?" Anastasia pointed to the far kitchen wall. He stood up and walked into the kitchen, breathing deeply.

Turning back to his sister, he blankly shook his head. "I can't smell anything." He looked at her for a moment with concern on his face. "Anastasia, are you okay? I mean, are you still upset about that incident with Stella? How about that guy next door?"

"Oh, no. I'm fine. I just ignore him. And that thing with Stella, I haven't thought about that at all lately. In fact, I haven't even seen Stella since it happened. How's she doing?"

Her brother looked annoyed at the abrupt change of

subject. “She’s fine, I guess. You know we don’t talk anymore.” He sighed and took his seat beside her again. “Actually, it’s Mom that I’m curious about.”

Anastasia leaned in. “Why? She isn’t sick or anything is she?” The vision she’d had at work flashed in her mind.

“No, that’s not what’s bothering me. What’s making me curious is that she’s been so pleasant lately, even nice.” They exchanged puzzled looks. “The other day, she even stopped me in the hall and asked how I was doing. And, you won’t believe this one. She even asked me if I might like a new pair of drapes for my room, ‘to brighten things up.’ I almost fell over. I said ‘sure,’ but didn’t mention that I’d never had any old drapes to begin with.”

Anastasia sat bewildered for a few moments. All she managed to do was to grunt her astonishment. She was preoccupied with the vision of her mother’s smile. She recounted the episode to her brother. He shook his head. “There’s something going on.” They sat quietly for awhile in thought.

“Well, anyway.” Her brother broke the silence. “Anything else going on with you?”

Anastasia smiled. Should she tell him about the mime? She glanced up at him shyly. He was so straight and strong. Sitting beside her was the ideal big brother, a guardian angel who came to her rescue in the middle of the night and comforted her. Should she confess to him about that wild and dangerous night she had instigated with a stranger? Would he think she was as bad as Stella? She decided to talk about work, and then they slipped into a conversation about the book he had given her. It was a pleasant evening.

Jim agonized over making the phone call. He would look at the number. He even memorized it, but it was Wednesday before he had enough nerve to call her.

“I don’t care what she looks like,” Jim whined to Anastasia the next day. “She just sounds so nice on the phone.

Her voice is so deep and sexy. I just gotta meet her."

"So, how does Skip know her?"

"Well, that's just it. He met her in a bar, but when she wouldn't sleep with him, he never called her. See, she's a nice girl! Too nice for Skip." Jim had such conviction in his voice, but Anastasia knew there had to be more to it. She gave Skip a scowl every time she ran into him at work. He would just grin back at her. What a bastard, she wanted to say out loud, but it really wasn't her affair.

The details of the night with the mime slowly began to fade into her subconscious. She convinced herself that it was a one night stand and quit looking for the details of his face in every stranger she met. The feeling that someone was watching her stopped. As for that strange man next door, Anastasia finally decided Mrs. Brown must have moved and he was the new tenant. She had mailed her rent check without a note. It wasn't her business anyway. Jim continued to report to her every morning about the details of all phone conversations with Julia, Skip's cast off with whom Jim was now in love. Jim still hadn't met her, but they were scheduled to meet for dinner and a movie that Saturday. Jim had also invited her to church on Sunday. Anastasia tried to talk him into going slow, but Jim was infatuated.

Friday evening, Anastasia had another visitor.

"It's freezing in here! What are you doing with the windows open?" This time it was Stella. She was carrying two bottles of cheap wine. Anastasia was wearing a sweater and sitting under the covers of her bed when Stella arrived. She shrugged. Her compulsion with ridding her apartment of the illusive smell was getting obsessive.

"I was just trying to air the place out." She closed the windows.

Stella took the wine into the kitchen and began pouring them both a glass without asking Anastasia if she wanted any. She handed her sister a glass and sat down on the floor. Anastasia watched with interest as Stella began sniffing the air.

"What's that smell?"

Anastasia jumped up excitedly. "You smell it too?".

"Yeah, smells like something died."

"Stella, you don't know how crazy I've been trying to find out what smells. I've torn this place apart."

Stella stood up and walked toward the kitchen. She stopped near the far wall. "I think your neighbor's got some garbage or something that stinks."

"That's it! It's next door, isn't it? That goof ball isn't taking out his garbage. It's getting rotten."

Stella shook her head. "Or something." She looked up where the wall met the ceiling, then took a drink of wine. "So, is Mrs. Brown back yet?"

Anastasia took note that Stella had called her neighbor "Mrs. Brown." This was the first time Anastasia had heard her sister call the neighbor by a proper name.

"No, I think she must have moved. All I ever see is that weirdo sticking out his head every time I come up the stairs."

Stella stiffened, but didn't say anything else about it.

They both took seats on the floor, leaning against the bed. "Well, little sister, you'll never believe why I'm here." Anastasia shook her head. "Mom wanted me to see how you were."

Anastasia looked puzzled. "What is the deal with her? Is she being nice to you, too? Our brother was here a couple days ago telling me how she wants to buy him new drapes."

Stella chuckled. "Yeah, it's really weird." She shook her head. "I can't explain it, but, listen to this." Stella poked her sister in the shoulder. "She said, 'I miss Anastasia so much. I wish she'd come back home.' Can you believe that?"

Anastasia stared down solemnly. The memory of her mother chasing her out of the house was vivid. It happened the day after her eighteenth birthday. The night of her birthday, she'd gotten so drunk she was sick and passed out on the bathroom floor. She'd awakened to her mother kicking her and screaming obscenities. Still sick, she stumbled out of the house, trying to escape her mother. She ran until she could run no longer, falling asleep in an open field. That was where her brother had found her, her hair tangled with burrs and her clothes stiff with mud and vomit. He had cleaned her up and sneaked her into his room until they could find her an apartment.

Anastasia looked back at her sister and shivered. "No way."

Stella chuckled again. "Hey, she said for me to tell you if you ever needed some help, found yourself pregnant or something, to come home and she'd understand." Stella leaned in toward Anastasia, anticipating a surprised reaction. Anastasia was bewildered. She just stared at the ground.

Straining for words, she stuttered. "Why? Wh-what's going on?"

Stella shook her head. "I have no idea."

Anastasia crossed her legs and rested her elbows on her knees. She held her head. She was playing back her sister's words in her mind. She jerked her head back to look at Stella. "Did she say pregnant?"

Stella looked thoughtfully. "Yeah, I thought that was funny, too." Then she looked seriously at Anastasia. "You're not pregnant are you?"

Anastasia shook her head without thinking. "No, of course not." The mime came to mind, but she shook her head again, refusing to give the idea any thought. "If I was, I'd get an abortion. I don't have the money to raise a baby, and I sure wouldn't want to raise one with Mom around it." Suddenly, the room seemed unnaturally quiet. Had her mother heard her say that? Stella even looked sober, staring at her sister. The quiet was eerie. Anastasia jumped up to get more wine, even though her glass wasn't empty.

The rest of the visit was pretty much ruined. They tried to engage in their regular conversation, but it was strained. Both of them were preoccupied. Anastasia no longer wanted to tell Stella about the mime. The details that had made the whole thing so exciting now seemed sordid and dirty. She was ashamed of herself. After finishing off the second bottle, Stella announced that she needed to leave.

After Stella left, Anastasia was grateful for the wine. It made her tipsy, but sleep was still difficult.

All day Saturday, Jim talked nonstop. He was finally going to meet his Julia. Anastasia normally would've been more tolerant, but she was depressed from her sister's visit the night before. She tried to make herself small and scarce, but Jim would seek her out, talking ceaselessly. Everyone, even Mr. Lowe, could not escape Jim's enthusiasm. Skip was the only one who seemed to be encouraging him. Anastasia didn't want to add another burden to her conscience, but she still had a foreboding feeling about the situation. When five o'clock came, she was the first one out the door.

Walking home, all the fears of the possibility of being pregnant hit her. They hadn't used any protection. She wasn't on the pill. Could she be pregnant? She was holding herself and walking quickly. Why didn't she look at the calendar at work? The phases of the moon were on it. She decided she would have to look for herself tonight, then every night until it was full.

Jim was walking quickly toward his home. For the first time, he was oblivious to the world around him. His mind was replaying over and over the details of all he needed to do before meeting Julia. Tonight, he mused, at the Chinese restaurant on Second Street at seven p.m. Finally, the day had arrived. He put out of his mind any worries about what she looked like or how old she was, or if she had any physical defects. None of that mattered. He had already decided he was in love with her. All that was of concern was whether she would love him. They had talked for hours on the phone about things that were important, things he had never discussed with anyone before. His friendless childhood, being teased because he was slow. His mother's death. She knew his whole life. She told him she was also teased for being different from the other children. She had moved away from her family when she was seventeen and was alone, too. They had so much in common.

He took a shower and was in his finest cloths by 5:45. Then he sat silently, watching the clock. Flowers, should I buy her flowers, he thought. No, no one really does that, do they? He debated in his mind the smallest details. Did he have enough money? Was he wearing enough cologne? Too much? He'd used a bottle of Old Spice that his mother had given him. It had belonged to his father. He rarely ever used it.

He was wearing a pair of grey slacks, a white button down shirt, a black tie, a multicolored sweater, and his Sunday shoes with black socks. His hair was still wet, combed back. He was newly shaven with only one nick on his chin. He did look his best, the way that made his mother proud. Sitting very still, he stared at the clock. He decided he would leave at six. Since he was the man, he decided he should get there first. He looked back at the clock, making a game of counting the seconds in time with the second hand. Finally, he jumped up and locked all the doors, quickly moving down the sidewalk.

He reached the restaurant within twenty minutes, and notified the hostess he was expecting a lady friend, so he needed to sit near the window, facing the door. "She's going to be wearing a blue dress," he announced. His waitress was also briefed on his situation and alerted that she should send any single, blue-clad women to his table post haste. Then he spied a clock on the opposite wall. It was 6:25. Only thirty-five minutes, he told himself.

The restaurant was less than half full when he arrived. A steady flow of people filled it to three quarters by 6:55. Any time now, he thought. He kept looking out the window and straining to identify the color of every dress walking in, even if it arrived with an escort. Finally seven arrived, but she still wasn't there. 7:05, now she was late. 7:10, did she have problems finding the restaurant? Wait, she was the one who picked it. 7:15, where was she? By 7:20, the waitress had asked him for a third time if he would like something to drink.

"No, I'll wait for my date," he said nervously. As his gaze was falling from the waitress, he spotted her. There, across the room, it was Julia. It had to be. She was tall, over six foot, slim, but large. Her hair was an unnatural shade of blond, shoulder length, and curled. Her makeup was heavy, but not gaudy. Her dress was modest, but a vibrant blue. Her age was hard to determine, not old, but not young.

Jim stood up, and their eyes met. Julia smiled and Jim sighed. The waitress was forgotten. He pulled the chair out for her. Then there she was, looking down at him. At 5'10", he had always thought of himself as average height, but Julia towered over him at least eight inches. He reminded himself of what she had told him. It was her height that had contributed to her miserable childhood.

She sat down gracefully as he scrambled back to his seat. Without the slightest idea of what to do next, he sat rigid and nervously folded his hands. He was looking at her meekly when she smiled again, laid her gentle eyes on him soothingly, and then spoke the first word. "Hello."

CHAPTER 6

Well, she was right. Anastasia was studying the calendar on the wall near a time clock. Tonight was a full moon, and she hadn't noticed any cramps, or the slightest sign of her period. She tried to push the worry out of her mind. Hadn't she heard of women who caused their periods to be late because of worry? She tried to forget about it.

Anastasia was surprised when she noticed Jim pushing his time card into the clock. She had beat him to work. This was a first. He looked chipper, whistling with a happy smile on his face.

"So, how did the date go?" Anastasia asked.

"Fantastic," Jim declared.

"Good, I'm glad to hear that." She stood dumbfounded as Jim sighed, then turned smartly and started work. It was so surprising to Anastasia. She was sure Skip had arranged the date as some cruel joke. Had it backfired? She only hoped for Jim's sake that it had.

Mr. Lowe walked onto the work floor. He seemed to be looking for someone. Jim noticed him, waved, and shouted "mornin'" from across the room. He nodded and waved. Evidently, he had missed Jim that morning and wanted to make sure he had made it to work. He turned to go back to his office when he spied Skip at the coffee pot. Skip fidgeted as Mr. Lowe drew near.

"Hello, there Mr. Morris." Mr. Lowe seemed to be intentionally making Skip uncomfortable.

"Mr. Lowe! Good morning." Skip set his coffee down and attempted to walk away.

"Skip!"

Skip stopped in his tracks and faced Mr. Lowe.

"Skip, I met the young lady, you introduced to Jim at church Sunday."

Skip looked away nervously.

"She certainly is a tall one, isn't she? Rather husky, as well."

Mr. Lowe was looking into Skip's face, with a stern look on his eyes. "Yeah, I believe that she may be Scandinavian," Skip muttered as he took a step backward.

Mr. Lowe raised one brow. "My mother is Scandinavian, Skip, and I'm sure that there isn't one similarity between them."

Skip just shrugged, putting another foot behind himself.

"Let me just say one more thing, Mr. Morris. James Ireland is a hard working, decent young man. He was raised by a wonderful, Christian woman. He knows how to support himself and take care of responsibilities. He might be slow, and you might mistakenly believe that his naivete is something to make jokes about, but the truth is you could learn a lot from James Ireland. Probably all of us could." Mr. Lowe was visibly shaken. There was rage in his eyes. "But, I guess the thing I want to make absolutely clear to you, is that Irene Ireland was a personal friend of mine. I will not stand by and watch you viciously make sport of her boy. Do we understand each other?"

Skip nodded, holding his cup and glancing at the floor. Mr. Lowe turned and walked back to his office.

Anastasia could see the exchange. She heard Jim's name, but she couldn't catch all of the conversation. She couldn't remember Mr. Lowe ever being that angry. In fact, this was the first time she had ever heard him raise his voice. Skip looked like a whipped puppy. She was curious, but at the same time, she really didn't think she could stand the burden of knowing, just then.

During lunch break Jim couldn't resist giving Anastasia the details of his date. He had obviously had the time of his life. His enthusiasm was so great that Anastasia had to give him a tired smile in spite of her apprehensions. He seemed more mature.

Maybe he really was in love. Hopefully, Julia was too. It would be too cruel if she wasn't.

The walk home after work was miserable. Half way there, she finally admitted to herself that she knew she was pregnant. She also knew she couldn't do a proper job of raising a child. Where would she get the money? She had to work all the time just to pay her rent. How could she afford child care, extra food, and a proper place for a child to grow up? She couldn't have a baby. She wouldn't even be able to afford the hospital stay for delivery. Anastasia wanted children, but not now, not until she could afford to give them the basic necessities, and especially give them her time. She wanted to be able to stay home with her children, at least until they started school. This was something she had thought about. She wanted happy, well-adjusted children. She wanted to be a good parent, and she knew she couldn't be her best right now, not yet. She hated the idea of an abortion, but the child had to wait.

She slumped up her stairs slowly, hardly noticing the man with the blond head sticking out of his door. The first thing that hit her when she opened her own was that smell. She spun around, angry. She was going to tell that crazy lunatic to do something about the stink. He quickly slammed the door when he noticed her turn toward him. She boldly stomped across the landing.

"Hey, open the door!" She pounded. "C'mon, I want you to do something about that smell! I'm going to complain to the landlord. I don't know what the hell kind of mess you've got in there, but that God awful smell is driving me mad. You hear me?" She was shouting at the top of her lungs and banging so hard her knuckles hurt. She continued to shout and pound on the door until she was hoarse. Then her screams turned into sobs. She broke down crying against the door. Slowly, she slid to the floor, crying hard. No one answered. She curled up into a ball, held her head, and rocked back and forth.

Loosing track of time, she had no idea how long she sat there crying. Finally, becoming aware of herself, she stood up and walked to the door to her own apartment. She just couldn't bring herself to go inside. Slowly, she grabbed hold of the doorknob and closed the door. She stumbled back down the stairs and started walking down the sidewalk. She was going to see her brother.

She let herself into her mother's home quietly, but without the usual degree of caution. He was sitting in his usual place on the bed, eating out of a bowl and reading. He hadn't even had the chance to say hello before Anastasia burst into his room, fell to her knees and hugged his waist, sobbing uncontrollably. He set his bowl and book on the nightstand and held her head, stroking her hair tenderly.

"Anastasia, what's wrong?" he asked in a whisper.

She was crying so hard she couldn't answer. She was making those hiccuping kind of sobs, like a child who is crying so hard that they can't take a breath. He continued to patiently hold her, rubbing her back and caressing her sweetly. It was a full five minutes before she could lift her head and rub her nose on the back of her hand. He offered her the end of a blanket. She looked up with big, red eyes.

"It's okay. It's washable," he reassured her. She wiped her whole face, then rested against his chest, shuddering occasionally.

"I think I'm pregnant," she said flatly.

He didn't say anything for a long time. He just sat there with his head against the wall, still stroking her hair gently. "Mother mentioned something about it," he admitted.

Anastasia looked up at him.

"How does she know these things? She knew before I did!" There was anger in her voice, a lifelong frustration.

"I don't know, but the thing is, Anastasia, she's not angry about it. She's, well, concerned." He looked down at Anastasia. "I know this sounds out of character for her, but she told me she wants you to move back in. She wants to help you and the baby."

Anastasia looked apprehensive. "Something's up with that, and you know it." She sat up on the side of the bed. "You know she's planning something. This whole thing just isn't right." The room had that eerie quietness. Their Mother was listening again.

"I can't have this baby." Anastasia shouted defiantly.

Her brother was clearly uncomfortable. He was almost afraid to speak. "I'll be there for you, regardless of what you decide," he whispered.

She turned and hugged him again.

"I love you so much," she whispered back.

He held her and replied in a hushed voice, "I love you, too."

They abruptly changed subjects, talked about books, Stella, current events, and everything but the details of Anastasia's decision. Someone was listening.

The view between her brother's new yellow drapes was growing dim. Twilight was on its way. Anastasia informed her brother that she should be on her way. He followed her to the stairway.

"There's a clinic on Second, near the bookstore. I pass it on my way to work. I noticed that it's open on Saturdays. You should go there for a physical." He looked at her seriously.

She nodded and descended the stairs.

"Take care", he said, bending down to touch her shoulder.

She looked up one last time. "I will." She smiled back.

She cracked the closet door and peeked out. She could hear the television in the next room. Slowly, she opened the door, then carefully shut it behind her. She turned to go back down the hall when something caught her eye. Her mother was suddenly standing beside her, looking directly at her. She froze.

"Anastasia," she said sweetly.

Anastasia looked up into her mother's face. Fear kept her from bolting.

"Anastasia, you look like you've been crying. What's wrong?" Her mother pronounced each word with such compassion, she would've fooled anyone else. Anastasia couldn't find her voice. She began to tremble. She really wanted to believe the concern in her mother's eyes. Did this woman really love? Had she ever loved? Anastasia wanted to leave, but was afraid to go.

"I-I-I'm okay." She shuddered.

To Anastasia's horror, her mother reached out and put her arm around her. "Now, you come in and have a cup of coffee with me. We need to talk." Anastasia stiffly moved in the direction her mother was pushing her. She was seated in a chair at the kitchen table, while her mother pulled a cup and saucer out of the cabinet. She then placed a hot cup of coffee in front of her daughter and sat down beside her.

"Anastasia," she said softly. She slowly reached out and laid her hand on her daughters forearm. Anastasia stiffened, staring at the steam rolling out of her coffee cup. "Anastasia," she repeated. "We both know why you're so upset. There's no need to pretend any differently. Now, we need to talk about your plans. Raising a child requires careful planning. I'm sure you'll make a wonderful mother."

Anastasia looked up at her mother in terror.

"Anastasia," she said, pleading. "You know you will. You're much better tempered for motherhood than I was at your age, or, let's be honest, than I am now, even."

Anastasia was amazed at her candid confession.

"And," she continued. "I'm perfectly willing to butt out of any of your parenting decisions. I just hope you'll allow me to offer you a home and financial help."

Anastasia stared at her mother, unable to answer. She felt like Gretle outside the witch's house, enjoying gingerbread shutters. Was this woman secretly planning to eat the baby? Something wasn't right. Anastasia could see through her mother's polished finish, but she couldn't figure out her plan.

"I-I-I'm tired. I need to go home and rest." The words were coming out easier. "I need to think things over, you know." She looked blankly at her mother, trying to keep her mind clear. She didn't want her mother to read her thoughts.

Marilyn's face was stony again, but she forced the corners of her mouth to curl. "Sure, I suppose this type of news takes a lot out of you." She helped Anastasia out of her chair, holding her with her right arm, as Anastasia walked directly to the closest door. She hadn't exited the house out of the kitchen in a long time.

"Take care," her mother said sweetly. Then she reached out and kissed Anastasia's cheek. Anastasia just stared in disbelief at her mother for a moment. Then she nodded and walked away. She noticed the door slam shut after she reached the sidewalk, but she never looked back.

That night, Anastasia had the most horrible nightmare. She dreamed the baby was born, and that it was lying on her bed, wrapped in a baby blanket. Stella and her brother were standing on either side of the bed.

"You should've gone to the clinic sooner," her brother shouted.

"Here, it's not too late." Stella offered Anastasia a large ugly knife. "Just cut off its head. It'll be the same thing."

Anastasia took the knife. She started cutting through the baby's neck. Halfway through, the baby started crying pitifully.

She stopped. "No, I've changed my mind!"

"Well, you can't stop now. Look it's already half off. You can't let it suffer with its head cut half off."

Anastasia looked back down at the pitiful, blood-covered baby. She held the knife over the wound, turned her head, and pushed the knife into the mattress. Screaming, with tears running down her face, she woke herself.

She jumped to her feet, and stumbled to find the light switch. She was shaking violently. Her legs went out from under her. She sat on the floor hard, holding her knees to her chin. She rocked herself, hugging her knees tightly.

Getting to work the next morning was difficult. She was tired, emotionally and physically. Her eyes were red and puffy. She was weak all over. In fact, she was so out of sorts she didn't even notice one significant matter until Joe mentioned it. Skip wasn't there. Jack Lowe, Mr. Lowe's son, stood next to the time clock and announced that Skip had been laid off due to lack of retail business up front. He told everyone that an increase in wholesale business more than made up for the declining retail sales, and not to worry about any further cut backs. Everyone nodded, but most of them knew about Skip's confrontation with Mr. Lowe the day before.

Jim was the only one who looked sad. Anastasia thought it was so ironic that the same person who had been the butt of so many of Skip's cruel jokes was the only one who felt bad about his leaving. She wondered what Jim would think if he knew he was the real reason for Skip's layoff. Did he realize the depth of Mr. Lowe's concern for him? That led her to the next question. What the heck did Skip do this time? Was it something about Julia? Now she was extremely curious. She had to get a look at Jim's new-found love.

She casually slid up next to Jim. "So, have you got a picture of her yet?" An immediate smile let Anastasia know that he knew who she was talking about.

"No," he said thoughtfully. "I'll ask her Friday. She's coming over to fix dinner at my house. She wants to see where I live." Jim took the opportunity to discuss in detail every conversation they'd had the night before. Since Anastasia had made the mistake of showing interest, she was now doomed to hear a replay of their nightly phone conversation. Love has a funny way of turning a normal person into a bore, and a boring person into a pest.

She nearly fell asleep at break, dropping a full cup of coffee onto the floor. Jack noticed how rough she was looking and let her go home early with pay. He could tell there was something wrong, but he didn't want to get so personal as to ask her about it.

Anastasia went home and slept until late afternoon. Feeling better when she woke up, she decided to visit the clinic her brother had told her about. She needed to confirm what she already knew in her heart.

The clinic was in the middle of a block of connected buildings. It was in an old, tired-looking part of downtown, but the inside of the office was clean and neat. The waiting room was full of women, a variety of ages and races, but all with a common, solemn look on their faces. No one talked. A television attached to the ceiling was showing a soap opera in the corner. Many of the women had their eyes fixed on it, but few seemed to be following the story. The receptionist was pleasant enough. She smiled at Anastasia and asked if this was her first visit.

"Yes," she replied.

"Are you here for birth control or a medical procedure?"

Procedure, Anastasia thought. So is that what they call it here? It was a much less emotional word. She decided she preferred it. Procedure was what she would call it from that day on.

"Well actually, I need to confirm that I'm pregnant, then set a date for a procedure if necessary." Anastasia was surprised at how calmly she had spoken.

"A complete physical is always required. Are you employed?"

Anastasia hesitated. Would anyone from work know about her visit here? "Why?" she asked.

"If you're unemployed or without health insurance, you can get financial aid," the receptionist explained.

"I don't have insurance. So how much would it cost? For everything?"

"Two hundred dollars, and it has to be paid in cash or money order."

The receptionist's warm smile was looking different now. It looked plastic and artificial, cold and unconcerned. Anastasia nodded. She promised to return on Saturday with a pay stub and birth certificate to prove she was a legal adult. They scheduled an appointment.

Anastasia scanned the waiting room one last time before she went out the door. Funny how no one made eye contact. It was like they were all ashamed of being there.

She stopped by the bookstore where her brother worked. She wanted to see a friendly face, someone who really cared.

"Hi there!" She waved to her brother as she walked in. He was standing behind the counter, studying a ledger.

"Hi! What are you doing here so early on a week day, skippin' work?" He was pleased to see her, but surprised.

"Oh, they let me out early. I've been working six days a week for so long now, I needed a few hours off." She was rummaging through a bin of old books. "I'm going to be taking Saturday off, too." She was talking without looking up. "I've got a doctor's appointment." Neither of them said anything else. He knew what she was talking about. There was no need to explain.

"So." He abruptly changed the subject. "I'll be closing this place pretty soon. Want to go out to eat? We haven't done that in awhile. I'll treat."

Anastasia lit up. "That would be great." She was relieved to have a good excuse not to go back to her apartment. She spent the next hour or so reading until her brother locked the doors. They walked to a small family restaurant a couple of blocks away. Anastasia ordered fish and chips. It was the first good, hot meal she had eaten in awhile. Everything tasted so good to her. She ate every bit of it. They discussed literature, mostly. He told her about a volume of Gnostic texts that had come in, explaining they were new translations of ancient books found in a cave before World War II.

"I really want you to read the *Gospel of St. Thomas,*" he said. "It has some interesting quotations attributed to Jesus. The whole book has a kind of Eastern feeling to it, difficult to explain, but then I believe St. Thomas was the one who supposedly founded a church in India."

Anastasia was fascinated. It felt great to be thinking of something besides her pregnancy. "As soon as you're through with it, let me know," she said with sincerity.

After eating, they sat drinking coffee and talking until they ran out of words. There was no excuse now. She had to go back to her apartment. He walked her home when it was almost dark.

"Do you want me to go with you Saturday?" he offered.

Anastasia struggled with herself. She wanted to say yes. "No, your life with Mom is difficult enough. She'd really be pissed if she knew you went with me." They were quiet for a moment, wondering if Marilyn was listening. "So, why do you think she wants me to have this baby so badly?" Anastasia almost whispered.

Her brother shook his head, looking around nervelessly. "Who can tell? I don't think we'll ever understand Mom. It's like she has a secret agenda. I don't think any of us, even Dad, know her." His voice trailed off. They both felt they had said too much.

They hugged good-bye. Anastasia started up the stairway. A large window above the doorway shed light onto the landing. Anastasia could see Mrs. Brown's door opening.

There he was again. She bounded up the stairs, eyes locked onto his, but before she could reach the landing he quickly slammed the door. She could hear him slide the bolt across. Aggravated, she let herself into her own apartment. God, how she hated that smell. It was beginning to make her nauseous. She opened the windows and crawled into bed.

CHAPTER 7

Work was so much quieter without Skip around. No one had realized how much he kept things stirred up. Even Jim was calmer. He was still just as enthusiastic about Julia, but a little quieter about it.

She told Jack she needed Saturday off for a doctor's appointment.

"Anything serious?" he asked.

"No, I've just been feeling run down lately."

He looked at her and nodded. She became a little frustrated. Did he suspect? "I think I'm anemic. In fact I know I am. I just need a stronger prescription vitamin or something." She was having problems reading him. She was usually so good at reading people. It must be because I've been so upset lately, she thought. She realized she was staring at him and felt embarrassed.

"It's okay, isn't it?"

"Oh, of course." He patted her shoulder. "I just hope you're feeling better soon."

She was still standing there feeling stupid when he turned and walked away. I have got to get a hold of myself, she thought, tilting her head back and taking a few deep breaths.

After work, she went back to her apartment, opened the windows, and relaxed with a book. She was feeling sleepy.

Soon after she dozed off, she heard a rustling sound on the landing, and then a knock. When she opened the door, she was amazed to see her mother standing on the landing with a bassinet. She was wearing a powder blue cape and a matching pill box hat.

"Mom?" She wasn't even aware her mother knew where she lived. Marilyn, ignoring her daughter's surprise, reached out and hugged Anastasia's neck.

"Darling, look what I've brought you!" She locked the legs of the bassinet in place and pushed it through the doorway. "I'm sure you don't remember this, but you used to sleep in it. So did your brother and sister when they were babies. Isn't it beautiful?"

Anastasia looked at the bed in horror. She didn't know what to say.

Her mother let herself in, closed the door, and set her purse on the floor next to the wall. She looked around, taking in the layout and contents of the apartment as she unbuttoned the front of a lightweight cape. She removed her hat, then stored both items in Anastasia's closet. Anastasia was still standing, mute next to the bassinet.

"Your apartment has a peculiar odor," she remarked, walking into the kitchen. She stared at the far wall, as if she could see behind it, then up at the ceiling. She then turned abruptly and looked straight at Anastasia. "Stay away from your neighbor. He's mad." She made the statement in a very matter-of-fact way. Then she softened her expression and moved to within a few inches of her daughter.

Anastasia wanted to ask more about her revelation, but she hadn't regained her power of speech yet.

"Anastasia," she said sweetly, taking her daughter's hands. "I know you're having a tough time, but I want you to know you don't have to be all alone. I'm here for you."

Anastasia was getting weak. She felt her mother was

somehow pulling the energy out of her. She wanted to break the circuit, to pull away, but fear kept her still and mute. Her mother's cold, blue eyes seared through her.

"Anastasia, dear, let me help you," she almost begged. "I know you're afraid, but I also know you'll make a wonderful mother. Of all my children, you are the most suited for parent-hood."

Her words were sending chills up Anastasia's spine. Why? Why was she so interested in this child?

"You know, dear, in some ways, you remind me of my aunt Elsa May." She looked up and away, dreamily. Anastasia had heard mention of Great Aunt Elsa, but almost as folklore from her grandfather. "Now she was a strong woman. She drove a stage coach out west, when it was still wild. She killed and fought off bandits, but she never lost a payload. When the stage coaches stopped running, she wandered the country, working gold mines, the railroad, she even cut timber up in the north. When the great war broke out, she tried to pass for a man and enlist." Marilyn shook her head, deep in thought. "They really made a big mistake when they made her leave after finding out she was a woman. She would have been an excellent soldier. Better than any they'd ever know."

Anastasia noted her mother's face was taking on an uncharacteristic look, a kind of forlorn expression. "I've never heard all of that before," Anastasia replied, loosening up a bit. "Grandpa mentioned her driving a stage coach, but he said he lost contact with her until just before she died."

"There's much that Patrick, I mean my father, doesn't talk about. He was busy being embarrassed about being Elsa's brother instead of being proud of her accomplishments. Men are like that when it comes to independent women. It's because strong women draw attention to how contrastingly weak they are. I guess that must be why he married such a silly woman."

Marilyn's words were now coming out with the familiar venom to which Anastasia was more accustomed. Marilyn suddenly realized it, too. This was not why she had come here.

She was quiet a moment, trying to compose herself again. She sighed and put the sweet smile back on her face.

"But, that's not the important matter here. You are the important matter, or should I say, the two of you? I'm so anxious to meet my new grandchild. You should hope for a boy. Boys are so much more fun to raise."

Anastasia was feeling uncomfortable again. Marilyn looked around the room. "Now, if you insist on living here, we could push your bed against the wall, and you could set the bassinet right here beside it." Marilyn walked to the side of her bed and pointed down. Anastasia only nodded. There was no way she would argue. She had already decided the only thing she could do was agree, keep her mind clear, and then go ahead with her original plans.

Her mother looked at her with suspicion, and walked near to her. She gazed intensely into her daughter's eyes, pushing her face into Anastasia's. "Don't tell me you're considering abortion," she shouted. "You know you can't do that. It's murder! How can you consider murdering your own child, Anastasia?"

Anastasia looked away, holding herself. Her mother grabbed hold of her forearms, shaking her slightly. "Anastasia, look at me!"

Anastasia looked up obediently, but trembling.

"Anastasia, you can't kill this baby! Why would you want to? I told you that we'll help you, your father and I. You can move back in. We'll pay for everything. You can quit working. I promise I won't interfere with your raising the child. In fact—" She looked away, then took much effort to soften her expression. "The fact is, Anastasia, I'm dying."

Anastasia's brows lowered in a curious expression. "There's a tumor in my womb. It's going to kill me soon. That's why this baby is so important. I want to know that life will go on. Your father will need his children around him. I just don't know what he'll do without me."

Now she was acting. Anastasia could tell. Was this story about a tumor even true? She pulled away from her mother's grip. "How long have you known?"

Her mother glared back at her. "You don't believe me, do you? I can't believe you'd think I'd make up such a thing. Have I ever tried to get sympathy from anyone? Never! Never, have I so much as complained. You kids and that good for nothing father of yours, none of you ever appreciate anything I've done, ever! But, have you heard me complain? So, why in hell would I make up something like this now?" She looked up at the ceiling, trying to compose herself.

Anastasia was beginning to realize just how difficult the situation was for her mother. She was used to being in complete control, and here was a situation she couldn't control. It was driving her crazy.

Marilyn took a deep breath then looked back at her daughter with a calm, but not so soft expression. "So, Anastasia, I'll say it one more time. I'm here for you, but it's up to you to make the right decision and have the baby. You would regret any other decision," she said evenly, almost threateningly.

Anastasia was trying to back away from her, but she was afraid to move. Marilyn put her face into Anastasia's again, turning her head slightly as she stared with intensity into Anastasia's eyes. "Abortion is murder, just as murderous as if you cut the baby's head off with a dull knife."

Anastasia sucked in a breath and held it in a horror-induced paralysis. Her mother was manipulating her dreams. How could she ever escape such a woman? Anastasia could not tell how long they stood facing each other. It seemed like an eternity before her mother finally turned, removed her things from the closet, and let herself out.

Anastasia paced back and forth for almost an hour, holding her head. She was so afraid. What would happen to her if she went through with the abortion? But now there was an even more compelling reason to have the abortion. Her mother was too anxious for Anastasia to have the baby. That meant there had to be some ungodly reason for her interest, something evil. But what? What was her mother's motive? Was she really dying? If so, why would this make her so interested in the baby?

Finally, Anastasia grabbed a pot, filled it with water and put it on the stove to boil. She decided to make herself some coffee. It was going to be a long night. There was no way she was going to sleep. The truth was, she was afraid to sleep, and would be until after Saturday. Maybe even after that.

Anastasia drank coffee continuously at work. She was looking every bit as bad as Tuesday, when her boss had sent her home. She tried to cover up her exhaustion, especially when either of the Mr. Lowes' were around. She didn't want to draw attention to herself.

After work, she decided she had to get some sleep, even if it put her in danger of another nightmare. Sleep came quickly. Soon, she became aware of the bassinet, only she knew there was something stirring inside it. She crept closer and looked in. There she could see the most perfectly formed toes, chubby little legs, and a penis. It's a boy, she thought happily. Then, she saw the plump tummy, and the little arms were flailing. But then, the head. She gazed in horror. The face was her mother's. Her mother's wicked blue eyes glared at her. She reached down, and the baby grabbed onto her hand and bit her fingers. Anastasia screamed and her baby-mother bit down harder, refusing to let go. Anastasia screamed again, until she woke herself. She immediately looked at the fingers on her right hand. They were purple on the ends with teeth marks at the first joints. She stared at them in horror for several seconds before deciding that during her nightmare, she must have bitten her own fingers.

She rolled off the side of her bed and looked at the clock. It hadn't even been an hour. Feeling wide awake, she looked at the bassinet wearily. After studying the hinges that held the legs in place she found they folded down easily. With the legs folded, she tried pushing it under her bed, but it wouldn't fit. She tried to put it into the closet. It was too long. She shoved it into the closet again, this time end to end. Then she slammed the door shut quickly, before it could fall back out. Sighing with relief, she realized that now she couldn't use her closet, but that was a small price to pay just to get the damn thing out of her sight.

She spent most of the night reading or pacing. She dozed off occasionally, but every time woke with a start. Sometimes she wouldn't remember what woke her, or it would be because of a sound. She couldn't tell if the sound was real or part of her dream. Most of the dreams were pure torture, except for occasional glimpses into something Anastasia began to find interesting. She kept seeing unfamiliar people in different times past. In one dream, she decided she must be her great aunt Elsa. She was whipping a team of horses, trying to outrun a bandit. In another, she had a vision of an old shack. A woman was standing at the door, shading her eyes with her hand, looking at something. Then, she saw even stranger surroundings— a vineyard in Europe with a castle in the distance. Finally, she felt the sensation of traveling fast on horseback, wearing something stiff and heavy, and only being able to see out of a hole in a helmet. She was holding tight to a long lance and rushing head long into a line of soldiers, also on horse back. They wore rags and animal skins. Every dream would wake her with a jolt. They all made her tremble and feel weak.

Every morning, she was happy to see the sun rise. She dressed for work and arrived early. Finally, it was pay day. The next day, it would be over.

The day dragged by. She was so miserable she was almost wishing Mr. Lowe would send her home again, but then what would she do?

Jim was in a vibrant mood. He was seeing his sweetheart tonight, and tomorrow they were going out dancing on the town. He wasn't sure what he'd do about the dancing part, but he was anxious to try.

He was still missing Skip. He couldn't understand why no one else did. Skip was always teasing him, but he was the one who had introduced him to Julia. That made all the rest okay. Mr. Lowe was acting funny, too. Jim was starting to think Mr.

Lowe didn't like the idea that he had a girlfriend. Whenever Jim mentioned Julia, Mr. Lowe acted like he wasn't listening. Once he even asked Jim to change the subject. Jim was becoming almost annoyed about it. Why should Mr. Lowe expect him not to be like everyone else? Most of the guys that he had gone to school with were married with children. Some were on their second wives. So, why did Mr. Lowe act so uncomfortable about him having a girlfriend? Julia told him that sometimes people were jealous of other people's happiness. Jim found it hard to believe, but maybe that was what it was.

CHAPTER 8

Well, she had made it. It was Saturday. She had managed to fall into a deep dreamless sleep for a couple hours during the night. But, it wasn't enough. She was still exhausted. She tried to perk herself up in the shower, afraid that they wouldn't preform the procedure if they saw her looking so weak and frazzled. She forced down half a bologna sandwich before leaving for the walk to Second Street. She had cashed her check the day before at the grocery store. She had $250 in an envelope in her purse. The closer she came to the clinic, the more she wished she had asked her brother to come with her. She was feeling so alone. Even the streets seemed deserted and empty that morning. As she turned the corner onto Second Street, she began feeling lightheaded. When she got to the block the clinic was on, she was dizzy. Crossing the last intersection was difficult. It seemed like she would never get to the other side. She sat down on the curb and held her head, trying to make it stop spinning.

"You okay there, lady?" It was a young man, tall and thin with dark, curly hair. He looked familiar. She stared at him a minute. Did she know him from the bar with Stella?

She nodded her head. "Yeah, I'm fine. Just tired." He helped her to her feet, then hesitated for a moment, still holding her arm. Anastasia looked down to see a wedding ring on his left hand. She looked back up into his face. He was staring at her with familiar eyes.

"Well uh, have a nice day," he stammered. For some reason, he suddenly appeared anxious to leave. Anastasia stood for a moment, watching him walk away. Could he be her mime?

She staggered on to the clinic, using her body to push the door open. There, behind the counter sat the lady with the plastic smile. Anastasia added her name to the bottom of a short list of names and appointment times. She noticed there were already four women with the same appointment time as hers. How many doctors were there?

Moving to an orange plastic chair near the TV, she sat down. For the first time, she realized sadly that now she wouldn't be able to afford her own TV. That would be just a small part of her punishment for getting herself into this predicament in the first place, she decided.

The plastic chair felt more comfortable than it looked. She found herself blankly looking at the television screen as the room quickly filled up. She wasn't sure how much time passed before her name and five others were called. The women were led down a hallway in a line, and one-by-one they fell out and were assigned individual rooms. Anastasia was assigned room number five. She took a seat on a black, vinyl-covered, flat bed with ominous looking stirrups and a strip of white butcher paper across it. She scanned the small room and noted it wasn't much bigger than her bathroom. There was a small metal cabinet on rollers across from her. Beside her was a silver pushcart, like the ones busboys use to stack dirty dishes. The only thing permanent in the room was a small, white, porcelain sink. A thought passed through her mind. She tried to remember what this building was used for prior to being converted into a women's clinic. She couldn't remember.

Shortly, a woman in a white suit carrying a clipboard entered the room and shut the door. She stopped in front of Anastasia and looked down at her clipboard.

"Hello, could you please pronounce your first name?"

"Anastasia," she replied.

The lady made a notation on her paper. "First we must give you a general physical and pregnancy test. If your pregnancy test comes out positive, I see here on your information sheet, that you'd like to have the procedure to terminate the pregnancy as soon as possible. Is that right?"

Anastasia nodded. "Yes."

"Okay, but let me also explain that, before you have the procedure, you are required to talk to a counsellor."

Anastasia panicked. "You mean I can't get everything done today?"

"Oh, there's no problem with getting through everything today. In fact, the part that takes the longest is after the procedure. You have to sit still for an hour before you can leave. Then you talk to a birth control advisor, who will supply you with birth control pills."

"You mean I can go through all these steps today before the clinic closes?"

The lady nodded. "No problem. We do it all the time."

Anastasia was perplexed. She felt like a car on an assembly line. The women quickly and methodically performed the physical, ending by giving Anastasia a plastic jar to pee in. Her instructions were to visit the bathroom at the end of the hall, print her name on the jar's label, then leave it with the receptionist and take her seat in the waiting room again.

In a matter of minutes, she was called back to the examining room and informed what she already knew in her heart. She was pregnant. She was asked if she wanted to continue with the procedure. To that she answered in the affirmative. She was then marched down the hall to another plastic chair outside a closed wooden door with the word counsellor printed on it. Anastasia waited quietly.

She could hear nurses talking about their plans for after work in one room, and a woman crying loudly in another. She tried to clear her mind and not think about anything. She stared at the ceiling.

Then the door opened. A young woman wiping her nose was directed out by a flabby arm. Anastasia watched the woman walk back to an examining room. Then, a short, chubby woman in a flowered dress stepped into the open doorway and looked at a clipboard.

"So, are you Anastasia?" she asked, peering over her glasses.

"Yes."

"Come right this way," she said.

Anastasia stepped into the room with apprehension. This room was a bit larger, with carpeting and comfortable-looking arm chairs. There was a potted tree in the corner and shelves filled with pictures of children and other family members. The lady took her seat directly across from Anastasia, only about an arms length away. She held her clipboard on her lap and a pen in her hand.

"Anastasia, tell me about yourself," the lady said cheerfully.

Anastasia looked at her blankly, "I live in an apartment downtown, and I work for a printer."

The lady nodded thoughtfully. "Do you live alone?"

"Yes."

"For how long?"

"Over a year now."

"Okay, so tell me about the baby's father."

Anastasia was uncomfortable. She felt ashamed of herself. "Well, actually I never got to know him very well."

"Does he know you're pregnant?"

"No."

"Don't you feel that he has the right to know?"

Anastasia cringed. "I don't even know how to get hold of him, or even his name." She looked at the floor with shame.

"I see." The lady started writing on the clipboard. "After the procedure, what type of birth control do you plan to use?"

Anastasia shook her head. "I wasn't planning to use

anything."

The lady frowned. "Do you plan to use abortion as a form of birth control?" She spoke with obvious disappointment in her voice.

"No."

"Well then, how do plan to avoid getting pregnant again?"

"Well, usually I just don't have sex during a new moon, but this time, well I just wasn't paying attention."

The counsellor looked annoyed. "Are you telling me that you think the moon has something to do with getting pregnant? How old are you?"

Anastasia felt foolish. She had forgotten that people outside her family didn't accept knowledge she had always taken for granted. She forgot they were different. "I guess I should start taking pills." She blurted.

"Well, if we start you on a program, will you take the pills? You have to remember to take them every day, or they won't do you any good. And believe me, sister, the moon has nothing to do with anything."

Anastasia was embarrassed almost to tears. "I'll take them," she promised.

The lady continued to write on her clipboard for several minutes. "Okay then, unless you have questions, you can go wait in the examining room. We'll need to do a gynecological exam next."

The lady looked at her sternly. Anastasia stood up to leave. She was anxious to get out of the room. Somehow, it had gotten smaller and less comfortable. The counsellor walked to the door and pointed down the hall.

"Go to examination room number four and undress. Take everything off. There should be a stack of paper gowns on the counter." Anastasia started down the hall.

Examination room number four was exactly like examination room number five, except for one difference. There was a window covered with white horizontal blinds. Anastasia stood by the window, pushed over the blinds and looked outside. It was raining. How fitting, she thought. The sky had darkened so that it looked like early evening, even though it wasn't yet noon.

She sighed as she slowly undressed. How had she gotten herself into this mess? She vowed it would never happen again. She couldn't go through this again. She slipped into the paper gown.

A different nurse knocked, then stepped into the room carrying the now familiar clipboard. Anastasia probably wouldn't have noticed it was a different nurse, but her hair was so dark. The first one had been blond. Both had worn white pant suits and had stethoscope necklaces.

"I'll need to get samples. Then the doctor will give you a pelvic exam and go right into the procedure. After he gets here, it doesn't take long at all." She smiled at Anastasia. She directed her to put her feet in the stirrups, scoot down and relax. "When the doctor gets here, he'll do a normal exam," she explained as she snapped on a pair of rubber gloves. "Then he will begin dilating you with larger and larger probes." Anastasia was becoming interested in the nurse's explanation, but the nurse's probing fingers were distracting. "Once you're dilated, he'll insert a type of suction hose that empties your uterus." Anastasia was beginning to notice discomfort in the pit of her stomach. She was feeling like she might vomit if the nurse didn't finish soon.

"Afterward, you get to sit in a lounge chair and eat cookies for an hour!" The nurse spoke almost too enthusiastically.

So will that be my reward for being a good patient, Anastasia thought.

The nurse left, and came back with a grey-haired gentleman in a white lab coat.

"Anastasia, this is Dr. Martin. He'll be preforming the procedure for you."

Anastasia nodded. The nurse had become a little too perky.

Dr. Martin barely acknowledged her before he put on a pair of rubber gloves and pushed aside the white paper that scantily covered Anastasia's private parts. He was a humorless older man who looked like he was at the end of a difficult life. Anastasia stared up at the ceiling as he performed the exam. Without realizing that she was crying, she noticed a tear run down the side of her face. She quickly wiped it away, hoping no one had noticed. They hadn't. She wondered if they treated everyone this impersonally, or was she just so upset that she felt that they didn't care? Maybe they were afraid any treatment besides this cold assembly line would make the whole thing more difficult to go through. Again, she tried to clear her mind and not think about what was really going on.

"Anastasia!"

"Oh, what? I'm sorry. I wasn't paying attention," she apologized.

The doctor stood up and looked over the paper sheet. "Did you say something?" He looked puzzled and annoyed. She noticed the nurse was looking at her quizzically, as well.

"I thought you called me."

"No, I didn't." He sat back down on his stool, returning to his task. Anastasia was feeling the nausea in her stomach again, but even more than before. Suddenly, it felt like he had shoved the probe all the way into her stomach. She whined and half sat up.

"Hey there! Hold still! What are you doing?" the doctor shouted.

Anastasia took a deep breath. The nurse moved up beside her. "I thought I was going to get sick." She explained breathing heavily with perspiration forming on her brows.

"Well, we're not going to be able to proceed if you don't quiet down. Just relax. Spread your knees," he ordered. Anastasia tried to relax, but the whole thing was beginning to feel more like a rape than a medical procedure. She clenched her teeth and squeezed her eye lids shut. It was unbearable.

"I said relax." The doctor was more than irritated. The nurse put a cold, wet paper towel on Anastasia's forehead. It was little relief. She didn't know how much longer she could force herself into this unnatural position. She was cramping badly.

"Anastasia!"

She heard it clearly now and opened her eyes in astonishment. That voice, it was her mother. She clenched her jaw tighter, trying not to yell out. She was now staring wide-eyed at the ceiling. Sweat mixed with tears ran down the sides of her face. She felt another sharp pain. She could bear it no longer. She screamed. "No! Stop! I've changed my mind!" she shouted.

The doctor looked over the paper sheet. "I can't stop now. We're halfway finished."

Anastasia screamed again, sobbing uncontrollably.

"Nurse! Hold her down. We've got to finish now. There's no choice." The nurse stuck her head out the door and called for help. Two other women ran in. They stood on both sides of Anastasia. One held her legs apart. The other leaned across her head, holding her arms and torso down.

Anastasia continued to cry and scream loudly. Finally, after what seemed like an eternity, the doctor announced he was finished and left the room. Anastasia dropped her legs, as though they were rubber. It was over. She was so glad it was over. She felt foolish as she looked around the room, noticing the first nurse was the only one left. She was quietly putting things away. Anastasia was embarrassed.

"I'm sorry," she sobbed quietly.

The nurse turned to her briefly. "It's okay. Sometimes that happens." She returned to her work, as though everything had went routinely. Was that whole traumatic experience just something the happens sometimes? Anastasia lay there wondering if she was just having another nightmare. Were these people real?

The nurse finished her task, and then left the room. Anastasia lay very still with her eyes closed. The nurse reappeared too soon.

"You can get dressed now. Then go to the end of the hall where you came in. There's a green door. You can go in there and have a seat in one of the recliners. There's juice and cookies. You should eat something. It will help you feel stronger. The attendant will tell you when your hour is up."

Juice and cookies, Anastasia thought. Just like in grade school. She slowly stood up and got dressed. She felt like she had been beaten and assaulted, but, it was over.

CHAPTER 9

Jim sat restlessly in front of the television. He was wishing the time away, anxious for his date with Julia. Last night had been wonderful. She'd brought over special groceries and fixed him a gourmet dinner. They had drank wine and talked until late in the evening. Then they'd spent a great deal of time necking on the sofa. Jim was head over heels in love. He had already decided that he wanted to spend the rest of his life with Julia. He didn't want to dirty their relationship— he wanted a proper white wedding. Julia had promised him that she was a virgin. He had admitted to her that he was, too. Everything was perfect. "Meant to be," as Julia would say.

Finally, when the time came, they met at the same Chinese restaurant of their first date. This time, she was wearing red. After dinner, they walked to a bar that offered dancing. Jim hadn't danced in a long time. Usually, when he went out, it was to a bar with pool tables and dart boards.

Arriving just before the place became crowded, they found a table close to the dance floor. The dance floor was made of white squares of plastic with colored lights blinking from underneath. A big silver disco ball hung from the ceiling, causing millions of little stars to swirl around the room. A disc jockey played music from a raised booth that stood to the left of the stage, against the wall. Jim was impressed. Julia had recommended the place. She had said it was the most popular bar in town.

As soon as they sat down, she began bobbing around in her seat. After the waitress delivered their drinks, she reached across the table, and grabbed Jim's arm.

"Let's dance," she shouted.

"No, not yet, let me have a couple drinks first."

Julia gave him an exaggerated frown, then she jiggled her head in a cute way, taking a sip from the straw of her mint julep. She eyed the crowd like a seasoned bar fly. A new song came on. She gave Jim an excited look, and grabbed onto his arm again so hard that it hurt.

"Oh, com'mon, this is my favorite song!" She was bobbing in her chair again with a pained expression on her face, pleading with Jim.

He motioned for her to let go. "Why don't you go by yourself? I see other girls out there dancing together."

She looked at the dancers. They were mostly women. She smiled. "Okay, but you come out for the next one!"

He was relieved. He waited for her to turn her back before he rubbed his sore arm.

She moved into the crowd. Expertly wiggling her hips, she turned, throwing him a sensuous smile. He was watching her closely. For him, she was the only one in the place. He couldn't even see the other dancers. She slowly turned her back to him, rotating her shoulders and grinding her hips. Her dress was gathered at the waist and billowed out as she swung around to face him again. He caught a glimpse of a black lace slip. It took his breath away for an instant.

Now she was facing him and motioning with her arms and eyes for him to come up onto the dance floor with her. He took a gulp of his beer. She moved her hands down her body, making a snakelike movement with her shoulders and hips. God, how he loved her. It almost hurt. She moved her hands to her head, gathering her hair between her fingers, then slowly raising her hands so that her trusses fell gently between her fingers and back to her shoulders. She motioned to him again. This was too much. He took one more gulp before jumping up to meet her on the dance floor.

He felt awkward at first, but soon she had him so distracted that he forgot his feelings of inadequacy. They danced for several songs. She seemed to get more excited with every new tune. At one point, she bumped him so hard that it knocked him into the couple next to them. Embarrassed, they both tried to pretend it hadn't happened. She discontinued the periodic bumps.

The feeling of awkwardness did return at the beginning of their first slow dance. She dwarfed him, and for some reason, they did have a problem synchronizing their steps. But soon she had him in a tight embrace, with her knees bent and her neck resting on his shoulder. It was an unnatural position, but it did make him feel more her size.

Finally, he led her back to the table. That was when they realized how crowded the place had become. People were standing thickly all around the bar. Even in the aisles, singles stood with drinks in their hands. Their own drinks went down fast.

Now they sat with empty glasses, their waitress nowhere to be seen. Jim wanted another drink. He could tell Julia was thirsty as well. That was when he offered to walk up to the bar. Julia agreed, fanning herself with a flyer someone had laid on the table.

Jim pushed his way through the crowd. Finally, he was standing behind another man who was ordering a drink. He stood, politely waiting his turn, when he began to realize that he knew the man in front of him.

"Skip," he shouted above the noise.

Skip turned around slowly. His red face and glazed eyes made it obvious that he was very drunk. His head bobbed as he focused on Jim. Then he showed a spark of recognition, but without a smile.

"Hey there, Jimmy," he said, reaching in his pocket to pay for his drink.

Jim was surprised, but not the least deterred by Skip's condition or demeanor. "Boy, Skip, we really miss you at work. Things are boring now. You always kept us laughing."

"Oh, well!" Skip shrugged, looking away. Even Jim could tell by Skip's tone that his recent layoff was not a subject that Skip wanted to discuss. Jim changed to something more pleasant— the love of his life.

"Hey, Skip, Julia's with me. We've got a table up by the dance floor," he nodded his head in the direction of their table.

Skip studied Jim for a moment. A drunken sneer crept onto his puffy red lips. "You still seein' that drag queen?"

Jim looked at him with a baffled expression, then smiled, trying to understand the joke. "Awe, she's a queen all right. I've never met a finer woman." Jim declared.

Skip chuckled, "So, you like your women with dicks, huh Jimmy?" He said this loudly. The people around them were starting to turn around and listen. Jim just stood glaring at Skip, without a smile. Skip continued. "I'll tell ya', when I saw her big dick, I got jealous!" Roars of laughter followed.

"What do you mean? You're not makin' fun of Julia, are you? I know she's kind of big boned, but she's the most beautiful woman there ever was. She's a nice person, Skip. I don't want to hear you talkin' dirty about her."

Skip just continued laughing harder, as more and more people near them were laughing and listening with great interest. Jim continued to stand his ground with a perplexed angry glare on his face. Skip just continued to laugh in an exaggerated way. Jim looked around him. It seemed that everyone there was looking at him and laughing. He was suddenly full of rage. Why was he always the one who didn't understand the joke? He scanned the crowd, their eyes following him and laughing. Now he saw the kids on the playground, laughing at him. Someone accidently bumped him. He shoved the woman hard. She screamed. The laughter died down. Several men came toward him.

He looked back at Skip while swinging at the men as they tried to restrain him. He kept his eyes on Skip. He wanted to get at him. He started kicking and swinging wildly, striking hard at the men who were trying to restrain him. He wanted Skip.

Skip had stopped laughing, but that evil vindictive smile was still on his lips as he leisurely watched the mob of men beating Jim to the ground with their fists. Soon the police arrived. He couldn't see Jim anymore, just a tangled mess of arms and legs. The police surrounded the mob and began peeling off the men, threatening them with their clubs. About this time, Skip looked past the fight and saw Julia watching with shock and surprise on her face, and something else, concern for Jim. Skip chuckled at the idea that maybe these two losers actually cared for one another. He took another drink. He never dreamed that his joke would go this far. He really wanted to see Jim's face the first time he saw Julia naked. But, never for an instant had he believed Jim would fall in love with her. Skip shook his head. What an ignorant looser, he thought, taking another slurp of his drink.

Finally, the police had worked their way to the bottom of the pile and were pulling Jim to his feet. Julia watched helplessly with her hands over her mouth. She wasn't sure what had happened, but after noticing Skip, she had a good idea.

She was trembling when the police pulled him up. His shirt was ripped half off. She could see his exposed chest. His hair was wet and mussed, covering his left eye. There was blood coming out of his nose and the corner of his mouth. She ran to him. The police pushed her back. She called out to him and managed to make eye contact. He only looked at her pitifully for a moment, then turned his eyes away.

"Jim," she cried. "Honey, what happened?" He ignored her, walking out between two officers. She glared dully at Skip, her eyes filled with hate.

"You loathsome son of a bitch!" Her voice raised with each syllable until the last word came out in a shout. Skip only looked at her with amusement and took another drink of his beer.

She walked close to him, slamming her fist hard onto the bottom of the upturned beer bottle. He fell backwards onto the bar. The bottle fell to the floor as he bent over, holding his hand against his face, blood running between his fingers.

"You freak," he screamed, blood spurting out of his mouth. "You broke my tooth!" Before any more blows were thrown, a policeman grabbed Julia's arms, twisted them behind her back and pushed her through the crowd after Jim. She spat defiantly in Skip's direction. The policeman slapped her on the back of her head.

Roughly, he pushed her through the door toward a patrol car. It was then that she realized that she was handcuffed. They're going to arrest me, she thought, panic filling her. She tried to turn to face the officer.

"Come on, turn around and get into the car," he ordered, pushing her toward the vehicle. Her eyes glazed over. She knew all too well what it meant when people like her were locked up in a men's jail cell. She looked down at herself, waiting for the policeman to open the door of the car. She thought sadly about how she was wearing her best dress.

Jim found a seat on a bench near the bars of his jail cell. There was the usual Saturday night crowd of derelicts, drunks, and red necks. The cell was large, but full to capacity. He had been arrested for fighting once before. Although he swore to his mother that it would never happen again, there he was. For once, he was grateful that his mother wasn't alive to see it. He leaned against the bars, quietly staring at nothing. He was completely sober. His face and body hurt, but he was too numb with depression to feel it. He wondered what had happened to Julia. He'd seen her handcuffed and being pushed into a police car at the time he was being questioned. He wondered if she had been arrested. Funny, but he didn't hate her. He was ashamed of his ignorance. How could he have fallen in love with another man? Was he that stupid? Now it was over. In just minutes, the love of his life was gone. In fact, she never really existed. He closed his eyes tightly. It was too painful to think about.

About this time, Jim noticed the men crowding around the bars. They were whistling and laughing. He looked outside, and there, within a few inches of him, was Julia. A guard was escorting her to Jim's cell. The guard yelled at the men to shut up and get away from the door. He pushed her through the doorway and yelled one more stern warning to the men inside to "leave'm alone!" She kept her eyes down, finding a seat near the bars. She jerked away from a man who mockingly grabbed her arm to help her sit down. Another man grabbed at the front of her dress. The first man jabbed him in the ribs and said, "That was no way to treat a lady." Everyone laughed.

Jim looked across at her with pity. She looked up and noticed him, then moved her eyes back down in shame. Now he knew it was true— Julia was a man. He stared at her gaunt torso. Her makeup was wiped off, and her hair was pulled back into a ponytail. Her features now looked rough and masculine. How could he have not known? It was so obvious to him now. Sitting across from him was a man in a dress. My God! Had everyone noticed but him? He banged his head silently against the bars. He wanted to cry.

CHAPTER 10

Anastasia was resting comfortably for the first time in a week. She was reluctant to get up and answer the door, but she did. On the other side was her brother, with his arms full of books. She hugged him lovingly. He was the only person she really wanted to see.

"So, how are you doing? Did everything go alright?" he asked, shutting the door behind himself.

"Yeah, I'm okay. Everything went fine," she lied, not wanting to relive the details.

"Well, you know Anastasia, you really do look good. In fact, for just having had a surgery, I'd say that you're looking better than you did the last time I saw you. You did go through with it, didn't you?"

Anastasia nodded. "Oh yeah, nothing to it."

He smiled with relief. "Well, I'm glad. I've been worried about you."

Anastasia crawled back under her covers. Her brother took a seat at the foot of her bed, setting the pile of books beside him. She watched him tilt his head up and sniff the air.

"Don't tell me that it's gotten so strong that even you notice it."

He looked disturbed and said, "That is a foul smell. Would you like me to talk to your neighbor? I know he's home; I saw him."

"I'd love it." Anastasia announced with enthusiasm. "Maybe you'll have better luck than I've had."

With that, her brother walked across the hall and began knocking, then banging on the door. He called out, but no one answered. Finally he gave up and returned to Anastasia's bedside.

"Is there a phone over there?" he asked, tilting his head.

"I don't know," Anastasia said wearily. "But I bet there is. When you get home, will you try calling over there?"

"Sure, we'll see if anyone picks up," her brother stated with resolve.

They entered into a light conversation. Then Anastasia ended up telling him about their mother's disturbing visit.

Anastasia pointed toward the closet. "It's still in there. I don't know what to do with it," she said referring to the bassinet.

He reached out and patted the lump in the blanket that was her leg. "I'll take care of it. Don't worry. I'll find out from Mom if she wants it back. If not, well, I'll just come and get it anyway."

Anastasia sighed. It was great to be the little sister.

"So," Anastasia started with fresh demeanor. "How has Mom been acting lately?"

"Quiet. In fact, she's been spending a lot of time in her room and in the basement." He looked at his sister mysteriously. "I'd sure like to know what she does down there, but I value my life too much to sneak around and find out."

Anastasia giggled. "Remember that time when I talked Stella into hiding with me in the furnace room?" She was hugging her knees, reflecting fondly. "It was when I first discovered that if I cleared my mind, sometimes she couldn't hear me, but she did. The only thing we saw her do was stand in the middle of the room with her head tilted up and her eyes closed. Then she walked right over to where we were hiding and pulled us up by our hair." She shook her head. "That was as close to death as I ever want to get."

They both laughed. Then it occurred to both of them that their fond, childhood memories were probably stories that other people related to their therapists as disturbing. The three of them had somehow learned to let things roll off their backs and be each other's therapists. If they hadn't had each other, well, they wouldn't have survived to adulthood. Marilyn's style of mothering would've killed an only child.

"Well, whatever it is she's up to, she failed at forcing you to do what she wanted." He spoke out loud before he realized. He looked at his sister in panic. Then the two of them were quiet for awhile. He was wishing he could take back his words. He could never be sure what his mother heard. Anastasia changed subjects.

They talked and eventually became involved in a card game. Her brother treated her to a pizza that he brought back to her room, and they had a nice evening together.

By Monday, Anastasia was anxious to go back to work. She had lain around all weekend, and was glad for the new surroundings. She even arrived early to clock in. Right away, she noticed that Jim was absent. As the room filled up, she became more concerned. Where was Jim? She had never known him to be late. That was when Jack Lowe came into the room and said solemnly, "I need to make an announcement. Could I have your attention please?" Everyone hushed. "I'm sorry to have to tell you this, but Jim is currently in the hospital in critical condition. It seems there was some sort of accident. He shot himself yesterday. The doctors aren't sure if he'll live." Everyone was quiet, in shock.

Anastasia followed Jack out of the room. Jack knew of Jim's special relationship with Anastasia and took her into his father's office so they could speak privately.

"Yes, it looks like a suicide attempt," Jack admitted. "My

father is at the hospital with him now. He's not allowed any other visitors."

"What about Julia?"

Jack's jaw clenched. "We think that Julia might have been the reason for it. Anastasia, have you ever met Julia?"

Anastasia noticed the careful way he pronounced Julia's name each time he spoke it. "No."

Jack looked uncomfortable. "Anastasia, Julia is a man." Anastasia looked confused as Jack continued. "Apparently he's one of those sorts who likes to dress up like a woman. You've heard of those people, haven't you?"

She could see that he was desperately hoping she had. "Yeah, a transsexual?"

"I don't know the terminology, but this guy did a really good job at convincing Jim that he was a girl, and, well, Jim hasn't had a whole lot of experience with women, so he fell for it, head over heals. There was a fight at a bar Saturday, so Jim was put in jail overnight. Then Sunday afternoon, one of his neighbors called the police because she heard a gun go off. They found Jim in his room with an old hunting rifle that had belonged to his father."

Anastasia and Jack looked at each other with watery eyes.

"Do they think he's going to make it?" She asked.

"They said Sunday that if he made it through the night, there was a good chance. He did, so maybe he'll be okay. The bullet went through his neck. He hit his head on his dresser when he fell. They said that the fall probably knocked him out. He almost bled to death before they got him to the hospital."

"Has he come to yet?"

Jack shook his head no.

"Let me know when he can have visitors, please." Anastasia wiped a tear off her cheek. "I'll tell my brother and sister. I wonder if they'd let us up?" She looked up at Jack.

He shook his head and hunched his shoulders indicating that he didn't know. They were quiet a moment then Jack assured her that he would keep her posted if he had any more information. He let her use his phone to call Stella, unfortunately Marilyn answered. Anastasia panicked and hung up, she decided that she'd wait till late tonight and sneak over in person. They returned to work. Everyone was unusually quiet that day.

After work, she found a note on her door from her brother. It said, "Anastasia, sorry but I haven't been able to talk to Mom. She's been in a bad mood, very bad. I'll come over as soon as I can to get the bassinet. P.S. I called your neighbor's phone, no answer."

Anastasia pushed her door open and walked inside. She was disappointed about the bassinet. Then it occurred to her that she was an adult and should take care of these things herself. She opened the closet and stared at the thing. She really did want it out of her apartment, but at the same time, it was a family heir-loom, so she couldn't just throw it out. Then she noticed the drawstring for the attic door above her head inside the closet.

She pulled the bassinet out of the way, then pulled down on the rope. A set of stairs rolled out, just like the ones at her mom's. She knew about the stairway, but she'd never had any-thing that needed to be stored away before. It looked dark and dusty. She remembered that she had a small pen light in her purse. She retrieved it and then awkwardly ascended the stairs with the folded up bassinet in front of her. She had to push the bed through the hole in front of her. Finally, she was standing with her back arched at the top of the stairs. The smell was worse, much worse. She shined the light around her. Most of what she could see was under a thick layer of dust. It looked like there were a few boxes and over stuffed bags on Mrs. Brown's side, but it was hard to tell what was discarded building materials and what was stored treasures. She became curious, wondering what the old woman might have stored away years ago and forgotten. She set the baby bed on her side, near the hole. Then she walked cautiously toward Mrs. Brown's half of the attic.

Part of the attic was unfinished, with bare floor beams showing. Anastasia had to watch her feet so that she didn't step in the wrong place and end up going through the ceiling. She noticed a stack of boxes and burlap or paper bags stuffed with clothes that peeked over the top of the bags. Everything had a thick coating of dust, except for a garbage bag that was sticking out from behind the boxes. She eased over to it slowly, afraid to make any noise, since she was kind of trespassing. The smell was also getting stronger. She wondered if she had found the source of the smelly garbage.

She shined the light over the stack of boxes, but the tiny beam of light would only illuminate a small area at a time. She arced the light around the boxes. There, she could see something like fur. Did Mrs. Brown have a fur coat, she wondered.

Finally, she decided to push the stack of boxes over slowly. How would Mrs. Brown remember the exact placement of the boxes? She pushed with her shoulder, then shined the light behind the boxes again. There it was, peeking out from the garbage bag. She reached over with the toe of her shoe and hooked it in the top of the bag. She dragged her shoe down, then shined the light back in that direction. The beam of light revealed the fur, but it was hair— grey curly hair. She continued to watch the beam of light as it then revealed a forehead, and then the open, dead eyes of Mrs. Brown.

Anastasia's scream could be heard on the street outside her building.

CHAPTER 11

Anastasia was holding her coffee cup with both hands. She was trembling so badly that she was afraid she might spill it. Her brother was gently rubbing her back. They were sitting on the edge of her bed while the police were going through the attic and Mrs. Brown's apartment.

They had to break the door down to get in. Inside, they found the disturbed blond vagrant huddled up on the floor in the bedroom. He refused to talk, but one of the officers recognized him as a local homeless man. Their first opinion was that Mrs. Brown had probably died of a heart attack. The police theorized that he may have wandered into her apartment and frightened her when she saw him. They were planning to do an autopsy after her niece in California identified her body.

Anastasia was close to collapse. Apparently, her mother did have some compassion for her, since she sent Anastasia's brother to her apartment and called the police. He had made it to her apartment on the heels of the first patrol car. Anastasia marveled that if everyone had her mother's abilities, the world would be a much different place.

She cried on her brother's shoulder yet again, and again he patiently held her, listening to her sobs. Then she had to tell him about Jim. It was all so dark and depressing, what more could go wrong?

The police had extensive questions, which she answered as best she could. It was well after midnight when they left. Anastasia was such a nervous mess that her brother bought her a pint of whiskey and had her take a couple shots before getting into bed. He stayed with her until she fell asleep.

Later, as he slowly walked home. He agonized over the plights of his siblings, feeling that their problems were partly his fault for not being around more. He knew that Jim was desperately lonely since his mother had died, but at the same time they had grown into such different adults that most of their visits were filled with expanses of awkward silence. He also wished that there was something more he could do for his sister. He realized that she needed company, as well. Then an idea came to him. It made him cheer up. He was going to wake Stella up and talk with her about it. It was time they began talking to each other again anyway. Besides, he did miss his oldest sister.

It was really tough getting up the next morning. Anastasia almost didn't, but then the ordeal with Jim came to her mind, so she did. She really wanted to find out how he was and when she could go see him.

She was late for work, so it surprised her that the employee entrance was still locked. She walked around to the front and it was open. Inside, Jack was waiting on a customer. "Sorry, Anastasia. I'm not used to opening up. I forgot to unlock the employee's door." Jack apologized. The man at the counter turned around. Anastasia was taken aback. He was tall, with a husky build, dark wavy hair, and the most striking blue eyes. He smiled at her and made her realize that she was staring.

"That's okay, Jack. Want me to unlock it?" she mumbled.

"Could you, please?"

"Sure," she said.

Then the man smiled at her again. "That is a beautiful name, Anastasia. That was my grandmother's name." The man had a wonderful, deep voice, with a slight accent. He was dressed in black with a long trench coat and was holding a pair of black leather gloves in his hand. He looked so European, Anastasia thought.

"Thank you," she said dumbly. She really wanted to say something clever, but it just wouldn't come. If only she wasn't so run down, she'd have been able to come up with something intelligent.

He continued to watch her as she walked across the room and through the, 'employees only', door. She couldn't get him out of her mind as she clocked in and got herself a cup of coffee. She took the coffee to her work area.

A few minutes later, Jack came around the corner looking annoyed. "Thanks for unlocking the door, Anastasia," he yelled across the room.

Anastasia remembered instantly what she had forgotten. "Oh, I'm sorry, Jack!"

"That's okay, kid. You were looking a little flustered out there. I wasn't surprised that you forgot. So, you want to know his name?"

Anastasia blushed.

"He's not married, either." Jack added.

"Now, how do you know that?" she asked, still embarrassed, but trying to cover it up.

"I know his father. His dad owns the Mattioli's Market. Mark, that's his name, is trying to help promote his old man's market by having coupon mailers printed up."

Anastasia noticed that Jack had emphasized the man's name, Mark. "Oh, that's nice of him. He must be a good son." She tried to say it coolly, but she was wearing a broad grin. Jack, who she had never known to play matchmaker before, smiled back and returned to his post at the front counter. Anastasia thought mildly that Jack must really like the guy, or he wouldn't have made such a big deal out of it. But then reality set in, and she knew that she was in no way ready for any kind of romance right now, nor for a long time. Even so, the distraction was nice.

In fact, she realized that no one there could even know about last night yet. She debated about whether or not to tell them. She looked around. The quiet was nice. No, she'd let them find out about it on the news or in the papers.

Marilyn paced back and forth across the basement floor. Her illness was getting worse, and she knew it. She could feel the growth in her entrails getting larger. She could see the grey mass getting thicker. It was eating away at her strength. A chilling fear swept through her. What if I die before either of my daughters gives birth? Would that mean the end of my long existence? All those lifetimes, the knowledge, would all of it be lost? What was death? She had long hoped that she would never know, that she would always defeat it. With each crossing, she had become wiser and more proficient. She no longer needed to kill for the ingredients of the witch's brew. Now she had become so strong that she could leave her body at will.

She walked across the room to a locked cabinet. She pulled a key out of her of pocket and opened the lock. Gently she pulled out a very old wooden chest and set it on the floor. The lid required extra care to remove. Age had warped its tight fit over the many years. Inside were the ancient relics that she had saved over the centuries. She softly laid her hand against an old book. It was handwritten, before the days of the printing press. She longed to open it up, but over the last hundred years, it had become so delicate that the pages fell apart at even the most gentle touch.

Beside the book was an animal-skin bag. She felt the suppleness of the leather. It had been the finest made in its day. She unknotted the drawstrings and laid it out flat. Blown glass jars, corked with clay stoppers were arranged inside, each wrapped in another piece of fine leather. The tops of the bottles were imprinted with different symbols to identify the contents. Most of them looked to contain dried black substances, long void of their individual characteristics. Marilyn knew what they were, each bottle. She examined every one until she located the original bottle of blood. She held it to her chest, closing her eyes so that she could visualize the circumstances in which she had gathered it.

She was known as Leigh the Victorious Warrior Chief. She remembered camping near the hut of an old witch— a druid witch who claimed to have known the secrets of the fallen angels who taught humans those things that were the building blocks of all higher knowledge. The witch had claimed she was taught by them the secret of eternal life, that she had borne a child by one of them, and that it was born white with red eyes. She claimed to have entered that child's firstborn, so that she was now blood kin to those Sons of the Gods whose knowledge built the pyramids and all the great cities of old.

Leigh wanted the knowledge, and he knew how to make the old woman interested in teaching him. He noticed how she watched him move and lusted after his youth and strength. He took advantage of his deep, sensuous voice and persuaded her to give him the knowledge that he was convinced she had. Then, even after she taught him all, he stayed with her until she died and was reborn into the baby of her granddaughter. He continued to keep track of the infant, returning every year, looking for signs that the child was the witch reborn. At each visit, he thought that he could see a glimmer in the eyes, but it wasn't until the third year that the child came to him and pronounced his name. He was confident that this was the witch, and so now he had the knowledge to beat the black unknown called death. It was the druid witch's blood that was contained in the bottle that Marilyn now held to her heart.

Leigh continued to visit the young witch until she was old enough to bear children. Then he took her for a lover until she became pregnant. He was past the prime of his life, but still strong. It was with the help of the witch herself that he entered the body of their child. Another male. Thus began his immortal journey.

Marilyn opened her eyes and sighed. How she longed to be that young man again, to feel her flesh tight and hard, to be able to walk tall and straight with a swagger, knowing that everyone held him in awe, frightened to disagree or challenge his words. Just to be a man, to watch other men tremble in fear and women tremble at his touch.

The other bottles contained blood and entrails of humans and animals that had been dissected over the years to ensure that there was a supply of the ingredients that were needed for the now unnecessary witch's brew.

The book was filled with rituals and chants to help obtain the altered state needed to enter an infant's body. Marilyn had them all memorized centuries ago. There was also a sword, Leigh's best. Marilyn held it by the hilt. It looked so primitive to her now, but she loved it still. There was a ring, a stone crucifix with Celtic designs carved into it, and a leather whip from her most recent past life. There were other treasures, too, mementos of lives gone by. She continued to hold each item, remembering solemnly the reason for its significance.

Now, what would she add from this life? She fingered her gold watch lovingly, then shook her head with contempt. Nothing, this lifetime had been a failure. All she wanted now was for Anastasia to supply her with a healthy host so she could be done with it.

She opened one of the bottles and sprinkled some of the contents carefully into a small jar that she pulled out of her pocket. Then she put the things back into the box and into the cabinet. She knew that she needed to hide the chest again soon, before she died. Then it would be several years before she could retrieve it. In the past, she had always buried it, but the fast pace of development had almost lost it for her the last time. A house was slated for the property where it was buried, and Patrick, her father, had moved the family so far away that she was barely able to run away from home to save it in time. She was only twelve.

Her father never trusted her after that, so she ran away again at thirteen and never returned.

This time, she thought she might try burying it in a graveyard. Surely, no one would disturb it there. She had considered buying a plot, but how could she be sure that after her death someone might not try to use it? That was when she decided that she needed to dig up an old grave and bury the chest on top of the current resident.

The next problem was her own feeble body. She didn't know if she had the strength to do it herself, and in one night, so she had come up with a plan. She was going to hire someone, stay with him until the work was completed, and then kill him. This seemed like the best solution. She would simply convince him to have a drink with her after he'd buried the chest. Then she would pick a spot on a deserted country road, maybe a bridge with a creek running under it. A poison drink would be the cleanest way to kill him. Finally, she would push this body into the creek, the best way to get rid of the evidence. Getting caught was of little concern. Marilyn knew that she would soon be dead anyway. Now she just needed to find a strong young man who wouldn't be missed, and who was in need of money. Her lips curled as someone came to mind.

CHAPTER 12

Anastasia was sitting in the front lobby of the hospital, waiting for Mr. Lowe. Jim was stable and in a private room. He couldn't speak, and might not ever be able to again, but he had written a note saying that he would like to see her.

Mr. Lowe was being overprotective with Jim and had asked that no unescorted visitors be allowed to see him. Anastasia had a hunch that the arrangement was made to keep Julia out. Mr. Lowe was complaining that Julia was hanging around Jim's room. He had even tried to have her arrested, but she just kept coming back. Anastasia still had not met her, so she was curious.

Exactly five minuets before visiting hours began, Mr. Lowe walked in wearing a lightweight, full-length coat and a hat. He looked like a typical businessman from the 1950's. They waved and smiled at one another from across the room. Then Anastasia threw down the magazine she was reading and started down the corridor by Mr. Lowe's side. They talked on the way to the elevator. Word had gotten out about Mrs. Brown, so Anastasia had been spending a great deal of time reiterating the story. It was tiresome, but good therapy. She was finally able to rattle off the last few weeks events without emotion. If only she could shed the trauma of her abortion so easily.

Anastasia noticed Mr. Lowe suddenly going tense as they rounded the corner to Jim's hallway. It was easy to locate the subject of his stare. Sitting among a row of plastic-seated metal chairs was a large figure in a dress. This has to be Julia, Anastasia thought. Mr. Lowe immediately marched up to her. Stopping, he stared directly down at her.

"I thought you were told to stay off this floor." There was a quiet thunder of righteousness in Mr. Lowe's voice. Julia sat motionlessly with her hands folded in her lap, her eyes cast down humbly. It was obvious that she did not intend to answer.

"Okay, I'll find security." Mr. Lowe bobbed his head around until he spotted the nurses' station. He marched to it and began talking sternly to a nurse behind the counter.

Anastasia stood silently with her eyes on Julia. It didn't require any special abilities to see Julia's pain. Julia continued to stare down at her folded hands. Her carefully curled hair, falling forward, blocked the view of her face. Anastasia could tell that she was quietly sobbing.

Mr. Lowe returned shortly with a security guard in tow. Julia was informed that she had been restricted from that floor and would have to leave. She never spoke, but only nodded her head with her eyes still cast down. She reached for her handbag, then got up and moved slowly toward the elevators. Anastasia couldn't take her eyes off the tragic figure until Mr. Lowe took her arm and abruptly walked her to Jim's doorway.

Mr. Lowe's face softened as he entered Jim's room. Jim turned his head from the direction of the TV and waved. His face lit up when he noticed Anastasia. They conversed about trivial things at first, with Jim scribbling little messages onto a yellow legal pad. Then Jim asked Anastasia about her ordeal, explaining that he had seen it on the news. She was almost happy to repeat the story. It kept the conversation away from his own unpleasant circumstances. Jim watched Anastasia intently, but she could tell that his mind was preoccupied.

There were a few minutes of silence where all three of them stared at the television screen. Anastasia could see Jim struggling with something that was bothering him. Finally, he carefully wrote another message, then reluctantly turned the pad so they could read it. Mr. Lowe's face went cold.

"Jim, what does it matter about this man, Julia? You do realize now that he is a man, don't you?" Mr. Lowe's voice was stern but caring, like a father.

Jim nodded, but was looking away.

Mr. Lowe continued. "Now Jim, what Skip did was hire this man to play a cruel joke. I'll never forgive either of them for the pain they've caused you, but it's over. You just need to forget about it and go on. You are a responsible, good-looking young man. The day will come soon when you'll meet a nice girl to have a family with. Mark my words!" Mr. Lowe emphasized his last statement by gently rubbing Jim's shoulder. The little speech had clearly drained him of his last bit of energy. Caring for Jim every day and spending so many emotional hours over the last week was clearly taking a toll on Mr. Lowe. He stood up. "I'm going to let you two young folks have some time together. I need to visit the shop, anyway. I'll bring a newspaper with me tomorrow, okay?" Jim nodded and waved good-bye.

As soon as he left the room, Jim looked Anastasia directly in the eyes, held up the same note and pointed at it.

Anastasia nodded. "Yes, she's okay. In fact, she was sitting outside in the hall when we came up."

Jim's face tensed. He was clearly taken aback at that last statement.

"Jim?" Anastasia waited for him to face her again. "Do you want to see her?"

Jim looked away again, seriously pondering the question. Slowly, he shook his head no, with a defeated expression.

Anastasia studied his face for a moment before she spoke. "Jim, I heard Mr. Lowe. I know he loves you like a son and wants to protect you. He's also from a generation that has a very narrow view on how men and women should behave and live." She was talking slowly, trying to use just the right words. "I'm sure that you've been thinking about life and how lonely it can be. Mr. Lowe is probably the closest person to you right now. I know you want to make him proud of you, but Jim, he'll always go home to his family at the end of the day. You, you are the one who needs to decide whether you want to be alone. You need to find out for yourself what makes you happy."

Jim was looking deep into her eyes. He moved his line of vision to the ceiling for several moments, then slowly wrote another note. Anastasia took the pad so she could read it. "I miss my mother," was all it said.

Anastasia sat silently, waiting for Jim to acknowledge her again. He seemed to be debating with himself. Finally, he took the pad, and with a spirit of determination, he wrote another note and gave the pad to Anastasia.

She smiled and nodded. "I'll be right back." She jumped up and ran out the door.

There, sitting in the same chair, was Julia. Apparently, she would wait for Mr. Lowe to leave the building, then go right back up and sit outside Jim's door.

Anastasia stopped in front of her. Julia looked up. She recognized her as being with Mr. Lowe and began reaching for her handbag to leave. "No, don't go. Jim wants to see you."

Julia looked surprised. "Really? Can I go in?"

Anastasia nodded.

Julia sat back down and opened her handbag. She pulled out a compact and began dabbing at her eyes. She was trembling excitedly. She did look frazzled. It was easy to see that Julia had been through a rough couple of weeks herself. After poofing up her hair with her fingers, she stood up and walked with dignity into Jim's doorway.

Jim watched her move into the room, silently assessing her appearance. Yes, now he could see the manly shape of her shoulders, the thickness of her waist. She sat at the chair beside his bed with her eyes still cast down.

Then, shyly, she looked up into Jim's face and smiled. That was all it took. His doubts melted away. All of those feelings that he'd had the first time he laid eyes on her came rushing back. He knew in his heart that he was still in love with this creature, regardless of who or what she was. He reached out his hand, and she took it, with tears welling up in her eyes. They embraced so tightly that Jim could once again feel that familiar loss of breath, but he loved it.

Anastasia backed out of the room. She realized that she was extremely happy with herself. She almost skipped down the hall, punching the button for the elevator. Once outside, she noticed for the first time that the sun was shining. There was a warm breeze gently blowing. She closed her eyes and tilted her face into the sunshine. Life is good, she decided.

There was one more happy surprise waiting for her on the landing in front of her doorway when she returned home that afternoon— a fairly large cardboard box with a note taped to the top of it. Anastasia read the note curiously. It was from her bother and sister. "Dear Anastasia, we decided that you could really use a companion."

Anastasia opened the box before she even had her door unlocked. She tore at the corners of the packing tape, then ripped it off. She threw open the ends and began digging at the white styrofoam inside. It was heavy. She held the sides of the box by bracing it between her feet. Then she pulled up with all her strength. She squealed with delight when she saw the glass screen. It was a portable television, and she could tell by the insignia that it was a color television— even better than the one she had planned to buy.

She spent the rest of the evening arranging the little antenna and trying out each channel. It was great. She wasn't alone anymore.

CHAPTER 13

Grey smoke curled up and around a dim neon light that was in the shape of a beer bottle. Inside, glowing letters spelled "Bu Bee." Stella chuckled to herself.

"Hey, bartender." She shouted. "Bring me another bottle of Bu Bee!" She laughed at her little joke, and then settled back onto her stool. The bartender appeared promptly, leaning against a sink with a not-so-amused look on his face.

"What do you want?"

Stella laughed again, losing her balance and nearly falling off her stool. "Bu Bee." She shouted, pointing with her eyes toward the damaged sign. The bartender looked behind himself, shook his head, then reached under the counter for another beer. He walked off humorlessly.

Stella finished the last of the beer in her nearly empty bottle. Then she wrapped her fingers around the new bottle. She looked down at her long red nails and saw an extra finger. This made her realize that if she didn't take a walk soon, she'd pass out.

She shook her head and slowly slid off the stool. The first

sensation of standing upright made her dizzy. She took a minute to compose herself before she grabbed her beer and turned around to lean against the bar.

The room had changed from two hours ago when she first sat down. Now it was full. A familiar drunk staggered passed her, giving her a wink. She acknowledged the greeting with a crooked smile, then took a swig of her beer. Too bad he doesn't have any money, she thought. She could knock him out before he had a chance to get his pants down.

After a deep breath, she felt strong enough to take a couple of steps away from the bar. Soon she was gaining momentum on her way toward the ladies room— too much momentum. She reached out and grabbed the back of a man on a barstool to keep from falling. He turned around angrily. Then his face softened when he saw Stella trying to regain her balance.

"Hey there, lil' darlin'." The big burly man wrapped one of his huge arms around her waist. "Don't hurt yourself, now."

Stella looked the man over. He was too big, she thought, and he was quite a bit more sober than she was. No, she told herself, this would never work out to my advantage.

"Thanks," she said politely. Then she pulled away.

She slowly worked her way down the aisle before deciding to rest. Leaning against the bar with one elbow, she was passively watching the crowd when she noticed another familiar face, but this one was from somewhere besides the bars. She squinted, peering intently at the man who sat halfway across the room.

Then it occurred to her— Lowe's Printing. That guy used to work with her. Then she remembered the name, Skip Morris. God, how she hated him. Such a smart ass. She even remembered him having the audacity to make snide remarks to her face. There were so many times when it took every ounce of her strength to keep from punching him. She remembered Anastasia pulling on her to get her to go home instead of waiting for him outside the employee entrance so that she could beat him up in the alley. Well, I'm not working for Lowe's Printing anymore, she thought. Maybe he'll even have a little cash on him. She stood up to get a better look. He was sitting at a table with someone. Stella peered around the group of men in front of her. She could see that Skip was involved in a conversation with a woman who was sitting with her back turned. Stella then remembered that Skip was a pot smoker. She decided to walk right up to him and ask if he wanted to step outside for a joint.

Taking several steps around a crowd of people, she suddenly froze. She was now close enough to get a side view of the woman. She squinted to be sure that she was seeing clearly. Quickly, she shrank back in astonishment. The woman was her mother.

Stella was flustered. Neither her mother, nor Skip had seen her, so she quickly turned and headed out the door.

Anastasia stopped by the bookstore on her way home so she could tell her brother how much she loved her new television. She was in a good mood. Things were beginning to feel the way they did a couple months ago. She felt that dawn had finally broken through. There was even a good feeling about the future. Great things were in store for her, and she knew it.

She skipped across intersections and defiantly raised her head and brows to the women's clinic as she passed by it. There was no turning back or wondering, 'if.' She had decided that she was done with all of that. Her life would move on.

When she arrived at the bookstore, her brother greeted her warmly. He was ringing up a sale. Anastasia began browsing the newest offerings at the clearance book bin.

"So, you're spending your evenings in front of the tube now?" he asked.

Anastasia smiled, laying aside the book she was looking at. "Sure am. It's great. I love it. In color even."

"You know, Dad went in on it, too. But don't let him know I told you. He's more afraid of Mom than anyone." The last sentence was whispered.

"Oh, someday Dad will find his voice. You'll see."

"Only if he outlives Mom." This was barely audible, but she could read his lips.

"Hey, by the way, have you noticed Mom being sick or anything?"

Her brother shook his head. "She doesn't complain, but I've never heard her complain about her health."

Anastasia spoke quietly and had a serious look on her face. "When she came to my apartment, she said that she was dying." She gave her brother a puzzled look. He seemed to be considering the statement.

"Did she say how or why?"

"Yeah." Anastasia was trying to remember her mother's exact words during that emotional exchange. "She said that there was a tumor in her womb, and that it was going to kill her."

Her brother had a bewildered look on his face. "It sounds like she knows." He pondered the information over.

Anastasia could see that he was upset. "Could she have just made it up? She was really kind of desperate about , you know." Anastasia was thinking it over now, too. Why did she have to bring this up?

Her brother shook his head, looking out the window. "No. She must have said that because it's true. I can't imagine Mom making up something like that. It just wouldn't be like her." They were quiet for a minute. Anastasia thought about how ironic it was that they should be upset about Marilyn.

"So, you haven't noticed her acting like she could be in pain or anything, have you?"

He shook his head no.

"Well, do you think you could ask her about it?"

He looked at his sister in panic. "And tell her that we were discussing her? And what she said to you in private? You know I couldn't."

Anastasia shrugged. "Well, I'm sure as hell not going over there to discuss her health over tea and cookies." They both stared at one another. It was almost comical. Trying to help Marilyn would be like trying to pet a rabid dog. "We're just going to have to wait for her to bring it up," Anastasia said with conviction. Her brother reluctantly agreed.

Later that evening, Stella stopped by Anastasia's apartment. "Well, at least it's starting to smell better over here," she announced. She was toting her customary bottle of whiskey with a quart bottle of beer for a chaser. After emptying the contents of her bag, she poured them both a drink. "It's nice to have the right crystal, you know, a shot glass for the whiskey and a beer glass for the beer." She made two trips from the kitchen so that they both had beer and whiskey. Then she grabbed both bottles so that she wouldn't have to make another trip, and plopped down on the floor at the end of the bed beside Anastasia, who was in front of the TV.

"In fact, we can even get fancy and do this." Stella dropped her full shot glass in her beer, then tipped the beer glass. Quickly draining the two glasses, she slammed them onto the floor so that the little shot glass dropped with a chink. Anastasia was almost impressed, but she had seen her sister do this before.

"So, noticed any new weirdos movin' in next door yet?" She sniffed and leaned back against the foot board of the bed, enjoying the burn of the whiskey hitting her stomach.

"Actually, no. In fact, I haven't even noticed them moving out Mrs. Brown's stuff yet, but then, I'm gone during the day, so who knows?" She was also leaning against the foot board with her knees up, nursing her beer and occasionally taking a sip of her whiskey. They were both staring at the television. It was the evening news.

"Well, I bet you'll never guess who I ran into at the bar the other night."

Anastasia shrugged.

"Well, first I noticed that jerk off, you know, Skip the dick."

Anastasia made a face.

"But, the thing that really, really was amazing was who he was with." She looked at her sister, pausing to build suspense. "Mom!"

Anastasia stared at her sister, wide-eyed. "Mom? Are you sure?"

"Yeah, she was sitting with him and they were involved in some deep conversation. They didn't even notice me."

"Wow, " She started to chuckle, then met Stella's alarmed gaze and decided that she should be more respectful. "Well, that is curious. I mean, have you ever noticed Mom in a bar before?"

Stella shook her head no. She was pouring herself another drink. Enough had been said. It was time to change the subject. "Were you planning on going anywhere tonight?"

Anastasia shook her head.

"Want to go out for awhile? It is Friday, ya' know."

Anastasia had a quick flash of the last time she had gone out with her sister. In fact, that had been the last time she had been to a bar. "Where?" she asked cautiously.

"Hey, don't worry. We'll go somewhere nice. Someplace where no one's dancing on the tables or anything."

"Somewhere that has a DJ so we could dance?" Anastasia asked.

"Yeah, okay. How about Billy's?"

That sounded tame enough. "Sure." It would be nice to get out of her apartment, Anastasia thought.

"Great. So sis, we'll just split the boys, huh?" Stella stretched her legs out and chuckled. They drank away the evening, watching TV until it was the proper time to make an entrance— not too early, but not so late that they wouldn't get a seat.

Both of them were in jeans with lightweight jackets. Fall had set in. Now the evenings were slightly cool. They were both feeling relaxed from the alcohol, but not drunk, as they casually strolled into Billy's, taking stools at the bar. They were in the habit of sitting at the bar. Stella liked to be able to get a drink without waiting and more men sat there. But, the reason Anastasia preferred the bar was that she had been in far too many situations where Stella had picked a fight with their waitress. Dealing with a male bartender was always preferable.

They were still on their first drinks when Stella nudged her sister and pointed. Anastasia looked down the row of men. She spotted the one that Stella was pointing at right away.

"Oooh," Stella cooed. "So, sis, which half do you want?"

Anastasia strained to see through the haze of smoke. "Oh, yeah, he looks kind of—," she stopped in mid-sentence. "Hey, I think that's the guy who comes to the shop. His dad owns Mattioli's Market."

"I don't remember seeing him in here before," Stella said thoughtfully. "Sure is nice looking!" She was openly watching him, waiting for him to look over and see her staring.

Anastasia was a little put out. Technically she had seen him first. "Well, I think maybe I'll go ask him about his printing," she said sliding off her stool.

Stella frowned. They rarely argued about men. Generally, they made it a point to never go out with someone that the other had dated, but unclaimed men usually went to whoever spotted them first.

Anastasia strolled over to him casually and tapped him on the shoulder. She had already noticed that he seemed to be alone. He turned his baby blue eyes on her and smiled.

"Hi, didn't I meet you at the printers the other day?" She said.

"Yes, I was there getting some printing done for my father." There was that hint of an accent again. God, he was gorgeous.

"I haven't noticed you in the area before. Did you just move here?" She wanted to know where that accent came from.

"I was born here, but my father sent me back to Europe for school. Then some family business kept me there. I just came back to the states to help him out at the market."

Anastasia was enchanted by his facial expressions, his perfect black hair, and his piercing blue eyes. It almost made her shiver to feel him looking at her. It was hard to maintain an aloof appearance.

"Where in Europe?" She tried not to sound too forward.

"Italy. That's where my father was from."

How could I have not known that, she thought. "Does most of your family live there?"

"Oh, most, but I have some cousins and an uncle here, besides my father. My grandmother lived here before she died. In Italy, I lived with an aunt. She's still there."

Anastasia caught herself staring at him after the conversation went cold for a few moments. She scrambled for something intelligent to say. Then, mercifully, he broke the silence, "Do you need a drink? You could sit here by me if you like." He gestured toward an empty seat beside him.

"Ah, sure." She realized that she had agreed too quickly, but without hesitation she moved her legs in beside him and sat down.

"So, have you always lived here?" He was motioning for the bartender.

"Born and raised."

"How long have you worked at the print shop?" The bartender finally noticed his gestures. "I'm sorry. First, what would you like to drink?"

Anastasia ordered a mixed drink.

"So, Anastasia, right?"

She nodded yes.

"So, Anastasia, how long have you worked at the print shop?"

"Oh, about three years now." She was wondering if she should ask him his name, or admit that Jack had told her.

"Well, that man, Jack Lowe, he's done good work for me so far. Hopefully, we will do much business together."

Anastasia was enchanted by his voice. It was so deep, and his words were like a lullaby.

"Tell me." He smiled and moved closer. "How did you get a name like Anastasia? You don't look Italian."

He was so close that it made her nervous. She was imagining his incredibly long black lashes tickling her cheek. "Ah, well, I don't know. I'm not Italian. In fact, my last name is

MacDouglas. My father's family is Irish. My mother's is a mix, but not Italian. She's the one who named us."

He nodded, listening to her intensely. About this time, the bartender interrupted, holding Anastasia's forgotten beer. "Hey, your sister down there." He pointed to an unhappy Stella. "She said to say that you forgot something." He set the drink in front of her and walked away. Anastasia leaned forward and waved at her sister.

Mark looked around her to see Stella for himself. "You didn't tell me that you were with someone. Why not invite her down here?"

Anastasia hesitated. How would he handle Stella, she wondered.

"Well, there's really no room."

"Oh, that's okay. I will stand." With that, he stood up and gallantly motioned Stella to come and sit. He didn't need to beg.

"So, Stella, this is an Italian name also. Why is your mother so in love with Italian names?" Neither of them had an answer.

"Mark isn't Italian, is it?" Anastasia asked. She forgot that he hadn't told her his name.

"Actually, I am named after my father, Mario. I just shorten it to Mark for less confusion."

"Mario," Stella interrupted. "That's the same as—." She was interrupted by the sound of breaking glass. There was some loud shouting and a woman's scream at the end of the bar. A fight was breaking out. Stella forgot about the conversation and stood in the aisle, watching with excitement in her eyes. She always found other people's fights extremely interesting. It felt good to her to see someone else in trouble.

The fight quickly escalated, involving several people. The bartender had even left his post to aid the bouncers in trying to get the fight under control. Stella had moved closer and was now lost in a thick crowd of gawkers.

"I don't like this," Mark said with a scowl on his face.

His hand was now on Anastasia's shoulder, as though he was shielding her from the violence. She brushed her cheek against his fingers, pretending that it was an accident. So warm and masculine, she thought dreamily. Mark didn't seem to notice, but then he tightened his grip and shook her shoulder with urgency. "C'mon, let's leave," he said. Anastasia scanned the crowd for her sister until she spotted her up in front, close to the chaos.

"Sure, we can stand outside 'til this is over." Actually, she would have followed him farther if he'd asked. He guided her out the door with his hand on the small of her back. She leaned in close to him. They slipped out double doors that muted the noises inside. She hadn't realized how loud it was until she stood in the quiet moonlit evening. The moon was almost full again, she noticed.

"So much better," he said. Billy's occupied a newer building that stood on the outskirts of the city. The area around it was mainly residential. Because of the absence of streetlights, the moon was all that brightened things up, except for a big neon sign near the street.

"This is a beautiful night," he said walking away from her with his eyes on the moon. He stopped, tipping his head up. His hands were folded behind his back. Anastasia wasn't sure what to do, so she just stood back and watched him. Finally, he turned and faced her. The light of the moon formed a kind of halo around him or, she thought to herself, a bright aura. There was something strangely familiar about him. She felt that she knew him well already.

His eyes were summing her up. She felt self conscious. Why did this man make her feel so shy, she wondered. It was a kind of sweet but forbidden feeling, as though maybe she was cheating on someone.

"So, tell me how it is that you know my name?"

Oops, she thought to herself. "Jack mentioned it to me, in conversation."

He smiled. He knew she had been interested in him the first time they met, and now she was blushing because she could read what he was thinking. "Oh," was all he said.

He strolled back up beside her. "So what else is there to do here?" He looked down at her, waiting for an answer. Her mind went blank. He was standing too close. "Um, there's a movie theater."

He nodded thoughtfully. "Maybe sometime we could go to the movies," he offered. She felt like she was losing ground. She had to think of something interesting, quickly.

"So, you said you were born here. Did you mean Center City?"

He nodded. "Yes, but unfortunately my mother died soon after I was born."

"Was your mother Italian?"

"No, in fact I'm told that she was very fair," he pointed to his eyes. "I think these are her eyes." He smiled again, but like a child. "I don't remember her."

Anastasia felt sad for him. "Your father never remarried?"

"No, he was too much in love with my mother."

"How about her family?"

"I don't know them, either. My father says that she was alone. I guess she must have been an orphan."

Anastasia was starting to worry that her questions were too personal. He was just so interesting. She really was curious. "I take it that you probably don't have any brothers or sisters?"

"No, just me, but I have many cousins. I was never in need of a playmate growing up." Anastasia could still sense a feeling of loneliness in his voice. She wanted to hug him, and tell him that she knew what it was like to feel lonely.

They became aware of sirens, and eventually two police cars pulled up and parked near the doors of the building. They stepped aside as the officers went in.

"So, how would you like to continue this questioning of me over coffee, somewhere quiet?" He teased.

To Anastasia, that sounded wonderful. It was a treat to talk to an intelligent, interesting stranger, to get lost in someone else's life for a change. She just hoped that she wasn't annoying him with her questions. “I would love to,” she agreed, feeling more comfortable with him now.

They continued to stand near the door, waiting for the police to come out so they could look for Stella. Anastasia would never leave her sister without an explanation. She felt bad enough abandoning her. Soon, the police led a couple of men out. A few people from the crowd of onlookers followed behind. Stella was among them.

Stella frowned when she saw her sister and the stranger that she’d seen first looking like a couple. It was a grey area in protocol that Anastasia was in violation of, and they both knew it. “Fine, I’m going to go in and have another drink,” was Stella’s only response after Anastasia explained their plans. Stella stomped back into the bar, leaving the couple alone again.

Now the question was, where to next? “We could walk to a little restaurant that my brother and I go to. It’s not far.”

“Walk? How about I drive?”

Anastasia winced. She didn’t like the idea of being trapped inside a vehicle that she wasn’t able to control, especially with anyone who could overpower her. She liked to stay in a position that allowed her to leave if she felt uncomfortable. She looked into his face again. Was he fooling her? She was just beginning to feel like her old self again. Was she reading him correctly? Could she trust her instincts yet?

He could tell that she was struggling with the question. “Well, I hate leaving my car here, but if you want to walk, we can.”

Anastasia exhaled with relief. They started down the sidewalk. He hesitated. “Are you sure that it is safe?”

Anastasia shrugged. “Sure, we always walk. I’ve never had a car.”

He raised his eyebrows. “You know, in Italy, many people walk or ride bicycles, but here in the states, I thought everyone had cars. I guess I was wrong.” He put his arm around her shoulders in a protective way as they headed toward the city.

The walk was pleasant for Anastasia, but Mark was tense.

He would stiffen whenever they passed someone on the dark sidewalks. Some of those people were familiar to Anastasia, especially the street people who she often knew by name.

By the time they reached the restaurant, Mark had developed a new respect for Anastasia. From the beginning, he had sensed that she was someone who could take care of herself, but now he was discovering that she could also protect and defend herself as well. He was developing an intense curiosity.

"So, Anastasia, how long have you lived alone?" He was helping her with her jacket.

"About a year and a half now." She slipped on to the bench window seat.

"You don't look so old to me. You must have been very young. Why?" Now he was getting personal.

"Well, my mother and I don't get along, so it was better for me to move out." She was careful how she worded the statement. She didn't want to get into the family closets yet. They didn't know each other well enough.

"I see. So, are you the youngest?"

Anastasia could tell that he was trying to find out how old she was. "I'm nineteen," she blurred out. "And yes, I'm the youngest of three children."

She could see Mark was doing some calculations. "So young to be all alone. I am just thirty-two, and still I live with my father. I guess I am a big baby." He smiled at her. "So, how about something to eat with our coffee?" He said picking up a menu.

"Sure," was the quick response. Stella's number one rule came to mind. Never turn down free food.

They slowly ate over a long conversation that spanned about two hours. The time slipped away quickly. Finally, they realized that the restaurant owner was wanting to close.

"So, Anastasia, will you walk me to my car so that I don't get hurt? Then I will drive you home. How about that?"

She could see in his eyes that he had additional plans. "I'll walk back with you, but I really should go home with my sister.

I'm sure that she's waiting for me."

"Okay, if that's what you want." Mark smiled at her, but she could tell that he wasn't done trying to convince her to let him into her apartment.

They walked back quietly. She was contemplating what she knew that he wanted. She was attached to him, but it was too soon. She was religiously taking the birth control pills that the clinic had given her, but sex was still out of the question. The desire to be close to someone like Mark was there, but she couldn't tolerate the idea of anything more than a kiss. She was afraid that they were about to end their only night together.

By the time they reached the bar, she had convinced herself that the only way to end the evening was abruptly. He did try again to convince her to let him drive her home. She refused, said good-bye, and stepped inside. After the door closed behind her, she did feel let down. Even though she didn't have a phone, it would've been nice if he'd asked for her number.

Inside, she located Stella at the back of the bar in a heavy conversation with a very drunk man. She stood a few feet away, summing up the situation. Then she decided to turn around and just go home.

As soon as she stepped outside, she notice a large, late model car pulling out of the parking lot. She had a gut feeling that it was Mark. Oh well, she told herself. She knew that she wasn't Cinderella, and this guy was obviously not her prince. He had taken her away to another place for awhile, but now she was back on earth. Time to get real.

She was wide awake when she made it home. She turned on her television and plopped down on the bed. The local news was on. She listened halfheartedly at first. Then the newscaster announced a breaking story. "The body that was found earlier today in a remote area outside the city was identified as Skip Morris."

Anastasia gasped and leaned forward. "An autopsy has yet to be performed, but the police suspect a drug overdose since no bruises or wounds were evident. Anyone who may have seen him or who has information should contact the police immediately. An investigation is currently underway." There was a snapshot of Skip with his arm around an older woman on the screen. Anastasia strained to look closer. Apparently, this was his mother. The next picture on the screen was of the same woman crying to a reporter about how she knew that her poor baby would never use drugs and that someone must have murdered him. She leaned back against the headboard of her bed. Anastasia knew that her own mother had something to do with this. But, why?

CHAPTER 14

A balsa wood glider still sat on the chest of drawers. If he looked closely at the side of the matching dresser, he could still see yellow crayon scribbles on it. A mirror over the dresser was rounded at the top, but it had aged so that the edges were black where the silver paint that made the reflection was flaked off.

This was the room of his childhood. In the corner was a rocking chair where his mother had rocked him to sleep, or so he'd been told. He wondered for a moment about this woman, and about his father's mother who'd died about the same time. He wasn't sure of the details, or even which one died first. His father would get confused on the few occasions when it was discussed. He didn't even know what killed them. All he was ever told was that they had gotten sick and died. Supposedly, there was no connection, but somehow he always knew that there was.

Slowly, he pulled himself out of bed. He really did feel pretty well for having gone out the night before. It must have been the food and conversation, he thought, but it had ended all too soon. He hadn't gotten what he wanted. Too bad, he thought, she was a beautiful girl— young, and somehow familiar. They hadn't even kissed. After all the deep philosophical conversation, it probably would have been like kissing a sister, he reasoned.

He stood up and looked at himself in the mirror. He grabbed a comb off the dresser and raked it through his hair. Then something occurred to him. That was what was familiar about the girl last night. She also had his mother's eyes. A brilliant blue. Maybe that was why he was so attracted to her. He smiled at himself.

Well, maybe he needed to get more printing done.

Stella reached for a soda cracker on her nightstand. She shoved a dry, jagged piece into her mouth, sucked on it, and then gently swallowed. Now she needed a Coke. She rolled over onto her belly, hugging her pillow. There was a throbbing in her head. She was beginning to notice something dry and flaky on her fingers. She looked at her hand in disgust— dried blood. Her plastic nails were gone, and there was blood under and in the corners of her own nails.

She was now remembering the details of the night before. Things had gotten messy. She had agreed to go to a motel room with a drunken service man. After having a good time with him, she was in the process of stealing his wallet when he woke up and caught her. He fell out of the bed trying to grab her, and he managed to catch her ankles before she could get out the door. She clawed at his eyes, kicking and screaming. Still, he was too strong for her. He dragged her across the floor and bolted the door.

She had been genuinely afraid for herself at that point. She could see blood in his eyes. She started frantically grabbing anything that wasn't bolted down and throwing it at him. Still, he kept walking toward her. She ran into the bathroom and managed to get the door locked before he came charging at it. He rammed it several times as she frantically tried to get the tiny bathroom window open. It was sealed shut. She hung by the shower rod, swinging her feet into the window to break it out. Then the rod broke. She fell hard, hitting her back on the tub. Panicking as the door was beginning to crack from the angry soldier's shoulder slamming into it, she had braced herself with the jagged end of the rod pointing toward the door. Just then, the door gave way and the man fell hard into the small room. Stella used his forward momentum to help her thrust the rod deep into his midsection. He doubled over and Stella ran for the door, never looking back.

She groaned. This was getting too dangerous. She knew that someday soon she was going to get killed. She needed to make a decision about whether she wanted to live or not. Did she have a death wish?

It was another busy Saturday. Anastasia never complained though, because she needed the money. What else was there to do except feed her new addiction to television?

Skip Morris's death had been the topic of conversation at the coffee pot that morning. Everyone was curious, but no one was especially surprised. Skip had a reputation as someone who enjoyed seedy company and drugs. Everyone knew about it. The question was, was it an accident? The vote was pretty much split on that one. Anastasia was happy that Jim wasn't around to hear the cold, offhanded remarks that were being tossed around. No one seemed to be the least bit grieved that Skip was dead. His death was just interesting conversation. Anastasia stayed quiet and listened.

It was late morning when Anastasia was surprised to see Jack standing in front of her, motioning for her to follow him. She turned off the machine that she was using and stepped up beside him.

"There's a customer up front that wants to talk to you."

She was confused. "Talk to me? Why?"

Jack was grinning at her. "He asked me, 'Who does the raised lettering on business cards?' When I told him that you did, he asked if he could talk to you about it."

Anastasia had never been asked to talk to a customer before. There was no task that she performed that Jack wasn't thoroughly familiar with. She was a bit perplexed until she entered the sales floor. There, standing near the counter, was Mark. They exchanged smiles while Jack busied himself with some paperwork.

"So, Ms. MacDouglas, could you please explain the raised lettering process?"

Anastasia blushed, then briefly explained, avoiding his eyes. He, in contrast, looked boldly at her, hanging on every word.

"You've convinced me to place an order," he announced after the explanation. She awkwardly motioned to Jack. Instead of taking the order for her, he gave her a form and briefly explained how she was to fill it out. She stepped back to the counter in front of Mark and began asking the necessary questions.

She was staring down, filling out the form when Mark reached out with his fingers spread and laid his hand on the form. Anastasia was forced to look up at him.

"So, why do you avoid looking at me?"

Anastasia couldn't think of an answer. Why did he make her so self-conscious? She looked away.

"How about dinner somewhere nice?"

Biting her lip, Anastasia looked back at him. She lowered her voice. "I'd love to."

"How about this Friday?"

"Sure."

"Great, so you have a phone number?"

She shook her head no.

"Well then, I'll just come to your home and pick you up. When and Where?"

Anastasia hesitated. She really didn't trust herself to be alone with him, not yet. She had a worried look on her face and was biting her lip again.

"Oh, don't tell me that you are still afraid to be alone with me." Mark was looking defeated. He sighed and stood contemplating for a moment, staring at the opposite wall.

"I know." He turned back to Anastasia. "How about if we make it a double date? You, me, your sister and my cousin?" Anastasia didn't know what to think. A double date with Stella? He obviously hadn't had a chance to speak with her sister the other night.

"I can ask her."

"Good, then. I will come back for these cards and you can tell me then if she said yes. Okay?"

Anastasia nodded. He looked up at the clock behind her, then slapped his leather gloves on the counter and announced that he had to leave.

"Take care, Anastasia, until we meet again." He smiled, nodded at her, then turned and left. As soon as the door shut, Jack walked up to her.

"Did he say a double date with Stella?" They both laughed. "So, how well does he know your sister?"

"I guess he'll be finding out soon. I know Stella will agree to a free night out. I mean, you know how she is." They looked at each other and laughed again. Jack knew full well about how Stella was. He was relieved when Anastasia confided to him that her sister wasn't holding a grudge against him for firing her. Jack was slightly afraid of Stella.

After work that day, Anastasia walked over to her mother's. She snuck around to Stella's window and knocked at it. It took several minutes, but finally Stella pulled back the drapes. Seeing her sister standing outside the window, she opened it.

"What's going on?" She whispered. "Did you see the news?" She was talking about Skip.

"Yeah, I know. Isn't it weird? Do you think it's a coincidence?" Stella shook her head no.

Anastasia debated about asking if she knew anything else about it, but decided it would be better not to. "Hey, I wanted to know if you want to go out with Mark's cousin Friday night."

Stella cocked her head. "Why? What's going on?"

"I want to see him, but I'd feel more comfortable if it was a double date. You know, so I wouldn't be alone with him. What do you say? It would be a free night out."

Stella pondered the question for just a few moments. "Okay, what time?"

They agreed to meet at her apartment early to have a few drinks beforehand, then have the guys pick them up at seven.

Anastasia quickly said good-bye and left. Then, as a second thought, Stella stretched her neck out the window. "Hey, so what does he look like?"

Anastasia turned and shrugged, running off through the back yard.

Marilyn could hear the exchange outside clearly. Her lips curled in an evil smile. She had been lying on her bed, contemplating the idea of possibly choosing a stranger's child, but it wouldn't be anything that she had done before. What if she choice an infant without her bloodline? No, Anastasia's child would be much better.

Her insides were cramping up. She could feel the pressure, even more severe than the cramps she'd experienced as a teenaged girl. She knew that she didn't have much longer.

The pain was interfering with her thoughts. During the last few days, she hadn't been as alert. The episode with Skip had taken more out of her than it should have.

Everything had pretty much gone as she'd planned. The chest was successfully hidden, although his body was found sooner than she had expected. She had always hated the man who made her offspring look like an idiot. It was satisfying to her to think that she had found a way to justify killing the useless son of a bitch.

She wondered how the autopsy would go. Could these twentieth century doctors correctly identify an ancient poison? Marilyn wasn't even sure that all the plants combined in the concoction even existed anymore, especially in North America. It would be interesting to follow the newscasts to find out.

Could they connect her to the murder? From what she'd heard and read in the newspaper, they weren't even sure it was a murder. Even if they did connect her with it, she would be dead soon anyway. What difference did it make?

"You are going on a date with your cousin?" Mario Mattioli Sr. was a round man. Standing about 5'10" and weighing over 200 pounds, he was a sober yet elfish-looking man. Friendly, but a hard worker who rarely had time for frivolous things. He was standing at the end of a counter, bagging a customer's groceries. He had always worked side by side with his employees. It never occurred to him that there was another way to run a business.

"A double date. Anthony will be with my date's sister," Mark explained.

"Oh, I see. You know these two sisters well?"

"I just met them, but Anastasia works at the printers—"

"Anastasia?" His father interrupted.

"Yeah, her name is Anastasia. Just like your mother."

"She's Italian?"

"No, Irish, but I believe she's Catholic." Mark said thoughtfully. "Actually, Dad, we are just going out. I thought it would be fun for Anthony, and besides, this girl is nervous about being alone with someone she hasn't known long."

"Does she have children?"

"No, never been married. She's still young."

Mario was looking pleased. "Well son, at this point, any young woman who will marry in the church and can have children sounds good to me. You need to settle down and give me grandchildren. I like it that her name is Anastasia. That's a good sign."

Mark was helping him pack the grocery bags. "You know, Dad, she told me that her mother was saying the same thing to her about grandchildren."

"You know her parents yet?"

"No, not yet." Mark found himself getting excited about the date. This was strange for him. Usually, he never even told his father about women he dated. For some reason, in this case he was kind of anxious for his father to meet Anastasia. He knew that they would like each other, and maybe it was time for him to find someone special.

"So, what about Anthony? He's happy about this?"

"Sure, when you can't speak English, it's hard to find a date." Mark explained.

"Does this girl know he can't speak English yet?"

"No, I haven't mentioned it. It won't matter, hopefully." They both chuckled.

Anastasia had spent extra time getting ready for work this morning. Mark's business cards were finished. She had personally taken care of the order herself, making sure all the details were just right. She was getting excited about the prospect of a real date. It had been a while. With Stella and his cousin there, she wouldn't have to agonize over the concern of being alone with him.

She did find him attractive, too much so. She just wasn't ready for sex, not yet. She was having problems with the birth control pills. Even though she was supposed to start her period, she hadn't. Instead, her body seemed to be following it's same old pattern with the moon. The nurse had warned her that it might take a couple months to regulate, but as long as she faithfully took a pill every morning, she was assured that her chances of getting pregnant again where close to zero.

"Anastasia!"

She turned from the machine she was working at. It was Mr. Lowe.

"I just wanted to let you know that the hospital has released Jim. He's insisting on going back to his house alone. I tried to get him to stay with my wife and I for awhile, but he wouldn't. I think it would be nice if we could check up on him regularly, you know, just to make sure he's okay. Don't you think so?"

Anastasia nodded. Mr. Lowe obviously felt that she would be beneficial to Jim's recovery. She didn't know if he was aware that she had encouraged Jim to reconcile with Julia. She did have a feeling that he knew about Julia and Jim seeing each other again. He just wouldn't admit or acknowledge it. He would never approve.

"I could stop by there tonight if you think that would be a good idea."

"Fine, then I'll stop by tomorrow night." He smiled at her.

She was glad to have Mr. Lowe's good will, and even happier that he took such an interest in Jim. Mr. Lowe was a good person. She just wished that he wasn't so ridged in his beliefs. It was making life hard for everyone.

Later in the afternoon, Jack motioned for her to come to the front. She knew it was Mark. She was getting butterflies in her stomach as she pushed through the door.

There he was, watching her enter the room. He was wearing that confident smile, and his eyes were boldly focused on her. She blushed, but was trying not to smile back or look embarrassed. It wasn't easy. She found herself avoiding his line of vision.

"These cards are beautiful," he said, holding one in his hand.

"Good."

"So, did you talk to your sister?"

"Yeah, she wants to. Is everything all set with your cousin?" She could look at him if the pace of the conversation was brisk.

"Oh, he's excited about it. I told him how beautiful your sister is."

"Good, I hope they like each other." She was searching for something else to say. "Oh, by the way, what does your cousin look like? How old is he?"

"He's about twenty-five. He came back with me this last time. He was born in Italy." Mark was worried that she would ask about his English, so he continued quickly. "He looks a lot like me, but has dark eyes and his complexion is a little darker. He's about the same size, etc." Anastasia looked interested, but not concerned. "So, now you need to tell me where to pick you up."

Anastasia explained how to get to her apartment. Then they talked about where they might go. She could have listened to him talk softly to her all afternoon, but they both had things to do.

Jack grinned at her when she left to go back to work. He felt like a matchmaker, as though he had kind of instigated the situation. It was an unusual feeling for him. He really wasn't sure why he was so happy with himself.

After work that day, she stopped by Jim's house. She was surprised by how healthy he looked when he answered the door. His neck was still bandaged and he couldn't speak, but there was a kind of glow to him. He looked happy. Anastasia had been to his home before. The last time he had invited Stella and her over to play cards and drink beer. It had been a pleasant evening, but Jim's house made people feel like they were visiting their grandmother. Stella was especially uncomfortable.

After saying hello, they sat down. Jim was wearing slippers and a robe with pajamas that looked new. Anastasia complemented him on them. He nodded again and wrote "Julia" on a pad of paper beside him. Anastasia smiled. So they were seeing each other. There was an awkward silence. Finally, she asked if he had seen Julia. This brought a broad smile. "She just left," he wrote again on his pad. It occurred to her that she probably had come over while Mr. Lowe was working to avoid running into him.

Anastasia couldn't help herself, so she asked, "Does Mr. Lowe know that you're seeing her again?"

Jim looked uncomfortable, then wrote, "Yes, but doesn't like it." He looked at Anastasia sadly. This was a man who had decided to live his own life, she thought. At the same time, she understood how disappointed he was that the only father figure that he had was unhappy with him.

"You know, Jim, I'd really like to get to know Julia. Maybe we could do something together, when you feel better."

Jim beamed. She could tell that he would like nothing better than to enjoy life with Julia in a normal way, with friends.

Anastasia decided to keep on the same subject, since Jim seemed to enjoy it. “So, what does Julia do, anyway? Does she work?”

Jim scribbled, “truck driver.” Anastasia's first inclination was to laugh, but she clamped her teeth together.

“How long has she been doing that?”

“Eight years.” This was getting interesting.

“What company does she work for?”

“Red Freight Tucking. She goes across country.”

Anastasia nodded. There were a million other questions, but none that she felt she should ask.

“I suppose she must have taken some kind of leave to be with you so much lately?”

Jim nodded.

“Does she live near by?”

“I've never seen home yet, lives in apartment.”

“Met her parents yet?”

“No, they live in Iowa.”

That must have been tough growing up, Anastasia thought to herself. She stayed for another hour or so, and they even had dinner together. They warmed up a can of vegetable soup, but Jim was having problems swallowing. Before he ate, Anastasia watched as he mashed the contents into a fine pulp with a fork, then ate every bit of it.

The walk home was pleasant. The weather was getting chilly, but by walking briskly, she stayed comfortable. There was a good empty feeling around her, with no overwhelming concerns. Jim was doing well. There was no feeling that someone was watching her, and thankfully, when she reached her building, no one popped their head out of the neighboring apartment door as she walked up the stairs. It was nice having something to look forward to, like her date with Mark. She decided that even if the date was a disaster, the anticipation felt good, and this was enough for now. Life was treating her well.

After putting away her jacket, she turned on the TV, as was her custom now, and settled into bed with a cold pastry. This was heaven, she thought.

Even when the news story about Skip Morris came on, she listened, but detached herself. Whatever her mother had done couldn't be reversed, and maybe she hadn't done anything. According to the report, the autopsy showed an unidentifiable drug, along with marijuana and alcohol. They now suspected that he had been experimenting with some new drug and overdosed. Anastasia gave a sigh of relief with the final announcement. Maybe he did O.D. by himself. It was possible. Everyone who knew him knew that he liked to experiment with drugs. She decided to close the matter in her mind and let it be forgotten.

CHAPTER 15

Friday, after work, Anastasia was just getting out of the shower when Stella came pounding on the door. Anastasia wrapped a towel around herself to answer it. She nearly gasped when she opened it. There was her sister with her pale blond hair all ratted and coated with hair spray. Her eyelids resembled colorful stained glass, and she was wearing a short, red sequined dress. She stood outside the door holding a familiar brown paper bag. Stella tried to judge the reason for her sister's startled look. Was it good or bad? Anastasia continued to stand in the doorway dripping until Stella spoke up.

"So, just get out of the shower?"

Anastasia regained her voice. "Come on in. You look, um, great!" Anastasia lied.

"Oh, good. You don't know how nervous I've been. Oh, and look." She waved her newly manicured red nails in front of her sister. "I hope you don't mind, but I've been seeing another beautician."

Anastasia marveled at her sisters demeanor. The whole idea that she had gone out of her way for this date was hard to believe, but she was even acting excited about it. "Stella, you know, I don't think I've seen you in a dress since we were kids, goin' to church in that big blue bus." Anastasia and Stella both chuckled.

"I don't think I've worn one." She laughed thoughtfully as she stood in the kitchen fixing them both drinks. "Except—"

She turned to her sister shaking a finger. “The prom that I went to with Ernie Chadwell.” She turned back around to continue the task of unscrewing the top off a wine bottle. Anastasia required no more clues to remember that incident. Stella hadn’t been as interested in going out with Ernie as she was at the opportunity to get dressed up like the princess that she secretly wanted to be.

Their mother had heartlessly teased Stella about the baby blue dress that she had bought herself. She told Stella that she looked about as out of place in the all too sweet prom dress as a toad in an evening gown.

“It’s just that, well, I thought it would be fun to go on a real date, you know, like on TV,” said Stella . “And, I haven’t gotten dressed up in a long time, so I went shopping this morning.” She moved to her customary place on the floor, but then hesitated and decided to sit on the bed for a change. She set their drinks on the windowsill behind the bed. “First, I went to that little clothing store on Main Street, and there was this really nice black lady who worked there.” Anastasia was listening but finding her ears hard to believe. “She’s the one that found this dress for me, and these shoes.” She raised one foot and dangled a metallic gold spiked heel in the air.

“Then,” Stella continued. “She told me about a friend of hers who works in a beauty shop a couple doors down.” She took a sip of her drink. Anastasia was following the story closely, but was distracted by the long black lashes glued to Stella’s eyelids. “So, then I went there and asked for Sadie, that was her name, and she did my hair.” Stella stopped to bob her head around, modeling her new hairdo. “Then she even looked at my dress and did my makeup and nails to match it! See my eyes?” She moved her face close to Anastasia and closed her lids. They were a kaleidoscope of colors. “Would you believe she used eight different colors on each lid! That’s the new way to do it so that it enhances your eyes and makes them look bigger,” she explained matter-of-fact. “Then she put liquid eyeliner and these lashes on my eyes.” Stella stopped again to bat her eyes at her sister. Anastasia nodded numbly with a smile frozen on her face.

"She did a really good job, Stella. It must have been expensive." Anastasia realized how important her approval was. She didn't want to disappoint her sister.

Stella took another gulp, trying not to smear her lipstick. "It was! But, I figure this one time, it was fun. Who knows, maybe this guy will be as cute as his cousin."

Anastasia was suddenly worried. What if they didn't show, or even worse, what if they did and laughed at her? She was sitting on the edge of the bed with a robe on and her hair in a towel.

"Hey, I'll wear a dress, too, and if they don't show up or something, we'll go out," Anastasia said quickly.

"What do you mean if they don't show up?" Stella frowned.

"Well, you know how flighty men are. I think they'll show up, but who knows? Let's give them 'til 7:30, then we'll just go without them. Okay?"

Stella looked annoyed. "Sure, I guess." Now Anastasia was really worried. Stella was placing a big bet on a blind date. She went into the bathroom to finish getting ready. It was already 6:30. She stood in front of the mirror, fixing her hair. She really did like Mark, but what would they think? What if they said something to Stella to hurt her feelings? She stopped and looked at herself in the mirror. Then she realized the answer. There really wasn't anything to decide about. If they said or did anything hurtful to her sister, she knew what she'd do. She'd tear them both up. With that resolution, she finished getting ready, adding extra makeup to make her and Stella more of a matched set.

She went through her closet, looking for her best dress. There really wasn't much to choose from. Luckily, she had been about the same size since seventh grade. Otherwise she wouldn't have had anything to choose from. Stella helped her decide on a blue dress that was so short it had matching panties. A strange thought came to Anastasia as she looked at herself and Stella. What if someone thought they were prostitutes? Well, as Stella would usually say, “Fuck em’ if they can’t take a joke.”

They sat together against the headboard and relaxed when Anastasia was finished getting ready. Drinking three quarters of a fifth of Jack Daniels helped.

“So, how’s Mom?” Anastasia asked casually.

“She’s not looking so good,” Stella admitted. “ Lately she hasn’t hardly come out of her room. She looks like she’s losing weight, and she’s pale.” Both of them looked solemn.

“And she still hasn’t said anything about what’s wrong?” Anastasia asked.

“Not a word.” They sat quietly in thought, sipping on their whiskey.

Several minutes later, they both heard someone opening the door at the foot of the stairs. They looked at each other and grinned. Neither of them moved at first. They just sat still and listened. There were two people coming up the stairs, talking low. They both strained to listen. At first it was just a mumbling sound. Then, Anastasia began to suspect that they were speaking a foreign language. Finally, a knock came at the door.

Anastasia got up nervously. She felt silly and conspicuous in her short dress. Suddenly, she hadn’t drunk enough. She fluffed up her hair, then opened the door. Mark was standing there in his long black jacket, his penetrating blue eyes boldly looking her straight in the face.

“Hello, I hope you didn’t have any problems finding the place.” She opened the door wide and stood aside so that both men could enter. The second man, Anthony, was shorter than Mark. He was slim, but well built. He looked to be about Stella’s age, younger than Mark. His eyes were a deep brown. He wore a black mustache, the same color as his hair. Anastasia knew that Stella would be pleased with his looks.

“Hello.” She nodded at Anthony. He nodded back with a smile, but without speaking. She introduced them both to Stella, who was sitting on the edge of the bed with her hands on either side of her lap, holding the mattress.

“So, Anastasia.” Mark moved up beside her. “Did I see a

picture of this stairway in the newspaper?" He looked at her curiously. "Wasn't there something about a dead women found in the attic?"

"Yeah, it was my neighbor," she answered awkwardly.

He looked at her with concern. "So, was it you who found her?"

"Yes." It was obvious that she didn't want to talk about it, so he changed subjects. The tender look in his eyes remained. Anastasia could see it whenever he spoke to her.

"Well, you both look lovely." Anastasia sighed with relief. "I hope you're not disappointed with us, two foreigners," he added with a shy smile. Anastasia marveled, there was something about Mark— he could make her blush. The truth was that he could be reciting the Pledge of Allegiance and make a woman swoon. It had something to do with his voice and eyes, Anastasia thought. Or was there something more. His aura just seemed to reach out and grab her.

Anastasia glanced at Anthony. He was looking fondly at Stella, but he hadn't spoken. She was relieved that at least neither of them seemed to find Stella's or her appearance as being offensive. Maybe, they were being extremely polite about it. Anastasia tried to focus in on Mark while he was looking away. She could sense a small amount of tension, but there was nothing coming from Anthony other than happiness. She could see that he was taken with Stella. The question was, why?

Anastasia looked over at Anthony. "Anthony, how long have you been in the states?"

Mark stepped up to her and answered for him. "Actually, only about three weeks. His mother is the one who raised me, so we are like brothers more than cousins." He continued to stare at Anastasia for a moment. She could tell that he wanted to say something else. He glanced at Anthony, then finished. "You know, he has not been here long enough to even learn English yet."

The two sisters exchanged glances. The way Stella was looking back at Anthony made it clear to Anastasia that it really didn't matter. "I'm sure he'll learn quickly," she replied, easing Mark's tension. The more she thought about it, the more she was convinced that Anthony's inability to understand English would probably work in Stella's favor. This might just work out, Anastasia decided.

"So, where did you want to go?" Anastasia asked.

Mark was looking around the apartment, noticing how small it was. She knew that he was probably used to nicer surroundings.

"Wherever you would like to go. We are just happy to be your escorts."

How charming, Anastasia thought. Just a hair too charming. The statement sounded well rehearsed. She could tell that he had used it before with other women. She looked at Stella, but knew that she wouldn't have a preference.

"How about Little Italy?"

Mark looked at her coolly. "You know, we are not confined to only eat Italian. Are you sure that is where you would like to go?"

"Unless you have a better suggestion, I like that restaurant." Anastasia tried to sound nonchalant to disguise the fact that she had never been there before.

"Okay, good, so do I. The food there tastes like home."

Neither of the girls had dress coats, so they pretended to believe that it was warm enough outside to go out without coats, in only their skimpy dresses. Luckily, Mark's car was parked in front of the building.

"Are you sure that you girls are going to be warm enough?" Mark asked. He had that concern in his eyes again.

"Oh yeah," they both said in unison. They also were wearing matching goose pimples. Mark's car was long and black. Anastasia got the feeling that it belonged to his father. It was comfortable inside with much room. The guys opened the doors and made sure both girls were safely inside before moving to the drivers side of the car. Once inside, Anthony gave Stella a shy smile. Stella smiled back.

The drive to the restaurant was too short. Mark had started an interesting description of his adopted home in Italy. He was wonderful with his descriptions. Anastasia could easily visualize everything that he described.

In the back seat, Stella was trying to have a conversation with Anthony. "So, do you like the United States?" She asked.

Anthony nodded and smiled. He pointed down. "United States." Stella smiled and sat back. He was trying to think of something to say in English. Finally, a thought came to him. He touched the hem of Stella's dress. "Very flashy." He smiled again.

Stella nodded and returned the smile. They both sat quietly until the car stopped. Mark let the three of them out in front of the restaurant, then parked the car. Anthony was trying almost too hard to be gallant. He stumbled over himself trying to help both ladies to the restaurant door.

Mark met them inside. He knew the host by name. Then a large man at a nearby table waved and called to him. He excused himself, then stepped up to a large burly man who was wearing a suit. They slapped one another on the back and began a lively conversation in Italian. He motioned for Anthony and introduced him to the man. Anastasia could see that this was annoying Stella. The reason was probably that they were speaking in a language that she couldn't understand. "They're talking about us," Stella sneered. "That big guy just nodded toward us and now they're laughing."

Anastasia was getting uncomfortable. The last thing she needed was for Stella to pick a fight. "Don't worry about it. If we make a fuss now, they won't buy dinner." She looked at her sister playfully as she was glaring at the men. "Come on, who cares what they're saying? We're dining with two gorgeous men. That's all that matters." Stella cooled down slightly, averting her gaze to a mural on the wall behind them.

Mark came up from behind and stood between them with one arm around each of their shoulders. "That was an old friend of my father's. He's my godfather." He was interrupted by giggles from both girls. Mark decided to ignore the interruption, "He told me he was jealous because we were in the company of such beautiful, young women."

Anastasia leaned forward and gave an 'I told you so,' look to her sister. Stella refused to completely relinquish her anger, but allowed Mark to guide her toward their table. Anastasia could see that Mark had an effect on her sister as well. His touch was like a warm kiss.

They were seated at a round table with formal place settings, a white linen table cloth, and a centerpiece with flowers and a lit candle. For Stella, it was one of the most romantic places she had ever been to. The restaurant was dimly lit so that the flicker from the candle gave their faces a warm glow. Stella looked beside her at the handsome, dark man. Even if the date ended right then, it would still be the best ever. Anthony caught her gaze and smiled back. He opened his mouth and gave her a helpless expression, then motioned with his finger to give him one minute.

He reached over to Mark and whispered something in Italian, pointing toward the centerpiece. Mark gave him a puzzled look, then answered. He looked back at Stella, lovingly, "You eye like candle."

She laughed softly. "Thank you." Her eyes did sparkle.

"So, Anastasia, you haven't mentioned your family too much. Do you have more than one sister?"

"No, just Stella. But, we do have a brother. In fact, it's kind of a coincidence. You, your father, and my brother all have the same name."

"No kidding? That is funny. Anastasia, Stella and Mario. Why is it that you all have Italian first names? You are sure neither of your parents are Italian?"

"I'm sure. I guess my mother just likes Italian names." Anastasia shrugged.

"You know, actually, I am only half Italian. My mother was like your family, a mixture." Anastasia had guessed that. "You know, my father says that your name is good luck. There is another coincidence; it was my grandmother's name as well."

"Didn't you tell me that she's dead now?"

"Yes. I can't remember her or my mother. Both of them died when I was very young."

"At the same time?" Anastasia felt that she was prying, but couldn't help herself.

"No, but close together. I don't know about the details. It still hurts my father to speak about either of them." He shook his finger at her gently. "You are lucky to have your parents both alive."

Anastasia kind of chuckled, but didn't say anything. Just then, the waitress came to the table. She was a young woman with long dark hair and a slight build. Her uniform was a colorful skirt and a blouse with white billowing sleeves and no neckline. Instead, the sleeves started a quarter of the way down her arms and the front fell low exposing her ample breasts, slender neck, and delicate shoulders. "Would you like drinks?" Her voice was heavy with an accent. Then her eyes lit up when she noticed Anthony. She began speaking to him rapidly in Italian. Anastasia could see Stella tighten. The waitress and Anthony both laughed and the waitress began wiggling her bare shoulders in a flirting way. Stella was turning red. She was wearing a very sober look, glaring up at the girl with dangerous eyes.

"Oh! Waitress?" Anastasia piped up rudely, interrupting the too intimate conversation. "I'd like a glass of wine."

The waitress looked at her dully, then made a notation on her pad. "What kind?" She asked flatly, annoyed with Anastasia's bringing a premature end to her exchange with Anthony.

"Ah, white," she answered in desperation.

The waitress looked up at her with contempt. "Honey, what kind of white? There are several."

Anastasia stared at the young woman. She didn't like being called 'honey' by this woman, especially in such a condescending tone. Mark was quietly watching the exchange, finding it entertaining. He decided that it would be wise to rescue his date, as well as the evening.

Speaking in Italian he ordered a bottle of wine. "I'm sorry, burt I hope you don't mind my ordering for you." He was looking at Anastasia lovingly. Something about the spark of anger in her eyes had aroused him.

As for Stella, she was relieved when the waitress left, but the anger was still there in abundance. Anastasia was sour as well, oblivious to Mark's eyes on her. Both girls looked across to one another, drinking their water, wishing it was something stronger. Anthony sat silently.

"They say the Irish are jealous lovers," Mark stated smoothly with a wink at Anastasia. She blushed.

She countered the only way she knew how. She changed the subject. "You told me that you had business in Italy. What kind?"

"Oh, just some apartment buildings. I have a good manager taking care of it for me while I'm gone."

"Are you planning to buy any buildings here?"

"I don't know yet what I am doing here. Right now, I am just on a long vacation. Helping my father a little."

"Are you going back?"

"I had planned to, but who knows?" He smiled warmly at Anastasia.

The waitress came back with a bucket of ice and two bottles of wine. Apparently, part of her exchange with Anthony involved his ordering a bottle of wine. She expertly opened the bottles and filled the glasses for everyone. "Do you need menus?" She asked.

Mark answered, "Yes, please."

She stepped toward the door and returned with a menu for each of them, then stood with her pen in one hand, the pad in the other, poised to take their order. Anastasia opened her menu and was agape when she realized that everything was written in Italian. She glanced up at the waitress, who was looking back at her with a sneer.

Stella slapped her menu shut. "Don't you have one

written in English?"

The waitress looked smug. "This is an Italian restaurant, we serve Italian foods, to mainly Italian customers. Or at least people who appreciate the country and know the language well enough to order food."

Stella was poised to jump out of her seat.

"I think I know what I want." Anastasia interrupted again. The waitress grunted and then stepped beside Anastasia's seat. Stella slowly melted back into her own.

"Ah, noodles with a white cheese sauce," Anastasia said quickly.

The waitress gave her an annoyed look. "What do you mean, 'noodles?'"

Mark came to the rescue again. "I think she would like fettuccine alfredo." He looked at Anastasia. "Any meat?"

She smiled at him with relief. "How about steak?"

"Fine," he answered softly. Then, to the waitress, he gave instructions in Italian and included Anthony by asking him a few questions. With that, the waitress gathered the menus and left abruptly.

Mark looked at Stella. "I hope you don't mind, but I ordered for you. Is that okay?"

She returned his smile and nodded her approval. Mark had a way of soothing even one of Stella's rages. He turned to Anastasia. "I see that you must be the one who keeps the order in your family." He said it quietly so that no one else could hear.

"No, not really," Anastasia answered. "My brother is the organizer most of the time. I guess it just depends on who's around."

Anthony and Stella were being very quiet on the other side of the table. Anastasia suddenly realized that she and Mark had been ignoring them.

"So, have you been following the news overseas?" Anastasia offered as group conversation.

Mark followed suit. "Not too much, which news?"

"Israel and Egypt are going to declare peace. Can you

imagine? After thousands of years of being enemies, their leaders are going to shake hands."

Anthony nodded his head, pretending to understand. Stella just stared at Anastasia across the table, unimpressed.

"Well, Stella, think about it. In biblical times, the Jews were used as slaves by the Egyptians. Remember the story of Moses leading them to the promised land while the Egyptians were pursuing them? They've been fighting to exist ever since."

Finally, Stella spoke. "Y'know that whole thing? I mean, I know that you and Mario are always talking about stuff from the bible and all those other old books that you two read, but seriously, have you ever seen those pictures of Israel on the news? I mean, really, all the pictures I've ever seen of the place, well, it's a desert, in the middle of the desert. It doesn't resemble the 'land of milk and honey' to me, so why did God give'em some worthless piece of desert? I think if He really liked them so much, He would have given them someplace nice, you know, like an island in the Bahamas or something."

Anastasia just stared at her sister for a moment. Mark was chuckling to himself. Anthony was nodding his head, agreeing with everything that Stella said, even though he had no idea what that was.

"You know Stella," Anastasia said thoughtfully. "I've never thought of it that way." She decided it best just to agree and move on.

The waitress arrived with a large oval tray with bread and individual salads on it. She totally ignored Stella and Anastasia, but gave long glances and smiles to both men. Stella scowled at her sister again. Mark ordered more wine. The girls were clearly out-drinking the guys.

Soon, the main course arrived. Despite the friction between the women, Anastasia couldn't help but admire the way the waitress could balance the large oval tray on one hand. Even with the tray packed full of heavy glass dishes heaped with food and condiments, she never faltered.

Then she used her other hand to unfold a small metal table

to set the tray on while she served the food. This bit of admiration was quickly overshadowed by something else as she slammed plates down in front of the sisters.

To Anastasia, the situation was now almost comical. Stella was fuming. Anthony had become aware of the seriousness of the situation. Anastasia could see the concern in his face as he watched her silently begin eating. What he did next was a small thing, but it made Anastasia want to give him a hug.

He reached over and tenderly squeezed Stella's shoulder with his right hand. When she looked up at him, he smiled warmly, then carefully placed his hand over hers. It was a small gesture, but it made Stella forget to be mad for a moment.

The meal was pretty quiet. Mark and Anastasia talked softly while Anthony and Stella exchanged smiles. Anastasia did notice Stella giving the waitress one last evil look as they were getting ready to leave.

Just as they where on their way out, Stella stopped and called to Mark. "Would you mind picking me up at the door? I need to go to the ladies' room." Mark readily obliged, but Anastasia looked hesitant. She knew there was something up. Mark gave her a small tug on the arm, so that she left her sister, who was now near the restroom door.

"I won't leave her, I promise." he smiled. Anastasia just smiled back and followed the procession outside. Mark was unlocking her car door when they all heard the crash. Stella was standing outside the building shortly after.

"So, Stella, did you see what happened in there?" Mark asked as she was stepping into the car.

She just shrugged. "Oh, I don't know. It sounded like someone dropped a tray or something." Mark turned back around with a bewildered expression, then put the car in drive.

Next, they went to a movie that Mark had picked. It was perfect. Even Stella liked it better than she thought she would. The evening was cool, but clear. If she had brought a coat, Anastasia would have rather walked home.

They stopped at a small bar after the movie and had a few

drinks together. Thankfully, Stella didn't see anyone she knew. She and Anthony were getting along fabulously. Anastasia wondered why she had never thought of fixing her sister up with someone who didn't speak or understand English. It was the perfect date for her. Now they were even talking softly to one another in a kind of pantomime. Both were smiling and laughing frequently.

Anastasia and Mark were sitting very close together. Mark had his arm around her. She had to put her face very close to his when she looked up to speak to him. They had discussed so many things. Finally, they were out of words, and just looked at each other. Mark leaned in closer. Anastasia kept her head up gazing into his eyes. Slowly, he turned his head and brushed his lips against hers. She let out the breath that she had been holding and closed her eyes. They parted lips and rubbed the tips of their tongues together. She wanted to use her teeth to bite his lip, but instead he pressed his open mouth against hers and sucked at her tongue. She moved her hand up to his cheek, then ran her fingers through his hair. He was holding her with both arms. They kissed for several minutes, until they became self conscious of their surroundings. Anthony and Stella were staring at them.

The drive home was full of tension. It was decided that Stella would be dropped off at Anastasia's, but whether the guys would be asked upstairs was still under consideration. Anastasia wanted Mark, but was still afraid. What if the pills didn't work? What if I'm not the same? And if she asked them up, well, as small as her apartment was, she could imagine how they might still end up spending the night. That was the mental picture that brought her to a decision. She would say good night and reach over and kiss him good-bye as soon as the car stopped in front of her building.

And that was exactly what she did, but she also told him how much fun she'd had. The kiss she offered did last a while. It was more difficult for her to say good-bye than she had imagined. But, there was something that Mark was reading from her. Somehow, he knew that she needed more time. He was feeling protective of her, like a younger sister that he'd never had. He let her go without a fuss. The two men walked the women to the door to the building. Stella was more reluctant to shut the door, so Anastasia did it for her.

Once they were upstairs, Stella was like a teenaged girl again. "Wasn't he gorgeous?" She said.

They had one last drink together and talked about the evening before Stella went home. Bed felt good to Anastasia, even though she lay awake thinking. Something magical had happened that evening, and it felt wholesome. It wasn't like the wild one-night stands she had acquired a taste for. This was something different.

CHAPTER 16

Morning broke, and the first thing that Anastasia became aware of was a pounding at her door. It was Stella.

"Mom's in the hospital. Dad found her passed out on the floor." Anastasia threw her coat on and quickly followed her sister. They walked fast down the sidewalks, running through intersections. Stella explained the details that she knew. Their mother was found unconscious on the floor. It wasn't until the ambulance came that they were able to bring her to. She was in pain, but awake when Stella left the hospital. Anastasia thought silently about the night her mother visited her. She was telling the truth. She was sick, but was she really dying?

When they arrived at the hospital, they found that their mother was still in the intensive care unit. The doctors were running tests on her. They found their father and brother sitting in a waiting room.

"Do they know what's wrong with her?"

"Well," their father began. "When I left her, she was explaining to them the problem. She said that she had a growth in her womb, and that it was spreading sickness through her body." He was staring at the ground in front of him as he finished the last sentence. Anastasia felt sorry for him. Such a quiet little man. How had he ever gotten involved with a woman like Marilyn, she wondered.

"Has she been to a doctor recently?" Anastasia asked.

He replied by shaking his head. "I don't know. I doubt it."

"She never complained about feeling sick?"

"No. I thought she was acting kind of unlike herself lately, but I work all day. When she quit fixing dinner a few days ago, well, I couldn't complain. I just figured that she was going through one of her spells. You know, she's always been moody."

How could two people be married for so long and not know each other well enough to confide an illness? Anastasia wondered, what was normal? The only couple she could think of that might fit the label was her grandparents, but she rarely saw them since they lived so far away. That reminded her.

"Has anyone called Grandma and Grandpa Polaski?"

"I did," said her brother. "They want us to call when the doctor's reports come in. Grandpa doesn't have much faith in Mom's diagnosis."

Curious, Anastasia thought. Her grandfather didn't seem to be the least bit intimidated by her mother. She knew that her mother's parents had problems controlling Marilyn all the time she was growing up. In fact, it wasn't until after Anastasia was born that Marilyn finally contacted them again. She had run away at thirteen and was never seen again by her parents until she sent them an invitation to Anastasia's baptism. No one was sure why this event caused her to want to see her parents again. After the shock of finding that their lost daughter was well, they did come to see their grandchildren occasionally, and sent them presents. Marilyn always put on a good show when they were around, but it was evident that there was no real love there. There was always an excessive amount of tension during their visits.

"I hope Grandma and Grandpa come. It would be nice to see them," Anastasia said softly. Everyone was quiet. This was a new experience for them. None of them had ever been seriously ill before. No one was sure what to do.

After a couple hours, a grey-looking doctor in a scrub suit stepped into the waiting room. He read Marilyn's name off a clipboard. Her family stood up and walked toward the doctor. He led everyone into a smaller vacant waiting room across the hall.

It was obvious that there was bad news. The doctor's sober eyes looked into each face with compassion. "I'm sorry, but there does appear to be a large mass in her uterus. It has to be removed. We'll get a biopsy then, but I know from experience that a tumor that size, well, it looks to be very serious."

Everyone was silent. No one knew how to act. Their father just kept looking at the floor, holding a paper cup of coffee with both hands. Finally, Mario noticed how despondent his father was, and knew the doctor needed consent for the operation. Mario stepped up and put his hand on his father's shoulder. "Come on Dad. Let's sit down." He led his father to a chair and explained to him softly that the doctor was waiting for him to sign a consent form.

He nodded. "But I don't know if she'd like that. I mean, what if she wakes up and gets mad?"

"But, Dad, the doctor said that it's very serious. She might die if they don't operate."

The father looked up at his son lovingly. "If you think I should, then I will." The doctor gave him the form, and he signed with a shaking hand. As soon as the doctor turned to leave, Mario's father dropped his coffee and clutched the front of his son's shirt.

Slowly, the family moved into the main waiting room, and Stella volunteered to call their grandparents.

"Y'know, your mother told me that she was an orphan for years." Their father began in an even tone. "It wasn't until Anastasia was born that I found out different. See, she would say that we were two of a kind, she and I, because my folks died when I was little, and she said her folks died when she was thirteen." Their father made a small laughing noise. "Boy, was I surprised when these two people came to the door one day and told me they were Marilyn's parents. I told them they must be mistaken. Then your mom pushed me out of the door and started huggin' them both, like she was glad to see them." He stopped as though he was lost in thought, then started again. "I guess she sent them an invitation to Anastasia's baptism, just like it was nothing. When I asked her why she lied about being an orphan all those years, she just shrugged. Said she might as well have been an orphan, and that it was just easier than explaining the truth. Then she just kind of dismissed me, you know, like she does." He was staring forward in thought.

Mario looked sadly at his father. Shouldn't this man be angry, he thought. Instead he just waited for her to throw another punch at him and then tried to duck. At least the kids had each other to talk to, but this poor man just took the abuse in silence, alone.

It was several hours before an attendant announced their mother's name. She gave the family the message that the patient was in recovery and would be in her own room soon. It would be the next day before they had the results from the biopsy, but the tumor was removed. They moved to Marilyn's room. The change in scenery was nice. Marilyn was brought in soon after.

She was rolled in still unconscious and wearing her surgical cap. There were IVs in each arm and she looked as if she were dead. Stella couldn't help but think how helpless and small she looked. When the nurse warned that she might be sleeping for quite awhile, Stella decided to go home and come back later. Mario stayed for his father. Anastasia wasn't sure why she stayed, but she did. The three of them were sitting silently, staring at a television that was mounted on the wall, high up by the ceiling.

"So, Mario, what was the name of the angel who presides over clamor and terror?" Anastasia asked quietly.

"Uriel," he answered.

"Do you think that he might be Mom's angel?" Mario flashed a look at their unconscious mother. She still lay there, lifeless. He looked at his sister in agreement, but didn't answer.

It was dark before she began moving around. Slowly, she opened her eyes. She asked for water. The nurse had left ice for her, predicting that she would be thirsty before she was able to sit up and take water. Anastasia tenderly held the crushed ice to her mother's lips. Mario and their father stood nearby. Everyone's eyes were on her. Suddenly, she looked annoyed. "What the hell's going on?" She asked in a slurred voice. It was as if she was drunk. As Anastasia explained, her mother's eyes grew sober. There was an unusual look of terror as she realized that she had completely lost consciousness. For the first time in her existence, she didn't know what was happening. She could have died without being aware of her own death. She went pale. How could she have lost control like that? It must never happen again, she vowed to herself.

She looked around, then glared suspiciously at the IVs in her arms. "What is this? I'm not to have any more medicine. Is that clear?" She looked sternly at Anastasia, who in turn nodded in agreement.

"Find out what this stuff is. I want to know immediately." Anastasia obediently left the room to find a nurse. Then Marilyn's gaze fell on her husband, who was trying to look as small as possible in the corner of the room. "What happened?" She demanded.

"Well," he started softly. "I found you on the floor and couldn't get you to wake up, so we called an ambulance. They took you here right away. That was when we found out that you were so sick that the doctor said you might die if they didn't operate right away. I would've asked you first, but you wouldn't wake up, and the doctor—"

"It's okay. You did the right thing," she announced, ending his torture. He immediately breathed a sigh of relief. Mario was relieved for him as well. She became quiet again. She seemed to be listening. Then her eyes followed the IV tubes up her arm again. A few minuets later, a nurse entered the room with Anastasia.

"You may leave the tubes, but I want to know exactly what is to be injected into them. I am not to have any more medicines that will cause me to be intoxicated."

The nurse, who hadn't spoken a word stared at Marilyn for a moment. "The doctor is in charge of what's injected into those tubes, I mean IVs. You'll have to talk to him about this."

"Well, then I wish to see him now."

The nurse looked confused. "I don't know if he's in the building, but I'll leave a message for him at the station. If you want to call his office in the morning, we have his number—"

"I am telling you that I will not allow any more medicine to be injected into these tubes until you've explained what the effects of the medicine are in detail." Marilyn glared at the poor woman with such fierceness that she was beginning to tremble. She seemed to be unable to speak, then turned and left the room. Anastasia and Mario glanced at each other, then down at the floor. How cruel it was to inflict their mother on these innocent people.

Marilyn relaxed, then looked at her family. "I need to rest now. Why don't you all go home? I'll call if I need something." They quietly lined up at her bedside and took turns kissing her good bye. It was a relief to be leaving the hospital.

"Now did that look like a dying woman to you?" Anastasia said in the elevator.

Mario looked at his sister. "She was sounding like her old self. Maybe the doctor is wrong about how serious her condition is."

No one answered.

Marilyn's parents came straight to her home the next morning. Mario greeted them at the door. It was a nice reunion. In the past, the kids had always enjoyed their visits, and now, without Marilyn there, the tension was gone as well. None of them could remember having a better time visiting with one another than they had over coffee that morning. Even Stella got out of bed and sat at the kitchen table with everyone.

"Where is Anastasia?" Asked Marilyn's father, Patrick.

"She has her own apartment now," Mario explained.

"Why, she is so young to be living alone. She is living alone, isn't she?"

"Yeah, she lives by herself there. Has for over a year

now."

"She having problems getting along with your mother?"

"Well, yeah, that's basically why she moved." Mario really didn't want to get into the details.

"It's a pity that your mother has to be so domineering." No one but Patrick talked like that about Marilyn. Everyone else just silently looked at him. "Anastasia was always such a good girl." He stared at the table a moment. "You know, it was your mother that made your grandma and I decide not to have any more children." He laughed. Everyone smiled timidly. "She was the strangest child. Never would talk to anyone. She just went about doing whatever she wanted, like she knew better than anyone else. To this day, I don't know half of what that child did after dark. When she ran away the first time, well, we had to bar the window in her room and put a lock on the outside of her door. Boy, was she mad. She hit your grandmother in the head with a table lamp, knocked her unconscious, then just left her there and ran away again."

Their grandmother reached over and patted her husband's hand. "Hush now, Patrick. There's no reason to tell all that now. Marilyn is their mother. Besides, that was along time ago."

Patrick pulled his hand away. "Sarah, they're all adults now. I think it's time that they knew just what their mother is capable of. For that matter, I think they need to be warned about the family."

Sarah sadly shook her head, looking down.

"What do you mean about the family?" Mario asked curiously.

"Every generation, there's born a real hell-raiser. The one before your mother was my sister, Elsa May. And before that was her grandpa, Ian. They're born mean and ruthless. And you know how they'll be when they're born, because just like your very own mother, they're born with a witch's veil."

Everyone was looking at him in amazement. This was something that no one had heard before. "What's a witches veil?" Mario asked.

"Just like an animal, like a dog. They come out in a kind of sac." He pointed his finger at his grandchildren. "If you ever have a child like that, kill it. Kill it right away. It's the devil's child." Sarah was shaking her head slowly and moaning. Patrick looked at her with sympathy, reached over, and put his arm around her shoulder. "Now Sarah, they need to know these things. My family has a cursed seed. They need to know about it."

Mario and Stella were staring at their grandparents with shocked expressions on their faces. Their father was wringing his hands and looking away in silence. "Grandpa, how? Why?" Mario was having difficulty speaking in whole sentences.

"Son, I don't know. I just know it's been going on a long time. It's always been something that no one talked about. When I was young, I'd hear whispers, but it wasn't until Marilyn was born that they confessed to me. My own mother knew about it, because of my sister Elsa May, but no one told me until it was too late. Now I'm warning you young folks. Maybe you shouldn't even have children. Maybe you should adopt. I hate to see my own line die out, but we've got a bad seed." He looked down, shaking his head sadly.

Marilyn's husband was listening, but remembering a strange conversation that he and Patrick had in private, soon after they had met for the first time. His father-in-law was asking him details about how the children were born. If they had been born in the hospital and if the doctor had told him anything about the births that was unusual in any way. At the time, he just thought it was odd. Now it all made sense.

"Well, I know that my children don't belong to the devil, not a one of them," he said. Mario and Stella were surprised by their father's outburst. Afterward, he got up and walked into the other room.

"Grandpa, what happened when Mom was born?" Mario asked, intrigued by the whole conversation.

"Marilyn was born proper in a hospital, even though my mother was against it. She wouldn't tell me why. Your aunt Elsa

May had come into town about a year before the birth. She was getting old and told everyone that she was retired. She was with us at the hospital. I guess she was interested in the baby since she never did have one, and by then she was too old. So, while Sarah was giving birth, Elsa May stepped outside. When the doctor came to get me, I went outside to fetch her, and that's when we found her dead. Died of old age, the doctor said on the certificate. But, anyway it was after all that confusion with Elsa May that the doctor took me aside and told me about the witch's veil. He looked like it kind of scared him. He said in all the years that he'd been a doctor, he'd never seen or heard of such a thing. Anyway, the baby was healthy. Right away, though, we started noticing things about Marilyn. She had these knowing eyes from the time she was born. She started talking before she could walk. In learning to walk, she'd go into these rages, like she was mad 'cause her little legs didn't do like she wanted them to. She was walking at six months. So many things no one taught her, she just seemed to know by herself. Then that secretiveness. We never knew what she did. She never confided in anyone."

Mario was fascinated. Stella just listened intently. "Have you ever talked to Mom about it?"

"Oh, yes, I tried to talk to her. Get her to confide in me. I was the only one who wasn't afraid of her. But she wouldn't say anything. She'd just clam up and sit there. And, y'know, my mother told me the whole time. 'Son there's nothing you can do, just let her be.' She said Elsa May was exactly like Marilyn, exactly."

"Where you close to Aunt Elsa?" Mario asked curiously.

"No, not too much. She was gone by the time I was ten. Before she left, though, I liked her a lot. She wasn't much of a lady, but she sure was good at rough housin'. She could shoot and ride a horse better than any man I ever knew. In fact, I was probably the closest one to her when we were young. But then she left and rarely came by the house after that. When I got to be a teenager, I guess I got to be embarrassed by her. She acted more like a man than a woman, and people would talk about it. It made me kind of ashamed of her. It wasn't until she was old and couldn't keep up with the kind of hard work she was always into that she came back home. I was busy with my business and new wife, then. Besides, I was an important person in the community by then and my masculine sister and her crazy escapades were nothing but bad gossip for me. It was bad business, so I tried to distance myself from her most of the time." There was a bit a of regret in Patrick's face. He looked like he might have been thinking about his youth with Elsa May.

"Well, she sure sounds like an interesting character," Mario offered.

"She was always good to me," Sarah mentioned quietly.

"Maybe we can talk some more, and I could write this stuff down, so we'll always have it?" Mario asked.

Patrick gave his grandson a sharp look. "Some things are best forgotten."

Mario didn't pursue it, but he knew that as soon as he was alone, he would try to remember every detail of what his grandfather had said and record it.

Patrick looked up at the kitchen clock. "Well, I think we should be getting up to the hospital now."

They filed out of the door toward the car, except for Stella. She offered to walk and swing by Anastasia's on the way there. Patrick wanted to pick her up, but Stella argued that the car would be too full. So she left on foot, headed toward her sister's apartment.

Stella was happy to be alone. She enjoyed her grandparents, but all the talk about devil children was giving her the creeps. Besides, she wanted to daydream about more pleasant things, like Anthony. They had talked on the phone just that morning, and the day before as well. It was a strained conversation, and most of the time was spent with dead air, but she felt a kind of electricity coming from the phone, just knowing that he was on the other end of it. She was dying to tell Anastasia that he had called her and wanted to go out again. There was just too much excitement in Stella's life to be depressed or upset about her mother right now.

When she arrived at Anastasia's apartment, she was relieved to find out that she was home. The first thing out of Anastasia's mouth was, "Where's your bag?"

"It's not noon yet." Stella spoke with an indignant tone. "What do you think? That I'm some kind of lush or something?"

Anastasia just shrugged. She had a mouth full of bread and peanut butter.

"Hey, guess what? Anthony called me, twice!"

Anastasia was taking a drink of juice. "I don't suppose that it could've been too much of a conversation."

"Well, he got his message across that he wanted to go out in the evening," she explained. "Or that he wanted a weenie," she added teasingly.

Anastasia laughed, choking on her juice.

"Anyway, Grandma and Grandpa are here. Everybody was on their way to the hospital, I just stopped by to get you. We're supposed to meet them there."

Anastasia nodded. "Yeah, I was just getting ready to go."

"So, I hear that Mom's acting like her old self. Mario said that she's already threatening the help." Anastasia could tell by Stella's bold statement that she was still high on Anthony. "You should've been at the house today. Grandpa was going off on some really strange shit this morning. It was kind of weird listening to someone talk about Mom that way, but he was telling us all about how she was when she was growing up and about a family curse." She kind of chuckled. "He said Mom was the devil's child." Stella started an all out giggle now, holding her stomach. Then she looked up at Anastasia and mouthed the words. "I could have told him that."

Anastasia wasn't laughing. She was listening. "What are you talking about, family curse?"

Stella begrudgingly stopped her laughing and shrugged.

"I don't know. Ask Mario about it. The whole thing kind of gives me the creeps."

Anastasia reluctantly gave up the conversation. She knew that Mario would be a better source for this kind of information anyway. "Well, I guess we should be on our way." Anastasia got up and put her juice glass in the sink. They started out the door together.

"So, have you heard anything from Mark?" Stella asked gingerly.

"How? I don't have a phone."

"Well, do you have his number?"

"No, but I figure that he can always get a hold of me at work."

"You're going to see him again, aren't you?"

"Oh, yeah. In fact, I've been thinking about it, and I think I'll go buy some groceries." She smiled at her sister. "Maybe even later today. Hey, want to go with me? Doesn't Anthony work at Mark's father's market too?"

Stella was beaming. "Yeah, he does. Sure I'll go."

They were silent for awhile, both in little daydreams about their new beaus. Suddenly, Anastasia had a flash of her mother smiling. She stopped abruptly, holding both sides of her head and trying to get her bearings back.

"You okay?" Stella asked.

"Yeah." Anastasia shook off the sensation and started walking again. Had her mother been listening?

Marilyn smiled. There was much pain in her body, but by separating herself from her body, she was able to avoid it. She was feeling more alert now. Her senses were sharp again. And now, after finding out that her daughter had a lover, she was feeling much better.

Patrick had annoyed her, but an old man telling crazy stories wasn't going to keep a healthy young person in love from reproducing. She felt confident of that. She had a deep-seeded affection for Patrick. It started when he was a baby. She remembered begrudgingly taking care of him as a child, but somehow she accidently began to genuinely have protective and loving feelings for him. It broke her heart when she realized that he was embarrassed about her. She continued to think that maybe he would grow out of it and go fishing or hunting with her again, but he never did. By the time he was out of that awkward, too self conscious adolescent stage, he was concentrating on becoming a respectable businessman. Having a sister like Elsa May just wasn't respectable. But, he was fertile ground for Marilyn to be born, even if he did prove to be less than adequate as a father. It was just too bad that he wasn't man enough to produce a son, she thought. Hopefully, Anastasia would.

Marilyn could hear voices. It was Patrick. She pulled herself together and gritted her teeth against the pain. This reunion was going to have to be a short one. She didn't know how long she could tolerate being in her pain-wracked body.

"Marilyn," he said softly, as he entered the room. Her face went pale and she continued to lie very still, with her eyes open. Patrick's face was filled with concern. He hadn't expected her to look so ill.

"Hello, Father." She closed her eyes as he bent and kissed her cheek. Sarah was close beside him.

"Why darling, you look like you're in pain," Sarah said with motherly concern. "Aren't they giving you anything for pain?"

"I'm okay. I told them not to." Both parents just shook their heads. They knew better than to argue.

Sarah took her turn kissing Marilyn's cheek, then her husband, and then Mario.

"So, have the doctors said how long before you can go home?" Patrick asked optimistically.

"The doctors think I'm going to die," Marilyn announced bluntly. "They think that I'm full of cancer and will probably never leave this hospital alive."

Sarah gasped. "They told you that?"

"No, but that's what they think."

Patrick looked annoyed. "Well, I think I'll confirm that diagnosis with the doctor, thank you. There is absolutely no reason for you to read such a grim prediction out of something that the doctors may have told you. It was probably nothing like what you're telling us." He shook his head. "I just don't believe that they have all of your tests back already. How could they think something like that without having all the tests back?"

"Well, Father, they do. Contrary to what they might tell you, that is what they think." Marilyn hated his condescending manner toward her. It infuriated her, in fact. If he were anyone else, she would have killed him years ago.

"Where is her doctor anyway?" Patrick demanded. He turned and stomped out of the room, heading toward the nurse's station.

The room went silent. Humbly, Marilyn's husband spoke up. "My, we certainly can see where you get your determination, dear."

Marilyn gave her husband a stern look. He shrank back and sat down. Intense pain was magnifying her cross mood. All she wanted was for everyone to leave. She was just about to say something when she noticed her two daughters come into the room. Their appearance surprised her. The pain was interfering with her thinking.

"Mother, you're awake," Stella said with fake enthusiasm. She stepped to her mother's bedside and kissed her cheek. Marilyn merely glared up at her.

"You look better today," Anastasia offered before kissing her mother as well. To this, Marilyn smiled faintly. It was apparent she was happy with this one.

"You look like a woman in love," Marilyn said with a slippery smoothness. Anastasia smiled, and then backed away from her. This was the woman who had caused her so much grief. Recent memories, still frightening, made her uneasy now that her mother was being especially kind to her.

"Why Anastasia," Marilyn said after reading her

daughter's fear. "I'm happy you found someone. It's unnatural for a beautiful young girl like you to spend all your evenings alone."

There it was again, the same tone she remembered from that night at her apartment.

"Well, fine then, I'll not say another word about it." Her mother declared. "Mario, what have you been up to?" Marilyn quickly changed subjects.

"Just working, Mother, trying to help keep your house in order."

"Don't suppose I'll be getting any grandchildren out of you any time soon," she said with immediate regret. As well disciplined as she was, sometimes the malice would unintentionally seeped out. "I mean, you're not seeing anyone are you?" She asked with mock interest, trying to recover.

"No," he answered, knowing she really didn't care.

About that time Patrick came storming back into the room. "Well, I guess doctors don't work on Sundays! God forbid anyone get sick on the Lord's day."

"Marilyn's not going anywhere, honey." Sarah rubbed her husbands shoulder. "We'll just call them tomorrow." Patrick drew in a deep breath and let it out in a huff.

"I hate to sound ungrateful," Marilyn started dryly. "But I really would like to get some rest." Her family immediately stood at attention, anxious to line up for the farewell kiss.

Patrick looked annoyed again. He hated the way everyone jumped every time his daughter cracked her whip. "Fine, then. I'll be back another day." He patted the blanket over his daughter's foot. He then turned and walked out, refusing to stand in line. Sarah hurriedly pushed in front of everyone so she could quickly kiss her daughter before her husband was too far down the hall. Anastasia was last in line.

"I'll be back soon, Mother," Anastasia promised.

"Good. But don't let me keep you from having fun."

Anastasia smiled and turned to go.

"Anastasia?" Her mother called her back. "By the way,

my angel is Azazyel."

Anastasia looked at her mother's smiling face with apprehension, then nodded quietly and left.

Stella was waiting outside the hospital room for her sister. "Are you going to stop by the house?"

Anastasia was in a fog, thinking about how her mother seemed to be too interested in her new romance. She peered up at her sister as though she couldn't comprehend what she had said, so Stella repeated herself.

"Oh, ah, I guess so. I'd like to see grandma and grandpa." She thought about this for a moment. It would be strange to enter her childhood home by the front door and to walk around without fear. She also very much wanted to visit her grandparents. It had been a long time since she'd seen them.

"Great, then after that, maybe we can go shopping, huh?" Stella said enthusiastically.

Anastasia nodded, but after visiting with her mother, she had lost some of her own enthusiasm. It pained her to realize she always had bad feelings whenever her mother was kind to her. There was a deep-seeded feeling her mother's motives for her every action were always self serving. It followed that Marilyn's approval of Anastasia's relationship with Mark was somehow beneficial to her. But for the life of her, Anastasia couldn't think of how.

"Stella," Anastasia started thoughtfully. "Has Mom ever acted like she wanted you to have children?"

Stella shook her head in surprise. "No."

"Well, I think she wants me to." She mumbled, still deep in thought. "And if it's grandchildren she wants, or someone to carry on the family line, why is it only me she's interested in?"

Stella chuckled. "Maybe it's just me. Maybe she thinks it would be better if I didn't breed." She continued laughing in a pathetic way. Anastasia only looked at her sadly. Her mother was an expert at making people feel worthless, and she had done an especially good job on Stella.

Walking right up to the front door of her parent's home

was almost scary. She knew they had just left her mother at the hospital, but she could still feel her mother's presence strongly as soon as she came into view of the old house.

They had just started up the sidewalk when they heard their father's voice calling them to the side of the house near the garage. When they walked over, they could see their grandparents were in their own car with the motor on.

"Oh, you're not going all ready," Anastasia moaned, walking up to the driver's side window.

"It's a long drive home, honey. We're getting old and don't like to drive after dark. We'll come back soon. I promise."

Anastasia looked at the sky. It would be another six hours before dark, and they didn't live that far away. Apparently, her mother had upset them. She decided not to argue. She could see a worn look in her grandfather's face.

"Okay, but I'll make sure I'm around to see you longer next time." He smiled and they kissed good-bye. She walked around the car to her grandmother's window and said farewell to her as well. She felt sad watching them back out the driveway. They all waved one last time in unison as the grandparents pulled onto the road and drove out of sight.

Anastasia looked at her family. There they were, all alone without their mother. All four of them seemed to realize it at the same time, looking from one to another, like four little orphans with no adult to supervise them.

Slowly, the corners of Anastasia's mouth curled. "Let's order a pizza!"

Stella said, "And I'll buy the beer!" Neither Mario or their father offered any words of agreement, but neither did they object. The four of them marched into the house with a new found, if only temporary, interest in life.

Later that evening empty beer cans in the sink, a discarded pizza box was sticking out of the garbage can, and in the middle, the four of them were playing euchre. Laughter and an occasional curse filled the air. None of them could remember anything like it before. There was this feeling of release. They were talking out loud with heartfelt laughter mixed with other human emotions. It was their first vacation together.

Earlier, Stella had forced Mario to drive all the way to Mattioli's Market for the beer. She was disappointed when neither of the boys were there. She had combed the place thoroughly, even sneaking through the 'employees only' door, much to Mario's embarrassment. Anastasia had stayed behind with her father. They both loved the opportunity to talk quietly alone.

CHAPTER 17

Jack was calling her into the front office again. She had a good idea as to why. Her suspicions were confirmed when she saw Mark standing on the other side of the counter, a faint smile on his lips.

"Come back to complain about those business cards, Mr. Mattioli?" she teased, cozying up to the counter in fount of him. Jack looked up, noting the difference in her demeanor since the previous week.

"Actually, I just wanted to show you how much I appreciate your fine craftsmanship by taking you to lunch," he said with a confident look. "Are you free?"

"Sure," Anastasia answered easily. She had the urge to casually kiss him, but remembered where she was.

"When can you leave?"

Anastasia looked back at her boss. He waved at her to go now, indicating he had apparently been listening to the conversation. She grabbed her coat and they walked to a nearby cafe.

"So, how was your weekend?" Mark started casually. Anastasia debated on whether to tell him the truth. It was such a new relationship that she wasn't sure if she should start out telling him her problems.

"It was okay. I really had a good time Friday. So did Stella. In fact, she said Anthony called her a couple times."

"Yes, I know about that. And for two people who don't speak the same language, they stayed on the phone quite awhile.

He called from work once." He looked playfully at Anastasia. "It was pretty comical to listen to. He kept putting his hand over the mouth piece of the phone and whispering words to me, asking what they meant." They both laughed.

They ordered lunch and then sat silently for awhile. Anastasia could tell he wanted to say something. Finally he asked, "Anastasia, I know this is going to sound strange, but what does your mother look like?"

"Why?" She smiled curiously.

"Well, I hope you don't think I'm crazy, but I had the strangest dream."

Anastasia froze. Mark noticed the tension immediately. "Listen, I usually don't pay attention to—"

"No, it's okay," Anastasia said. She realized he couldn't understand her reaction. "I have strange dreams all the time. So, what was it about?" She really did want to know.

"First tell me, does she look a lot like you? Maybe taller, blonder hair?"

Anastasia nodded. "What happened in the dream?" There was more urgency in her voice.

"To be honest at first I thought I was dreaming of my mother. I don't know what she looked like, but the woman in this dream, she looked familiar to me. Anyway, soon I began to realize she was thinking only of you. It was as though she was interviewing me for you." Mark laughed and looked nervously at Anastasia. "I'm not sure what it meant. I just saw her looking at me kind of quizzically. Then there was this kind of spark in her eye and she smiled at me. But, she never really said a word."

Anastasia was looking at him. Feeling awkward, Mark continued. "So, tell me. What do you think? Maybe I'm worried about your parents? You think that is it? I don't know why it bothered me so. Kind of silly, huh?"

She swallowed hard, looking carefully for the right words. "Mark— my mother— she's a very strong person. Maybe she did come into your dreams. She's also very sick right now. In fact, my father had to rush her to the hospital Saturday morning. She's still there."

"Why didn't you tell me?" Mark looked concerned. Then a thought came to him. This was why her mother was speaking to him. He decided that the dream must have been because she was sick and worried for her daughter.

Anastasia kind of shrugged. "I didn't want to depress anyone, I guess." Mark instantly snapped back from his thoughts and continued listening to Anastasia. "She's convinced herself that she's dying. The doctor still hasn't finished all the testing on her yet, so we don't know for sure."

"That is terrible. But, Anastasia I want to know of these things. Don't spare depressing me, okay?"

Just hearing that made her feel better. "Sure. And, don't worry that I'll think you're crazy for telling me about your dreams. I know it's important to listen to them. Sometimes you tell yourself things in a dream that you don't realize you know."

"Yes. I believe that," Mark said enthusiastically. "In fact, since you seem to understand these things, let me ask you something. Do you think maybe we talk to each other this way too? I mean, if you and I and everyone has a soul, don't you think sometimes we can communicate soul to soul?"

"I know we can," Anastasia stated flatly. "And when your body is resting, it's easier to separate and communicate 'soul to soul,' as you put it."

Mark's face lit up. It was as if he had finally found someone who understood the things most people thought he was crazy for believing. "How did you learn about these things?"

Anastasia looked thoughtful. "You know, it's just something I've always known." She looked him in the face carefully, trying to judge just how much she should reveal. "In my family, there are ideas we just grew up believing. I always thought everyone else did, too, until I started making friends and working. It was kind of funny, because I'd just start talking about something like it was common knowledge and the person who I was talking to would look at me like I was crazy. Finally, I slowly figured out that our beliefs were different from other people."

"So you are saying all the members of your family share these ideas?"

Anastasia nodded.

Mark sighed and explained. "Well, let me tell you, my family doesn't. As for me, I can't figure out where they came from." He shook his head. It was such a relief to have someone to confide in. "I thought maybe I was an alien or something. I mean with my blue eyes, I always knew I was different. But these thoughts I have sometimes, I still don't know where they came from."

"Mark, you aren't from another planet, unless I am too." They both smiled at one another.

It was a messy job, but someone had to do it. Mario grasped a beer can in each hand, holding them upside down over the sink. He wasn't used to cleaning, except for his own room. His mother had always taken care of these things. Then again, he couldn't ever remember having a mess like this in the house. It really wasn't bad, but Marilyn had always kept the house spotless. Parties were never allowed, even for the family. She would've went into one of her rages if she could have seen the house just then.

It was 5:30 in the afternoon, and Stella was still in bed. She had went out the night before, after Anastasia left. He was still angry with Stella for her continuing behavior. She was out to all hours of the night, and was still managing to come up with room and board money for their mother every week. He had a good idea what she was doing, and regardless of the way every-one else in the family turned their heads, he couldn't turn his. His sister was going to get killed or be thrown in prison. Somebody had to do something.

He was stewing over what to do about his sister and washing dishes. Their father would be home soon, and he wanted to get the place cleaned up before they left to visit their mother. He was going to have to wake Stella in time to get ready to go with them.

A few minutes later, a car pulled up into the driveway. Mario watched his father pull in close to the garage. He was just finishing the dishes. They greeted each other. Mario dried his hands then hung up the dish towel.

"I'll go wake up Stella", he said before rounding the corner to her room.

First he tried knocking on the door. There was no answer. "Stella!" he called. He turned the knob and pushed the door open slowly. The drapes were pulled shut, making the room dark. "Stella?" he said again. The door caused a light to fall on a familiar lump in the blankets, but she didn't stir. Mario entered the room and stood beside her bed. She was laying on her side, facing away from him with the blankets pulled up over her head. "Stella, wake up," he called. She still refused to stir, so he gently pushed on her shoulder. There was no reaction. He looked around her room. There was an opened package of soda crackers on the nightstand, and her clothes were scattered all over the floor. Then something caught his eye. He looked down on the floor and picked up her blouse. It felt stiff, but it was hard to see in the dark room so he turned on the lamp by her bed. Then he could see the dark stains better. They were what was making the material stiff. It looked like blood.

He quickly looked back at his sister and pulled her over onto her back. She moved slightly, moaning painfully. Her hair was stuck to her bloody face, and one eye was swollen shut.

"Stella! You okay?" he asked in a panic. She moaned again, struggling to open her eyes. "Can you hear me?" he asked desperately. She nodded and made a small noise. Mario moved his face closer to her. "What did you say?"

She wet her lips and tried again. "Water."

Mario turned and quickly came back with a glass of water. He gently slipped his hand between the pillow and her head and lifted her so the glass met her lips. She took a small sip. The blanket fell, exposing her naked and bruised chest and arms. Mario winced. He carefully laid her back down and pulled the covers to her neck. He left again, returning with a warm, wet wash rag. Tenderly, he began wiping the blood from her cheek. She moaned and tried to push him away.

"Stella! Be still, I have to see how serious this is. You probably need to go to the hospital."

"No," she cried pitifully. She managed to get one eye partially open. Mario could see that the white of it was red. Then he realized both eyes were swollen. Her nose looked as thought it might have been broken and, there was more blood underneath.

"Do you have any other cuts besides your face?" He was too embarrassed to pull the blankets back.

She swallowed with difficulty. "No."

"Should I call the police?"

"No." She said louder.

He shook his head with disgust. "Stella, this has got to stop. Don't you see? You're going to get killed." His voice became strained, it cracked on the last word. He bit his lip.

Stella looked up at him with her one eye. She was surprised at the emotion in his face. He continued wiping the blood from her. She gritted her teeth and closed her eye without another complaint.

Their father came to the doorway as Mario was leaving to wash out the rag. "What's going on?" he asked, glancing inside her room. Mario shook his head and stepped past his father. Their dad entered the room, looked down at his daughter, and gasped. When Mario reentered the room, his father was still standing over the bed staring down. "What happened?" He asked softly with a bewildered look on his face. Stella turned her head away from her father. He looked at Mario helplessly.

"Dad, let's talk about it later." Mario put his hand on his father's shoulder and gently pushed him away. He obediently left the room, but there was a hurt, confused look on his face. Mario bent down beside his sister and continued cleaning her face and neck. She lay quietly. Next, he carefully lifted her head and traded pillows for a clean one. "I'm going to go talk to Dad. Do you need anything?" She shook her head slowly, then closed her eye and turned her head away.

Mario walked out of the room and deposited the soiled linen in the bathroom. He found his father standing in the kitchen, staring toward the window. Mario walked up to him slowly, not knowing where to start. Their father had always been a shadow. He tried to stay small and out of the way. The children loved their father because they had no reason not to. He was just an agreeable man who lived in the house and brought home a paycheck. No one ever remembered him having a personality. He certainly wasn't someone any of them confided in. The truth was, it never occurred to anyone that he might care or want to know.

Mario felt sorry for him. His father seemed to have no clue as to what was going on with any of his children. "Dad, I think I should stay here with Stella. Can you tell Mom I'll be up to see her tomorrow?"

His father nodded, with his eyes still focused on the window. Then he raised his right arm he pointed straight ahead. "Looks like that window could use some caulking. Guess I better get to it before it gets much colder. Maybe this weekend."

Mario gave a small sound of agreement. He was relieved he wouldn't have to explain Stella after all. He really didn't know where to begin.

Anastasia had an urge to walk by her parent's house before going to see her mother at the hospital. She told herself it was too far out of the way and walked directly to the hospital instead. When she entered her mother's room, her father was already there. She stepped up to her mother's bedside and kissed her hello. "Where's Mario and Stella?" She asked.

"Stella wasn't feeling well so Mario stayed home with her," her father answered.

"Stella," Marilyn said loudly, "got the shit kicked out of her."

Anastasia and her father both looked at her in surprise. He hadn't said anything about it to her. He didn't even explain why he was alone. One thought passed through his mind. Everyone seemed to know what was going on but him. He quietly stared up at the silent television. He had long ago realized he was ignored, but for the first time, it really bothered him to be excluded. They had been a family just last night. They had played cards and drank beer together. He had woke up that morning thinking he felt closer to his children than he ever had before. And tonight, tonight he realized he still didn't know who they were.

Anastasia didn't ask any questions. She knew it was best to just go over there later. She glanced at her father. As usual he was staring in another direction, looking as though he hadn't heard a word.

"Are you feeling better today?" she asked hoarsely.

"I'm beginning to heal from the surgery. I'll be around for awhile yet." She smiled. Anastasia wanted to know if the doctor had talked to her today, but she knew better then to ask. "So, how is that new boyfriend of yours?" her mother asked pleasantly.

Anastasia really didn't want to talk about him to her, but she nodded politely and explained he was doing just fine. Marilyn stared at her a moment, then looked away.

Very few words were exchanged during the whole grueling, one hour visit. Then, mercifully Marilyn announced she wanted to go to sleep. They lined up for their customary kiss good-bye and left.

In the hallway Anastasia's father offered to give her a ride to the house. She accepted. They traveled to the house quietly. It would've been out of the ordinary for them to exchange more than a few words, even in the best of circumstances.

Anastasia made the same kind of gasping noise her father had made when she got a look at her sister. She immediately shut the door and drew back the covers. There were bruises all down her sister's back and buttocks, as well as purple finger prints around both forearms. Whoever did this was serious, maybe even attempting to beat her to death. She had a good idea of what happened.

Stella was crying silently when Anastasia gently pulled her onto her back. Tears were running down her swollen cheeks and she was unable to speak between the little gasps of breath. Anastasia was filled with pity. She knew what ever had happened to Stella, Stella had brought it on herself. Still, her big sister was hurting. Anastasia sat on the side of the bed and bent over her sister, gently holding her close. Stella broke out into louder sobs. Anastasia held her tighter.

Patiently, she waited for the sobs to subside, then she left the room to return with a cold wet rag. She gently wiped Stella's face. Then she laid a plastic baggy of ice their bother had prepared onto the more swollen eye.

"Stella can you tell me what happened?"

Stella nodded then swallowed back her tears. "Um, it was this big sailor. About two weeks ago, I took his wallet. He tried to beat me up then, but I got away." She sniffed and made a kind of hick-up sound. "He chased me outside, behind Billy's Bar, and this time he got me." She let out a big sob. "I couldn't get away from him. He kept hitting me, and when I couldn't get up anymore he started kicking me on the ground. Then he lifted me up by my collar and threw me against the dumpster. He was trying to kill me." She started sobbing again. Anastasia wiped the tears and waited for her sister to continue. "Then I kind of blacked out and fell on the ground again. I was laying there waiting for him to kill me and this big black dog came out of no where and jumped on him." She looked up at her sister in amazement, as though she herself had just realized what had happened. "The dog just started biting and tearing him up. I saw it grab hold of his hand. It wouldn't let go, and when it had him on the ground, it went after his neck. Somehow he rolled over and got up and took off running. I thought it would come after me next, but then it just looked at me and walked away. There was blood all over the place. I don't know which of us was hurt worst." She was sitting up now, trembling. Anastasia held her again, gently rubbing her shoulder while she cried.

Neither of them could judge how much time had elapsed before Stella was able to compose herself again. Finally, she sniffed and pulled away from her sister, and looked at her through her one eye. “Anastasia, what will I tell Anthony? I don’t know how long it will take for this to go away. What will I say?” Stella had finally met someone she could have a normal relationship with, and now this happened.

“Well, we’ll just have to tell him you were in some kind of accident.” Stella thought about this a minute.

“Maybe, we can say I was hit by a car while I was walking.” Anastasia nodded approval and it made Stella feel better.

“So, Stella, don’t you think it’s time for you to look for a real job?”

Stella looked at her sister wearily. “Anastasia, I’ve tried. No one likes me.”

Anastasia was aware of part of Stella’s problem. Stella was so hostile, she unintentionally scared people. Even on a good day, Stella came across as cold and threatening. Now Anastasia looked down at her brute of a sister with pity. “Listen, Stella, I’ll help you look. We’ll find something.” She gave her sister a reassuring pat on the arm.

Mario knocked on the door. “Anastasia, does Stella want some soup?” Stella nodded.

“Yes, with lots of crackers,” Anastasia called back. “Oh, and milk.” Stella formed a faint smile. She must be feeling better, Anastasia thought. If she’ll eat, she’ll live. Dutifully, she left the room to return with her sister’s lunch.

Mario had stopped her in the hallway. He asked her how their sister was, really. Anastasia took time to explain that she thought Stella would make a quick recovery and not to worry. When he continued to look at her seriously, she added that the two of them had agreed she needed a new line of work. Mario looked relived at that. “Maybe this will do it,” he sighed.

Everyday after work, Anastasia stopped by her parents house to check on Stella before she left with her father and brother to visit their mother. Marilyn's prognosis was grim, but nonetheless, she seemed to be feeling better every day. They started her on chemotherapy by the end of the week. After one session, she refused to take another. Marilyn knew she was to die soon, but at the same time, she also declared she alone would decide when. As usual, no one could talk to her about it. As far as Stella was concerned, Marilyn never asked about her. The family all knew she had a hand in her rescue, but Anastasia wondered if she also arranged the beating. They would never know. No one knew just what Marilyn's limits were.

Mark was a regular visitor to the print shop. He took Anastasia to lunch every day. It was a wonderful outlet for her. They talked steadily the whole time they were together. Mark was the first person she had ever met who gave her the close feeling she had when she was with her brother. She knew when she spoke to him he was genuinely interested in what she was saying, fascinated even. They talked about things she had only talked about with family before. She still wouldn't mention her mother's strange powers— that would've been too much— but she did mention other things, and feelings. He soaked up every word, often expressing surprise and relief to find someone who understood his own ways of thinking. They had so much in common. When Anastasia mentioned Stella's accident and how she needed to find a job, he offered to give her a job at the market. Stella, of course, thought the idea was wonderful. Maybe things were working out.

Mark wanted to take her out again Friday night. There was no fear anymore, except of herself. She had been taking the pills for two months now, but her body still hadn't adjusted to them. She still bled at the full moon, and when she was supposed to be on her period, there was nothing. She had stopped by the clinic and talked to the nurse. The nurse assured her that her cycle would eventually adjust to the pills. All she had to do was continue to take a pill every day at the same time. Anastasia left the clinic feeling that surely this trained professional knew what she was talking about. They had already made it perfectly clear to her that they knew much more than a nineteen year old high school drop out.

CHAPTER 18

His hair was still damp from the shower, even after blowing it dry. He still wasn't used to the hand held hair drier. Everyone seemed to be using them, but if he wasn't especially concerned with his appearance tonight, he would've let it dry naturally. He was going out with Anastasia, and hopefully, tonight would be the night they made love.

He was more anxious about this girl than he had been about a woman in a long time, maybe more than ever before. Even his father had noticed the change in him. He wanted to meet her, and for the first time, Mark wanted his father to meet this girl as well. He was confident the two of them would hit it off. Mark was euphoric. Everything seemed to fit together, even his and Anastasia's personalities. They were a matched set.

He splashed cologne on his face and smoothed it over his neck. He slipped the newly pressed white shirt off the hanger and put it on, carefully buttoning it, starting from the second button. He sat on the edge of his bed to pull on black trousers with a leather belt, and lastly, the matching suit jacket. He stubbornly stuck to the wool and cotton blends. The polyester and other synthetics that were so popular were just too stiff and plastic for him.

He also preferred natural foods. He could taste the chemicals and preservatives in many American foods. They would leave a kind of aftertaste in his mouth, it surprised him that no else seemed to notice.

Looking in the mirror one last time, he practiced his most charming smile. He would do his best to woo her. The idea of undressing her excited him so much he nearly slipped into a daydream about it, but he shrugged it off. It was time to pick her up.

He passed through the living room, where his father was in an easy chair reading the paper with the television playing loudly. He tapped him on the shoulder to let him know he was on his way out. Mario smiled, and a pleased look lingered on his face. He was glad to see his son finally serious about a girl.

Mark stopped at the car wash on the way to Anastasia's apartment, paying extra to have the interior cleaned as well. The attendant hung a little pine scented air freshener from the rear view mirror. Mark was in the process of looking for a new car, but for the time being, his father's old car was a little large for his taste, but comfortable.

He parked on the street in front of the door to her building. The part of town she lived in would've been safe enough for him, but the idea of her living here alone, walking the city streets at night, did worry him. Although he knew she was tough and smart enough to handle herself well, still, it was dangerous. Her strength would have intimidated a weaker man, but Mark Mattioli wasn't intimidated. There was a familiar, more vulnerable person behind those blue eyes of hers, and he knew that person better than two weeks would allow. Somehow, some way, he was confident he had known her before and loved her then as well.

Consciously slowing himself down, he tried to climb the stairs casually. Once at the top, he rapped on the door. After a shuffling sound the door opened. There she was, tall enough to almost look him straight in the eye. Like a goddess, her eyes glittered with iridescent eye shadow. Her blue eyes sparkled. Her smile glowed. He felt the urge to take her right there and then. Instead, he sighed. He placed his hand on her neck and drew her to him then kissed her tenderly on the mouth. He felt her tense up. There was desire there, but hesitation. He would have to overcome that somehow during the course of the evening. She blushed and cast her eyes down, opening the door for him to come inside. He wondered mildly if other men made her blush so easily.

He stepped inside, slipping his hands inside his overcoat and into the pockets of his trousers. He looked around the room. Her apartment was so small and plain. He really did admire the way such a young girl could work and support herself the way she did. His next thought was of how he could give her so much more than she had ever had before. He turned back around and faced her. She was wearing blue jeans and a billowy black satin blouse. She looked slightly embarrassed.

"I hope this is okay." She held her arms out and glanced down at herself. "I wasn't sure where we were going." Mark continued to look her up and down with a neutral expression on his face. Anastasia really couldn't tell what he was thinking. She was wearing her best. She didn't own anything except blue jeans and a few very old and out of style dresses.

Finally, he smiled at her. "On you, even a paper sack would look beautiful." She blushed again and turned toward the closet for her coat.

He stepped close to her, holding the back of her jacket so she could slip into it easily. He gently gathered her hair and pulled it out from inside her coat. She stood very still, and he couldn't resist kissing her neck softly. He could tell by the way she tightened up but rolled her head to the side that she enjoyed it. Again, he sensed she was trying to keep herself from getting lost in the moment. He would have to remedy that before the end of the evening.

They moved reluctantly out the door. The long black car looked like a limousine in the moonlight. He opened her door and stood to the side so she could enter. She noticed his tight fitting black leather driving gloves. She admired the deliberate way his one hand gripped the door handle while the other brushed her shoulders, gently guiding her into the car. He was so tender, yet strong. She could only imagine what kind of lover he was.

Their first stop was the same Italian restaurant they visited last week, but this time they sat at a very small table in the most remote corner. A little flame from a candle in the center of the table barely cast enough light to read the menus. Mark helped her into her seat and moved his chair so he was seated next to her. He immediately laid his arm across the back of her chair.

Anastasia thought mildly about another date she had been on where the man sat so close. She had told him to move his chair back and not to crowd her. For some reason, Mark was different. She enjoyed being close to him. During their afternoon lunches, she had felt the impulse to move to his side of the bench, but never did. Now they were as close as possible without her being on his lap.

"Hey, you remember the waitress we had last time?" Mark asked after they had sat quietly for a moment.

Anastasia felt a wave of panic pass through her body. "Yes." She answered nervously.

"Well, my father comes here often. He is friends with the owner. That waitress, Maria, is the owner's niece."

Anastasia tried to look casual. "That's nice. Is she from Italy?"

"Yes. But, what I was going to tell you is that the night we were here-" He looked at Anastasia to catch the expression on her face. She was staring down at the menu. He could sense the tension. "The same night when we left, she had a terrible accident." Anastasia was visibly tense, which greatly amused Mark. "She fell with a big tray full of hot food. I guess she was burned on the face from the food and also hurt her leg from the fall." Anastasia nodded and made a sympathetic sound. "And you know the crazy part?" Mark studied her face as he deliberately waited a few moments. Anastasia didn't want to know, but looked at him politely with mock interest. "She said someone kicked the back of her knee and made her fall on purpose!" He was looking at her with sober eyes, but the corners of his mouth were slightly curled.

"Wow," was the only word she could think of. "Did she say she knew who did it?" Anastasia looked away as she asked, then focused again on his face. He stared into her eyes a moment, making her very nervous. There was a slight smile on his face.

She realized he knew it was Stella, and somehow he found it amusing.

"Well," Mark continued. "Of course she claimed it was Stella. It was easy to see they didn't like each other. I'm sure she was just jumping to conclusions. I mean, Stella was with us. Right?" Anastasia nodded in the affirmative. She was anxious to change subjects. She noticed his smile broaden as he motioned for the waiter. "How about a bottle of wine?"

"Great, the kind we had last time was good," Anastasia offered anxiously. He was staring at her again. It was hard to keep his eyes off her. There was something wild and exciting about this women, and he liked it. He spoke to the waiter in Italian. The waiter left then returned with the wine in a bucket of ice with two glasses.

"Let's drink to us," Mark declared, holding out to her a full glass of wine. They toasted, looking deep into each other's eyes while they brought glasses to their lips.

Mark ordered for her again, and after eating he told her about his plans for the rest of the evening. "You told me you had never been to an opera, but were curious. So, I bought us tickets to see *The Marriage of Figaro.*"

She looked up at him, smiling brightly.

"This opera is in English and is also a comedy, so it will be a good one for you to try out."

Anastasia was happy, but then she looked down at her clothing. "Won't a theater be kind of dressy?"

Mark winced a little. "Probably most women will be in dresses, but you will be so much more beautiful than the other women, no one will notice your blue jeans."

Anastasia was embarrassed, and still uneasy about her appearance, but she was glad to finally have the opportunity to see a live opera.

The theater was in a larger city about an hour away. Anastasia had only heard stories about the old theater and how beautiful it was. She still wasn't prepared for what she saw as they rounded the corner. The front of the building was large and ornate, with beautiful gold trim and an old fashioned marquee with the information about the performance. Everything was lit and glittered from the street lights. Well dressed couples walked passed them in fur coats and fancy hats. Anastasia felt like a pauper. She vowed to herself that she would buy a new dress with her next check and save for a nicer coat. Mark noticed her watching the other couples and put his arm around her. He pulled her closer, taking her attention away from everyone else.

"I asked for good seats, but you never know." Anastasia knew he was just trying to make conversation to keep her from being so self conscious. He held her close, guiding her through the double doors. Once inside, she noticed the marble floor. Then she saw a beautiful gold pillar in the center of the great room. Her eyes followed the pillar to the ceiling. It was covered with murals and trimmed with gold. A marble staircase went up the back wall to a glorious mezzanine.

Anastasia stood still with her mouth agape, trying to look everywhere at once. Mark was watching her face. He was pleased with her reaction. This was what he wanted, to show her something wonderful she had never seen. He led her to a velvet sofa to wait while he picked up the tickets. She was noticing the detail in the statues lining the walls and decided that even if she wasn't allowed into the theater, she would still leave happy.

Luckily, Mark was able to push their way into the inner lobby. He stood in front of her and handed their tickets to the usher. Anastasia gasped as she entered the theater. Red velvet covered the walls and stage, while gold gargoyles guarded from above. It was wonderful. Sitting next to Mark made it even more special. She was in love.

He quietly told her the story of Figaro, and pointed to the important parts in their program. Anastasia studied it thoroughly. She already enjoyed the opera before it had even started. Mark held her hand through most of it.

Afterward, he escorted her out of the theater by hooking

his right arm in hers, his other hand resting on her forearm. They made a good looking couple. The drive back was pleasant, they decided to pick up a bottle of wine on the way back. Anastasia opened it in the car and they drank champagne out of paper cups. She dreaded seeing the familiar landmarks that told her they were near her apartment. She didn't want the evening to end, and she wasn't sure what to do. She wanted him to come upstairs, but she also knew what that would lead to.

She was uncomfortably sober by the time they reached her apartment building. They parked in front again. Mark looked over at her, not sure of what to do next. She smiled back nervously. Slowly, a crooked grin crept across his face. It was as if he were reading her mind. He knew she wanted him. All he needed to do was ask, so he did. "You know there is another bottle of wine in the back seat?"

She smiled shyly. "Well, you might get drunk if you drink it all by yourself." He refused to say anything else. He wanted her to invite him up, so he waited silently with a smile and his blue eyes focused on her. Anastasia was blushing and uncomfortable. She knew he was teasing her, and it was difficult for her to look at him. Finally she asked, "So, Mark, would you like to come upstairs? We could drink the wine in real glasses."

"Sure, I would love to." He was still smiling at her, but now he opened his door, then went to her side and let her out. They climbed the stairs side by side, and he even held her purse for her as she unlocked the door. She had a small flashback of the last time she had entered her apartment with a man. It had been the night she got pregnant. But that couldn't happen this time she told herself. She had been taking the pills consistently. It was an impossibility.

Mark noticed her getting tense. He wondered if there was going to be a problem. He handed her the bottle of wine, looking her square in the eye, biting his top lip slightly. She was making him nervous. She took the bottle into the kitchen. Then she took off her coat, and offered to put his in the closet as well. She still wasn't looking at him. It was starting to bother him because she wasn't smiling anymore, either.

He followed her into the kitchen, and wrapped his arms around her. "Anastasia," he whispered in her ear. "Why are you so tense?"

She didn't answer.

"Anastasia, I promise we won't do anything that is not your idea, okay?"

She had this sudden urge to cry, but held it back. He kissed her earlobe, and then her neck. She spun around and kissed him passionately, running her fingers through his hair, then wrapping her arms around his neck. He was holding her firm but gently, with his hands supporting her back. She felt something wet on her cheeks and realized she was crying. She slid her head against his chest and wiped the tears away, hoping he hadn't noticed them.

"Oh, Anastasia, you are such a complicated woman." Mark pulled away so he could put his hands on her cheeks and force her to look at him. She was having problems looking him in the eyes again. He sighed. "Anastasia," he whispered, moving his face close to hers. "Anastasia, I want so much to make you happy. Tell me what you want."

She swallowed back the tears and answered by kissing him on the lips again. He wrapped his arms around her and hugged her close to his chest. They stood in the kitchen embracing for several minutes, before she could compose herself.

"C'mon, lets just sit and talk," she said. She took two glasses and the wine and led him into the next room. She realized they would have to sit on the bed together since it was her only piece of furniture. She set the wine and glasses onto the night stand and motioned for him to have a seat on the edge of the bed. He quietly sat down. She could see he was uncomfortable as well. She had never been so embarrassed about her meager things before. This was the first person she had invited up who's opinion she was the least bit concerned about. Her family and the one night stands she had dragged up there in the past were never a concern. Mark was a different story. He mattered.

"I guess I need a couple chairs up here." She laughed nervously, making herself small against the head board.

"This is fine. You are single and alone, you don't need a big set of furniture. I admire how practical you are." Then he decided he should clarify the remark. "I mean, so many women are silly for things they don't need." He looked at her in a matter-of-the-fact way. She nodded back and smiled. The evening was going from passionate to polite, Mark thought. He realized he was losing ground and needed to change the mood fast, before they drank much more of the wine. "So, Anastasia what do you do up here alone for so much of the day?"

She took a swallow of her wine. "Well, I watch TV now." She pointed to her new set. "See what Stella and Mario bought me?"

Mark looked puzzled. "You mean you didn't have a television before? Wow, I thought all Americans spent most of their time watching TV. What did you do before?"

"Read."

"What?" he asked, taking a sip of wine.

Anastasia looked thoughtful. "Well, actually, my brother has been giving me these old books. Ancient books. I find them really interesting."

Mark lowered his eyebrows. "What do you mean, ancient books? Like the bible?"

"Yes. I find the bible fascinating. I also read other books that are just as old. There are many books that have been forgotten over the years, and some that have been hidden and rediscovered."

Mark was truly interested. Anastasia was still surprising him. He leaned toward the nightstand, spying a book laying there. "What is that?"

Anastasia carefully picked up the book. "*The Gospel According to Thomas.* It's a Gnostic text discovered hidden in a cave." Mark kicked off his shoes then moved next to Anastasia. He put one arm around her while she was still holding the book. "Read to me." He smiled.

She looked around and shrugged. "You want me to read one of my favorite parts?" Mark nodded.

She turned a few pages to a marker.

"Jesus said: If those who lead you say to you: 'See, the Kingdom is in heaven,' then the birds of the heavens will precede you. If they say to you: 'It is in the sea,' then the fish will precede you. But the Kingdom is within you and it is without you. If you will know yourselves, then you will be known and you will know that you are the sons of the Living Father. But if you do not know yourselves, then you are in poverty and you are poverty." She stopped and looked at Mark. He had been reading over her shoulder.

"This is saying you make your own heaven?", he asked curiously.

Anastasia nodded. "That's how I understand it. Do you think heaven is what we make on Earth?"

Mark looked down at her thoughtfully. "All I know is it would be sad to waste a lifetime unhappy. I think we should try to cram as much pleasure as we can into our lives, because they turn out to be so short." He drew a heart on her cheek with his finger. "And I have found making other people happy gives me the best pleasure." He curled his finger under her chin and kissed her tenderly. He moved his hand down her shoulder and held her in both arms, kissing her with more passion. She dropped the book.

They slid down the bed. Now he was over her, kissing her down her neck. She tingled with excitement. He moved his face down the neckline of her blouse and began unbuttoning it, kissing her as he worked his way down the row of buttons. She tangled her fingers in his hair, and kneaded his shoulders. He was pushing up her bras and sucking on her breasts before she had a chance to refuse him. He began to unfasten her pants.

"No," she said, blocking his fingers from her zipper.

He stopped abruptly and looked at her. "Why?" he asked softly.

She laid her hand on his cheek, not knowing what to say.

"I don't know." She could never tell him about the abortion. But he knew there was something serious.

"Anastasia, what is it that is keeping you so tense? You have been with a man before, haven't you?"

She nodded yes. "Mark, there's just been too many things happening to me lately. I— I'm not ready."

He tried to read her, but there was something that bothered her so much she didn't want him to know. He decided not to push. He was leaning on one elbow, but close to her face.

"How about this," he said quietly. "How about if we spend the night together, but not have sex?"

Anastasia thought this over. It would have sounded suspicious to her if anyone else had suggested it, but she really didn't want him to leave. "I think I would love to wake up in your arms," she admitted.

He smiled coyly. "Then we can get rid of this?" He asked, pulling at her blouse. She stood up and he watched her with interest as she removed all of her clothes. This was almost too much for him. "No sex?" He reiterated in a small voice.

"You promised," she reminded him, pulling at the covers.

He looked at her as if in pain, then stood up and undressed. She tried not to look at his large uncircumcised penis, but he made sure she knew he noticed her looking. She blushed. When they met under the blankets, he found a comfortable spot for his head between her breasts. It was a long time before he was able to fall asleep.

In the morning, Anastasia found herself pinned to the mattress. Mark was sleeping soundly on her chest. She felt safe and comfortable. It had been like Christmas night when she was very young and had slept cuddled to her brand new doll all night. "Mark, you're better than a Christmas doll," she said softly, combing his hair with her fingers.

He moaned. "And you, Anastasia, are so soft and warm that you made me crazy all night." Anastasia was surprised he was awake. He popped his head up and kissed both of her nipples, then her mouth. "You know, my father is expecting me to help him with some things this morning, but there is one thing I have been laying here thinking about."

Mark got to his feet and pulled the blankets and sheets completely off the bed. Anastasia raised herself up on her elbows watching him. He looked down at her naked body hungrily, then firmly grasped her left knee and pushed her legs apart. Slowly he lowered his face and put his mouth on the soft white inside of her thigh. He sucked and gently kneaded her skin with his teeth, just enough to send electricity down her spine. Then he gently kissed her thigh. She closed her eyes and breathed deeply as he did the same to the other leg. She was almost ready to give in. Then he stopped, stood up, and moaned once more looking down at her. She opened her eyes and tried to compose herself. Now he was putting on his shirt.

"So," he said coyly. "Now I will leave you with something to think about." He laughed and quickly finished dressing. He looked over at her once more with confidence. "Maybe, I will be back, huh?"

Anastasia rolled over to him, and pulled him down to her with a kiss. "Please," she said with pleading eyes. He laughed again, then let himself out.

She came to with a violent spasm. The pain was a tidal wave over her. She looked at her husband scornfully. Why did he have to wake her? He was standing over her like an idiot, and now the pain was rushing through her body.

"Hi, honey, I hope I didn't wake you. Feeling better?" he asked cheerfully.

She didn't answer him. Instead, she just glared at him silently until he shrank back and sat down. He was trying to be consistent with his visits. He arrived every day at the same time. He thought this would make her happy, but nothing ever did. No matter how hard he tried, he just couldn't guess right. He never could. Clenching his jaw, he began staring at the television.

Marilyn closed her eyes and tried to separate herself from the pain. She had been happy just a short while ago. Anastasia had a lover. This was perfect, and none too soon. All Marilyn wanted now was to shed this deceased, pain ridden body.

Physically, the doctors were amazed at how quickly she had healed from the surgery. But as they suspected from the beginning, the cancer was unstoppable. They gave her no more than six months to live.

"Tell Stella," Marilyn said. "To look in the pantry for a metal canister with purple flowers painted on it. Take a small scoop of the herbs in it, tie them in a clean white cloth, and then dip it in a pan of boiling water until the water starts to turn yellow. If she lays with this poultice on her swollen eye, it will help it go down, and heal faster."

Her husband nodded, making a mental note of her instructions.

"Did you get that?" she said a little louder, in an annoyed voice.

"Yes, Marilyn, I'll tell her. She's been real upset about her face." He said, standing at attention beside her bed, holding his hat.

"I know," she answered.

One more day was nearly gone. Mario Mattioli, Sr. was feeling tired. The old man's eyes were bloodshot and his back was aching. He shuffled to the end of a grocery counter and began sacking one of his customer's merchandise. He was moving in a type of well rehearsed dance. Snapping a bag open expertly, he set it just so on a small shelf below the counter. Canned goods on the bottom, macaroni next, bread on top. He couldn't phantom the number of times he'd preformed this ritual along with all the others he did daily.

"Dad, why don't you go home?"

Mario looked up and smiled proudly at his son. He

looked so tall and handsome. “I will soon.”

Mark moved up beside him and began filling another sack for the same customer. “I can do this. I came in late today. I will work till closing. Don’t worry, I will make sure everything is taken care of.”

Mario knew his son would be able to handle the store alone. He was so proud of how hard he worked. Most young people weren’t such hard workers. “By the way, when am I going to meet this girl who makes you late?”

Mark smiled again, as he had done all day. “Soon, I promise.” He continued to sack the groceries, then finished his fathers bag and carefully placed both sacks in a shopping cart. Mario was standing a pace away, admiring his son working.

Mark casually noticed someone coming in the door, at first not paying it much attention. Then he quickly looked back at the entrance and smiled broadly. Mario looked behind him to see what his son was staring at. There was a beautiful tall girl with blond hair and blue eyes. Mario was enchanted. There was something exciting and familiar about her. He forgot about his son until he noticed him approaching the young woman. Then he happily realized this was Anastasia. She was exactly the way his son had described her, and even more charming.

Mark greeted her with a teasing smile, grabbing the back of her cart and refusing to let her pass. She was embarrassed to be there in the first place, and here he was, making a scene. She blushed and looked away, wishing she hadn’t noticed everyone staring at her. Mark took his eyes off her for a moment and glanced at his father, then back to Anastasia, still smiling. He took his foot off the end of the cart and stepped beside her, touching her shoulder.

“Hey, you here to pick up the groceries for me to make you dinner with tonight?”

She hadn’t thought that far ahead, but it sounded good to her. “Yeah, just like we planned.”

He looked deep in her eyes and wanted to kiss her, but remembered his father was watching and waiting nearby.

"Anastasia, I want you to meet my father." He turned and motioned for Mario to come closer. The proud parent moved toward them timidly, and he reached out and took Anastasia's hand. His smiling eyes were locked on hers.

"You are even more beautiful than my son described."

"Thank you," she said modestly. Without knowledge that this was the continuation of another type of love affair, but one daughters have with their fathers.

Mario suddenly realized he was still staring at her. "Mario," he said, turning to his son. "Why don't you help this young woman with her shopping? I'll stick around little bit longer so you don't have to worry about the store." He smiled and glanced in Anastasia's direction.

Mark said something short in Italian. Mario turned back to the grocery counter and Mark and Anastasia pushed forward.

"It sounded strange to hear you called Mario," Anastasia said once they had moved out of ear shot from his father.

"He refuses to call me anything else. He says my mother had named me."

"It's too bad she died so young." Anastasia said this so solemnly that Mark knew she truly meant it.

He stopped the cart abruptly near a rack of bread. "This will work," he said grabbing a long loaf of French bread and throwing it into the cart. They moved to the back of the store, where there was a meat counter. Anastasia was surprised to see Anthony standing behind it. He saw her and shouted a greeting in what she assumed was Italian, or very bad English.

"Hello, Anthony." She smiled, walking toward the glass cases. He greeted her warmly, reaching over the counter to take her hand.

"Stella?" he asked, looking around her curiously. Mark explained something to him in Italian. He nodded with a disappointed look on his face. Anthony said something else in Italian, obviously asking Mark to be his interpreter. Mark nodded and turned to Anastasia.

"Anthony wanted to know how she was doing. If she

would be healed enough for company soon."

Anastasia looked at him, not knowing how to answer. She had already told Mark the lie about her accident. He was keeping Anthony updated. Anthony and Stella were still speaking regularly on the phone, but their conversations were never as informative as Anastasia's updates through Mark.

She looked at Anthony seriously, while Mark translated in Italian. "She's embarrassed by the swelling and bruises. That's the only reason why she hasn't been able to see you again. Her right eye is still swollen more than half shut. My brother wants to take her to the doctors, but she doesn't want to go."

To that Anthony said something short in an irritated voice. "Why?" Mark translated.

Anastasia didn't know how to answer. "She's never been to a doctor before. Our mother has always taken care of us. The problem is that our mother is in the hospital right now."

Mark turned toward her. "She has never been to a doctor?"

Anastasia shrugged. "When we were in school, we had to go to the health department for shots, but that's all."

"None of you has been sick or hurt?"

Anastasia shook her head. "No. My brother once cut his leg open when we were climbing a fence. That was probably the worst accident. My mother cleaned the wound and tied strips of cloth around his leg to keep the wound closed 'til it could heal. That's kind of what she always did. She was our doctor."

Mark looked at her with astonishment. He had never heard of an American family that didn't visit doctors. Anthony was asking Mark to explain what was being said. He turned to his cousin and explained in Italian. Anthony's reaction wasn't as puzzled as Mark's, but he looked thoughtfully at Anastasia, nodding his understanding.

"Please tell her for me, that I miss her and would like to see her soon." Anthony pronounced each word carefully in English.

Anastasia nodded. "I will." Mark proceeded to give his

cousin directions in Italian about the meat he wanted and how it was to be cut. Anthony complied quickly and with an expertise that led Anastasia to believe he had been a butcher for a long time. They stood quietly at the counter, Mark watching her closely the whole time. Anastasia tried to pretend she couldn't feel his eyes on her. She watched Anthony cutting the meat.

He handed a package wrapped in white paper to Mark, who threw it in the cart. They waved to one another and continued on toward the dairy case. Mark nuzzled Anastasia's ear. "You know I just can't keep from thinking of you?" She rolled her shoulder over her ear, trying to keep the tickling feeling at bay. She looked at him and then kissed him quickly on the jaw. He smiled and gave her a little squeeze.

He moved closer to the dairy case, selecting a few packages, and then a small container of cream. "Now what kind of spices do you have?"

She looked at him with a little embarrassment. "Salt and pepper?" He laughed and led them down an aisle with spices and baking supplies. After throwing several more bottles and packages into the cart, he led her to the wine. There, he carefully examined the bottles and put two of them into the cart.

"I think this will do it," he announced. She looked down at all the items, thinking surely he knew she didn't have enough money to pay for all this.

He looked at her and chuckled. "Now, let me take you through the check out counter so I can pay for all this." She looked up at him, surprised. He seemed to be able to read her mind. She had never known anyone outside of her family that could do that.

Going through the check out was awkward for her. Everyone knew Mark, and they were looking her over and smiling. She felt very conspicuous. It also embarrassed her when he pulled out his wallet and paid for everything. She didn't like for anyone, even strangers, to think someone might be keeping her. She also wondered what his father thought. Did he know his son had spent the night with her? Mark was sacking her groceries when he stopped suddenly and looked up at her.

"How can you carry all of this home? I will have to bring it to you when I finish work." He then looked at her again. "You live a long ways from here to be walking." He looked around, raised a finger, and motioned for her to stay put for a moment. He left to find his father, they said a few words to one another, and then Mario looked up at Anastasia and smiled.

Mark moved back to the counter. "Anastasia, my father said he would drive you home. He was just leaving anyway." Anastasia panicked. She did like the old man, but this would be putting her in an awkward position, being alone with her boyfriend's father, who she had just met. Mark could see her apprehension. "Please Anastasia, it would make me feel better, and he really likes you. He would feel bad if you said no." Anastasia quickly realized she had no choice. It would be a short drive anyway.

It wasn't until she was being packed into Mario Senior's car that it occurred to her how Mark had just manipulated her into doing exactly as he wanted, even though it was totally not at all what she wanted. He carefully closed her car door, just as she was about to protest. Then he waved at her through the glass. At the same time, his father stepped on the gas and sped away. She dropped back in her seat and tried to relax. Mario was looking over at her with a big friendly grin. She smiled back and nodded.

"So, you are a city girl, huh?" Mario asked softly. "Have you always lived in the city?"

It was easy for Anastasia to see he was trying to make her feel comfortable. "I grew up in a house near downtown, but I've been living alone in the same apartment for a couple years now".

"You look so young to be away from your parents. Maybe you are older than you look, huh?"

"I'm nineteen."

"You moved away when you were only seventeen?"

"Actually it was the day after my eighteenth birthday."

Mario was silent a moment. "So, when is your birthday?"

"March twenty-first."

"Ah, the first day of spring! That is a wonderful day to be born on."

Anastasia had to smile. He was so full of love, she could almost see it glowing around him. She wondered if he was always so kind or if his son had put him into an especially good mood. Then she caught a feeling that part of his enthusiasm was because of the prospect of his son having a girlfriend. She remembered Mark telling her he wanted grandchildren. What was the deal with grandchildren anyway, she marveled— first her mother, now Mark's father. Still, something about Mario told her his motive wasn't rooted in some self serving reason like her mother.

"Do your parents still live nearby?" he asked.

"Yes, my mother is in the hospital right now, though."

"Ah, yes, my son told me the bad news. I hope she is able to come home soon."

The car was silent again. Anastasia could tell he was trying to think of something to say, without being too intrusive. "So, do you like having your son home?" She asked this knowing it would be a happy subject for him.

"Yes! He is so much company to me. And he is a good son. Hard working and smart." Now he was beaming again. It was Mark who was giving him that glow.

"Do you think he plans to stay here in the states?"

"I hope so. We have business still in Italy, but I'm hoping we can work out some kind of deal with my brother. He would like to buy the apartment buildings we own there. He's taking care of them now. It's just that he doesn't have enough money, so we would have to let him pay for them slowly, or something. I don't know, but we'll work it out. Maybe you can keep my son busy so he won't want to go back, huh?"

Anastasia smiled. When they arrived at her building, Mario insisted on carrying up her groceries. She fumbled with the keys nervously as he stood beside her on the landing, holding a bag in each arm. She wasn't sure if she wanted him to see her dinky little apartment. Finally, she pushed the door open. He politely walked behind her as she showed him to her kitchen counter. After he set the bags down, he nodded and smiled, looking around.

"This is nice, very nice. Just right for a single lady."

She knew he would have said the same thing even if she lived in an outhouse, but it was kind of him. "Thank you." They stood in the kitchen for a moment in awkward silence. "Would you like some juice? I can make instant coffee."

"Oh no, I need to go. I just promised my son I would make sure you got home safely." He smiled broadly. Anastasia wasn't sure if she liked the idea that Mark felt she needed protection, but she smiled back just the same. "So, I will just get going now." He turned and walked toward the door. Anastasia held it for him. They said their farewells and waved. She shut the door quietly behind him. Then she let the breath out that she had been holding. Meeting a guys parents was tough, no matter how nice they turned out to be.

Stella sighed, then slid out of bed. Her father and Mario were at work. She had been sleeping most of the time over the last week. She was feeling better, except the swelling in her eye was stubbornly refusing to go away. Today, she had fallen asleep with a poultice on her eye. She had constructed it in the manner her mother had dictated, through her father. Now she was anxious to see if it had helped.

She shuffled down the hall and into the bathroom. She flicked on the light and slowly pulled the bundle of herbs from her eye. The swelling had went down, but it was far from normal. Makeup would never hide the dark purple and yellow bruises. She feared the skin under her eyes would never return to the light pink that matched her complexion. She had known women who had been beaten until their eyes seemed to have a perpetual dark ring under them. She couldn't stand the thought of being one of them.

She was dying to see Anthony again. He was so worried about her. She smiled. He was so worried about her, she thought. He had talked to Mark's father for her, and she was supposed to start work there as soon as she was well enough. Anthony said he would teach her to cut meat if she wanted. Then they could work together.

She looked at herself again in the mirror. If only her face would heal. It looked as though her nose might be broken. It was still swollen, but when she tipped her head back she could see one of the openings was half closed. It looked as though the bone going down the center of her nose was bent. She could live with a crooked nose, but that eye— if only the swelling would go down.

Then a thought occurred to her. She knew her mother would know what to do, and she had already offered help. Maybe she would help some more. Stella and everyone else had already accepted the fact it was Marilyn who was responsible for the dog attack. No one knew how, but everyone knew it was her, especially Stella. This did prove one thing to Stella. Her mother must care for her a little. Otherwise, she would be dead right now.

That settled it in her mind. She was going to the hospital and talk to her mother. She showered and dressed, then tried in vain to cover the bruises with makeup. She was never very good with makeup in the first place, so after several minutes, she surrendered and left the house out the back door. She walked most of the way with her eyes cast down, avoiding people's stairs. Now she knew what it was like to have a disfigurement. Luckily for her, it was only temporary.

Her mother was laying very still with her eyes closed when Stella arrived. She stood over her mother's bed, not knowing what to do except watch her sleep. Suddenly, her mother shook violently. Stella panicked, but stood wide eyed as her mother stiffened, then opened her eyes and stared unblinking at the ceiling for what felt like several minutes. Her complexion seemed to change to a pale gray. Then, without warning, her eye flashed and focused on Stella.

"God, he certainly made a mess of you, didn't he?" were her first words.

Stella swallowed, this was going to be harder than she had anticipated. "Thank you for telling dad about the poultice."

Her mother smiled faintly. "So, did you enjoy making it?"

Stella wasn't sure how to answer, but come to think of it, she had kind of enjoyed putting it together. "Yeah, I guess it was kind of like cooking. I've never done that before."

Marilyn's smile broadened. "Who knows, maybe there's hope for you yet." Marilyn groped for a glass of water from the stand next to her bed. Stella helped her hold the cup. It was a strange feeling for her to be holding the cup to her mother's lips. Marilyn was staring up at her daughter the whole time. Slowly, she took a sip and tipped her head back onto her pillow. Stella put the glass back on the table as her mother sank into the mattress. Then, under her breath she murmured, "You know that foreign boy wouldn't have anything to do with you if he even knew about half of your sleazy life."

Stella stiffened.

"Those Italian men," Marilyn continued. "They are only interested in a woman who can cook and clean. You don't stand a chance with that kid if you can't do both."

Stella looked down thoughtfully. This was the closest she'd get to a traditional mother daughter talk, and she knew it.

"There's an old cook book over the stove," Marilyn explained in a louder voice. "You could practice on your dad and brother. I'll never be coming home from this hospital, so we'll just say I'm appointing you head chef." She laughed at her little joke. Stella stared at her without a smile. The realization of her mother's condition hit her suddenly. Her mother was dying.

Marilyn stopped laughing and glanced over at her daughter with a puzzled expression. She had never considered that her daughter might love her. She certainly never thought she might be missed. Marilyn never allowed herself to have sentimental feelings. They were a sign of weakness. Marilyn would never allow herself to be weak. She quickly pushed the feelings aside.

"So, Stella, wasn't the real reason for your visit so that I could give you some advice about that swollen eye?"

Stella wasn't as surprised by her mother's intuition as she should have been. "Do you know how to make it heal faster?"

"Turn on the reading light and move a little closer."

Stella quickly obeyed her, moving her face close to her mother. Marilyn reached up and held her daughter roughly by the jaw. Stella whined, but didn't complain. "I believe the bone near your eye is cracked." She turned Stella's head to the side then pressed on the swollen eye. Stella gritted her teeth. Her eyes began to water. "The crack is irritating the skin and causing the swelling. The swelling is causing the bone to separate and not heal." Satisfied with her diagnosis, she released her daughter and dropped her hand to her side. Stella grabbed a tissue off the table and dabbed her eyes, gently. When she looked back at her mother Marilyn was staring at the ceiling again, pondering her daughters problem.

"I know what would help, but it's no longer available." She said more to herself then to Stella. "You need to get the swelling down. Try goats milk, add some vinegar to make it curdle, then add some yeast. Mix it into a paste. It's going to smell awful, but smear it thick over your eye, put a towel under your head, and sleep with the paste on there. That should help." Stella nodded gratefully. She had complete faith in her mothers cures. Marilyn took another look at her daughter's face. "If the bruises don't fade, leaches will take the black away." Stella swallowed hard at the last remedy, but nodded dutifully.

"Thank you, Mom." She said sincerely. Her mother's acknowledgment was a roll of her eyes, before she closed them. Stella reached over her and kissed her cheek good-bye before leaving the room.

She walked down the hall sadly. She was committing the cure to memory, but all the while she had this feeling of doom. Her mother was dying, and for maybe the first time in her life, she was thinking she might miss her. A panic went through her body.

Who would take care of them, and watch over them? What if something terrible happened to one of them again? There'd be no one to call the police, to tell Mario where to find them, to protect her from men who want to kill her. She stopped, standing in the center of the lobby, staring at the floor. They would be all alone, she realized with terror. Their protector was dying.

Slowly, she became aware someone was patting her on the arm. She looked up at a nurse, who was bending her neck, tying to look Stella in the face. "Are you okay?" Stella shook her head slowly, and then with more vigor. "No," she shouted, with tears starting to run down her swollen face. She pulled away from the woman and ran out of the building.

Warm water cascaded over her naked body. She was scrubbing every inch of herself with scented soap. Tonight would be the night, she decided. She couldn't keep her life on hold forever, she needed to forget and move on. She had also come to the realization that she was in love with Mark. She couldn't ever remember having such a crush. Even more importantly, she couldn't remember ever meeting someone she could talk to and confide in as she did with Mark. She had told him about things other people just couldn't understand, at least no one that wasn't family. She marveled at this. Where did this understanding come from? He had told her over and over how she was the first person who understood him. How was it the two of them could be so different from other people and yet so much like each other?

She turned the water off and was just stepping out of the tub when she heard knocking at the door. Groaning, she knew it was probably Mark. She had wanted so much to look nice when he got there. He was earlier than she expected, and here she was, looking like a wet dog. She grabbed a towel and wrapped it around herself quickly.

Grasping the towel together in the front with one hand and holding the door knob with the other she pushed her shoulder against the door and called out, "Mark?".

"No, it's a wolf," he teased.

Anastasia opened the door just a crack. "I was in the shower." He had been leaning against the door frame for several minutes, listening to the noisy pipes. He had waited for the water to go off before he knocked, so her dripping hair was no surprise. She slowly opened the door enough for him to enter, but he didn't. He continued to lean in the doorway, staring at her while she made a little puddle on the wooden floor. She was beginning to look around nervously while the cool air from the open door was making little goose bumps.

"So, are you coming in?" she bit her lower lip.

He looked contemplative. "You know you are making a mess on the floor."

She immediately looked down at her feet to the puddle of water, then back up at Mark.

"I think—" Mark began. "You should clean it up with that towel." He pointed to the towel she was still grasping with her right hand. She took a glance around, and relaxed her grip. The towel fell to the ground. Mark's eyebrows raised. His aloof expression changed to one of extreme interest as his eyes followed the fullness of her bare breasts to the curve of her waist, down to the brown curly hair between her legs, and rested on her soft white thighs. He walked inside, closing the door behind him.

Anastasia stood in place, self conscious, but refusing to make any motions of covering herself. Mark bent down in front of her and sopped up the water with her towel. She stood her ground as he then grasped one calf in each hand. She refused to quiver as he pressed his lips once more against her inner thigh, nibbling tenderly. Her head involuntarily rolled back and to the side as he worked his way up, pulling gently at her pubic hairs with his lips. She managed to remain standing, but reached out and grasped the door knob to keep her balance as his tongue sent lightning through her body. Her back arched, her nipples went granite, and she clamped her jaws together, trying to hold back the loud gasp and moan. She finally let out a breath with a shudder. Her body turned to rubber instantly and she fell forward, bending over Mark and holding him against her.

"Come on." She took hold of his hand and pulled him to his feet. This was just what he wanted. He moved slowly toward the bed, letting her pull him, as though he was reluctant. "Mark! Quit teasing me," she pleaded, kneeling on the mattress. He laughed at her, sitting on the edge of the bed, letting her undress him. The tickle inside her was almost an ache before she was able to get him to remove his pants. Finally, his firm nude body was laying across her bed. His head was on her pillow. She caressed his chest as she slid her leg across his body and mounted him. His penis was stiff and long. She rubbed it against her tummy then pulled herself up and carefully sat back down. Slowly, she pushed it up into herself deeper, and deeper, until she was sitting flat on him. She arched her back again, moving her hips, grinding him even deeper into her.

He pressed his fingertip into her buttocks, helping her move vigorously in an ancient rhythm. She leaned back and braced herself by grabbing hold of his thighs, bending her back to the limit. Her breasts were pushed out and her nipples were pointing up. Finally, she threw her head back, showering his naked legs with water from her wet hair. He pressed her firmly against himself for his own climax. Still throbbing, he braced her against his knees and buried his mouth on her heaving breast.

Anastasia wrapped her arms around him while he still suckled her breasts. She knotted her fingers in his hair and tipped his head up looking him straight in the eyes. "I love you," she whispered. He reached up and held both sides of her face in his hands, pulling her lips to his and then pulling both of them to the mattress. He rolled her over, laying his body on hers and answered her with Italian words that she understood.

CHAPTER 19

Mark continued to take her to lunch each afternoon, but now he was also spending every night with her as well. They couldn't get enough of each other. Monday he had arrived with a change of clothes, but by Wednesday they were doing their laundry together and he left his clean underwear beside hers in the top drawer of her dresser. His pants and shirts were hanging in her closet. All the while, they were telling each other they needed to go slow.

She was visiting her mother every day after work. The way her mother was acting bothered her. She was just too kind again. In fact, she was even being more considerate to the rest of the family as well.

One afternoon, Anastasia arrived at the hospital before the rest of the family. Her mother was laying with her eyes open, as though she had anticipated Anastasia walking through the door. She smiled at her daughter and called her over to her bed side weakly. Anastasia kissed her cheek.

"Anastasia, darling," she said. "There's something I want you to have." She held out her arm, and to Anastasia's surprise, she unfastened the clasp on her gold watch. "I'm not sure how much you care for this old watch, but it has a lot of sentimental value to me, and I want you to have it." Anastasia grasped her mother's arm and helped her slip the watch off her wrist. She wasn't sure what to say or do. She simply stood there with the watch in her hand, staring at it.

"Are you sure, Mom?"

Marilyn closed her eyes and nodded slightly. "You're the

more sentimental daughter. I think you'd take care of it better than Stella. It's an expensive watch. Maybe you can give it to your first born."

The first thought Anastasia had was maybe now she could get it fixed, but then to her astonishment she looked down to see the second hand was moving. Her mother was watching her daughter's expression.

"All you need to do is set the time correctly."

Anastasia looked at her mother, she had never known the watch to work.

"Just slip it on," her mother urged her. Finally, she sighed and explained. "Watches don't work for me, it's something about my body, I guess, but it should work for you. I've been telling you children for years, it's not broken."

Anastasia slipped it onto her left wrist. It was so delicate, solid gold, with a thin band and small oval face. There was a clasp and a small gold safety chain. Anastasia wiggled her wrist causing the lights to glitter off the shiny gold metal. It looked like it had just been cleaned and polished. "Thank you, Mom," she said with genuine enthusiasm. She bent and kissed her mother's cheek again. Marilyn was smiling broadly.

"Remember, Anastasia, take good care of it so you can hand it down to your first born. I'm sure they'll love it, too." Anastasia smiled and nodded. That was a wonderful idea, she decided.

Mario MacDouglas climbed down the attic stairs dressed for work with his coat laid across his arm. He could smell something cooking. It smelled like very hot grease. Then, he heard the unmistakable sound of something being tossed in a pan to fry. When he came out of the closet door, he was surprised to see Stella in front of the stove. He knew she had been spending most of her time studying her mother's cook book. She had showed it to him the day before. When her mother told her it was old, she wasn't kidding. The thing dated from before World War II.

Next, he noticed his father sitting at the kitchen table with a cup of coffee and a newspaper in front of his face. He was surprised to see she had even set the table with plates, silverware, butter and syrup.

"Good morning," he said cheerfully to both of them. Stella looked up from her cooking briefly. She had an uneasy expression on her face. It was obvious things weren't going so well. "That smells good," he said, trying to be supportive. Stella nervously smiled and cast her gaze back to the cast iron skillet. "Your eye looks better, too," he said with a little too much enthusiasm. She glared back up at him with a annoyed expression.

"Thanks," she answered. Sleeping all night with that nasty gook on her face was what woke her up so early, but it did help the swelling.

She had decided to start her cooking adventure with pancakes. Mario was staring into the pan with a puzzled look on his face. "Well, I've learned the difference between baking powder and baking soda today." She tossed a green pancake onto a platter. Mario slowly backed away and got himself a cup of coffee. Against his better judgement, he took a chair beside his father. Stella plopped the platter of pancakes on the table in front of him. He looked down at the pile of emerald fried cakes with a disagreeable look on his face. "They're okay. They taste just fine. It's just that I used baking soda instead of powder. Try one!"

Mario poked at one with his fork, then he noticed his father peeking around his newspaper. He was interested in how well his son stood up after ingesting one. Mario looked back at the pancakes. He knew how much it would mean to his sister if he would just eat one. He had never seen her take this much interest in anything before. He bravely lifted one onto his plate. He plastered it with butter and then saturated it with syrup.

Stella was standing behind their father, looking at Mario anxiously. With his father still peeking at him from behind his newspaper, Mario cut a large piece with his fork, closed his eyes and stuffed it into his mouth. He had decided large bites, swallowed whole would be the least painful route. Maybe the bite was too large, or maybe the pancakes had taken on a life of its own with no intention of giving it up without a fight, but he started to gag. He swallowed hard again and managed to keep it down. Quickly cutting another hunk and swallowing it in the same manner, he jammed the last piece in before the first had hit bottom. He looked up at Stella from his clean plate. She was smiling broadly. He nodded at her and smiled back, pushing his chair out and going into the bathroom.

He managed to spit the last bite into the toilet, but there was a definite knot in his gut from the first two bites. He rubbed his middle and washed his mouth out, scooping water with his hands, using them as a ladle. He did it, and it made his sister's day, he thought as he dried his face on a towel and walked back out. He grabbed his coat, kissed Stella on the cheek, and complemented her on her new success. "I have to go now, but make sure you fry up at least three of four of those for Dad. I'm sure he's going to love them." He smiled at his sister, and winked at his father as he passed him and walked out the door.

The tiny little kitchenette fit just right pushed up against the back wall. Mark had bought it brand new. He had come clunking up the stairway with it earlier in the week. It was just right for two people, and there was a flap that pulled out to make it larger. Now the two of them could have breakfast together and dinner in the evening.

She had a pot roast and potatoes in the oven. The little table was set. Now she was just sitting there, quietly fingering her new watch, waiting for Mark to get home. She smiled, remembering her mother's words. She was to give the watch to her first born. Normally, this wouldn't have had any meaning to her, but now it did. She pondered the idea of having children with Mark. He would make a wonderful father, she decided. Would he be a wonderful husband? She smiled to herself. She knew he would.

She looked at the face of the watch and remembered she hadn't set the time yet. Carefully taking it off, she pulled the little stem out and turned the hands so the time matched the clock on her stove. She snapped the stem back in place and wound the watch gently. Holding it to her ear, she listening to the barely audible ticking. She stroked it in her palm, and then turned it over in her hand. That was when she noticed something scratched on the back of the watch face. Bringing it closer to her eyes, she could see the scratches were an engraved message. She strained to read the small lettering. It said, "To my beautiful wife, from her loving husband."

"Hum," she mumbled to herself. She had never known where the watch came from. So, it was a gift from her father. That was wonderful. It truly was a keepsake.

Shortly, she heard Mark coming up the stairs. She listened to him climb the staircase. His steps were far apart, and when he got to the landing, she could hear a soft thud. It sounded like he was coming home with another package. She stood up and opened the door. Sure enough, there he was, standing beside a box that looked to be about three feet tall and two feet across.

"What's that?" she asked curiously.

He looked tired. Apparently, whatever it was, it was heavy. "This is for me. I hope you don't mind, but I like cold juice in the morning."

She cocked her head. "A refrigerator?"

"Yes, just a small one. It even has a freezer." He lifted the box back up and stepped past her and into the kitchen. He threw his coat off and into the closet, and then started unpacking the box. Anastasia was smiling brightly. She held the box as he pulled the refrigerator out. It was a small white box with a little door on the top and a slightly larger door on the bottom.

Mark was happy with her reaction. She was beaming. He looked at her over the new appliance. "So where do you want it?"

She shrugged, looking around. "Um, I guess it would fit in the corner. I think that's were the old one was." Mark nodded, then set it in the corner and plugged it in. It looked ridiculous, being so short, but it would do for now. Maybe he'd buy her a short cupboard to sit it on next, he told himself. He stepped back, put his arm around her, and gave her a little squeeze. She wrapped her arms around his neck and kissed him.

"Oh, Mark, this is great. Now I have a real kitchen." She hugged him again.

"It smells good in here, what are you cooking?"

She used two folded hand towels as pot holders and pulled the roast out of the oven. Mark moved behind her, wrapping his arms around her waist and looking over her shoulder. "So, was it your mother who taught you how to cook so good?"

Anastasia shook her head. "Not really. She didn't like anyone in the kitchen with her. I just kind of figured things out for myself."

"Well, you've taught yourself well," he said, kissing her neck. She turned around and faced him, remembering about her watch.

"Look what my mother gave me today!" She held her arm up proudly, displaying the new watch.

He took her arm and examined it closer. "That's very nice. She gave it to you?"

"Yeah." Suddenly, she realized her mother had given it to her because she was dying. She looked down at it sadly. "My father gave it to her a long time ago. I can't remember seeing her without it."

Mark could read her pain, and he knew the gift was an ominous one. He rubbed her shoulder reassuringly. "It's nice. Now you will always have it to remember her by." She bit her lip, then hugged him tightly, burying her head in his chest. He wrapped his long muscular arms around her, holding her lovingly.

They embraced for several minutes. Mark was thinking about Marilyn's serious condition. "So, Anastasia." He massaged her back. "When am I going to meet her?"

Anastasia pulled back and looked at him thoughtfully. “I know she would love to meet you. I’m sure she’d like you.”

“Well, let’s do it soon, then.”

Anastasia continued looking at him and nodded yes.

Mark was curious to meet Marilyn. Whenever she came up as a subject, he could sense a strange mixture of feelings in Anastasia. He wanted to know why.

CHAPTER 20

Stella was standing in front of the bathroom mirror with every bottle, tube, and cake of makeup she could find laying in a pile on the counter in front of her. The swelling had finally gone down. Now she was trying to cover the bright yellow and deep purple marks that covered her face like a Halloween mask.

She moaned and took a sip out of a tall glass filled with ice and an amber liquid. Looking perplexed, she picked up a bottle of liquid foundation she hadn't used since last summer. It was called 'deep suntan.' She filled her palm with the beige liquid and smeared it over her face. She spread it like plaster over the contours of her cheeks, then carefully smeared it with her finger under and over each eye. As soon as she felt the thick coating was uniform, she picked up a hand held hair drier and began blowing it directly onto her face at high speed.

After a few minutes, she set the drier down and took another drink of her whiskey. Then she slowly looked at her own reflection, still holding her glass firmly. The dark lines and patches of bluish purple were still noticeable. She sighed then began rummaging through her collection of colored bottles for something white. Finally she grabbed hold of a tube of white eyeshadow and held it up to the light.

She unscrewed the lid and squeezed a good amount on her index finger, then rubbed it into an especially noticeable patch of purple above her cheek. She was happy with the result, and set to work adding a layer of white on top of the other dark bruises. She picked up the hair drier and flipped it on again, blow drying her face with one hand, lifting the whiskey glass to her mouth with the other. Next, she gently applied yet another coat of liquid foundation over the white patches, carefully, so as not to disturb the layer of white eye shadow.

She stopped and looked at her face as a whole again. "Good enough," she said aloud, picking up the hair drier again. She smoothed some of the foundation to her neck. Then she applied dark blue eyeshadow and mascara. She spent some time on her hair, and then moved to her bedroom to get dressed.

She was on her way to see Anthony at the market. It would be only the second time they saw one another in person, although they had been spending many evenings on the phone together. They were beginning to understand each other better all the time. In fact, she was fairly confident he knew she would be there to see him today. He told her he wanted her to meet his uncle Mario, since he had been trying to arrange for her to have a job there.

She threw on a pair of blue jeans and a modest button down shirt. Then she dug through her closet for a pair of walking boots. The weather was getting cold and sloppy out. It was mid November, and the snow had already started coming down in occasional flurries.

She sprayed perfume on her neck, took one last look at herself in the mirror, then grabbed her coat and shoulder bag. Once outside, she looked up at the sky. It was dark and cloudy. She decided it would be better for her if it snowed rather than rain. She was worried her many layers of makeup would run off her face if it got wet.

It was nice to stretch her legs again. She hadn't hardly been out of the house since the beating. The incident was still giving her occasional nightmares, but for the most part, she was feeling better than she had in a long time. Having something to look forward to was a new feeling for her, and home was so much different with her mother gone. She didn't want to admit it to herself, but having the burden of her mother's presence lifted from her shoulders was liberating. Still, she did feel guilty for not seeing her as often as everyone else had been. She was using the excuse of being ill to avoid going to the hospital. But she knew her mother understood the truth, and the danger of her mother's wrath did nag at her. The other part of her mother's absence was the liberation of her father and brother. She couldn't remember ever having so many enjoyable conversations with either of them in broad daylight. There was a new sound filling the walls of their home lately— laughter.

She moved expertly across intersections and through crowded streets. Finally, reaching her destination, she looked up at the big sign that ran the length of the front of the building. "Mattioli's Market", it read in large black script. It was hand painted on the white building itself.

She walked in casually, heading straight for the meat counter in the back of the store. She was mid way down the bread aisle when a big strong arm grabbed her by the waist. Her first instinct was to swing, but when she spun around she quickly recognized Mark's smiling face.

"Stella! Say, you weren't going to hit me, were you?"

She laughed nervously. "No, you just startled me."

He hugged her like a brother. "It's so good to see you again! You look good. Do you feel okay?" He was looking at her with genuine concern.

"Yeah, lots better. I just wish these bruises would go away!" She couldn't help but mention her face. It was worrying her.

He examined her face carefully, glancing in her eyes. "You can hardly notice them." He announced, then he looked at her with a mock curiosity. "So did they ever catch the guy who hit you?"

Stella quickly looked away from him. For some reason, he reminded her of her mother when he asked that. She had the feeling he knew the truth. "Ah, no," she said, shaking her head.

"Well, maybe the police will catch him." He decided to let the issue rest. He knew she and Anastasia were lying, but he didn't know why. "Anthony's behind the meat counter."

"Thanks." She started walking away, anxious to get away

from him.

"See you later," he said after her. She waved over her shoulder. He watched her walk down the aisle curiously. 'I'll find out some day', he thought to himself before turning back to his work.

Anthony had a line of customers waiting at the counter, but he waved enthusiastically at Stella when he saw her approach. He handed a white package to a heavy set middle aged woman in front of him, then, to the rest of his customers' dismay, he walked to the other end of the counter where Stella was standing. He reached across for her hand. "Stella, I miss so much!" He massaged her hand gently smiling into her receptive blue eyes.

They had been gazing into each other's eyes lovingly for a few moments when a short round woman walked up beside Stella. "Excuse me, but I believe I'm next."

Stella looked at the woman with great annoyance. Anthony dropped her hand, turning his attention back to his customers. "Sorry, what you want?" He motioned for Stella to stay, then returned to his post, pulling out a tray of meat the woman was pointing at. Stella watched him work hastily on two more orders, as three more customers walked up. She sighed impatiently. It looked as though she'd be standing there for awhile. Then she noticed Mark coming around the corner, and quickly turned her back, hoping he wouldn't notice her.

She was staring at a display case full of dead chickens when Mark walked up behind her. "Maybe you should get back there and help him?" He walked passed her and behind the counter. He took the next customer, alternating with Anthony until the crowd disappeared. Finally, they were down to just a couple of people, and Mark motioned for Anthony to leave. Anthony thanked him in Italian and wiped his hands on his apron before removing it and letting himself out. Putting his arm across Stella's back, he led her to the 'employees only' door.

"We drink coffee here," he explained, guiding her through the door. He led her to a row of chairs next to a vending machine. She sat down as he drew coffee from a large pot in the corner. “You like?” he asked, pointing at the sugar and cream dispensers.

“Sugar,” she called back. She wanted to say, “a lot of sugar”, but decided against it. Her brother was always badgering her, telling her the reason she craved so much sugar in everything was because she was an alcoholic. Of course, she knew better.

He handed a cup to her, then took a seat beside her. “How you feeling?”

“Much better, thanks,” she replied.

He looked thoughtful. “Maybe they catch the guy, huh?” He nodded seriously, taking a sip of coffee. Stella nodded back, indicating she really didn’t want to talk about it.

“So, do you like working here?” she asked, changing the subject.

“Yes. I do same thing at home in Italy.”

“Do you like living in the U.S.?”

“Yes. More money here.” He pointed down, but she knew he was referring to the American economy. Surely this little grocery store couldn’t pay much, she thought.

“When you want go out again?” He asked, looking at her.

“Anytime.” She answered too quickly.

“I don’t have a car,” he stated. “We go again with my cousin and you sister?” He took another sip, waiting for her answer.

She was trying to pace herself, worried she was too anxious. If the weather had been warmer she would have suggested the two of them walk, but Mark’s car equated comfort to her.

“Maybe Friday?” he suggested.

Stella nodded.

“I talk to Mario”. There was an awkward silence. Finally, Anthony thought of something. “So, you still want to work here?”

Stella was glad he asked her. “Oh, yeah, um, who should I talk to about that?”

Anthony looked at her thoughtfully. “I speak to my Uncle

Mario, before. They ask when you want to start."

Stella looked puzzled. "You mean it's all set? I just need to tell you when I can start?"

Anthony nodded his head.

"How about a week from today?" she asked.

Anthony nodded again. "Okay, they put you on schedule."

Stella wanted to ask how much they paid, but decided not to complicate things. Even minimum wage would pay her board, and that was all she really needed.

They managed to pass time with small talk and to slowly finish their coffees, then Anthony announced he should go back to work. They both stood nervously looking at each other, wanting to kiss good-bye, but both felt awkward. Stella wasn't used to being with a man in broad daylight and totally sober all at the same time. Anthony just wasn't sure what would be appropriate. Finally, he slipped his arms around her and gave her a little squeeze. Once in an embrace it was easy for them to mutually kiss one another on the mouth. As soon as they felt the soft warmth of each other's lips, the difficulty was to stop kissing. For Stella, kissing Anthony reminded her of her first high school crush. She would be absolutely giddy for the rest of the day.

"So, until Friday." Anthony said, so close to her face she could feel his breath on her cheek. He kissed her once more. The noise of a stockboy entering the break room was what finally caused them to break apart. He walked her to the door and waved good-bye.

On her way home, she stopped at a grocery store closer to her house and bought a few things with money her father had given her to shop with. The whole domestic thing was beginning to appeal to her. After a few small successes, she was feeling more confident in the kitchen all the time. Tonight she was planning on trying out a spaghetti recipe, with cornbread and chocolate brownies for desert. She had been reading tips on how to make a balanced meal. They suggested a meat, a starch, a vegetable, and a bread. From that, she concluded the hamburger and spaghetti would suffice as meat and starch, and the cornbread would serve as a vegetable and bread. And as for the chocolate brownies, well, she just had the craving. Besides, she thought of it all as good practice, and her father and brother made great guinea pigs.

The house was located on a corner in an old part of town. It used to be a grocery store with the living quarters on the second floor. Inside, it looked like a bachelor's home. The furniture was old and worn. It was easy to distinguish which chair was his favorite. The upholstery was so tattered he had thrown a blanket over the whole thing. There was a collection of framed photographs on top of the television and along the walls. Anastasia could easily identify the subject in most of them. Mario's love for his son shined through the house. The only other pictures were photos and prints of landscapes, and she guessed they were probably of Italy. Crucifixes were also present in every room. It looked like a home that had been well lived in for many years, but there was another feeling here, one of loneliness.

A familiar smell permeated the air, and when they sat down at the kitchen table, she noticed Mario's fettucini looked suspiciously like Marks. Apparently, they were using the same recipe. "So is this recipe an old family secret?" Anastasia asked after her first bite.

Mario looked at her fondly. "Yes and no. My mother made her sauce this way, but she would make her noodles from scratch."

Anastasia cocked her head. "My mother makes noodles, too." Mario looked at her with surprise. "She would start out in the morning making the dough. Then she'd roll it out, cut it into strips that would have to sit out on the counter all day so she could use them to make dinner that night."

"Ah, just the same as my mother." Mario nodded. "So, is your mother Italian?"

Anastasia laughed. "Everyone asks me that. But no, and my father isn't either."

"But you are Catholic aren't you?"

Anastasia wiggled in her seat uncomfortably. Mark had warned her his father would be concerned about this. Mark could see she wasn't sure how to answer, so he jumped in for her. "Papa, Anastasia wasn't raised with any particular religion."

"She has no religion?" Mario's shocked expression was making her even more uncomfortable. "You believe in God?" Mario asked quietly, not meaning to frighten her.

"Yes. I just don't go to any church," she explained delicately.

Mario just nodded thoughtfully. This bothered him, but the last thing he wanted to do was offend Anastasia. Then a thought struck him. "So, if you have no religion, maybe you can take Catechism and become Catholic like Mario? Huh?" He asked in a pleasant tone.

Anastasia didn't know what to say, so she looked at Mark for guidance. He was smiling with a look of anticipation. She could tell he wanted her to agree, so she did.

"Good, I will ask my friend Father Roberto when you can start the classes." He offered enthusiastically. Anastasia was slightly alarmed. She hadn't expected things to move so quickly. "My friend is the priest at St. Mary's. We have been friends since he first moved to this parish, before Mario was born."

Anastasia was trying to conceal her apprehension. Mark patted her hand. She looked over at his grinning face as he mouthed the words, "I love you." She smiled and blushed when she realized his father had noticed the exchange. But, to spare Anastasia further embarrassment, he looked down at this plate and only smiled to himself.

After eating, they cleared the table and sat back down with a bottle of wine. Anastasia loved listening to the old man's stories about living through the "great war" in Europe, but losing his father. He and his mother had managed to flee to the United States, only to find themselves in the middle of the depression.

He talked about how badly the foreigners were treated then, how they had to cling together and stay away from white American girls or risk being beaten by her parents. He had been born at just the right time to see the world change in dramatic ways. He knew the value of money, and believed strongly in the traditional family. He clung to his church. It had supported him though many a crisis, including the death of his wife. Anastasia wanted to ask more about Mrs. Mattioli, but she knew it was a sensitive issue with him, so she didn't.

There was a break in the conversation. Anastasia tipped up her glass of wine, and the soft light from an overhead chandelier glittered off her watch. Mario watched with interest.

"That is a handsome watch, may I look at it."

Anastasia happily reached across the table giving him her hand. He examined it with interest, turning her wrist over. There was a intensely curious, almost worried look on his face. Then he swallowed and shook his head. He looked up into Anastasia's eyes, then shook his head again and released her hand. "Very nice," he almost mumbled, then stood up and retrieved another bottle of wine.

Mark also noticed his strange behavior, but he and Anastasia only exchanged glances and chose not to ask any questions. The old man's mood seemed to have changed after that. He wasn't as jovial as he had been. There was almost a nervousness about him. They left shortly afterward. Mario warmly embraced Anastasia and his son before they left, gently reminding Anastasia of the Catechism classes. She knew this was important to him, so she nodded and asked him to let her know when they started. This made him happy.

As they were driving back to the apartment, Anastasia couldn't help but ask Mark, "Your father was talking about how American's looked down on immigrants and Italian men had to be careful about even talking to American woman."

Mark nodded. "I thought your mother was American?"

"Yes, she was," Mark explained. "But she was an orphan, so there was no one to speak for her. You understand? Sometimes, I get the feeling my mother wasn't in such a good position when she met my father. I don't exactly know how to explain it, but I get a feeling from talking to my father and the few friends of his that knew her, that maybe she was living a rough life at the time when my father met her. I just don't know very much about her, really. It makes me curious though."

Anastasia felt sorry for him. He had never taken his eyes off the road, but the tone of his voice told her the subject troubled him deeply.

"Maybe someday your father will feel more like talking about it," Anastasia said, trying to console him. But, at the same time she had a strong feeling he never would. There was something deep and dark there, and now she was curious, too.

Stella was looking more like her old self. The swelling had went out of her face, leaving her nose with a slight bend, and a small knot at the top. But, it wasn't as noticeable as the remaining bruises. She had carefully concealed them under layers of makeup, but the bright yellow rings on her cheeks were still visible. Despite all her healing wounds, she was in a chipper mood when she knocked at Anastasia's door carrying her familiar brown paper bag. This time she had brought wine, although the term was being used loosely. This was one of the cheap, high alcohol wines that was popular with winos. Anastasia was thinking this when she removed the bottle from the bag, but didn't say anything. "In honor of our two Italian men, I thought I should learn to start liking the stuff," Stella announced taking off her coat. "I noticed they seem to like the red kind, so that's what I bought." Anastasia quietly took down two glasses and unscrewed the top.

"So, where are they going to take us tonight?" Stella asked, sitting down at the little table. Then, looking as though she just realized what she had done, she looked up at her sister with a surprised expression. "Where did this come from?"

Anastasia smiled, setting the glasses and bottle on the

table. "Mark came home with it the other day. He also bought a brand new refrigerator." She pointed at the little square box in the corner.

"Oh, that's so cute," Stella exclaimed. Then she slapped the table. Looking at Anastasia, she whispered, "You mean, he's living here?"

Anastasia kind of giggled and nodded in the affirmative. Stella let out a little squeal. "That's great! Do you think you'll get married?"

Anastasia let out a breath and sat back in her chair. "We haven't even discussed that. In fact, we keep telling each other we need to slow down." She shrugged. "Stuff just happens. I mean, we never discussed living together, either, but he came over one night, and just never went home!" She laughed and shrugged at her sister. It was fun to have someone to talk to about her situation, and Stella thought it was wonderful. For Stella, this was her fantasy, and for the first time in her life, she thought the dream might come true for her as well.

"Does Mario or dad know yet?" Stella asked excitedly.

"No, you're the first person I've told. I just don't know how to explain it to anyone yet. They don't even know him, and here we are, living together." The two sisters stared at one another for a moment.

Then Stella gasped. "How about inviting everyone over for Thanksgiving?"

Anastasia looked at her with a puzzled expression. "In this little apartment?"

"No, at my house!"

"But Mom's in the hospital."

"I know, I'll cook." Anastasia looked curiously at her sister. "I've been practicing! Mom gave me her old cook book. She told me Italian men expect their women to be good cooks, so, I've been practicing. I'm really pretty good at it. Ask Dad and Mario."

Anastasia found it hard to believe what she was hearing. She couldn't imagine Stella anywhere near a stove. Suddenly, she realized she was staring. "Um, I think that would be great. We can ask the guys about it when they get here."

They began discussing what Anastasia should wear and if Stella needed to borrow anything. Hair was the next topic, and then they discussed whether Stella would get to be alone with Anthony that night. Everything was new and exciting. They were young girls in whirlwind romances.

Mark came home early with Anthony in tow. Stella watched in awe as Mark boldly stepped up to Anastasia and embraced her, kissing her on the lips. They were really a couple, Stella thought dreamily, and that was what she wanted more than anything she had ever wanted before. When she finally quit gawking, she realized Anthony was watching her from the other side of the room. They had already greeted each other from a distance, but now he was walking toward her. She smiled shyly as he stood beside her and asked, "How you doing?"

Before long, they were en route to a destination which only Mark seemed to know. "An indoor park?" Anastasia asked curiously.

"Yeah, I heard about it from a friend of Dad's. I guess he has a restaurant there. It sounded nice. We'll have to see for ourselves." He looked over at his sweetheart and winked.

After close to an hour of driving, they finally exited the expressway. Everyone was impressed when they drove up to the large glass dome. They parked and Stella grabbed hold of Anthony's arm. The two couples cuddled close against the cold on the way to the entrance.

Inside was the echoing of children's excited voices and a choir singing somewhere in the distance. There was a damp feeling, kind of like the feeling of walking into a thick forest. Real trees lined the cobblestone path that led them past the main gate. Then, a log cabin was nestled between the trees with the entrance lit, inviting patrons inside. They continued passed, walking toward the sound of running water. In front of them in their path was a babbling brook with a wooden plank bridge built over it. They stood on its edge, looking over at a Indian village hiding around a bend.

Anastasia instinctively looked up. The evening sky with all its stars was clearly visible overhead. Searching the sky, she found a full moon. She smiled to herself. Her body had finally adjusted to the birth control pills, she thought. For only the second time in her womanhood, there was a full moon and she wasn't on her period.

They walked on to a cluster of log cabins with little shops inside. Mark noticed one was selling custom painted Christmas bulbs. He urged everyone inside. They walked up the little path. An artificial tree was filled with ornaments with names and miniature paintings on each one. They marveled at a display over the fireplace mantel which included photographs along side painted portraits of the same. Even children's faces smiled sweetly from the round glass bulbs. There were paintings from photographs of pets, cars, and houses. There was a beautiful miniature landscape, and it looked even more lovely than the photo propped up beside it. This gave Anastasia an idea.

She walked over to the busy artist, a young woman who seemed to be more interested in the painting she was working on then talking to new customers. Her eyes were cast down, busily working on her current masterpiece. The lighting was bad, and her fingers seemed to be gripping the globe in an unnatural way. Anastasia felt uncomfortable watching her work and even more uncomfortable interrupting her. She remained quiet for a full minute before the artist began spouting off a well rehearsed sales pitch, complete with prices and a timetable for completion of a new painting, without raising her eyes. Mark stepped up beside her. "We want one." The artist sighed and dutifully set her current painting aside.

"Which one you want?" she asked, finally looking up at her customers.

Mark pointed to a dark blue bulb with a pair of love birds kissing from a tree branch. There was a large yellow moon shining down on them in the background. "Can you add our names to it?" he asked. Anastasia looked up at her boyfriend and smiled.

"Sure." She reached behind herself and pulled out a box filled with similar ornaments she had painted in advance. "What did you want on it?" She pulled out an ornament with one hand and held a pen to a pad with the other.

"For my beautiful Anastasia, Love Mark." The couple were looking romantically into each others eyes as he spoke.

"Can you spell that?" The artist asked with what sounded like contempt in her voice. Mark spelled out both names. The artist worked quickly with a fast drying paint to add the message, then wrapped the ornament in tissue and placed it in a box.

As Mark was paying, Stella and Anthony where standing in line behind them, Stella was happily cradling an ornament with Mary tenderly holding the baby Jesus in her arms. The two had decided to have their names painted on one as well. Their's simply read Anthony and Stella, but Stella would cherish it always.

Just as they were about to leave, Anastasia bravely approached the artist one more time, asking for an address so she could send a photo. The artist looked at her doubtfully and explained she couldn't promise to have anything finished and mailed back before Christmas, but she'd try. Anastasia returned to her party and asked Mark if he could secretly obtain one of his fathers photographs of Italy for her. "I have the best idea for a Christmas gift," she exclaimed.

They wandered further down the cobblestone road to a village with a stage set up and a live performance underway. They watched for a while, and then slowly wandered through the village. As they passed down the narrowing road, a tall storefront gave way to a giant ferrous wheel. The girls gasped. Anastasia turned around to look excitedly at her sister.

They walked briskly to the operator. Even though there were a good number of people at the park that day, it was as though the two couples were all alone that evening. The wheel came to a slow stop and each couple took a car to themselves.

The view was glorious. They could see the entire park as

they approached the top. They shouted and waved at one another when Stella's and Anthony's car was moving behind them. The wheel seemed to move especially slow as they reached the top most position. Anastasia reached over and pulled herself under Mark's arm. They kissed on the way down. Their first instinct when the car stopped was to go again, but now there was a line forming, so they exited.

They walked completely around the complex, exploring every feature, finally finding themselves in a large screen theater. As soon as the lights dimmed, both couples moved together, cuddling in the dark.

Shortly thereafter, Stella began plotting how she could discreetly get Anthony alone for the night. She knew he was living in Mark's father's home, so that was out. Could she take him to her house? Her mother wasn't there. If only she could sneak him past her brother. Her father would simply pretend he didn't see a strange man in their house. She knew that. Then a thought occurred to her, what if her mother did find out? She knew from past experience about how that happened. No, she decided, they needed a hotel room. She unintentionally sighed out loud. Anthony looked down at her sweetly and kissed her forehead, before returning his glaze to the screen. Stella looked up at him glumly and realized that this was the guy that was every mother's dream. There was no way in Hell she was going to get him into a hotel room.

In the car on the way back, the subject of Thanksgiving came up. First they had to explain to Anthony what it was, but as soon as he understood the concept, he was whole hearted in accepting Stella's invitation. "Of course your father is invited, too," Anastasia added.

"I doubt he would come. He has a friend that spends holidays with him. They have done this for many years."

Anastasia cocked her head. "A girlfriend?"

"Oh, no. Father Roberto. Remember, Papa mentioned him at dinner the other day?"

Anastasia nodded, feeling embarrassed at jumping to

conclusions.

"You will meet him at church Sunday, huh?" She had forgotten her promise to attend mass with Mark and his father. It would be the first time she'd been to church since she was a child.

She wondered if they were grooming her for marriage. Mark unexpectedly patted her on the leg and winked at her. Could he read her mind? She watched him for awhile as he drove. Finally, he turned to her with almost an annoyed look and put his arm around her, forcing her onto his shoulder so she couldn't stare anymore. If he couldn't read thoughts, then he was still more sensitive to other's feelings than anyone she had ever met outside of her family. "Quit trying to analyze and just enjoy the ride." He said to her finally with a little squeeze. She looked at him once more with suspicion.

When they arrived at Stella's, it was easy to see she wasn't ready to go home. She invited everyone in. Mark declined for Anthony and himself, explaining the two of them had to be to work early the next day. It didn't take a mind reader to understand Stella's expression. Mark tried to change the subject. "So, I've put you on the schedule for Monday, right?"

Stella's expression changed to one of interest. "Sure. What time?"

"Six a.m. Anthony said he would train you to work at the butcher counter. Sound good?"

Stella shyly looked at Anthony. "Yeah." He smiled back at her.

"But, now we have to go. So, Anthony, why not walk her to the door?" He pointed to the house while looking at his cousin. Anthony nodded and got out of the car, walking to Stella's side to let her out. She flashed an angry look at Anastasia as she gathered up her packages and stepped out. Anastasia bit her lip, trying not to laugh. She knew full well what was on Stella's mind.

When they finally arrived back at the apartment, Mark claimed to be tired, but as it turned out, he wasn't too tired to make love. This had been happening every night since the first time. He knew she was taking birth control pills, so the two of them felt safe. She never did explain to him about the abortion. She had given it long thought and decided it was too painful to explain about, and it had nothing to do with the two of them, anyway. She wanted the memory to fade away forever.

Beautiful stone statues adorned the outside of St. Mary's Cathedral. Anastasia had noticed the building before and had always wanted to see the inside. Now she was about to get the chance. She was wearing a simple dress she had bought the day before, holding Mark's arm as they climbed the stairs. His father was supposed to meet them inside. After a lifetime of attending the same mass at the same church, Mario senior had a special place where he always sat, so Mark knew exactly where to find him in the enormous chapel.

Inside was breathtaking for her. The high, arced ceiling was adorned with paintings and stained glass windows that told the stories of the bible. Several beautiful painted figures lined the walls and hung over rows of red devotional candles. Behind the podium was a large painted figure of Jesus crucified. A large red candle hung from a gold scone nearby, with a perpetual flame flickering. Anastasia had to keep a grip on Mark's arm to keep from tripping as she marveled at her surroundings. Then she heard him hailing his father in Italian.

She turned to see him smiling broadly and motioning for them to sit near him. He had reserved half of a pew for them. Mark was shaking hands with several people and introducing her, but mainly speaking in Italian. Apparently, these were old friends that were like family to one another. They spoke and laughed loudly, shushing one another occasionally.

Mark genuflected before entering the aisle, Anastasia looked around with embarrassment, and quickly made a similar motion. They moved onto the bench, pushing Mario farther to the inside so Anastasia was sitting on the end. Then, before he sat down, Mark kneeled and prayed silently for a few minutes.

Anastasia looked around herself helplessly. She wasn't sure what to do. Mark turned halfway around, giving her a reassuring pat on the arm and a wink before finishing his prayers. She sat quietly with her hands folded in her lap.

When he finally sat back in the pew, he whispered in her ear. "I thought you were baptized Catholic?"

Anastasia nodded. "Yes, but that was the last time my parents took me to church."

Mark simply nodded and then stood with the rest of the congregation as the Priest entered. The responses, standing, sitting, and kneeling took some getting used to. Finally, she was handed a missal that proved to be helpful in keeping pace.

Father Roberto was an almost bald man in his sixty's. He was of average height, but with slightly slumped shoulders. Anastasia liked his quiet manner. There was no shouting or crying in this church. It was unlike any service she could remember.

During the homily, her thoughts began to wander. She remembered her last experience with church. When she had been about ten, a church bus used to stop at her house on Sunday mornings and pick her and her sister and brother up. Their mother permitted it because it provided her with a free sitter for the morning and part of the afternoon. At first, the children believed the church was full of nice caring people who were out to save their souls, and teach them how to save others, including their parents. All three of them dutifully read the little bibles they were given. They each were also given a work book with a lesson to study for the next Sunday school session. Even Stella was coaxed into doing her workbook and memorizing the weekly verses that were assigned. During the week they would scour the neighborhood for soda bottles so they could return them and donate the money to the collection plate. This was when Mario became interested in the bible, he read it everyday, and even aspired to be a preacher for awhile.

They were so interested in doing what was right by God, and the formula they were taught to achieve this was outlined in the bible. “And those that were saved were baptized and added unto them...” This three step process was explained to them as follows. First they were to be saved, which meant they had to go before the congregation and announce they had accepted Jesus Christ as their savior. They pledged their whole selves to him and his mission of converting any who were lost. Second, they had to participate in a baptizing ritual and be submerged in a large tub of water by the minister. Then the third step was to be added as a contributing, paying member of the church, having their names listed in the official directory.

The first step was the most difficult, but they bravely held hands and walked down the center aisle of the big church in front of everyone. Then they stood facing the minister as he and his wife held them and sobbed in a contagious manner that caused even Stella to shed a tear. Finally, they were asked to kneel with a few others that had answered the call that day, and mercifully the minister announced they were saved.

The very next Sunday, the three of them asked to be included in the next Baptism ceremony. Unfortunately, the next one wasn’t to be held until the following spring. They were disappointed, but mostly worried. What would happen if they died before the ceremony? Would they go to hell for not completing the three steps? Mario especially lamented over the question, but thankfully all three of them survived. The ritual was being held during a special evening service, which meant they had to walk the ten miles since the bus was not running for it. They made the journey in record time, which they were sure was divine intervention.

After they had completed this important second step, the minister’s concern for their parents was even more pressing. He would remind them every Sunday of the importance of sparing those loved ones from the catastrophic miseries that awaited them in Hell. They were so filled with compassion and fear for their parents that Mario even dared to ask his mother to attend church. She laughed at him. Anastasia still remembered how her mother told Mario that he and his sisters were silly fools. She said they were being led about by an unscrupulous man who simply wanted them as slaves to make him wealthy. He wasn't really interested in them, but in her and their father, because children didn't have enough money. "He's working you like a pimp! You're scouting out more members to give more and more money."

Mario backed away from his mother and ran passed his two sisters, returning to his room for the rest of the day.

His faith had been shaken, but he rode with his sisters on that bus the next Sunday. The three of them were eager to see their names listed in the new directory. Finally, they would be added unto them, they would be on their way to heaven. Unfortunately, after Sunday school, when they were finally able to obtain a copy of the new directory, their names weren't listed. Mario search madly, flipping pages and reading every name. They weren't there! Confused, he frantically tracked down the youth minister with his two little sisters in tow. He explained there had been a mistake. The three of them had been saved and baptized. Their names should have been listed in the directory of members.

Anastasia remembered the look on the youth minister's face. He looked so casual about their problem, and annoyed they were making him late for the sermon. "I have to go, I'm in the choir," he explained in almost a shout. Couldn't he see how urgent their predicament was? Their souls were in limbo. Finally, to get away from them, he explained hastily that only children who's parents belonged to the church could have their names in the directory.

Anastasia remembered the stunned look on her brother's face. The three of them were so surprised and disappointed. Weren't their souls important? She remembered the tears welling up in Mario's eyes as the three of them stood mute for several minutes after the youth minister hurriedly disappeared down the hall. They didn't stay for the church service. The three of them slowly and silently walked home, never to return.

Thinking back on it, Anastasia wondered if what happened to her brother was equivalent to a nervous breakdown. He was quiet and stayed in his room for months afterward. He became obsessed with ancient texts, biblical and otherwise. He read the Book of Mormons, the Koran, the Torah, and even a book titled, Satan's Bible. Religion and it's origins became a kind of obsession with Mario and a hobby for Anastasia. Stella just became indifferent and cynical of all religion in general.

Mark nudged Anastasia. She suddenly realized the priest had stopped talking and everyone was standing. This jumping up, sitting down, and dropping to your knees was beginning to remind her of some strange exercise routine. At the same time, she was beginning to think she would never catch on. Then there was the praying and talking in unison, and how did all these people know how to answer the priest's questions? Did they memorize the answers before the church service? She felt a bit overwhelmed.

After several prayers, including one where everyone held hands, the service stopped and everyone began shaking hands. The priest even came down the aisle and hugged her, introducing himself. Mario embraced him as well. Anastasia couldn't understand what was going on, but she did find it curious. Then Mario reached around his son and grasped her left hand in both of his. He pulled her close to him and kissed her cheek lovingly. She noticed his eyes stopped on her watch. He almost said something, then shook his head and mumbled to himself. She could sense confusion, but decided to shrug it off.

When their aisle rose to take their turn for communion, Mark stayed behind with Anastasia. When the parishioners from their aisle returned, Mario sat beside Anastasia instead of returning to his original seat. He said a quick prayer from his knees then turned to Anastasia. He pointed to her watch and smiled. "Would you mind if I took a closer look at your watch? Could you take it off for me?" He asked quietly.

Anastasia nodded her head in agreement, unsnapped the clasp, and slipped the watch off, handing it to Mark's father. He was trembling slightly as he accepted the precious gift. Then carefully he flipped it over. His face became contorted with a strange, fearful expression. Mark and Anastasia both watched him with concern as he read the inscription over and over. Finally, Mark reached around Anastasia to his kneeling father. "Papa, you okay?"

Mario looked up at his son, then straight into Anastasia's face. He seemed to be looking for someone through her eyes. Finally, he spoke. "Where did your mother get this watch?"

Anastasia looked at him uneasily. "My father bought it for her."

Mario read the inscription one last time before he slowly handed the watch back to Anastasia. Then he turned and closed his eyes in prayer. He never explained his strange behavior. In fact, he was quiet and stayed after the service was over, saying he wanted to say a novena for his mother. They parted, leaving him behind. Both of them felt uneasy about it.

On Monday morning, Anastasia was surprised to see Jim back at work. He was looking good, even better than he did before he shot himself, Anastasia thought. There was one addition to his wardrobe though, hanging from a long chain around his neck was a small spiral note pad with a pencil clipped onto it. It seemed he still couldn't speak, and according to the doctors, he never would. The bullet had destroyed his voice box.

He was smiling broadly as he strolled up to Anastasia, patting her on the back, then hugging her warmly when she pulled him close to her. She asked him if he was feeling well, and he nodded yes enthusiastically. Then, in a lower voice, she asked, "Is Julia doing well?" He nodded his head again.

Then she noticed Mr. Lowe looming ominously behind Jim. Jim quickly sobered when he spun around to see who Anastasia was looking at. The two men exchanged glances before Mr. Lowe hurriedly turned the corner and disappeared into his office. The expression on Jim's face when he turned back around to face Anastasia was heartbreaking. She wished so much that Mr. Lowe could soften his 1950's morals, just enough to let

Jim be happy.

Then a thought struck her. "So, Jim, what are you and Julia doing for Thanksgiving?" He looked at her curiously and shrugged. It wasn't until after he accepted her invitation that she realized that he had never visited her mother's house. She wondered how her father would react. Once he had secretly looked at a school photograph of Jim that Anastasia had offered him. But, he refused to keep it. He just looked at it a few moments then handed it back to his daughter. He never spoke of the whole incident. He acted as thought he had no recollection of it. Then she wondered mildly what Mark and Anthony would think of the odd couple. She was comfortable that her family would accept another outcast, but her family wasn't the average. Well, if nothing else, she decided, it would be fun to watch the expressions on their faces. She decided then that she wouldn't explain the details to Mark and would see how long it took him to figure it out. It made her chuckle in an naughty way whenever she thought about it.

Stella had awakened easier than she had expected. It had to be because she was excited about starting her new job. The sun was still a few hours from rising— it was only 4:30 a.m. She had set her alarm so she had a full hour to get ready. All those layers of makeup over her bruises took time to apply. Most of them were now a bright yellow, the last stage before fading, but they were still difficult to cover up.

This will never happen to me again, she vowed with conviction. She was starting a new life, the life of a normal twenty-three-year-old woman. Just like on TV, she thought. Suddenly, she stopped and stared at herself in the mirror. Could she really be like the women on TV? Could she really have a normal life? For the first time in her life, she realized she had always observed others, thinking they looked happy and interesting, but never, never had she ever felt as though she was one of them. She had never felt she was like other humans. It was always as though she was an alien from another planet, just observing some remote life forms.

She shook the thoughts from her head and forced herself to begin getting ready for work. There just wasn't time for daydreaming.

CHAPTER 21

She had calculated that based on the chart in her mother's cook book, she needed to have the turkey stuffed and in the oven at six a.m. so it would be cooked by four p.m. that afternoon. She truly wanted everything to be perfect, so she had made the stuffing the night before. She had just completed stuffing it into the bird before sunrise. It was now exactly six a.m., so she carefully lifted the pan with pot holders and was gently lowering it into the open door of the oven.

She had been studying the old cook book for the last month now, and finally she was beginning to feel more at home in the kitchen. Looking around herself with confidence, she noted the main course was in the oven, so now she could make the pumpkin pies for desert.

According to the book, one medium sized pumpkin would make two pies. Her first step was to cut it in half. This task proved to be more difficult than she had anticipated, and she ended up sawing it with a large butcher knife. She scraped the slippery, slimy seeds out of both halves, then began peeling the hard, outside shell. This resulted in the loss of some blood, and it took more time than she had anticipated. Finally, she was cutting the pealed pumpkin into smaller slices, rinsing, and dropping them into boiling water. She looked anxiously at the clock and decided everything was still under control. She had plenty of time.

The pie crusts also took longer to prepare than she had anticipated, and despite starting over several times, they never did hold much resemblance to the illustration next to the recipe. She popped them into the oven anyway. After draining the water off the pumpkin slices, she mashed them with a potato masher and noticed hair like fibers running though the mashed pumpkin.

Perplexed and tired, she decided these pumpkin hairs must cook away or something. They had to, she told herself, they weren't mentioned in the book. About this time, the pie crusts were done. She opened up the oven and let out a little scream. The sides had fallen into the middle. Now she had to start all over. She tossed the crusts into the garbage and looked up at the clock. I still have plenty of time, she told herself again.

This time, before she put the pie crusts into the oven, she had an idea. She laid a plate on each pie pan, holding the crust in place. She chuckled to herself, and how clever she was as she set the two pie pans carefully on the rack over the turkey. She returned to mixing the pie filling. This went pretty smoothly, but the pumpkin hairs still bothered her. They didn't seem to be melting.

She was beating the pie filling with a wire whip when she heard a pop and crash noise coming from the oven. She ran to the stove and opened the door to find the heat from the burners had caused the plates on her pie crusts to shatter. She groaned and pulled the porcelain filled pie shells out of the oven. She burned her fingers on pieces of the broken plate, but under the glass fragments was a decent looking pie crust. The second crust was the same way, almost perfect, except for the broken glass. She stared at the matching pie shells and bit her lip. Carefully, she removed every bit of glass from each pie shell. She blew on them and patted every inch of both of them searching for small pieces of glass. There were none, so she decided to use them. Who would ever know, anyway?

The rest of the dinner would be a snap— mashed potatoes, canned corn, and fresh bread she brought home from the market. Anastasia had mentioned to her that cranberries were traditional, but she told Anastasia she didn't like cranberries, so no else needed them either. Besides, she was worried enough about the turkey and pies. Cranberry sauce might have put her over the edge.

When she finally felt she had everything under control, she opened a bottle of whiskey and took it with her into the bathroom, where she drew herself a bath. She sat on the edge of the tub and took a swig out of the bottle. Ah, the burn. She told herself how much she deserved a good drink. So what if it wasn't noon yet? Who made up that silly rule anyway, she thought, leaning against the wall. The bath proved so relaxing, she nearly fell asleep in the tub.

The stale air in the upstairs apartment seemed to be intermixed with another, sour odor. Anastasia raised her body slowly. She crinkled up her nose and tried to determine the source of the smell. She threw Mark's arm from her middle and slid off the side of the bed. The stuffy odors were making her nauseous, so winter or not, she opened the window. She bent her naked body so she could lean against the sill, inhaling deeply. The streets outside had a gray look. Winter seemed to have come early, sprinkling a fine layer of powder in the cracks of windows and the corners of buildings. The sky was overcast. It looked as though it would snow more today. She sighed. So what if it snowed? It was Thanksgiving, and she was looking forward to the big get together. She didn't mind that it meant exposing Mark and Anthony to her unusual family.

"You are going to catch pneumonia!" She felt Mark step behind her and put his hands on her hips. He pushed her bottom against his manhood, kneading her skin. She sighed again. For some reason, her usual enthusiasm for sex seemed to be missing. She pushed herself away from the window and tried to muster some interest. He moved his hands up the front of her body, massaged her breasts, and nuzzled her neck. She hunched her shoulders from the tickle and spun around to meet his lips. They kissed passionately, rubbing their cheeks and noses tenderly.

Marks fingers prodded her, carefully making way for his penis. Then, gripping her behind, he pushed her gently onto him. She raised her left leg and rested it high on the side of the bed. He maneuvered his knee between her legs and thrust himself into her full while holding her back, so she could keep her balance.

Anastasia let out a small animal sound as Mark moaned. He released and thrust again, pushing himself further inside her. This time he held her tightly, spending himself slowly with another moan. They stood embracing each other tightly for several seconds. Finally, Anastasia couldn't stand the cramping in her leg any longer and set it on the floor. Mark began massaging her back again. He pulled away and looked into her eyes, kissing her one last time. He spoke to her softly in Italian, words she now easily identified as, "I love you."

They moved apart and Anastasia sat back on the bed and immediately became aware of that odor again. She made a face. Mark was looking at her. "I guess I should take a shower now. My feet stink." Anastasia scooted back against the head board and wondered, is this what marriage is like? She could hear Mark chuckle before he shut the bathroom door.

She made coffee, showered, and dressed. It had already been decided. Today was the day Mark was to meet Anastasia's mother. They had planned to go to the hospital before Stella's dinner.

Bundled up for the cold, they headed out. Mark opened the car door for her. She had grown to love his father's old car. In the mornings now, he even dropped her off at work in it. She wondered mildly if Mark was making her grow lazy, with all his amenities. She was aware of her steadily growing dependence on him. But, for some reason, it didn't worry her. He reached over and kissed her cheek after he let himself in and shut the car door.

She folded her hands in her lap and stared forward out the windshield. The idea of introducing Mark to her mother suddenly made her sick to her stomach. She wasn't sure why. It wasn't that her mother wasn't glad she had met someone. Mark had already been warned of Marilyn's temper. Nothing could go so terribly wrong, she thought. Mark reached over and patted her arm, searching with his hand for hers. She warmly obliged, weaving her fingers though his.

Their first stop was the hospital gift shop. Mark insisted on bringing Marilyn flowers. Anastasia helped him pick out an arrangement that had a red rose as the focal point. They arrived to her room to find it empty, except for her mother's quiet body laying with a blanket tucked under her arms. Anastasia moved slowly to the side of her bed. The IVs still hung ominously from each arm. Mark stepped timidly behind her. He held the vase of flowers awkwardly with both hands.

To him, she looked dead. She was thin, white and had a hollow look to her closed eyes. Motionless, her light colored hair laid in loose curls behind her oval head and looked almost transparent around her face.

Then he felt it. A presence surrounded him. He turned abruptly, looking behind and around himself with an almost paranoid expression. He looked quickly at Anastasia. She seemed to be oblivious to the gathering cold that was encircling them. She was staring at her mother's body, waiting patiently for her to awaken. Mark's eyes were drawn to the ceiling, and slowly his gaze moved to the area above Marilyn's bed. Then, like a puff of smoke, she seemed to inhale the presence, shuddering violently. Anastasia reacted with no more than a blink. She patiently waited for her mother to open her eyes.

Slowly, Marilyn raised her eye lids, looking first at her daughter and then searching the room for Mark. He knew she was searching for him. He could sense her questioning thoughts. It almost scared him. Those pale blue eyes, almost white, with a ring of red around the pupils— he could see them resting on him. Two ice blue glass globes with small black pupils focused on his face. He wanted to take a step back, but forced himself to stand firm. She smiled as though she knew him already.

"Mario Mattioli," she said slowly with perfection. She smiled at him, then accepted a kiss on the cheek from her daughter.

The two of them were still staring at one another as Anastasia properly introduced them. Mark swallowed and nodded his head cordially. He had never expected this meeting to be so uncomfortable. The thing that would bother him afterward was why he was so uncomfortable. The woman had done nothing to provoke the indescribable feelings he had while he was in her presence. It was a feeling of fear, unprovoked, but total fear. He was almost trembling as he mutely offered her the flowers he was holding.

"Thank you," she said. "Roses are my favorite."

Anastasia took the flowers out of his dumb hands and made a place for them on the night stand.

"So, you and my daughter are in love," Marilyn said sweetly.

Mark was fighting with this feeling of panic, trying to get a hold of himself. "Yes. Very much so." He forced the words from his mouth.

"That's nice. And, by the looks of you, I can expect blue-eyed grandchildren, can't I?"

Anastasia's eyes flashed away, with red faced embarrassment. This made Mark smile in spite of his fears. Marilyn gleamed, taking advantage of the light moment. She truly wanted to make Mark comfortable. He was an important instrument for her, and also she admired his strength. He reminded her of someone long ago. "Oh, Anastasia, don't be so embarrassed, you should be lucky to have this man's child. He has the look of a strong warrior. I think his child would be handsome and strong."

Mark stared at her with apprehension. For some reason, he had the feeling she knew him much better than possible. Now he was curious. This woman reminded him of himself.

Marilyn suddenly looked at him with more interest. "So, your father has the market down town?"

"Yes. Do you know him?"

Marilyn made a thoughtful sound, then answered lazily, "I don't believe so."

Mark looked at her with suspicion. He wasn't sure she was telling the truth. But, why would she lie, he wondered.

"Mother," Anastasia began. "Did you hear who's making dinner tonight?"

Marilyn shook her head, patronizing her daughter.

"Stella! She's been practicing with your cookbook. Now

she wants to make Thanksgiving dinner!"

Marilyn smiled and offered some words of encouragement. Mark could tell the news was old to her. If Anastasia noticed, she pretended she didn't. They continued with the small talk until Anastasia's father and brother walked into the room. They greeted one another then Anastasia and Mark announced they should leave so Marilyn could visit with her husband and son.

Anastasia leaned over the railing of her mother's bed and kissed her cheek. Marilyn then motioned for Mark to do the same. He moved timidly to the side of her bed and leaned over carefully between the tangle of IV tubes. Marilyn surprised him by reaching up and holding the sides of his head. He could feel her run her fingers through his hair while she held him firmly to her face. She tenderly kissed his cheek. He returned the kiss on the left side of her face. Then, suddenly, he felt her pull several hairs from his head. He pulled away quickly and looking at her with surprise.

"I'm sorry dear," she apologized in a weak voice. "I must have gotten my wedding rings caught in your hair."

Mark smoothed his hair with his hands and nodded to her, but with a look of suspicion. She smiled back in a motherly way. Anastasia took his hand and led him out of the room.

Once outside, Anastasia hugged Mark affectionately as they walked down the hall. "I hope she didn't scare you. I told you she was intimidating. See what I mean about grandchildren? I don't understand what the big deal is."

Mark could tell she was still embarrassed by the way she was rambling. He smiled at her reassuringly, but inside he was scared and didn't know why.

Stella had inserted the leaf in the kitchen table to lengthen it to accommodate company. She had covered the table with a white linen table cloth and set it with her mother's fine china. She had carefully filled the matching salt and pepper shakers and put a stick of margarine in the butter dish. Now she was deciding what bowls to put the vegetables in.

Mario came creaking down his attic stairs and turned the corner into the kitchen with a book in his hand. He stopped in his tracks taking a long look at the table. Stella watched him with a look of anticipation. "Stella, this looks beautiful! Smells good, too," he said sniffing the air.

Stella was pleased, she so wanted everything to be perfect. "I hope so."

Her brother walked over and gave her a supportive pat on the back. That was when he also got a whiff of the whiskey on her breath. He started to give her a disapproving look, but then decided to let it go. She was trying hard to change. He didn't want to risk discouraging her. Her alcohol problem would have to be dealt with later.

The guests began to arrive on schedule. Mark brought Anthony, as well as Anastasia. Stella greeted Anthony awkwardly at the door with an embrace. He kissed her warmly on the mouth. They took seats in the front room while Anastasia helped her sister finish setting the table. She was famished, poking her fingers in everything to get a taste before setting the bowl on the table.

In the front room, Mario was engaged in a conversation with Mark about his coming from Italy, and their family history. "My father always bragged that our ancestors were soldiers in the crusades." Mark added to the conversation.

Mario kind of laughed. "That must be a popular claim. My grandfather on my mother's side told me the same thing about our English ancestors. He even gave me a name, 'Leigh.' He said this man was a commander of an army that invaded eastern European countries."

Mark nodded with an impressed look on his face. "Well, it makes for an impressive story."

Mario shrugged. They both laughed.

"So, sir, what about your roots?" Mark asked Anastasia's father, trying to include him in the conversation. "I suppose they are from Ireland?" The somber middle-aged man had been listlessly staring in the direction of the television since Mark had arrived.

"Probably. I was an orphan, so I'm not entirely sure."

Mark looked defeated, this apparently wasn't a good question to start out with. He tried again. "That certainly was a beautiful watch you bought your wife. You know, Anastasia is wearing it now."

He frowned. "Yeah, you're right, that is a beautiful watch. But the truth is, Marilyn was wearing it the day I met her."

Mark looked puzzled, then embarrassed. Had she been married before? He made a note to himself to ask Anastasia when they left. Deciding not to chance embarrassing himself again with another question, he fell silent.

About this time, the door bell rang. Mario answered the door. There was a curious couple standing outside. The man looked fairly normal, except he was wearing a small notebook on a string around his neck. A pencil also dangled from another string attached to the first. His companion was just as odd. She stood almost a foot taller, with a husky build. Her hair was carefully arranged and affixed in place with several coats of hair spray. She had one of those dangerous hair styles, the kind you had to be careful not to get to close to or risk losing an eye. Her makeup included a rainbow of eye shadow and deep red lipstick.

Mario suddenly realized he was staring. Then he remembered, this must be Julia. "Hello," he said quickly. "You must be Julia." He reached out with one hand to shake hers, then hugged Jim, patting him on the back at the same time. "Come right in. We've been waiting for you." He spoke almost too sweetly, trying to compensate for his staring.

The two entered quietly. Jim looked around the room till his gaze fell on the man who was his biological father. He was able to identify him mainly because of photos that Anastasia had shared with him over the years. Jim was disappointed when the man refused to make eye contact with him, instead he continued to stare into the direction of the television.

Anastasia was close behind her brother, having heard the door bell. She embraced both guests warmly. Julia was especially happy to be reacquainted with the woman who helped her and Jim become a couple again. This was the first time they had seen one another since the incident at the hospital. Anastasia took their coats and introduced them to the rest of the dinner guests. She especially watched the perplexed expression on Mark's face. Although she had explained to him the extenuating circumstances of her relationship with Jim she had omitted the details of Julia. She was curious to find out if he could guess Julia's true sexuality. There was an immediate look of apprehension on his face. He knew something wasn't as it appeared, but was he reading Anastasia, or could he tell by looking at Julia? Anastasia was amused. Anthony, on the other hand was totally accepting of Julia and her masculine features. He, in fact, seemed to be more interested in Jim's notebook. Anastasia explained about Jim's inability to speak as tactfully as she knew how.

"How this happen?", Anthony asked innocently.

Anastasia looked back at him uncomfortably. "An accident with his rifle." She answered slowly, looking at Jim for approval. He nodded, taking a seat near her father.

"Julia, why not come in the kitchen with my sister and I? The women seem to be gathering in the kitchen while the men have been gathering around the TV. Typical Thanksgiving, huh?" Julia tried to giggle, but it came out as a kind of a deep chuckle. She followed Anastasia anyway.

Jim noticed the football game on the television right away. He made himself comfortable, then nudged Anastasia's father's arm. He looked curiously at Jim who was writing something down on the notebook he was wearing.

"Score," he wrote, then pointed to the football game.

Anastasia's father looked at he television then back to Jim with a blank look on his face. "Hell, if I know. I'm not even sure what teams are playing!"

In the kitchen, Julia was happy to be included in the girls

circle. She offered any advice she possessed about cooking and table arranging. Soon, they were calling into the other room that dinner was ready.

They agreed Mr. MacDouglas should sit at one end of the table, and Mario would sit at the other. Then the women sat on one side and their corresponding dates on the opposite. It was decided this would be most appropriate.

Stella had proudly set the turkey on a platter in the center of the table. It looked surprisingly like the picture in the cookbook. Julia had explained that the head of the household should do the carving. At first, the two sisters were at a loss, explaining their mother was in hospital. So, the job went to their father. He looked at them blankly as Stella pushed the handle of a carving knife in his hand. "I don't know how to do this," he said with indignity. He then tossed the knife to Mario, who wasn't expecting to have a knife thrown at him. The knife handle bounced off the back of his hand.

"Here, I have an idea," Mark offered, picking up the knife. "Let's get the professional to do it." He then handed the carving knife to Anthony. They all agreed this was the best solution.

The main course went smoothly. Everyone complemented the blushing cook. Stella was on cloud nine, warning everyone not to eat so much they didn't have room for dessert. Anthony would give her an occasional endearing look. Jim and Julia were happy just to be included as a couple. They smiled at everyone frequently while Julia lovingly shredded Jim's meat. She mashed the rest of the items on his plate with her fork until they were indistinguishable from one another. Everyone else winced and turned their heads politely as he ate.

The only unfortunate incident happened was when Anthony leaned forward over his plate at the same time Julia was bending over the table replacing Jim's. This resulted in Anthony getting a poke in the eye from Julia stiff hairdo. His eye watered and turned red, but he refrained from complaining after his initial yelp. He simple sat holding a napkin to his eye until it quit tearing.

As soon as Stella noticed a few people were sitting quietly at their empty plates, she went to the counter and brought out plates with slices of pumpkin pie on them. She removed empty dinner plates and set a small saucer of pie in front of each guest. Another round of oohs and ahhs went up. She was in an absolute giddy mood, almost pirouetting back to her seat to sit down.

Then Julia, Anastasia, Jim and Mark began taking bites of their pie. Anastasia was the first to find a pumpkin hair. She could feel it in her mouth, but wanted so much not to spoil her sister's glorious mood, she forced herself to swallow it. Julia was the next to make a face. She smiled painfully and nodded at Stella. "Good, very good", she cooed.

Then her father started to take a bite, but with much less tact. Before he even put the fork to his mouth, he noticed one of the strings and began dissecting the slice of pie with his fork. He then dug his fingers into it and pulled out one of the strings. "Stella, did you have someone with orange hair helping you make this thing?"

Stella looked at him sharply. "No, it's just part of the pumpkin. I followed the directions. I guess they're supposed to be there. Just eat around them."

No one else made mention of the strings. In fact, the conversation had died down to nil when Julia made a sharp sound, and suddenly put her hand to her mouth. Everyone watched with concern as she tried to discretely spit two somethings out of her mouth. One was a piece of her tooth, the other a small piece of porcelain. Finally, she wiped her mouth with a napkin, and then held the napkin in front of her face and announced. "Why Stella, dear, I'm afraid I've chipped a tooth on your pie." She let out a nervous laugh. Then she let her hand down to reveal that a triangular chip was missing from her front tooth. It was very noticeable.

Stella had a miserable, irritated look on her face. Everyone stopped eating. Stella looked around the table with anger. "So, I broke a couple plates on the crusts! Just don't eat the crusts, okay?"

Everyone picked up their utensils and looked over each bite carefully before putting it in their mouths. Anthony seemed to be a bit confused, only understanding that Stella was upset. He studied her with furrowed eyebrows. When she finally noticed him, he smiled at her sweetly. Her angry expression instantly softened and she smiled back. Everyone else at the table let out a sigh of relief.

The rest of the evening went smoothly. Everyone, even Jim and Julia, stayed for after dinner drinks. Julia was a good sport about her tooth. She made everyone laugh when she flashed her broken toothed smile. After a few more drinks, Jim started a game of hang man with his notebook.

Something else Anastasia noticed was the more Stella drank, the more she stared at Anthony. She was taking on a catlike look, as though she might spring and jump on the poor guy at any moment. Words weren't necessary to explain to Anthony what was going on. Anyone could see the thoughts running though his mind. He clearly was feeling like the prey. Anastasia was watching with interest. She could sense he was interested, but unsure of himself. He wasn't sure if it would be acceptable to spend the night there in her father's house. He was trying to calculate the best course of action, one that wouldn't spoil his relationship with the family but would allow him some time alone with Stella. Then their father got up from the table and announced he was going to bed. Anthony watched the old man leave. When his line of sight passed over Stella, she was driving a hole through him with her stare. He kept his eyes on her for awhile, licking his lips nervously.

Anastasia began getting excited herself, just watching the two in their courting dance. Somehow, she soon found herself on the other side of the table on Mark's lap. He was quietly watching her watching Anthony and Stella. When Anastasia looked down at him, she realized it at once. "So, what do you think?" she asked him quietly.

He moved his head slightly from right to left in a sexy way, then hummed softly. "I guess they are both old enough to take care of themselves." Jim and Julia were in an animated conversation with Mario, who was doing most of the talking. Anastasia looked over at the trio, admiring how her brother was a natural teacher. It seemed anyone who spent any time at all with him ended up engulfed in an intellectual conversation that always left them enlightened about subjects they never knew they were interested in. It was just the way he was.

"So, do you think we'll end up leaving him here?" Anastasia asked. Mario looked as though he was giving the situation some thought.

"Do you think he will be safe?"

Anastasia laughed. "Well, I don't think we have to worry about him being permanently damaged." He looked up at her again, and they kissed with a slow passion.

The conversation at the end of the table began to lose its fast pace. Stella and Anthony had retreated into the front room. Anastasia was still sitting on Mark's lap. Mario looked over at his sister with a tired expression. She could tell he wanted to go to bed. It was late, and these were her guests. She stood up and asked if anyone wanted coffee. Julia recognized the cue to leave and announced she would pass on the coffee, preferring to go home to bed. Jim looked around, oblivious to the hour, preferring to continue the party. He was having a good time drinking and chatting with Mario. Julia stood up and griped his shoulder. "Come on, honey, everyone is tired and wants to go to bed." Then she winked at him. "Including me." Jim blushed and stood up.

Anastasia brought out their coats and she and Mark walked them to the front door. Everyone was embarrassed as they passed the couch where Stella and Anthony were tangled together in a heap. It looked as though Stella had managed to unbutton his shirt and trousers. Her blouse was open as well, with her bra pushed up around her neck. She was sitting on top of him, straddling his lap between her knees, and was in the process of grinding her breasts against his naked chest when they entered the room. Everyone averted their eyes. Anastasia was wishing she had sent them out the back door. Stella kept her mouth on his, encouraging him to ignore the commotion behind them.

It was decided, that Anthony would be retrieved in the morning. Mark was concerned about leaving him there without his oral consent. Anastasia again reassured Mark that Stella wouldn't hurt him. If at any time Anthony did begin to feel he was in danger and called out, Mario would come to his rescue. She even had Mario promise Mark he would keep his ears peeled. They left out the kitchen door.

Marilyn wound the strands of Mark's hair around the index finger of her right hand. She brought the hairs to her nose, and inhaled deeply. She was trying to get even the slightest fragrance, but all she could smell was shampoo. Giving up, she lay her hand back to her side with disappointment. She missed the natural smell of humans. Deodorants and cleansers seemed to have made modern people's odors stronger when they weren't being used. The unnatural stench of bodies and feet after being bound for hours in plastic clothing and shoes that didn't breath was especially offensive to her. But, the natural smell of humans after bathing in a stream and washing their hair with sand, maybe even rubbing it afterward with lilacs or some other fragrant plant, that was wonderful. She even missed her own smell. There had been a time when she could sniff the air and recognize the presence of her family members or close friends. Those days were gone, she thought sadly. Now she couldn't even pick up the scent of her own offspring.

She moaned quietly, forcing herself to take inventory of her own decaying body. She could feel the knot in her womb. If only she could block her body from feeding the growth. She concentrated on the area around it. If she could just slow down it's rate of growth long enough for Anastasia to give birth, she could give up her diseased body for a young, healthy one. She needed to hold on for just a few more months.

She enjoyed the idea of Mark being the father. He was a handsome man. He should be more than capable of fathering a strong, healthy son. He would work just fine, she thought to herself. She couldn't have produced a better father.

CHAPTER 22

Business was always slow after a holiday that involved such a big feast. The old man busied himself by marking down the few overstocked items that were perishable.

Anthony and Stella were now lovers. This fact was apparent to anyone who paid attention. It was made obvious by the way they looked at one another, and by all of the new giggling and touching that went on. It embarrassed the old man to see them always touching each other. Maybe he should talk to Anthony, he thought. Even though Anthony was technically his cousin's son, Mario always considered himself Anthony's uncle. It was his duty to say something. Anthony's father was dead, and his mother was in Italy. He had promised his cousin he would watch over her only son like she took care of his own son for all those years he lived with her. Mario made a mental note to himself that he would have a man to man talk with Anthony over dinner that evening.

Mark's tall body coming around a corner distracted Mario's thoughts. He returned a smile from his son and the two embraced warmly. "Papa, did you have a nice Thanksgiving?"

The old man held his son's arms, not wanting to give up the embrace. "Yes, thank you, and Father Roberto sends you his love. You should go visit him sometime soon. He misses you."

"Yes Papa," Mark stated with exasperation. "Anastasia said she enjoyed going to church with us last Sunday. She said she'd take the classes, too."

Mario smiled. To hear this made him very happy. "If she begins right away, she can take her first communion on Easter."

Mario's smile faded and he dropped the grip on his son's arm. There was a subject eating at him. He had been trying to shrug off his fear and convince himself his suspicions were an impossibility. The truth was, he had been discussing it at length with Father Roberto the day before. He had told himself he needed to clear up any questions in his mind, so he asked, "Son, have you met Anastasia's family yet?"

"Sure, we had dinner together last night."

"How about her mother?" he asked nervously.

To that, Mark took on a more sober look. "Yes, just yesterday. We went to see her at the hospital."

Mario looked up into his son's eyes with a bit of pain in his own. "What did she look like?"

Mark could see a strange look in his father's eyes. There was some greater importance to these questions. "She was laying in a hospital bed, very ill. But—" He struggled for the best description. His eyes wandering the display of vegetables. "She had light hair and very pale blue eyes. I think she is probably in her forties. Her face is strained from the illness, and she is very thin, but I think she was once beautiful like her daughter."

Mario went cold. Like a statue, he stood staring and thinking of something far away. Mark looked curiously at his father. There was something there, something important he needed to know. "Papa, what's wrong?" he asked in Italian.

His father looked back at him, and forced himself to go on. "Her father, you met this man as well?"

Mark nodded. "Yes, he's a very quiet man."

Mario pushed himself farther. "The watch." He spoke hoarsely. "It was a beautiful gift to his wife. He must love her dearly."

Mark narrowed his eyes. The watch, what was the significance of the watch? He wondered to himself. "Actually, I found out Anastasia was mistaken. Her father told me his wife had the watch from before they knew each other."

Mario's face took on a horrified expression. Beads of sweat formed on his forehead. He looked away from his alarmed son, shaking his head.

"Papa, what is wrong?" Mark moved closer to his father,

laying his hand on Mario's shoulder.

Mario shook his head and pulled away. "I'm not feeling too good. I ate too much yesterday." Breathing heavily, he turned back to his son with a sudden look of resolution. "I think I will go home for awhile and rest." He tried to look natural, aware his son was alarmed at his behavior. "I am fine son, just a little sick to my stomach. A nap will fix everything." He patted his son's shoulder and walked away. Mark watched him leave curiously. There was something there, but what was it?

Mario went into the office for his coat. He knew what he had to do. He had to put an end to his fears. He had to visit the hospital.

The sky was still an ominous grey color. Snow was building up in the clouds. The air was dry and bitter. A biting wind pulled at his tattered, buttonless coat. He kept meaning to buy a new one, he just hadn't gotten around to it. Approaching the front doors of the hospital, he drew the grubby sides of the coat together. That was when he realized he was still wearing his white apron from work. He hesitated for a moment, then told himself it was too late to turn back now. He just gathered the front of the coat so the apron was covered.

When he arrived at the hospital doors, he stopped suddenly and realized his fears. What if she was there? What if it was her in that bed? He began to tremble. He shook himself, trying to belay the fears and convince himself he was going to find out once and for all that his imagination had been working overtime. He was simply going to meet Anastasia's mother.

With renewed strength, he pushed the door open and entered the lobby of the hospital. He went to the information desk and asked for Marilyn MacDouglas' room number. The nurse consulted a book on her desk then informed him she was in room 213 on the second floor. He thanked her and turned to the hall that led to the elevators.

His mind began racing to the day his son was born in that

very hospital. He had walked the same hall, only turning just before the elevators into the maternity ward. His wife had given birth so quickly that by the time he was able to reach the hospital, she was already finished. His mother had met him in the lobby. She was excitedly giving him the news. He had a healthy son. He and his mother had walked this hall together, anxious for the mother and child to be moved to a room so they could visit. A tear formed in his eye, remembering his mother at his side as they peered through the glass of the nursery. They watched a newborn being placed into a bassinet marked, "Mattioli boy." The two of them had hugged and excitedly exchanged phrases in Italian, not caring if those around them were offended or not.

Then, less than a year later, he was back. Only this time, it was to claim his mother's body. This time, police officers walked him to the cold basement, away from the rest of the hospital, where they kept the dead. He realized tears were starting to roll down his cheeks. A sob was building in his throat. Embarrassed, he realized the other people waiting for the elevator where looking at him. He tried to clear his mind. He wiped his eyes with his sleeve. He swallowed back the tears and cleared his throat. The elevator stopped. He made a motion for the others to proceed first, putting him near the doors. He reached over and pressed the second button. Then he straightened himself and stared at the closed doors in front of him.

When the doors finally opened, he moved briskly out of the elevator and walked toward a sign with arrows that pointed the direction of rooms 200 - 220.

He noticed the odd numbered rooms seemed to be on his left, so he moved to the left side of the hall. He watched the numbers on the doors increase. He swallowed hard and slowed his pace wearily as he passed room number 211. Then, just before he approached Marilyn's room, number 213, he involuntarily stopped. His heart was pounding. Sweat was beading at his brow. His feet seemed to be glued to the floor. He realized his jaw was clenched so tightly it felt sore. He wiped his face with his hand and tried to convince himself he was about to find out his imagination had gotten away with him. How could Marilyn be his Maria? The watch was probably purchased from a pawn shop.

He forced himself to take another step toward the door. Then another so that he was at the threshold. He took in a deep breath and looked around nervously. It felt as if someone were watching him, but there was no one. Then he stepped inside the room. It took a few seconds for his eyes to adjust to the darkness. The blinds were drawn and a curtain was pulled almost completely around the bed, exposing only the foot of the bed. There, through the curtains, he could see the form of a woman. She was laying very still with IV tubes in both of her arms. He stepped a bit closer and waited for his vision to clear. Squinting into the darkness, his heart stopped. He clutched the front of his coat with both hands and stood rock still. He stared in horror at the form of an old woman who resembled his Maria.

A familiar shockwave pierced through her body, shaking it violently as she reemerged with a smile. She opened her eyes and looked at the old man standing near the foot of her bed. His eyes were wild and round like an owls. His medium complexion had went white as he stood mutely staring at her with an open mouth, clutching his tattered old coat.

"My Mario." she hissed slowly.

He made a kind of gasping, anguished sound and placed both hands on the sides of his head. He bolted out of the room.

Marilyn laid back on her pillow. She sighed sadly, missing the time when they had talked fondly to one another as lovers. If only that nosy old woman hadn't come between them. She floated back into a dream, raising above her pain riddled body.

Her thoughts went back to the day she had met Mario Mattioli. He was working in a grocery store in a poor part of town. She was only fourteen and hungry, after recently coming out of the woods. She had been eating small game she killed with an old rifle she had kept from her life as Elsa May. Finally, she had run out of ammunition and her clothes were worn and thin in places, that they looked almost transparent. Her desperation was great, she was even considering prostitution. She walked into the store rubbing her empty stomach and wanting to stealing something to put in it.

She was aware the young man was watching her. Her threadbare, dirty appearance made her stand out, regardless of how she tried not to attract attention to herself. She knew he was wanting to catch her shoplifting. She walked quickly down one aisle, and then another. He pursued her. Finally, she turned to him and focused her ice blue eyes on his. She could sense immediately there was more than a man trying to catch a shoplifter. There was a young, poor, Italian immigrant. He was also hungry, but for an American life and a woman to share it with. Her angry expression quickly melted into one of sincere desperation. She remembered an old Italian language she hadn't spoken in many years. In a quiet, pleading voice she told him she was an orphan named Maria, and then she moved close to him and begged him for something to eat.

He looked at her in bewilderment. He was astonished at her Italian words and infatuated with her beauty and her desperate plea for help. He was immediately snared in her trap. Hesitating only a moment, he looked around himself and picked up a package of cookies. He told her to hide them in her clothes and he would follow her out so his boss would think he was chasing her out of the store. He was speaking to her quietly in Italian, looking nervously around himself the whole time. His plan worked and she stayed close to the rear doors of the store the rest of the day, waiting for him to get off work.

He took her to the home that he shared with his mother. Even the old woman took her in like a daughter. The three of them lived together in a small, one bedroom apartment. At first, she slept with the old woman. Then she and Mario were married secretly by a priest. They were never legally married because Marilyn claimed to be an orphan with no record of birth, but, they were married by a young priest named Roberto who was friends with Mario. That was good enough for the old woman. She relinquished her bedroom to the young couple. Soon, the long hours Mario worked allowed them to purchase a small store with a two bedroom apartment over it. It had a dirt floor basement.

These were happy times. She learned to cook and clean from the old woman. And from Mario, she learned to enjoy making love every night. Somehow, being female became almost acceptable to her. The small details of life became a joy she hadn't experienced in many lifetimes. She planted roots by digging a hole in a remote corner of the basement where she hid her precious chest. Soon, she found she was pregnant. She bore a beautiful son. Mario bought her the gold watch as a gift. He had the precious inscription engraved inside the face of it. Never had she felt so comfortable being female as she did in those days, nursing her baby as she rocked him to sleep. She admired the simple gold band around her finger and beautiful gold watch around her wrist.

Then the dark day when Mario's mother had surprised her by coming down the basement stairs when she was getting something out of her hidden chest. The basement was a dark place with no electric lights. It was really more of a root cellar with shelves along the walls for storing canned goods, potatoes, wine, and apples. When she heard the woman creaking down the wooden steps, she hurriedly pushed her chest into the shadows and rushed to meet the old woman at the bottom of the stairs. She thought she had satisfied the woman's curiosity by explaining she was only retrieving potatoes for dinner. But, then late that night she was awakened from her sleep She felt her heart leap. Someone was going through the things. She could feel them grasping at bottles, touching the book, holding her sword. She crept out of bed, so as not to wake her sleeping husband. Then she bound down the stairs to the basement. A candle glowed in a the far corner and there she found her mother-in-law with her back turned, hunched over the chest. She was rummaging through her things and dropping them carelessly on the dirt floor!

Marilyn dropped her robe and rushed to retrieve her precious treasures. She gasped when she saw a fragile glass vial being tossed to the ground. The old woman turned suddenly to the noise and faced her daughter-in-law standing naked in the eerie candle light.

With a frightened look in her eyes, the old woman shouted, "Maria! Where did these things come from? Did you bring them here?" She spoke in a stern but trembling voice. Marilyn stood motionless, trying to think of the best course of action. The old woman's shocked gaze wandered up and down her daughter-in-law's naked body. Then, sensing that she may be in mortal danger, she gathered up the candle in her right hand and took a step back from her daughter-in-law. "You are a witch!" She spat straight into Marilyn's eyes.

Marilyn looked around, nervous that her husband might hear. Just then, the old woman bolted toward the staircase. Without another thought, Marilyn chased after her. She grabbed the old woman around the waist and threw her to the floor. The woman shrieked and rolled to the back of the basement. Marilyn picked up her sword. She kicked the flailing body onto it's back. Then she grasped her sword with both hands and held it over the hysterical old woman. She plunged the blade deep into her body, piercing her heart straight through, instantly stopping the maddening noise.

Marilyn stood very still for several moments, listening. Had he heard anything from their room on the second floor? Probably not, she decided. Expertly, she held down the dead woman's body with her foot as she pulled the blade back out. She wiped the blade clean with the dead woman's black dress. Then she retrieved the candle. It had landed upward with the flame still flickering. She moved the light over the old woman's face. Her eyes were protruding from their sockets. The mouth had formed an eternal scream.

She felt only an angry regret for murdering the old woman. Now her happy life was in jeopardy, and it was all because of her meddling mother-in-law. She set to work collecting her things, cursing her mother-in-law the whole time. Then, she carefully replaced the lid of the chest and set it back into the hole in the ground. She pushed the dirt back over it and sighed as she stepped over the old woman's body and picked up her robe. She began to plan an explanation while walking naked up the stairs.

She poured herself a small glass of wine and pondered the possible courses of action. Then she decided the best thing to do would be nothing. She'd let her husband find the body and blame it on an intruder. How would anyone even suspect that a delicate, young mother like her could do such a thing? Confident in her decision, she went back to bed.

She remembered Mario searching the house the next morning, looking for his mother when she didn't have breakfast ready for him the next morning. First he let Marilyn convince him that his mother must have went out before he woke. This would have been unlike her, but there was no other explanation. Then, shortly after he opened the doors of the store for the day, he remembered the basement. Marilyn was washing the morning dishes when she heard his wild screams as he charged back up the stairs like a madman. By that time, her body was cold and stiff, and there was already a slight odor. Marilyn did a good job acting surprised and calling for the police. When they arrived, Mario was still hysterical. The police were sympathetic. They all knew him well, but a few days later, he was arrested. He was the only possible suspect in a gruesome murder.

Marilyn remembered those days sadly. She worked at the small store alone with the baby. She answered relentless questions and endured the gossip and whispers quietly. Silently, she clung to the possibility of regaining her once happy family. With the help of father Roberto and a few of her husband's good friends on the police force as character witnesses, they finally let Mario go for lack of evidence against him. The case was left unsolved. Her grieving husband finally returned home.

But things never did fall back into place the way they were before. Mario never recovered. She would find him often in the basement, squatted down over the place where he found his mother's body. He refused to give up the search for her killer. He couldn't accept the idea that someone entered their house without breaking a lock or window, only to kill his mother with a double edged sword. The intruder never stole a thing. "How could this happen?" he would mumble to himself as he paced.

Then the horrible day when she was at the health department getting shots for the baby. Her ears perked up. She could hear him kicking the dirt away from the hole. She could see him fall to his knees and dig with his hands. She raced out of the health department without an explanation. She ran down the city sidewalks to their home and bounded down the stairs with the baby still in her arms. There he was, standing near the open chest, holding her sword by its hilt in his right hand. He looked up at her strangely, as though in a dream. She stood mute in front of him with both arms wrapped tightly around their child.

Her heart felt like it would burst as he stared into her face and whispered. "What kind of woman are you?" There was no denying the chest was hers. He knew it was, just as he knew she had murdered his mother. Suddenly, his face turned a bright red with rage. Then she felt it, something she had never felt from him— hate. If she hadn't been holding their baby, he would have slapped her, and she would have let him. As difficult as his pain had been for her to bear, this final burst of rage and hurt was overpowering. He flung the sword to the ground and thundered passed her and up the stairs. She stood silently, listening to him slam the outside door. She never did know where he went for those three days. She didn't try to envision where he was. She only gathered up what was her's and used those days of his absence to remove her things from the house. She left the baby with a neighbor and never returned.

Now she stared at the hospital ceiling. If only the old woman hadn't been so nosey.

The high pitched voice of the cashier grated on his nerves. He gritted his teeth and nodded to her in agreement, hoping she would soon run out of words if he refused to contribute any of his own. He had already chewed and swallowed a handful of stomach antacid tables, and countless doses of aspirin. Still, his head pounded and his stomach was in knots. His thinking was even dull and slow. He decided he was just too old to drink anymore, at least not the amount he had put away last night. Slowly, he became aware of his son walking toward him from the back of the store. He stopped sweeping the floor and leaned against the handle, wearily waiting for his son to reach him. "So, you just get here?" he asked with a forced smile.

Mark nodded, but was looking at his father with concern. "Papa, you feeling okay?"

Mario looked down sadly, shaking his head. "No, son, I need to talk to you. Let's go into the office." He set the broom against the wall, then turned to a stock boy and instructed him to finish the job. When he turned back to his son, he tried to smile. There was no fooling Mark. He knew there was something seriously wrong. He could feel it.

When they reached the office, Mario flopped down in a chair behind an old metal desk. Mark pulled up a folding chair from against the wall. He sat directly across from his father with the desk between them. "So, what's wrong?"

Mario looked thoughtful for a moment. He started out with slow, deliberate words. "Son, I've been thinking about it, and I think you should go back to Italy to take care of the apartments. Your cousins don't know how to run things the way you did."

Mark's expression seemed to be frozen. "What are you saying, Papa? You want Anastasia and me to move to Italy?"

Mario turned his head and stared at the closed door of the office. "No, you don't need to take Anastasia. Just go by yourself. It will give you a chance to think things over."

Mark leaned against the desk, moving closer to his father's face. "Papa, are you saying you don't want me and Anastasia to be together?"

Mario hesitated, then firmed up his chin and answered. "I've noticed you are always with her, and this kind of arrangement clouds a person's vision. Maybe you are rushing into something you might regret." He looked soberly at his son. "I just think if you spent some time apart, maybe you would be able to see things more objectively."

Mark looked away and pushed himself back in his chair, trying to make sense of his father's sudden change of heart. "Papa," he said softly after a long silence. "Why? What is the reason you feel this way all of the sudden?"

Mario tried to look as if he didn't understand his sons question, and shrugged. "I just think it would be best. I am your father and I love you. I don't want you to make a mistake. And, besides, the business—"

Mario stopped suddenly when his son slammed his open hand loudly on the top of the desk. "Why Papa? What has happened to change your mind?" He was now talking louder, in a demanding but controlled voice.

Mario looked away, visibly shaken, and tried desperately to think of the right words. How could he convince his son not to marry this girl without explaining why? He vowed when his son was an infant he would never tell him the truth about his mother. How could he tell his son his mother was a murdering monster? He never wanted him to know he had this bad blood running though his own veins. He shielded him as best he could, sent him to be raised in Europe, lied even to his own relatives about the death of his wife and the truth about the death of his own mother. Now, how could he tell his son everything was a lie and his mother was the same murderous witch that lay in a hospital bed only a few miles away. The woman he loved and slept with every night was his own sister. Tears of desperation filled his eyes. His son stood up on the other side of the desk, watching him, waiting for an answer.

Mark marveled when he began to notice the glazed look of his father's downcast eyes. He shook his head. There was something so wrong, his father was starting to cry. Mark's look softened. He moved to the other side of the desk and kneeled down in front of his father. He offered his arms and hugged him tenderly as he sobbed. As Mark held the old man and patted his back, the questions kept running though his mind.

When Mario was finally able to stop shaking, he lifted his head and moved his face close to his son's. He told Mark he was still feeling ill from yesterday. They would have to finish their talk tomorrow after he'd rested some more. Mark felt helpless. He wanted to find out why his father was so upset, yet he was concerned for his father's health. The old man looked pale and sick. He reluctantly agreed and walked him to his car, promising to take care of the store.

Mario lovingly patted his son's shoulder. Then, impulsively, he reached up and hugged his son, kissing his cheek. Mark, kissed him back and asked him one last time if he was going to be okay to drive himself home. Mario assured him he just needed some rest and not to worry. Then he left. Mark watched the car drive slowly out of the parking lot. Curiosity was eating him up.

Anastasia was waiting anxiously in the kitchen. The table was set and the food was sitting on the stove on a low temperature. Mark was late. She was in a melancholy mood, contemplating her situation. A growing suspicion had finally caused her to admit to herself, that she was pregnant again. This morning, she had gotten sick, and despite taking her pill every morning without deviation, she still had not started her period. She had decided to tell Mark this evening. She also had made up her mind that if he thought it would be prudent to get another abortion, she would. She had decided to leave it up to him. The last time she was forced to make the painful decision herself. This time, she was going to put the burden on Mark.

She rubbed her stomach unconsciously. Then she quickly folded her hands together on the table. She was not going to allow herself to even consider she was carrying Mark's child. She didn't want her heart to become the least bit fond of this unborn child until she had talked to Mark, not until he made the decision.

He was almost an hour late when she heard him unlocking

the door. She continued to sit at the table, listening to his footsteps as he drew closer to her. Finally he was standing in front of her looking down.

"Why so quiet?" he asked as he bent down to kiss her. She shrugged, trying not to let on about how nervous she really was. "Sorry I'm late," he said. "I had to check on my father. He hasn't been feeling well the last few days."

"Oh, what's wrong?" Anastasia asked with genuine concern.

"I'm not sure." He answered as if in a fog, staring at nothing. He had already decided not to tell her about his father's change of heart about their relationship, but he did need to tell her something. "He says he's tired. He's left work early two days in a row now. He did look sick to me today, so I stopped at the house to check on him. He was sleeping. Anthony said he's been drinking too much. There were several empty bottles in the garbage." He shook his head absently. "I just don't know. It's not like him to drink alone, especially enough to make himself so sick." The concern in his eyes made Anastasia forget her own dilemma. She patted Mark's hand and stood up to bring their dinner to the table.

Mark looked up at her from his seat and forced a smile. "So, how was your day?"

"Good. Jim told me he and Julia are looking for a new house together."

"I thought he already had a house?"

Anastasia walked to the cabinets for bowls. "Julia has finally convinced him he needs to get out of that house and buy one that would be theirs together. I agree." To that, Mark quietly nodded his head unwilling to get involved in the discussion.

She filled both of their bowls with stew and began tearing a new loaf a french bread apart. She then buttered a piece for both of them.

"You know," Anastasia started cautiously. "Since you've been living here, I think I've gained weight. I'm not used to eating regular meals like this." She smiled. Mark was beginning to sense she was leading into something more serious. He looked down at his stew, not anxious for another serious discussion. Anastasia watched his tired look and wondered if she should put off the news. She went to the refrigerator carrying her glass. "Do you want anything to drink?"

"No."

She sat back down and began eating slowly. Mark tried to ignore his suspicions, but found himself glancing over at her solemn profile. "Okay, what's wrong?" He asked in a defeated voice.

Anastasia looked over at him, stirring her stew unconsciously. She didn't know how to begin. Now Mark was convinced there was something very wrong. He set his spoon down and stared into her face. Patiently he waited for an answer. Finally, not knowing how else to say it, she simply blurted out, "I'm pregnant."

Mark's expression changed to one of shock, but his body maintained the same position. His eyes were quietly fixed on Anastasia, as though she still hadn't answered. She immediately became worried. Mark had failed to react, except for the look of shock. Had he heard her? She said it again. "I'm pregnant."

He suddenly realized he needed to respond. He shook the astonishment out of his head and sat back. The news had completely taken him off guard. The concern for his father had so preoccupied his mind that he was in no way prepared for such a shock. He looked with confusion at Anastasia. "I thought you were taking pills?"

Anastasia plunged into a state of remorse. She wasn't prepared for his reaction. He didn't look at all happy. "I was," she answered defensively. "They just didn't work!"

"How do you know? Are you sure?"

"I haven't been to a doctor, but I have all the symptoms." She hung her head, looking sadly into her bowl.

Mark wiped his face with his hand nervously, then reached over and rubbed her shoulder. "I'm sorry if I sound upset about it, it's just such a shock. I wasn't expecting it."

Anastasia kept looking down, not wanting him to see the tears of disappointment building up in her eyes. "It's okay," she mumbled. "I'm not very far along. I'll make an appointment."

Mark softened, unsure of what she was trying to say. He moved closer. "For the doctor?"

She nodded, quickly wiping a tear away as it slid down her cheek. Mark still felt confused. "Do you need money?"

She wiped at another tear. With her head still bowed, she nodded. "200 dollars."

Mark gasped. "What? Just for a test?"

She glanced at him with her red, tear filled eyes, and then moved her eyes back down in shame. "For everything." She answered with a bit of anger in her voice.

Mark jumped up and squatted down next to her chair, he placed his hand on her cheek and forced her to look him in the eyes.

"What do you mean, everything?"

Anastasia didn't want to say the word. "For the procedure." She choked weakly.

Mark's eyes took on a sharp look of comprehension. Now he was staring back at her with a sober look that seemed almost angry. "You want an abortion?"

Anastasia pulled away, embarrassed to look him in the eye. "What do you want me to do?" She didn't want to see him answer. She didn't want to face him if he said he did.

Mark stood up and walked nervously behind his chair. His father's words slipped through his mind. Then he looked at Anastasia, who was now sobbing quietly. Without thinking, he instinctively moved behind her and wrapped his arms around her, kissing her neck.

Then, from his heart, he whispered, "I want us to be married as soon as possible."

Anastasia let out a loud sob and hugged his arms tightly. It was exactly what she was wanting to hear, but not daring to hope for.

It was decided they would meet for lunch like usual the next afternoon, but go to Mark's doctor instead. They wanted to get blood tests done so they could apply for a marriage license.

When Mark arrived at work the next morning, he was surprised to find that his father hadn't gotten out of bed. Anthony had driven himself to work. This worried Mark, but did allow him to avoid telling his father the news. He decided not to tell anyone. If Anastasia wanted Stella to know, then he'd let her do the honor of telling her. He simply informed his cousin he would be taking a long lunch that afternoon.

Anastasia didn't mention their plans to anyone at the print shop, either. She only told Jack she needed the afternoon off. His response was a shrug. "Sure." Everyone was used to seeing her leave for lunch every afternoon with Mark, so no one thought anything was out of the ordinary. They left quietly in Mark's car, heading toward his doctor's office on the other side of town.

"Do you think there'll be any problem with us not having an appointment?"

Mark made a face as he drove. "No, I never have an appointment."

Anastasia wanted to ask something, but was uncomfortable. "Mark?" She waited for him to answer. "What if the tests came back and I'm not pregnant?"

This was something he hadn't had time to consider. He looked at her blankly. "Would you still want to get married?"

Anastasia thought she could sense that he would still want to, but her emotions were so out of whack, she was afraid her own hopes were clouding her senses. "Would you?" She asked, feeling as though she might cry again.

Mark could tell she was getting emotional. he looked at her, wondering if it was because she was pregnant. Then he patted her leg reassuringly. "Yes."

Anastasia let out a breath she had been holding. Mark felt the tension escape her. "So, let's just do it. You don't need the pregnancy test if you don't want to. Then we can just tell people we eloped and didn't know you were even pregnant. How about that?" He winked at her. Anastasia was still having problems getting a grip on her emotions. She wiped a tear from her cheek and nodded in agreement.

Then a thought occurred to her. "Did you say anything to your father at work today?"

"He's still sick. He didn't come in." He left the subject at that, not wanting Anastasia to have any ideas about the last conversation he'd had with his father.

There were only a few people in the waiting room. Mark signed them in and they had a seat. A few minutes later, the doctor read Mark Mattiolli on the check in list. Then he opened the door and looked around the almost empty waiting room.

"Young Mario," shouted the elderly physician. "It's good to see you! When did you get back to the states?"

"Just last summer. I think I'm going to stay this time." He motioned to Anastasia. "Anastasia, this is another of my father's friends, Dr. Thomas." Addressing the doctor, he introduced Anastasia. "This is my fiancee'. We are here for blood tests."

The doctor made a surprised sound and walked across the room to shake Anastasia's hand. "This is wonderful! I know your father must be pleased." Mark only smiled, but didn't answer. "And such a beautiful bride. Are you from this area?" He asked kindly.

"Yes, born and raised."

"Well, that's great." He looked back at the clipboard in his hand. "Just one more patient in front of you. It won't be too long of a wait. Your father will be happy about this, won't he?"

"Yes. I'm sure he will," Mark answered.

Anastasia could see the lie. As soon as the doctor was out of sight, she asked. "Why doesn't he want us to get married?" Mark knew he was caught, but still didn't want her to know the truth.

"He's old fashioned. I know he would want us to get

married in the church." He lied again, but with enough conviction that Anastasia was put at ease.

"Maybe we could have another ceremony after I take those classes," she offered.

"That's a good idea."

Soon, Dr. Thomas called their names and led them into separate examination rooms. Anastasia was embarrassed to find out that part of the requirements for the marriage license involved a pelvic exam. This was only the second time she had to endure this type of indignity, and it was especially embarrassing knowing Mark was old friends with the doctor. Happily, Dr. Thomas was quick and professional. Anastasia decided she liked this man. Still, she didn't ask for a pregnancy test. She already knew she was pregnant.

They met in the lobby and drove the paperwork to the courthouse downtown. Once they found the right counter, they stood in line together, anxious with excitement over this important step they were taking.

After quietly thinking to himself as they were standing in line, Mark explained to Anastasia about a bed and breakfast he had heard about outside of town in the country. "If you want, we could take a long weekend and drive there. I'm sure there would be someplace nearby where we could get married, and then spend our wedding night at the Inn. How does that sound?"

Anastasia sighed. "That sounds wonderful. You mean this weekend?" She was a little caught up in the whirlwind pace their romance had taken on.

Mark shrugged. "Why not? The sooner the better. It would be better for the baby." He whispered the last part. Anastasia smiled with a new exuberance. The baby! She was going to have a baby. Soon she was going to be a respectable wife and mother. She suddenly felt as though she might burst with happiness. Life is wonderful, she thought to herself.

"So, what do you think?" Mark nudged her again, bringing her back to Earth.

"Oh, Mark, it sounds great. Let's do it."

He reached over and kissed her just before the clerk called them to the next window.

Once they had the license in their hands, Mark dropped her off at the apartment and drove back to work. Anastasia made herself a sandwich. Looking around the apartment, she realized she was just too excited to stay there. She decided to go shopping for a new outfit for the ceremony.

There was an empty knotted feeling in Mario Mattioli's stomach. He sat alone at his kitchen table, staring at a plate of toast. He was trying to convince himself to eat some of the toasted bread. He needed something bland in his stomach, something to comfort his middle and help to cause his headache to go away. He held his head with one hand and slowly inserted the toast in his mouth with the other. Chewing was almost painful.

He tried to refocus his mind on the problem at hand. His son, had already grown to love Anastasia, but this unholy union must be undone. But to tell his son the truth about his mother after all these years, how could he do it? How could he explain that the vicious witch of a woman was his mother? There had to be another way. Then a thought occurred to him. What if he spoke to Anastasia? What if he explained it to her? Did she love his son enough to leave him without explanation? Then another realization hit him. She would have to know anyway. Why not explain things to her first? Maybe he could convince her to leave Mark quietly, and if she didn't, he would still be spared the pain of telling his son.

He ate half a slice of toast, gathered his hat and coat, and went out the door. He knew Anastasia worked at Lowe's Print Shop. He intended to catch her before she left work.

The weather had turn bitter cold and he was without a car. Without considering the biting wind and the near zero temperature, he trudged steadily toward the downtown area where the print shop was located. He was disappointed when he found she had left work early. Without hesitation, he stepped back out into the cold, gathered the front of his tattered wool coat, and headed for her apartment.

When he arrived, he realized how tired and cold he was. He looked wearily up the steep set of stairs that led to her upstairs apartment. He grasped the hand rail and began the slow ascent. He was only a quarter of the way up when he notice his heart racing. He stopped to catch his breath. After a few more steps, he stopped again. It was several minutes before he reached the top, only to find the apartment empty. He banged on the door several times. He hoped in vain for an answer that never came. He was so sick and exhausted he sat down on the landing, leaning against the stairwell. He waited there until his breathing became normal and the tightening in his chest eased up. Sadly, he stood up and began his decent. He had to stop several times because he felt dizzy and nauseated. Eventually, he made it to the front door. He gritted his teeth and gripped the front of his coat together, trying to keep the biting wind from ripping it off him as he headed for home with a defeated feeling inside.

In a hospital bed not too far away, a terminally ill woman smiled victoriously.

CHAPTER 23

Thursday morning, when Mark found out his father was still home sick, he had a serious talk with Anthony. He asked Anthony if he knew why his father was acting so peculiar lately.

"I don't know, cousin." Anthony spoke in his native tongue. "Your father is sick. He doesn't want to get up in the mornings, and he stays up late and drinks too much wine. I hear him sometimes in his room, but I'm not sure what he's doing." Then, with sober eyes, he looked up at Mark. "It sounds like he's crying."

Mark could only stand there mutely. He knew that somehow he was the one who was causing his father this pain. But, his love for Anastasia pulled at him. How could his father ask him to abandon his only true love, without an explanation? Surely he didn't want his son to remain single all his life? What could have changed his feelings for Anastasia so much? Then he realized Anthony was still staring at him, waiting for a response. Mark had none that he could give. He just patted his cousin on the shoulder and thanked him for the information. He never mentioned the last discussion he had with his father.

That afternoon, Mark put on a false face as he listened to Anastasia talking excitedly about her shopping trip. She relayed to him the information she had gathered about the bed and breakfast he had told her to call about. She had made the preliminary arrangements over the phone that day at work. Mark reached into his pocket and handed her a credit card to use for payment. She accepted the card, then looked at him seriously. She could sense there was something bothering him. Her excitement had temporarily blinded her.

Mark knew he had to be truthful with her, or she'd know he was lying. He down played the situation with his father. "I'm just worried. He is still ill. I'm going to visit him after I drop you off at work."

Anastasia was worried his illness might cause a snag in their plans, but then she felt immediately guilty. "Do you want me to go, too?" Mark thanked her for the concern, but assured her he was probably worried over nothing. After all, everyone gets sick occasionally.

They finished their lunch together earlier than usual. He dropped her off at work and headed for his father's home.

The front door was locked. He tried knocking, but there was no response. He used his key to unlock the door and called out softly for his father. No one answered. The television was off and the front room was in disarray. An empty wine bottle laid beside his easy chair, along with the brown paper bag he carried it out of the store with. He noticed some old picture albums stacked on the floor on the opposite side of the chair. He immediately recognized the albums that were filled with photos of himself growing up in Italy. His Aunt took his picture regularly and mailed them to the states. His father would tuck them securely into the albums. He passed by this and into the hall. He called out occasionally, but got no response. He looked into the kitchen and moved down the hall, rapping on the bathroom door as he passed it. Finally, he made his way up the stairs. He went straight to his father's room. The door was shut. He rapped on it gently, calling out softly. There was no response. He opened up the door. Immediately, he could smell sickness. He saw his father laying naked on his bed with the blankets in bunches under and around him.

Mark ran to his father's side. When he stepped closer he could see the sweat gleaming on his father's face. His hair was wet. His mouth was hanging open wide, and he seemed to be laboring hard for each breath. Mark didn't like the unnatural color of his skin, either. He pulled at one of the blankets and then threw it over his father. He laid his hand on the old man's forehead. It was very hot. Mark squatted beside the bed and put his hand on his father's shoulder and shook it gently. "Papa," he called. The old man just tossed his head, breathing noisily. "Papa, wake up!" Mark shook him with more vigor and called louder, with mounting panic in his voice. "Papa, it's Mario!"

At that, the old man moved his lips. He attempted to repeat his son's name. His brows furrowed and his face took on a look of confusion. "Papa, wake up! I want to talk to you."

Slowly, Mario managed to open his eyes. He blinked, then strained to move his head to face his son. "Mario," he gasped.

Mark smoothed the few stands of sweat soaked hair away from his father's face. "Papa, I think you need to see the doctor. Maybe I should drive you to the hospital. You are very ill." Mario made a sound of disagreement and smiled at his son weakly. Then he turned his head to the side and fell back to unconsciousness. Mark stood up in a panic. He looked around the room. It was in a shambles. Dirty clothes were all over the floor, and another empty wine bottle was laying next to the bed. Then his eyes fell on something else, another photo album. This one was different than the others in the living room. He didn't recognize it. It was padded with white cloth and had lace around the edges. He stooped down and picked it up. It looked like a wedding album. He flipped open the cover. On the first page was an image of his father, only younger, thinner, and with a full head of hair. Beside him was a young woman. Mark pulled the book closer to his face. She looked amazingly like Anastasia. She was wearing a white dress that reached her knees and a white veil was pulled back to reveal her face. Long tresses of blond hair fell to her shoulders and her eyes were a radiant blue. Mark realized this beautiful woman must have been his own mother! This was their wedding picture. He flipped another page. There was a photo of his father and mother again, but with his grandmother standing between them. He recognized her immediately from older photos he had grown up with. The three of them were standing close together with happiness on their faces. The two women were looking down a the bundle in his grandmother's arms. He knew the baby must be himself as a new born. They looked so happy. How he wished he could have known these two women.

His father tossed and threw the blanket off. Mark suddenly remembered he was about to call the doctor. He set the album on the night stand then walked down the hall to the phone on the wall in the kitchen. He called information. Then he dialed the number for doctor Thomas. The doctor agreed to come to the house. Next, Mark called the store and informed Anthony he wouldn't be coming in until he had seen to his father. Anthony quickly offered to stay until closing if necessary.

He walked back downstairs and sat in his father's easy chair, waiting for the doctor's knock. He pondered his father's strange behavior.

After work, Anastasia walked briskly to the hospital to visit her mother. She had decided to tell her the good news. The weather was cold and crisp, but refreshing to the bride-to-be as she happily bounded down the sidewalks. There was a bit of snow here and there, but no real accumulation. She had felt nauseous early that morning, but by late morning, she was feeling even better than usual. She couldn't help thinking about how she was going to be married the next day. Everything had been arranged and paid for with Mark's credit card. They had a two o'clock appointment with the Justice of the Peace.

She was surprised to see the door to her mother's room was ajar. She pushed it slowly the rest of the way open and stepped inside. She pulled it closed behind her. When she walked around the corner, she saw the head of her mother's bed was raised and her mother was wide awake and smiling. Anastasia was filled with a new kind of joy as she rushed to her mother's side and enthusiastically kissed her on the cheek. Her mother's eyes glowed like a cat's in the dark room. She looked thin and weak, but in much better spirits than Anastasia had seen her in a long time.

"Guess what." Anastasia said excitedly.

"What?"

"I haven't told anyone else this," she said. "Mark and I are going to get married at two o'clock tomorrow!" Marilyn looked at her daughter fondly. She had already known this. Anastasia knew her mother could never be surprised, but this game of guess the news that other mortals played was fun, and they were both enjoying it.

"Wonderful! Now maybe I'll see some grandchildren," she said with enthusiasm. She paused to see if her daughter would reveal the rest of her news. Anastasia did contemplate it, but reminded herself she and Mark had decided to wait until after they were married to tell anyone.

Marilyn chuckled and turned her head to the side, closing her eyes. The pain had eased a bit, but now her body felt weak. She thought mildly of how shocked her daughter would be to find out the identity of her husband-to-be's mother. As for herself, she was unconcerned about the dangers associated with a baby born to such a couple. She had inhabited the body of a babe born of incest before.

Anastasia took this gesture from her mother as a sign that she wanted to be left alone now. So, she kissed her again on the cheek and left. Carefully, she closed the door behind her.

Before Marilyn heard the door close, she was already drifting down the hall and moving to a room on another floor of the hospital. She looked fondly at the elderly form of her old lover. The doctors had placed a plastic oxygen tent over his head, but she could see his face though the plastic. Old and pale, Mario was unconscious, but breathing better now.

His only son sat in a chair beside his bed, watching his father's chest move up and down, unaware that Anastasia was just leaving the same building. Curiously, he moved his focus to Marilyn. It was almost as if he could see her hovering over his father's bed. Marilyn blew a kiss to him sweetly. He closed his eyes. She reached out and stroked his hair. When she moved away from him, she noticed a tear in his eye. Odd, she thought. How could he love a mother he never knew.

Mario's condition was serious, but not critical. Doctor Thomas had informed Mark his father was suffering from pneumonia. There seemed to be an irregularity in his heart beat as well, but getting the fluid out of his lungs was paramount.

Mark had talked to the doctor at length. He debated whether he should cancel the plans for the marriage until his father's condition was better. He was struggling with this now as he drove home. They still were without a phone, so he had no way of telling Anastasia where he was. He left the hospital about the time he would normally have left work. His father was still sleeping. He had never regained consciousness.

Earlier, Mark had called Anthony and broken the bad news about his father's illness. Anthony again offered to cover for the two of them for the next workday. Mark hesitated a moment, but never did tell his cousin about the marriage plan. Now he sat in the driver's seat, agonizing over whether he should ask his bride-to-be if they could cancel their plans.

He was greeted at the door by a negligee clad Anastasia. When she wrapped her arms around his neck, he could smell lightly perfumed oil. She felt all soft and satiny in his arms. He held her to his breast for a long time, comforting himself in the crook of her neck. He sighed. How could he break their date for tomorrow? She kissed his mouth, tugging at his top lip with her own. Then she kissed him again and rubbed her tongue against the roof of his mouth. He kneaded her shoulders, surprised by the surge of passion he suddenly felt.

He wrapped his right arm behind her, reached down, and swept his other arm behind her knees, scooping her up into his arms. He carried her to the bed, and laid her down gently. He squeezed her. Crushing her chest with his face while reaching down her leg with his left hand, he found the hem of her nightgown and pulled it up. Still kneeling beside the bed, he leaned over and kissed the inside of her right thigh, then the left. Then he became so filled with passion he quickly pulled off his own clothes. They made love. All thoughts of postponing the wedding were forgotten.

CHAPTER 24

"Where am I?" the old man demanded of the nurse beside his bed.

"Mr. Mattiolli, are you feeling better?" she asked while writing something down on a clipboard.

"What is this? A hospital?" He was trying to pull away the plastic tent over his head.

The nurse gently pulled his hands away and answered. "Yes, your son brought you here yesterday. You have a bad case of pneumonia. It looks like maybe you're feeling better."

Her cheerfulness was a bit of an annoyance. "My son? He brought me here?" He asked gesturing with his hand. Then he saw for the first time that an IV tube was attached to his wrist. "Where is he now?"

The nurse looked contemplative. "I don't believe he's been back here today, but Doctor Thomas is in the building." She added cheerfully.

"Well then, let me talk to him." The nurse continued to make notes on her clip board then smiled politely and left the room.

Mario pulled the plastic tent off his head. He was surprised at how tired the small movements made him. Then he lay back into his pillow and waited for the doctor, straining to breath.

It was nearly noon before the anxious couple pulled up to the bed and breakfast where they had reservations. Anastasia was starved, but was more interested in finding their room so she could change into her new dress.

The inn looked like a large old house that had been refurbished. They pushed open a large wooden door that was round at the top. It reminded Anastasia of a hobbit's hole. An old man standing behind the counter looked up as they entered the lobby. The couple moved to the counter and Mark introduced them as already having reservations.

"Oh, you're the newlyweds." He smiled.

"Well, almost," Mark answered. He looked at the phone at the front desk while the old man leafed through a large book behind the counter. "You have phones in the rooms, don't you?" He wanted to check on his father.

"No, but there's a pay phone." The clerk gestured with his head to an old fashioned booth.

"There haven't been any calls for us, have there?" Mark asked. The man shook his head, still looking in his book.

Anastasia looked at him uneasily. "Do you think we should have postponed this?"

Mark shook his head. "No, he's probably fine. I just want to check on him."

Anastasia continued to look at him in an uneasy way.

Just then the clerk found whatever it was he was looking for in his book and interrupted them. "Here we go. Mr. & Mrs. Mattioli, right?" Anastasia forgot her concerns and smiled, nodding her head in agreement. "Now, could I have one of you sign here and fill this out." He turned the book around for Mark to sign then pushed a form across the counter for him to fill out.

Soon, they were led up a grand circular staircase with polished wood banisters. Anastasia glided her hand up the railings as they ascended. She had never been in such an ornate, fussy place. Her eyes widened as she took in the glossy wooden floors and floral wall paper with the matching floral borders. It could have been a movie setting for some romantic turn of the century film. Anastasia was glad she had chosen a frilly white dress with a gathered waist for the ceremony. It looked old fashioned, like the inn.

The decor of their room was similar, with a different, but complimentary, style of floral wallpaper with matching borders.

The bed was layered with pastel colored blankets and comforters. A ruffled skirt peeked out from under the blankets and the whole thing was topped with more than half a dozen pillows of all shapes, sizes, and colors. The whole thing was sitting on an oval area rug with an oriental pattern. Anastasia impulsively wrapped her arms around Mark's neck and kissed him. The old man simply smiled and quietly backed out of the room.

"Listen to me, Robert. I don't care about my condition, I just want to talk to my son. There is something important I need to speak with him about. Please just dial the store for me and put the phone to my ear." Mario was having difficulty trying to talk and breath at the same time.

Dr. Thomas looked at his old friend, who was also his patient. He had talked with Mark on the phone earlier this morning. He knew Mark was to be married in less than an hour. Mark had also explained to him that he hadn't had the chance to explain his plans to his father before he left. Now the doctor was in the awkward position of not knowing how much to tell his old friend without giving the new couple the opportunity to break the news personally.

"Mario, he's not there," he said flatly.

Mario's face took on a puzzled expression. "Where is he? You know where he's at?"

The doctor looked down nervously then back at his friend. "He and his fiancee' went away for the weekend."

"What?" Mario looked alarmed. "What fiancee'? You mean Anastasia? Where did they go?"

The doctor was now becoming concerned about his patient's condition. He was too excited. His blood pressure was rising. "You need to calm down, Mario. You're not well. Your heart is beating too fast—"

"Tell me where my son is!" He leaned forward in this bed.

Dr. Thomas moved to the side of the bed and rested his hand on Mario's shoulder, pushing him back into his pillow.

"They are staying at a bed and breakfast a couple hours out of town."

"What is the name? I need to call there and talk to him." He shrugged the hand off his shoulder and tried to sit up. The doctor now reached across him and applied both of his hands to Mario's shoulders, trying to push him back into his bed.

"Mario, they're not there now! They have an appointment. He told me he would call here later to check on you."

"Why would my son leave for the weekend when his father is in the hospital? Who is watching the store? And, what do you mean, 'an appointment?'" Mario temporarily gave in, laying back on his pillow, waiting for an explanation.

"I'm sure young Mario took care of everything before he left. And, I know he considered canceling his plans when you got sick, but we knew your condition was not critical. He's not so far away. He didn't want to disappoint that lovely fiancee' of his."

"Why do you keep calling her his fiancee'? How do you know this girl, anyway?"

The two men were very close together. At this point the doctor was sitting on the edge of the bed with his hands still placed on Mario's shoulders. The doctor looked into Mario's eyes and answered in a defeated voice. "I met her when they came into my office for blood tests."

Mario gasped. "What? Why?" Then the light of comprehension burned in his eyes. "Don't tell me they are getting married." He pushed the doctor away.

Dr. Thomas looked up at the nurse, who was already close to calling for an orderly. She nodded at the struggling doctor and poked her head into the hallway, calling for help. The doctor continued to struggle with his patient, who was determined to get out of his bed. Mario was shouting. "You don't understand! I must stop this! Please! Tell Mario, this is *in'tfesto*" Pulling the IVs out of his arms, he nearly had his feet on the floor when two large orderlies entered the room and wrestled him down from both sides of the bed. They pinned him to the mattress. The disheveled doctor moved close to the bed with a syringe. With an apologetic look on his face, he plunged the hypodermic needle into his friend's arm. Within seconds, Mario's writhing body relaxed and he fell into a deep sleep.

Before the doctor could finish checking his patient's vital signs, the phone rang. He picked it up, and it was Mark.

"Dr. Thomas? Lucky I called when I did. How's Papa?"

Dr. Thomas hesitated, not wanting to spoil Mark's day. Still, he felt obligated to give a truthful answer. He looked down at his clip board. "Well, his vital signs where good the last time his nurse checked them. He seems to be recovering quickly. He was conscious earlier, but he's sleeping now."

"Good. Good." Mark sighed. "Now I can get married without my mind being preoccupied. Thank you so much. You are a wonderful doctor. I know you're taking good care of him for me."

Dr. Thomas acknowledged the compliments, but felt a nagging guilt for not being completely honest. Mark said good-bye, and the doctor gave him his best wishes and hung up.

He turned and looked at Mario one last time before he left the room. The nurse was busy reinserting the IV in his arm. He couldn't help but wonder why Mario had become so violent. It wasn't his nature. What was so urgent? What was *in'tfesto*? He was sure the word was Italian, but he didn't understand the language. Then he decided this must be a family affair. Whatever reasons Mario had for not wanting his son to marry Anastasia were personal and none of his business. He turned toward the door and walked out of the room.

The little town only had one traffic light. There was a small block of shops, three churches, and four gas stations. City hall was a small white building opposite the row of shops. They arrived at 1:50. Mark was in a grey suit with a black shirt and tie. Anastasia wore the lacy white dress that came to her knee, with a full skirt gathered at the waist. They made a handsome couple.

Inside the building was simple and void of any ornamentation. A middle-aged clerk worked at a desk on the other side of the counter. She looked up over her reading glasses when the couple entered the room. She stood up and walked to her side of the counter with an inquisitive look on her face. Mark explained they had a two o'clock appointment. The lady frowned and bit her lip. "I'm sorry, but the judge was called away unexpectedly. He had to fill in for Judge Armstrong in Clearwater. I'm not sure when he'll be back."

Their faces fell. They looked at one another disappointedly. "Listen," the remorse clerk said. "Why don't you have coffee across the street, and I'll call you when he gets in."

Anastasia was starved. She nodded her approval at Mark. What else could they do? They left their car in the parking lot and walked across the street. In the center of the block was a restaurant-lounge called "One Eyed Jacks." A pirate with a knife between his teeth and a patch over one eye was painted on the top half of the door. They both chuckled and entered through the heavy wooden door. Inside was dark. It looked more like a neighborhood bar than it did a restaurant. As their eyes adjusted to the abrupt change in lighting, they noticed three stocky regulars in baseball caps on barstools. They were looking at the couple curiously as they walked past. Beyond the bar was half a dozen small round tables with condiments and silverware wrapped tightly in paper napkins.

They looked around for a host or waitress to seat them. Then a booming voice came from behind the bar. "Just sit anywhere. I'll get Rose for ya." The voice belonged to a rough, stubble-faced bartender with long grey hair. He looked a bit like the pirate on the front door. He ducked into a doorway that was behind the bar. Mark and Anastasia took the table farthest from the entrance. Mark instinctively sat with his back to the wall. Soon, a short thin woman with a grubby white apron came through the door the bartender had went though. She looked about fifty, or maybe younger but badly aged. Her brownish-gray hair was pulled up with clearly visible hair pins. She looked tired and annoyed by having to make an appearance.

"What can I get ya?" Rose asked, pulling a pad and pen out of her pocket. "Anything to drink?"

They looked at one another. "What kind of wine do you have?" Mark asked politely. The waitress eyed him suspiciously.

"Where you from?"

Mark swallowed, then put on a friendly smile. "I was born not far from here, in Center City, but moved to Italy when I was a baby."

She nodded her head slowly with comprehension. "Well, we got white, red, and pink."

This answered Mark's question. He now knew better than to order a bottle. "I think we will both like a glass of red." He glanced at Anastasia for approval. He talked slowly, straining to pronounce each word without an accent.

The waitress ran her tongue across her top row of teeth as she wrote on a pad. "You gonna eat?"

Anastasia wanted to say yes. Mark remembered her remarking about being hungry on the way to the city hall. "I guess so. We are waiting for a call from the judge. The clerk said she would call us here."

Rose peered at them while sucking something out from between her teeth. "I don't believe he's gonna be back for awhile. He's fillin' in for Judge Armstrong in Clearwater."

The couple were both surprised the waitress had this information, but only looked back at her mutely. "I'll go get the menus," she muttered as she turned and walked away.

She returned a few minutes later with their drinks and two laminated one page menus under her arm. Luckily, Anastasia was having a craving for a hamburger, because that was probably the safest choice on the menu. The waitress stood poised with a pen in one hand and the pad in the other. She leaned on her right leg with her hip in the air. They quickly skimmed through the short list of items and gave her their orders. When she walked out of ear shot, they couldn't help but cover their mouths and laugh quietly.

At first they took their situation lightly. But slowly, as

they ate their burgers and sipped their second glasses of wine, they both began to worry that the ceremony wasn't going to happen. Mark glanced at a clock behind the bar. It was after three o'clock. "Let's get dessert."

The waitress made a face when Mark waved her over. "I'm sorry," he apologized. "But do you have pie?" He asked meekly.

She took a deep breath. "Yeah, apple."

Anastasia nodded at Mark. "Two, please."

The waitress wrote on her pad once more then disappeared into the kitchen. She reemerged shortly with their pie. "So, what do you want to see the judge about, anyway?"

"We were supposed to get married. I hope he gets back soon."

She stared thoughtfully toward the clock on the back wall, then shook her head doubtfully. "If he ain't back by four thirty, he ain't gonna come back."

Anastasia's face fell into a frown as she looked sadly at her apple pie. Mark felt obligated to say something uplifting. "Don't worry, Anastasia. If he doesn't make it back here today, we'll come back tomorrow."

Anastasia looked up at him with glassy eyes. "Tomorrow's Saturday. He won't be here tomorrow."

Mark looked at her with determination. "Well then, we'll find a minister or someone else!"

They sat silently eating their pie. Mark kept having flashes of his father telling him not to get married. He wondered mildly if this problem was a sign. Then he quickly put the negative thoughts out of his mind. He remembered seeing a phone near the door and wondered if his father might be awake by now. They ordered more wine. They had drank all of the red and white, so now they were drinking the pink. It was good neither of them were wine snobs. Finally, Mark looked up at the clock. It was almost four. He stood up and announced to Anastasia that he had to use the toilet and wanted to check on his father with a phone call. She nodded silently.

Anastasia gloomily watched him walk away. The day had started out so happy. Why wasn't the judge there for their appointment? Was it an omen? She was on the verge of tears when she noticed the waitress standing near her. She looked up with tear filled eyes at the rough looking bar maid. Surprisingly, Rose was looking back at her with what appeared to be compassion. She refilled their glasses from a one gallon glass container. Then she sat the bottle on the table and looked directly into Anastasia's eyes.

"So, why do you want to marry that foreigner for anyway?"

Anastasia's emotions were so out of kilter from being pregnant and the delay in getting married that she couldn't tell if the waitress was attempting to be funny, concerned, or just hateful. All she could do was burst into tears and speak straight from her heart. "Because I love him," she sobbed.

The waitress' face went soft. Her painted on eyebrows raised even higher. "Well, if you've got your heart set on marryin' this guy today, I'll just get a hold of the mayor. He'll do it for ya."

Anastasia's heart leaped. "You know the mayor?"

"Sure, everybody does." She turned and walked back toward the bar and shouted to the bartender. "Hank! Git your brother over here. Those two want to get married today!" To Anastasia's astonishment, the greasy haired bartender immediately picked up a phone behind the counter and started dialing.

Mark was just stepping up to the pay phone, unaware of the conversation between Anastasia and Rose. He picked up the receiver and dialed the number of the hospital from a piece of paper he had stuffed in his wallet. He asked for his father's room. The phone rang several times. Finally, a nurse answered. "Hello, this is Mark Mattiolli, is my father awake?"

There was a short pause on the other end. "No, sir, we don't expect him to wake up until late this evening at the earliest. The injection the doctor gave him was pretty strong. He'll be sleeping for a while."

"Injection?" Mark asked.

"Yes, the doctor had to give him a strong sedative to calm him down. It took two big orderlies to hold him. He's quite a fighter." She chuckled just a bit, and then realized Mark wasn't laughing or even responding to what she had said. "You know about this afternoon don't you?"

"No, what happened."

She was worried she might have violated her patient's privacy. "He was struggling with the doctor this afternoon, right after he came to, and the doctor had to sedate him."

"Let me talk to the doctor," Mark demanded.

The nurse swallowed. "He's not here now. Would you like me to get a hold of him and have him call you?"

"Yes, immediately. Tell him to call 'One Eyed Jacks' in Devyn. I'll be here, or at my hotel. He knows the number." He hung up the phone abruptly, angry at the doctor for not being truthful with him.

He was half way to the table before he noticed the cheerful expression on Anastasia's face. "Mark," she exclaimed. "You won't believe this, but the mayor of Devyn is the bartender's brother. He's coming here to marry us!"

Mark was dumbfounded. "Are you serious?"

"Yes! The bartender's talking to him on the phone right now." Mark turned to see Hank talking into the telephone behind the bar. He quickly forgot his anger and decided not to tell Anastasia the latest news about his father.

They waited and watched anxiously as the bartender hung up the phone and motioned for Mark to come to the counter. He walked across the floor briskly, then leaned against the counter toward the burly bartender.

"My brother said he'd be out here as soon as he finished dinner. Probably less than an hour." Mark sighed with relief, then looked at the bartender with appreciation. He stuck his hand out politely. The bartender took it reluctantly. "Thank you so much," he said with deep gratitude. The bartender looked a bit embarrassed, then nodded and turned away. Mark moved quickly back to the table and informed his bride-to-be the ceremony would indeed still take place that day. They both relaxed and soon were engaged in a lively conversation about their plans for the future as man and wife.

Mayor Piggett was an interesting character with short grey hair and a round, chubby face that went with his round, chubby belly. Wearing a winter cap and scarf, he reminded Anastasia of a snowman. He hung his coat, hat, and scarf on a hook near the door. He acted quite at home. It was easy to see he was a regular visitor. The two men who were at the bar when Mark and Anastasia came in were still sitting on the same bar stools. They were still drinking beer and watching a small television hanging from the ceiling. Both men waved and grunted at the mayor as he came in.

Mark stood up and walked toward the man. No one had introduced them yet, but both Anastasia and Mark were confident this was the man they were waiting on to perform the marriage ceremony.

The mayor was in a conversation with his brother, who nodded to Mark as he approached. The mayor turned and looked Mark over, leaning against the bar. As Mark reached him the mayor stuck out his hand and introduced himself. "Mayor Piggett, here. My brother tells me you want to get married?"

Mark nodded his head. "Yes sir, if you would."

"Well let tell me you, son. First off, I charge fifty dollars for the service and another fifty for workin' after hours."

Mark nodded again in agreement. "That will be just fine."

"And you got cash, I hope." Mayor Piggett was pulling reading glassed out of his shirt pocket.

"Yes, I do." Mark reached into this back pocket for his wallet. He noticed the mayor and his bartender brother both leaning forward to see inside his wallet as well. He pulled out two fifty dollar bills and handed them to the mayor. Then he pulled out an envelope with the unsigned marriage license and handed it to the mayor as well.

"Okay, it seems everything is in order." The mayor counted the money and put it into his pocket. Then he opened the envelope and examined the license through his reading glasses. "Do you have a ring?" The two men watched carefully as Mark reached into his pants pocket again and produced a small box. He turned his back so Anastasia couldn't see what he had. Then he revealed to the anxious brothers the diamond ring. They both frowned with appreciation and glanced at each other. Now the other two men on the bar stools as well as Rose the waitress were straining to look.

Anastasia bobbed her head around, trying to see what was going on. She was still sitting at the table. She and Mark had briefly discussed rings, and had decided to wait until they were settled in a larger apartment before spending the money on unnecessary things like wedding rings. However, she was suspicious maybe he had other plans. Now she was pretty sure everyone wasn't crowding around her husband-to-be just to look at the marriage license. This was so exciting, she thought. Never would there be another moment quite like it again.

Mark took the ring out of the box and carefully put it into his shirt pocket. "So, where are you going to preform the ceremony?" Mark asked.

"Well, right here. I suppose. I'm sure not gonna go back out into that cold again, unless you wantta pay me double."

Mark shook his head. "No, this is fine. I'll get Anastasia." He turned and walked back to the table, leaving the mayor as his brother was handing him a mug of beer.

He looked seriously at Anastasia as he approached with an apologetic arm around her shoulders. "I'm sorry Anastasia, but this isn't going to be like we had planned..."

"Oh, it's better," she said with a smile. "Just think of the story we can tell our son when he grows up. This is going to be a very memorable ceremony."

He brightened and kissed her once on the lips as she rose from her seat. It wasn't until they were walking back toward the bar he realized she had said, “our son.” This made him give her a little squeeze.

“You’re gonna need two witnesses.” The mayor began, taking a long drink from his mug. “Rose, here, says she’ll sign for ya, and my brother, can be your other witness, if that’s okay.”

Mark looked at Anastasia for confirmation before he nodded his agreement. Rose wiped her hands on her apron and took her place beside Anastasia. Hank the bartender came out from behind the bar and stood beside Mark. The mayor sighed, set his beer on the counter, and cleared his throat.

“We are gathered here today to witness the marriage of—” He pulled out the license and searched for their names. “Mario Matt— i— how the hell do you pronounce this?”

“Mattiolli,” Mark offered politely.

The Mayor glanced up at him over the license. “Mattiolli and Anna — what?”

“Anastasia,” he offered again.

“Anastasia MacDouglas. MacDouglas, now there’s a proper name.” He pulled a small book out of his vest pocket and began reading. “We are here to join these two young people in holy matrimony by the power vested in me as Mayor of Devyn, in the state of New York. Do you, Anastasia, take this man to be your husband?” He looked up at her over his reading glasses.

She looked into Mark’s eyes and answered, “I do.”

Just then, the phone began ringing. Hank looked around nervously as though he wanted to answer it. It rang again. The Mayor turned his head in annoyance to one of the regulars who were both watching the ceremony with interest. “Pete, will you get that? Tell ‘em Hank’ll call back.”

Mark watched the man reach over the counter and grab the phone. He wondered if it might be the doctor. Then the Mayor interrupted his thoughts by asking, “Will you, Mario, take this woman to be your wife?”

Mark refocused his attention to Anastasia. Looking her in the eyes he answered, “yes I do.” He then turned back to face the Mayor and noticed Pete waving at him.

"It's for you," the man whispered holding the phone to his ear and using his other hand to point at the handset.

The Mayor turned a stern eye at Pete and shouted, "Tell whoever it is he'll call back. Can't you see we're in the middle of a sacred ceremony here?" Mark was suppressing an impulse to interrupt the service to take the call. He was a bit relieved the mayor had taken the option away.

"Now, hand over that fancy ring!"

To Anastasia's delight, Mark reached into his pocket and produced a thick, gold wedding band. It was decorated with a cluster of diamonds. She gasped and squeezed Mark's arm. He savored the look on her face as he passed the ring on to the mayor.

"This must of set you back a pretty penny," the mayor remarked as he turned the ring between his fingers. "This continuous circle of gold is a symbol of Mario's never ending love for Anastasia." He looked it over again as though he was reluctant to give it back. Then he handed it to Mark. "Put it on her left hand," he instructed gruffly. Mark took the ring in his right hand. Then he reached for Anastasia's hand with the left, holding it tenderly. He carefully slipped the ring onto her finger. Without knowing her ring size, he seemed to have guessed well. The ring slipped over her knuckle easily and felt secure on her finger. Anastasia looked down at it solemnly. She was thinking to herself about how Mark had placed this ring of gold onto her hand. Now she would never allow it to be removed.

"I now pronounce you man and wife," the mayor announced quickly, slamming the little book shut and placing it back into his vest. "You can kiss the bride now."

First Mark kissed her lightly on the lips. Then Anastasia threw her arms around his neck and kissed him passionately, hugging him so tightly she had to stand on her toes. She never would've known just a few months ago how happy this ceremony would make her. Now they were married. Now the child she was carrying would make them a family.

There was a fuzzy feeling in his head. He wasn't sure where he was at first, but slowly it all came back to him. He looked over to his left, at a window. There was only a crack between the two halves of the drapes, but through it he could see only blackness. He gazed straight up at the ceiling remembering with a defeated feeling what the doctor had told him. They were to be married at two o'clock. Surely, the ceremony was long ago completed. The room was dark and empty. He could see a light coming from an open door beyond the foot of his bed. He couldn't detect any sounds from the hallway, so he guessed the hour must have been late.

He lay silently, agonizing over the events that led up to his current predicament. How could he let it happen? How could he have buried his head in the sand all the years, not telling anyone about Maria, especially his own son? All he had wanted was to protect him, and spare him from knowing his mother was a wicked, murderous woman. He couldn't bear thinking his innocent son might grow up feeling he had this evil inside of him. Father Roberto was the only one he had confided in. At the time, he agreed with him that his son should never know the terrible truth. Mario pondered the conversations he had long ago with the priest. Had this man of God been wrong, too? What were the chances his son would fall in love with his own sister? How did they meet? Then a thought occurred to him. Was Maria somehow responsible for this?

He sighed, remembering the image of her, beautiful and young, nursing their son as she rocked him. Then he recalled seeing her in that damp basement. He was covered with dirt from digging a hole with his bare hands. He remembered the strange feeling he had holding the weapon responsible for his mother's murder. He could still see Maria running down the steps, holding their infant son in her arms, trying to convince him she had nothing to do with his mother's death. Now this same woman lay in a bed dying. In fact, he thought, she was in this same building with him.

He pondered this for a moment. Then, with angry conviction, he decided he needed to put these questions to the person responsible for his torment. He decided to visit with the woman now calling herself Marilyn.

"Can you say that again?" Mark asked the doctor while cupping his hand over his other ear. Subconsciously, he thought this might cause the doctor's words to be more clear.

"I'm sorry I don't understand Italian, but it sounded like, *in'festo*."

Mark concentrated, trying to think of all the possible words the doctor was trying to repeat. "Could it have been i*n'tferto*?"

"I'm sorry, Mark. I'm just not sure. I guess you'll just have to talk to him yourself. I hope I didn't cause you any grief by not being totally honest, but I didn't want to ruin your honeymoon. I promise you, his health is much improved. I really don't know why he had such an outburst. I just thought it must be some kind of family matter you already knew about."

"That's alright." Mark sighed. "I'll talk to you when I get back, unless his condition changes. Then I want you to call me immediately."

"I will," the doctor promised.

After he hung up, Mark continued to sit on the stool in the old fashioned pay phone in the lobby. He was mentally running though a list of words that could have been the one his father had asked the doctor to relay back to him. The only one that seemed to fit was *incesto*. This meant incest. How could this be? Surely, this couldn't be the word his father had used. He knew his father's family was in Italy. His mother had died an orphan. How could his father know who her relatives were when she didn't know herself? No, he told himself. The doctor must be mistaken. He must be pronouncing the word wrong. Maybe it was *incerto*. This meant uncertain or doubtful. Why had his father become so cynical about their union? Mark shook the worry from his head and stood up. His new bride was waiting for him upstairs.

A thick gloom seemed to emanate from her room and into the hallway. Even the lighting grew dimmer as he approached. He suddenly felt weary and overwhelmed, but he had to push himself. He had to confront his mother's killer.

He leaned against the door frame for a moment. He gathered his strength before he opened the door. Inside was total darkness. The blinds and drapery were closed, not even allowing the light of the moon or stars to enter. When his eyes adjusted, he turned to where her bed should be. Curtains were pulled completely around it. He entered quietly, silently pulling at the curtains to expose her bed. There she lay, as if dead. Her body was covered to her chest with a white hospital blanket. Her arms lay straight at her sides with IVs in each wrist. Her eyes were closed and sunk into her white, sagging skin. He remembered how beautiful she once was. Now she looked as though her body was an empty vessel, completely used up.

He stepped to the side of her bed, leaving the door open for the dim light to enter. He wanted to reach over and touch her, to wake her, but his hands wouldn't obey him. He stood with his arms resting on the bed railing, staring at her lifeless body.

Suddenly, her body jerked to life. It was as though a shock wave had shot through it. Mario watched with suspicion and fear. Her eyes jerked open with a surprised look that lasted only a moment before narrowing and moving to the side to focus on the terrified old man.

"Nice to see you again. You forgot to say good-bye the last time."

Mario began to tremble. His voice was gone.

"So, what have you come here to discuss?" she asked.

Mario slapped his hand over his mouth, pulling at his lips and rubbing his face. He was trying to massage life back into his being. He swallowed hard and forced himself to take his eyes off the old hag so he could compose himself. Finally, his voice returned in a hoarse squeak. "Why? How could you do this to our son?"

"Why, my darling husband, what are you referring to?"

Mario choked. "You know! Somehow you arranged for them to meet, didn't you?"

She chuckled. "Why, they're not properly related. We were never properly married. Besides, his mother is dead, isn't she?" Marilyn made a shrill laughing sound.

"Well, I am glad you find this amusing." Mario shouted with anger. "We cannot let these two marry. They are brother and sister." He finished in a hushed voice.

"I believe they are already married," she interrupted quietly.

Mario sighed deeply. "Yes. This is probably so, but we have to tell them."

"Why?"

"What do you mean, 'why?' Because they cannot stay married. They cannot have children!"

"Again, my dear Mario," she said quietly. "I believe you're too late."

Mario froze, with an alarmed expression on his face. He stared wide-eyed at his former wife. "What do you mean? She's not pregnant."

Marilyn nodded her head with a victorious smile on her lips. "You will soon have a grandchild."

Mario let out a kind of silent scream, grabbing his chest and bending over in the middle. Marilyn stopped smiling and carefully listened. Even in her wicked heart, she worried she might have inflicted a fatal injury to this man she loved. He sat himself on the floor, with his legs in front of him, knees bent. He leaned forward, holding his chest, and gasped for breath.

Marilyn closed her eyes. She visualized the man on the floor. She placed her hands on his heart and massaged it gently, squeezing and loosening her grip in a regular rhythm. She could feel his tension. She moved her head next to his and pressed her chin into his shoulder, using it to caress and loosen his tense muscles. Slowly, she felt him sigh and begin to breath in a regular, steady pace.

When he finally became aware of himself again, he realized he was sitting on the floor in Marilyn's hospital room. He gripped the railing on her bed to pull himself up. There she was, slowly opening her eyes again staring at him like a cold fish. He looked away. He tried to remember how it was he found himself on the floor. Then he heard her words again in his head. Anastasia was pregnant by her own brother. He took in a deep breath and tried to steady himself. Whatever happened had taken the energy out of him. He felt dizzy. He slowly moved his eyes back to Marilyn's still body.

"What have you told them?"

"Nothing," she stated flatly.

"Your new husband. What does he know?"

"Nothing! No one even knows about my first son. There was never a reason to tell anyone, so I didn't."

Mario looked at her curiously. What kind of person was this? The memory of his mother's death entered his mind, but he put it away. There were matters of the living to attend to at the moment. "Then we are the only ones who know?"

"Yes." She narrowed her eyes and looked at him passionately. "Why do we need to tell them at all?" Mario listened to her silently. "You have told your son his mother was dead. When he finds out you've lied all these years, he will hate you. When he finds out how he has to give up the love of his life and kill their unborn baby, it will kill his soul. He will never recover from it."

"But the child!" Mario leaned closer to her. "Children born of these types of unions are idiots."

"Not always," Marilyn corrected. "The fact is, there is already incest in our son's blood! It happened often in the olden times!"

Mario stared at her, wide eyed. His mind was racing. He averted his gaze from her and ran his fingers through his hair. He knew full well what she said was true. His only son would never recover and never love him again. This would kill his soul as well. He was a lonely old man, too close to death to be so all alone. Tears filled his eyes, and a sob broke his lips. He turned and moved toward the dim light that fell from the doorway and returned to his own hospital bed.

Mark bound up the staircase with enthusiasm, putting all unpleasant thoughts out of his head and thinking only of Anastasia. He knocked on their door lightly before he pushed it open. He found his new bride sitting in front of the vanity, combing her hair. She was wearing the same white negligee she wore once before, but this time she was still wearing the white hose she had on for the ceremony. She didn't seem to be wearing anything else.

He smiled at her, walking to meet her in the center of their room. She was glowing. Mark wondered absently if it was from the ceremony or because she was pregnant. In any case, it suited her well. They embraced, kissing passionately for at least a full minute before he swept her up in his arms and lowered her onto the bed.

He ran his hands across the silky stockings, pushing up her nighty. At the top, he found the elastic garters that held them up. She purred as, he bent over her, unable to resist kissing the inside of her satiny thigh. He nibbled on her gently, just barely pinching her skin between his teeth. Then he thrust his hands farther up her negligee and kneaded her breasts, one in each hand. She moaned and began pulling at the back of his shirt, managing to pull it over his head without unbuttoning it.

There he was, above her with his thick grove of black curling hair that rolled over the mountains and valleys of his chest. She tangled her fingers in the hair, pinching his nipples just before he crushed himself against her. Running her hands down his back, she pushed her fingers into his pants, squeezing the cheeks of his buttocks. It was easy to push the unfastened pants down enough to expose his penis. She maneuvered his firm manhood inside her, while he kissed her neck and chest passionately. They made love with more intensity then ever before. Rolling entangled in each others arms. Joining and forming one person with three souls. Lovers now converted into husband, wife and child.

CHAPTER 25

Anastasia burst through the front door of her parents home and enthusiastically hugged her brother's neck. He hugged her back then anxiously pulled away to ask what the occasion was. Mark stood quietly, just inside the door as Anastasia pulled her left hand out to show her brother her wedding ring.

"You're married?" he asked with a broad smile.

Anastasia nodded excitedly as her sister came running out of the kitchen.

"What's going on?" She looked at her sister's hand that was still extended. "You got married?" she shouted, pulling her sister away from her brother so she could hug her herself. After squealing and hopping a few times while still in an embrace, Anastasia pulled away and looked around for her father. He was sitting on the edge of his chair, watching the whole display of emotions quietly. Anastasia ran over to him. Bending down, she wrapped her arms around him and gave him a little squeeze. He returned the embrace in his usual awkward manner. He was happy for her.

"Look, Daddy," she said, sitting on his lap like a child and showing him her ring. He glanced at the ring, but then his eyes lingered on his daughter. He remembered when she fit better in his lap, not so long ago. He patted her back and smiled warmly. Anastasia noticed his eyes were glazed. She leaned over and kissed his forehead lovingly.

Mark stepped beside the two of them and offered his hand to Anastasia's father. "I hope you're not angry we eloped."

He accepted Mark's hand graciously. "Whatever makes

my daughter happy."

After a brief, but comical account of their wedding, Anastasia announced they wanted to leave for the hospital so they could share their news with her mother. They agreed to come back afterward and share a bottle of wine.

"Before I forget," Mario interrupt as they were getting up to go. "You have a package here." He went into the kitchen and retrieved a small box from the table. It was addressed to Anastasia MacDouglas. Anastasia took the parcel from her brother and looked it over carefully.

"Oh, look Mark, it's here already," she said, turning to him excitedly. "The present for your father," she explained. She took in a breath, then pinched his shoulder. "We can see him after we visit my mother and give it to him." Mark gave her a nervous smile, trying desperately not to let her sense his apprehension. He had hoped to speak to his father privately to give him the news. How could he explain to his new wife that his father was against their marriage, especially since he didn't understand it himself.

They left and drove directly to the hospital. Anastasia carefully held the parcel on her lap. "Think we should open it up before we get there?" Anastasia asked.

Mark glanced over at her, wondering if it would be wise to warn her about his father before they got to the hospital. He didn't know where to start. "Anastasia, I think I should tell you about something."

She forgot about the package and looked at him seriously. "I know there's been something bothering you concerning your dad, something besides his illness. I guess I didn't want to hear anything negative this weekend."

Mark looked over at her with awe. "How is it we are so much alike?" He chuckled, then a thought suddenly struck him. He remembered the doctors message, *in'tfesto*. He shook the thought from his head. "Anastasia, the truth is, my father has been acting strange lately. Just before we made arrangements for this weekend, he took me into his office and told me he was having second thoughts about our marriage." He paused and looked over at his new wife. She was staring down at the package in her lap. "I don't know why. In fact, he was ill at the time, so maybe this all has something to do with his sickness. I don't know." Mark stared at the road ahead. Anastasia sat silently. "Whatever, the problem is, we will work it out. I just wanted to warn you in case he said anything." He reached over and rubbed her knee. Anastasia just continued to sit, staring out the window vacantly.

They parked the car and walked quietly toward the hospital, side by side. Anastasia still carried the package. "Well, I know my mother will be glad to hear we're married."

As they approached her room, Mark couldn't keep a creepy shiver at bay. He wondered if Anastasia was even aware of how dark and gloomy things became as they neared her mother's room. There was something unsettling about his new mother-in-law. But as long as she was Anastasia's mother, he'd do his best to try to ignore it. He paused for a moment at the threshold of her room. The darkness and smell of death was almost overpowering. The room seemed to reek of evil. He pushed through the door, forcing one foot in front of the other.

Then, through the blackness, he could see the contours of her limp body in the white sheets. He couldn't help but glance over at his wife, who was smiling brightly. They both stood silently while they stared at the body and waited for that ominous current to surge through it and jolt her back to life. Then it happened. Mark watched with a sour look on his face. What was that about, he asked himself. Unconsciously, his lips curled into a painful expression.

"There she is, the beautiful bride!" A raspy voice cut through the silence. Mark winced as long bony fingers reached up and touched his wife's face. His teeth clenched as he watched his wife bend forward and kiss the cold white flesh of her mother's cheek. "And now I have a new son." Marilyn smiled hideously at Mark. He tried to look pleased, but there was no way he was going to kiss the old hag again. On the occasion of the first time they'd met, kissing her made his stomach churn.

“Mother! Look at my ring!” Anastasia waved her hand in front of her mother’s face.

Marilyn took her daughter’s hand, but seemed to be eyeing the old watch more than the ring. “Why, it’s beautiful!” She moved her hollowed eyes slowly up at her daughter, but continued to hold her hand. She couldn’t help but look back at the watch fondly. “You won’t forget to make a gift of the watch, will you?” she asked meekly.

Anastasia looked at her curiously. She couldn’t remember her mother ever making such a humble request. It was almost a plea. “Yes, I promise.”

Marilyn smiled, then averted her eyes and lost the grip on her daughter’s hand. She seemed to nod off and grow limp again. Mark remembered this was their cue to leave. He was grateful to see Anastasia bend down and kiss her mother good-bye.

It wasn’t until he had quickly stepped out of the room and was waiting for his wife in the hallway that he noticed she had tears in her eyes. He put his arm around her shoulder and felt guilty for being so eager to leave. It was obvious that the life in Marilyn’s body would soon be extinguished.

They walked down the hall to the elevators and headed for Mario’s room. Mark was feeling uneasy about his father. He was glad he and Anastasia had discussed the situation in the car. This whole ordeal with their parents was too stressful, Mark thought. He wondered if his father would ever get to meet Marilyn.

As they stepped out of the elevator, Mark noticed Anastasia was still cradling the unopened parcel. They stepped quietly into this room, side by side. His room was a stark contrast to Marilyn’s. It was bright, with sunlight flooding through the open blinds. He was sitting up in his bed, staring up at a television set. When he saw the two walk in, the corners of his mouth involuntarily curled up.

Mark was glad to see the faint smile and his healthy complexion. He looked much better than the motionless, sick old man Mark had left at the hospital just a few days before.

"Papa! You look so much better!"

Mario's smile broadened a bit, but there was still a look of sadness in his eyes. Mark moved swiftly to his father's bed side. He reached around him with both arms in a warm embrace. He was disappointed when his father didn't return the hug. He pulled away slowly.

"The doctor said your pneumonia is almost gone. He said you'd be coming home soon" Mark made his voice sound cheery, trying to ignore his father's lack of enthusiasm. He knew there was still something radically wrong. Mario just looked blankly at his son. Mark looked back at his father with mounting anger. He decided to ignore his father's blank stare and just proceed on with telling him the news about he and Anastasia. "Papa, did you hear the good news yet?" Mario continued to stare mutely. "Papa, Anastasia and I were married last Friday." At this point, he was leaning over the bed railing with his face close to his father's. His eyes were focused unblinking on his father's eyes.

Finally, Mario spoke softly. "Yes, I know this." His gaze dropped from his son, down to the sheet covering his legs. Mark became flustered. His father's behavior was such a mystery to him, and this feeling of helplessness was driving him to anger.

Mark threw up his hands in a large gesture of aggravation. "Papa, how can you not be happy for us? For me, I have finally found the love of my life. She's a beautiful, loving woman. Look at her!"

Mario continued to stare down at his lap. He was emotionally drained. Numbing himself was the only way he could keep himself from crumbling from the guilt, from bursting with the fear for his son's happiness and his own sanity. He tried pushing everything out of his mind, voiding all thoughts and letting his emotions rest. Here was the person who he loved the most in all the world standing in front of him with anger in his eyes, demanding an explanation of those things he dared not to explain.

Mario closed his eyes. "I'm sorry son," he said weakly. "I am still ill."

Mark continued to stare at his father for a few moments. He snatched the package from Anastasia's hands and tossed it into his father's lap. "This is an early Christmas present from your new daughter. We hope you enjoy it." With that, he spun around on his heels and walked out of the room.

Mario carefully held the box in his fingers. Glancing up briefly, he saw Anastasia still standing at the foot of his bed. She stood quietly, looking at the old man with sad concern. Their eyes locked for a moment. They exchanged long, sad looks. Then, without a spoken word, Anastasia slowly turned and followed her husband down the hallway.

Several minutes after they were gone, Mario slowly began pulling at the packaging tape on the outside of his parcel. He worked at it slowly. He loosened the end of the tape with his fingernail and gently pulled it away from the brown corrugated box. On top lay a familiar photo his sister-in-law had mailed him from Italy. He cringed at the idea that someone had went though his precious photo albums to remove the photograph. It was a breathtakingly beautiful view of his home town, taken from the top of a mountain.

There was something else in the package. Inside, there was a smaller white box nested in a bed of crumpled newspaper. He pulled the white box out and opened the top carefully. Inside, he found something was blanketed in white tissue. He wrapped his short fingers as best he could around the round, fragile object. Carefully, he pulled away the tissue. He gasped. There, on a round white tree ornament, was a miniature painting of the same photograph of his home town. Every detail of the little village was there, but in even more vibrant colors than in the old photo. This was how he saw the old village at night when he closed his eyes to sleep.

He swallowed the lump in his throat and remembered this was a special gift from his son and new daughter-in-law. He threw his head back against his pillow in anguish, remembering the words of the dying woman who was his son's mother. He finally admitted to himself what he knew in his heart. Marilyn was right. There was no other course for him to take. He declared to himself at that moment that the best thing he could do for his son and himself was to let the identity of his son's mother go to the grave with her. God forgive him, there was no other way.

CHAPTER 26

"Well, brother do I get a raise? Or, maybe some kind of special treatment now that we're officially related?" Stella inquired in a teasing way.

Mark shrugged. "Sure, now you get to work fifty and sixty hours a week with no overtime, too." He laughed at her frown, then spun around and moved quickly down an aisle toward the front of the store.

"He's no happy with his papa," Anthony said quietly. He was lifting a large slab of ham onto the meat slicer.

Stella looked down at him with one hand on her hip. "Why?"

Anthony shook his head, looking down at his task. "I don't know, but he ask me to get his papa from hospital today. So, I leave early." He looked up at Stella to make sure she understood he would be leaving her alone for the afternoon. "I come back to pick you up, okay?"

Stella nodded. She watched lovingly as he quickly sliced the entire slab of meat with remarkable speed and expertise. When he finish, he looked up at her. She became aware that she'd been staring. Anthony darted his eyes around the store, then reached up and kissed her on the lips quickly. Stella smiled at his timid ways, then realized this was part of her attraction to him. He was like her little bulldog— loyal, loving, and protective of her.

The smell of tuna filled the air, making her feel sick, yet

hungry. For Anastasia, being pregnant seemed to involve a multitude of conflicting emotions. She paused when she heard someone on the stairway outside her apartment. Mark must be home early, she thought, as she continued to drain the oil off the can of tuna. She was surprised when she heard a knock at the door. Setting the can down, she wiped her hand on a towel, then went to answer it.

She put her ear next to the door and called, "Who is it?" She placed her hand on the knob.

There was a hesitation before a hoarse voice answered. "Your father-in-law."

Anastasia froze. She was completely unprepared for this meeting. She didn't even know he was out of the hospital. Then, realizing she still hadn't unlocked the door, she twisted the knob, and opened it. He stood awkwardly on the landing, holding his hat, looking pale and full of remorse.

"Come in." She opened the door wide and motioned with her hand for him to enter. He stepped in quietly, with his head slumped down slightly. She closed the door and turned to face him. There was only about three feet between them, but an ocean of awkward silence. Mario wasn't sure what to say first. Anastasia was having problems reading him. She could tell he wanted to make amends, but she could sense there was something still troubling him that he didn't want to discuss. She wanted to know why he disapproved of her.

Finally, Mario thought of a way to start the conversation. "Thank you so much for the lovely gift. I will treasure it always."

Anastasia nodded. She realized he was sincere in his appreciation of the gift, but this wasn't why he was here. There was another silence.

Anastasia noticed that he was still wearing his coat with his hat in his hands. "Could I take your coat for you?" She stepped next him and began helping him remove his coat. He froze when he felt her knuckles brush against his shoulder. Her warm sweet scent drifted to his nostrils, reminding him of her mother when she was young. Anastasia pulled his coat off and laid it across the crook of her arm. As she started to pass him to the closet, he reached out and grabbed her by the waist pulling her to him in an embrace.

"I am so sorry." He sobbed into the nape of her neck. "I feel terrible for causing you pain on your wedding day!" He held her tightly. She hugged him back. "I am a foolish old man. I just want so much for my son to be happy!"

Anastasia pulled away from him enough to look him in the eyes. "Then why do you disapprove of me? Why didn't you want us to marry?"

Mario looked down, unable to answer. "I do approve of you, Anastasia. I couldn't have found for my son a more beautiful, loving person."

She focused all of her intuition and attention on the old man. "Then what is it?" she demanded. He fumbled for words, stammering in his frustration. She was looking at him like his son did when he would catch him in a lie about his mother. Mario knew she had the gift too. She could read him exactly like his son and his son's mother could do. He tried to clear his mind and remember the words he had practiced earlier that day.

"Anastasia, I was confused. I was so ill, I began to panic. If you had only one person in the world, if you were alone with only one son, you would become crazy with fear for him, too. You don't trust anyone with his heart. That was the problem. I just became sick with worry."

Anastasia continued to gaze into his eyes. She knew this was only half of the truth. He was hiding something from her.

"Anastasia please. Find it in your heart to forgive a foolish old man. I just want for us to be a family."

Anastasia softened, feeling pity for this man who she had already grown to love. He looked at her with imploring, tear filled eyes, still holding her tightly. She broke. She returned the hug, feeling a wealth of love in his arms. Whatever his reasons were, she decided they could stay private. He was too much of a treasure to let his regretted feelings keep her from loving him.

They embraced for a few minutes. Finally, she rubbed his

back and asked him if he had eaten. He shook his head and tried to get his emotions under control. "Well, I'm not fixing anything fancy for dinner. In fact, I'm afraid it's just tuna casserole, but you're welcome to stay. Mark should be home soon."

Mario nodded, feeling embarrassed for his tears. "I would like to see my son." He frowned slightly. "I don't believe I've ever eaten tuna casserole," he said thoughtfully. "But I would enjoy sharing a meal with you."

Anastasia smiled. "Good. I think that would be nice, too." She turned to the closet and hung his coat up and laid his hat on the shelf above. When she turned back, his eyes were still on her. "Why don't you have a seat in the kitchen? We can talk while I finish dinner."

Mario watched as she methodically prepared the casserole. They talked about simple things, as well as his ambitions for the store and the reinvestment of money from their apartment complexes in Italy into American businesses. His pride in his heritage and gratitude for his life in the United States was apparent in the conversation. It warmed Anastasia's heart to think this man would be her child's grandfather. She wondered if he knew. She was confident Mark hadn't told him, but she had the feeling somehow he had found out.

The casserole was simmering on low and Anastasia was sitting at the kitchen table with her father-in-law when they heard Mark unlocking the door. They looked at one another nervously. Anastasia stood up to greet him as he came in.

"Did I hear you talking to someone?" he asked while still holding her near the doorway.

She kissed him quickly on the mouth before answering. "Your father is having dinner with us."

Mark looked around. "My father?"

Anastasia nodded, still holding him. About this time, Mario walked timidly out of the kitchen with his hands folded in front of him. He stood a few feet away, looking apologetic at his son. Mark stared at him for a moment, reading his face and posture.

"Son?" He started quietly moving closer to the couple. Anastasia let go of her husband and made room for her father-in-law. "I hope you can forgive me for my behavior lately. I'm sorry." Anastasia looked at her husband anxiously, not knowing how he would react. His face was firm, eyebrows furrowed, but his eyes were piercing as he seemed to look beyond his father's features and into his heart.

Then he softened. "So now will you tell me what the problem was?"

Mario tried to clear his mind again, going though the same steps as he had earlier with Anastasia. "I don't know how to explain it. I just panicked. You know how much I love you." He paused, wetting his lips. "I just worry too much, that's all."

Mark wasn't satisfied, but he didn't want to upset his wife with whatever the whole truth might be. "Sure, I understand."

Mario looked up at him with surprise. Then realized his son was intending to discuss things with him further without Anastasia around to hear. Still, this truce was enough to make him happy. He had missed his son. They came together in a warm embrace.

"So, you're sticking around for some of Anastasia's famous tuna casserole?"

Mario nodded, grinning with happiness.

CHAPTER 27

AUGUST 19, 1974

Her pulse and body temperature had dropped so much, the doctors were amazed she would still slip in and out of consciousness. Her body was a pain wrecked, decrepit carcass she avoided as much as possible. Instead, she hovered over her husband, children, and her lost love, Mario. She remembered with fondness the time they had spent together. Somehow, his gentle ways had revealed to her, for the first time in her existence, that there could be joy in being female. His seed had rooted and flourished in her womb, bringing her unexpected happiness in motherhood. Never before had she believed that womanhood could be anything but a weakness. Never had she found a special warmth in a man's arms. For this, she still had a place in her heart for this man. Even though later, after she left him, she cursed the trap society had set for her. She hated men like the ones she had been in other lives, who put limits on her existence. But she couldn't help herself from loving the man who taught her to enjoy being a woman.

Now she hovered quietly, watching her daughter. Mark was sitting faithfully at her side as she lay writhing with pain in a hospital bed. She was soaked with perspiration. She gripped her husband's hand so tightly it caused him pain, but he sat patiently without complaint.

Marilyn watched, wishing she could be so patient. The thought of abandoning her useless body for this healthy newborn's was causing her such anxiety, she couldn't help herself from coaxing the baby into being born a bit prematurely. She focused on the infant, trying to penetrate its little body. She needed to push its shadow of a soul out and fill its mind with her own. It fought her more than any before, or was she growing weak? It was a male. She smiled to herself. She could once again be strong and dominant like her nature.

Anastasia moaned. She let loose of Mark and gripped the side rails of her bed with a ferocious pain. Her body was trying to expel this foreign presence. It caused an itchy irritation that combined with the piercing labor pains. Together, the sensations were driving her mad. Marilyn's presence was like a grain of sand in a clam shell. Anastasia's body was forming a protective skin around the infant and the offensive entity was burrowing its way inside it. Anastasia cried out, arching her back, unaware of her husband rushing to the doorway and calling for help. She was unresponsive as the nurse checked between her legs and tried to assure Mark the baby was still not ready to come. Mark looked down at his miserable wife, contorted with pain. He grabbed hold of the nurse, refusing to let her leave the room, imploring her to give his wife something for her pain.

"I'm sorry, Mr. Mattioli, we can't give her anything that would interfere with her labor. Please let go!"

Mark looked down at his hand, realizing the grip he had on the woman's arm. He released her. "When can you give her something?"

"Not until the baby's head starts out of the birth canal," she explained, rubbing her arm. Then she hurried out of the room. Mark looked back at his wife's tense, sweat soaked body, feeling angry at his helplessness.

Hours slowly passed as Marilyn took hold of the infant. She had almost succeeded in pushing his little soul out when she felt a sharp jolt. Something pulled her away. Startled and shaken, her spirit was being whisked away, out of the room and dragged unwillingly back to her own hospital bed. There, she glimpsed in horror as a group of men and women in white were gathered around her body. Against her will, she realized she was inside her own body. She opened her eyes to see those same faces above her. They had pressed flat round objects against her skin that filled her body with an electrical charge.

"She's back!" One of the nurses shouted in triumph. The air was suddenly filled with sounds of joy and congratulations. All of them were patting one another on the back.

Marilyn stared up at them with a plastic mask over her mouth and wild look in her eyes. How could they do this? She shouted in her mind. You idiots! She wanted to scream. They only gazed down at her with wide proud smiles and patted her arm with a reassuring glow. Marilyn winced as one of the nurses stayed behind to wipe the jell off her skin and cover her naked body with a clean gown. Unable to contain her anger any longer, Marilyn struck out at the nurse. It was a feeble attempt, since her withered body was nearly void of any strength. It did cause the nurse to lose her maddening smile and finish her task quickly to leave the room.

As soon as the nurse left, Marilyn saw her husband humbly walk in with a sheepish grin on his face. Marilyn glared at him with all the venom she could muster. She moaned, rolling her head from side to side. He quickly moved beside her bed and removed the plastic oxygen mask.

"What the hell was that?"

"They saved your life. You had stopped breathing."

"Get the hell out of here," she yelled. "And lock the door behind you. I don't want anyone coming in here again! From now on, they are to leave me the Hell alone."

He backed away with a confused, fearful look in his face, and then charged toward the door and out. Obediently he locked it behind himself.

Marilyn closed her eyes, trying to calm herself and focus on the room where her daughter now silently lay.

Mark, happy with the lull, sat beside his wife, quietly watching her breath. He listened to the reassuring beep of the fetal monitor that was attached to her. She was resting with her eyes closed.

Then, a surprised look of fright lit Anastasia's eyes as Marilyn began her second assault on the weary infant. The jolt of electricity seemed to energize Marilyn as she struggled for control of the child's mind.

Anastasia screamed out as she rolled and gripped the sides of her mattress with white knuckled fists. Mark jumped to his feet and watched his wife with a helpless anxiety. He lunged for the door again, shouting into the hallway for someone to help.

"Mr. Mattioli!" This time it was an old grey haired nurse who shouted back as she entered the room. "If you can't control yourself, I'm afraid you'll have to leave your wife's room." She walked past him to Anastasia. She ignored the screams and writhing movements of her patient, and forcefully pushed the mother-to-be's legs apart to checked her dilation. "Well, she's almost ready," the woman announced gruffly. "I'll call the doctor now and we'll push her into the delivery room." She stood in front of Mark with her hands on her hips and a stern look in her eyes. "I'm afraid you're too emotional to go in there with her. You'll have to sit in the lobby."

Mark nodded quietly, too overwhelmed with grief and worry to argue. He just looked at his wife miserably and prayed these people really knew what they were doing.

Meanwhile, a battle was underway inside Anastasia, and Marilyn was now gaining control of the infant's body. She struggled with all her energy to push this child's soul out and fill its mind with her own. Slowly, forcefully she pushed, enveloping its body. Then, with one final surge of strength, it was done.

Anastasia let out a breath she had been holding and suddenly became aware of herself and her husband. She reached out and clasped his hand, breathing loudly. Mark stood again, panicked by her sudden change in her demeanor. At that point, two men in a blue scrub suits came to move her to the delivery room. Mark watched deliriously while they disconnected the monitor and unlocked the wheels on his wife's bed so she could be moved. He swallowed hard, refusing to let loose of his wife's hand. He walked beside the moving bed instead, lovingly moving the sheet over her exposed leg as they raced down the hall. He rubbed the hand that clutched his the whole way, then leaned over and kissed her before she was pushed inside the double doors. An orderly instructed him to stay out. Then he stood looking through the glass window in the doors until she was pushed out of sight around a corner. Grasping his head and pulling at his hair in anguish, he sadly turned and sat in a chair lining the wall.

Quietly holding his head with his hands, he became aware of someone's hand on his shoulder. He looked up at his father standing in front of him.

"Son, tell me, is she okay?" Mario asked gently.

Mark sat up in his chair, trying to relax the muscles in his face. "She's in the delivery room. I guess everything is okay."

Mario sat down beside his son. "When you didn't show up for work this morning, I called the hospital."

Mark looked wearily at his father. "I'm sorry, Papa, but she woke up in the middle of the night. I didn't have time to call anyone." Mario reached out and rubbed his son's back compassionately as Mark continued. "Ever since she woke up in pain— it just seems to be relentless— I couldn't leave her side." He rubbed his forehead and face nervously.

Mario continued to look at his son sadly. He remembered the helpless feeling. He was sick with worry the day when his son was born. Then, clenching his teeth, he remembered that the same woman lay in a room nearby. Don't think about her, he thought to himself as he watched his son.

Mark looked up at him suddenly. "Papa, there's something I never told you about. It's about the day when I brought you here to the hospital." Mario listened intently to his son. "When I was sitting next to your bed as you were unconscious, I saw something. I think —" Mark hesitated, staring at nothing, still holding his head. "I think it was my mother."

Mario turned his head away and straightened himself in his chair, crossing his arms. Mark looked at him curiously. He wondered why his father would react so strangely when he talked about his mother. "Papa, I didn't mean to upset you. For some reason, I just remembered it and thought you might be interested. That's all." Mark stood up and looked down the hall.

Mario stood up and placed a hand on each of his son's arms. "I'm sorry, son. It's just that I loved your mother so much, it bothers me to talk about her." Then he brightened. "Are you sure maybe it wasn't your grandmother's spirit you saw? I'm sure she watches over you, always."

Mark hunched his shoulders. "I don't know." He shook his head, tired of the discussion. "I'm going to look for coffee." He wearily pulled away from his father and walked down the hall. Mario watched him with sad eyes.

The fresh ink on newsprint was a blur as it moved rapidly past him and into a separator. He had been working for the newspaper all his life. First at as a paper boy, selling the papers from a bag slung over his shoulders. Now as a aging adult, working in production. He couldn't remember ever missing a day of work, only coming in late after the birth of each of his four children. He managed to make it in on time this morning, even after seeing his wife's lifeless body being resuscitated. She hadn't even said thank you, he thought, and he was the one who called the nurse because the monitor by her bed had went flat. Instead of being grateful, she was angry. He stood dazed, almost hypnotized by the flurry of color passing smoothly in front of him.

Then he felt a hand on his shoulder. "Hey, there's a call for you." His manager delivered the message with concern in his eyes. "I'll watch the press."

He walked toward the phone silently, wondering to himself if his wife had died. Instead of a doctor, he heard the frantic voice of Stella. "Dad, Anastasia's in the hospital! Anthony's going to give me a ride there and pick up Mario on the way."

He felt an unexpected relief. "I'll meet you there," he said in his normal, unemotional voice. He hung up the phone and explained to his manager that his daughter was in labor and he was going to have to leave. His manager nodded at him reassuringly. He seemed grateful for his co-worker that it wasn't bad news about his wife.

Stepping into his car, he thought again about Marilyn laying in a hospital bed. Every morning before he went to work and every evening after work, he visited that room. Now, he wondered for the first time if he should be. Maybe she really didn't want him there. All along, he had told himself she was ill and needed him. Maybe she didn't want him. He pushed the unpleasant thoughts from his mind. A car horn brought him to attention. He hadn't noticed the traffic light in front of him had turned green. He followed the now familiar route to the hospital as if in a dream.

He moved methodically through the building to the information counter and inquired as to where his daughter could be found. The clerk looked though the pages of a large white book in front of her. Then she explained that according to her records, Anastasia was still in the labor room. He stepped away from the counter, remembering from years ago where this area was located. He remembered how it was Anastasia's own birth that brought him to the delivery waiting room last.

The first thing he noticed as he turned the corner was an elderly man sitting in one of a line of chairs against the wall. He quietly sat on the opposite end, minding his own business and quietly looking straight ahead at a blank wall. He ignored the old man staring at him. He never acknowledged someone staring at him, avoiding the possibility of engaging in conversation or a confrontation.

Soon, the staring was interrupted by someone calling his name. He turned his head to see Mark coming down the hall toward him, carrying a paper cup in each hand. "So, I see someone must of called you, huh? Sorry I didn't, but your daughter had me so worried. This being a father thing is too much!" Mark was much more relaxed. The walk had done him good. He stood awkwardly in front of the two men and offered the extra coffee to his father. "Did you want a cup?" He asked Anastasia's father.

He shook his head no, now looking more closely at the man sitting next to him.

Mark realized they hadn't met. "Oh, this is my father, Mario Mattioli." Turning to his father, he said, "Papa, this is Anastasia's father."

Mario looked curiously at the man who was now married to his son's mother. He smiled and nodded politely at the man, wondering to himself about what kind of person he must be.

"So, how is your wife?" Mario asked politely.

"She's fine." He wasn't interested in going into details. Mario nodded, then settled back into his chair. Mark had a seat between them.

Soon, Stella, her brother Mario, and Anthony came noisily down the hall toward the three men. "Has she had it yet?" Stella called down the hall.

Mark smiled nervously. "They haven't said. We're still waiting."

Mario drew his eyebrows together. "So, who's watching the store?" He called excitedly. Anthony turned red and explained in Italian he had left the head cashier in charge. Mario looked at him thoughtfully. He softened his stare and decided this was a special occasion that warranted some slack. He took a noisy swallow of his coffee.

A half hour later, Dr. Thomas pushed open the delivery room doors. He looked at the family with a forced smile, but Mark could tell something was wrong.

"The mother and child are doing well. I'm pleased to tell you that you have a son."

Every one cheered or made some sound of approval except Mark. He wanted to know what the problem in Dr. Thomas' face was about. "Are you sure everything is okay? Any problems?" He pronounced each word carefully, reminding the doctor with his eyes about another occasion when he hadn't been so truthful.

"Yes, the health of the mother and child are good. The delivery was normal, no anesthetics, but there was something a little out of the ordinary."

Everyone became quiet. Anastasia's brother and sister looked at each other.

"The baby was born with a kind of membrane sack covering it's body."

Both of the siblings jerked their gazes downward then back at each other remembering their grandfather's words. Mark could hear the words that were being repeated in someone's head— "witches veil." He glanced around the group, trying to figure out where the stray thoughts were coming from. He noticed his brother-in-law avoiding his eyes.

"I've never seen anything like this before," said the doctor. "But, everything else seems to be normal."

"So, when can I see my grandson?" Mario perked up, apparently unconcerned with the details of the birth.

"They will be placing him in the nursery window any time. Then we'll move the mother back to her room." Mario pushed his way to the doctor and shook his hand with a large smiling face that was void of resentment before the doctor could excuse himself.

"Well, I am going to wait by the nursery window so I can get a glimpse of my new grandson," Mario announced. There were some sounds of agreement and everyone turned to follow him down the hall. Anastasia's brother Mario followed as well, until he felt a hand on his shoulder pulling him back.

He turned and faced Mark. "So, tell me, brother. What is a witches's veil?" Mark spoke with an unavoidable direct look into Mario's face.

Mario blinked nervously. "It's just some story my grandfather told us."

"And the story is?"

Mario knew he wasn't getting away from his brother-in-law without an answer. "He told Stella and I this story about how some of the children in our family are born with a kind of veil over them." Mario tried to make the story sound trivial.

"Does the veil make these children special somehow?"

"He said they are smart children, and well, usually they're very difficult to raise." Thinking a moment, he continued. "My mother was born that way."

With the last statement, Mark froze. The thought of his infant taking after that strange woman frightened him. "Well, then it sounds like I'm going to have my hands full, huh?" He smiled at his brother-in-law and patted him on the back. They turned and followed the rest of their group toward the nursery.

As they crowded around the window they could see a nurse lowering a naked infant into a sink with a shallow tub for the baby. She began washing it. Holding it by the ankles, she lifted it up and laid it on a type of table that was also a scale. Everyone smiled as the infant began howling indignantly as it was held upside down for a few seconds. She quickly weighed and measured the newborn, applied a disposable diaper, and expertly wrapped it in a blanket.

It wasn't until she laid the infant down in a plastic bassinet that she stopped to look it carefully in the eyes. It seemed to be watching her. She shook the idea out of her head, telling herself this was absurd. Then she went to a nearby counter and made up a little sign. She walked over to the bed and inserted it in a plastic sleeve in front. She couldn't help but look at the baby one last time. She was shocked to see it's head was turned toward her and its eyes seemed to be focused on her as well. She backed away and then walked quickly out of the room.

Anastasia's father stood awkwardly in front of the door to his wife's room. He thought she would want to be included in the good news, but her threatening words were still fresh in his mind. He didn't want to make her angry by disturbing her again. He stood staring at the closed door for several minutes until a nurse walked toward him. "Mr. MacDouglas?" she asked timidly.

"Yes."

"I just have to take your wife's vital signs. I can't put it off any longer. I hope she'll be in a better mood about it." The young nurse pushed the door open.

They stood still in the doorway for a moment adjusting their eyes to the darkness. Then the nurse pulled the curtains away from the bed. They both stared at the still body a moment before the nurse gasped. "The monitor! She disconnected it!"

She excitedly moved over to the still body, grasped the limp wrist, and checked for a pulse. The arm felt cold. The nurse stood still for several seconds feeling for a pulse. Then she ran past her patient's husband and called excitedly for emergency personnel. Her patient had stopped breathing.

He stood helplessly at the foot of his wife's bed, looking at her with hopeless eyes, not knowing what to do. Then a nurse told him to leave the room and wait in the hallway. He complied quietly as the emergency personnel flooded the room with their equipment in tow. He listened to the ominous sounds of the equipment and those trying to bring life back to his wife's body. He heard a beep, a woman shouting directions and then a thump after the strong current of electricity surged through Marilyn's body. He heard those sounds repeated three times. Then, after a several seconds of silence, he heard a round of cheers. He heard one of the men yell, "Good work, Regena! You did it!"

His heart lightened. She had been revived.

Mario sat back in his chair, carefully accepting the sleeping infant into his arms. He looked lovingly into his grandson's face. He wondered to himself why he had been so worried. This child was an angel sent by God. How could he have ever questioned its right to exist?

Everyone in the room was moved by the sight of the old man tenderly holding his grandson. Even Stella had to look away for a moment before she asked the new parents what they where intending to name the child. "I hope its not going to be another Mario!"

Anastasia and Mark smiled at one another. Anastasia had combed her hair and applied some makeup, but she still looked and felt exhausted. It was only the rush of adrenaline from having the baby that kept her awake. She answered her sister. "Well, we thought about it, but that would just make too many Marios. We were thinking about Leigh."

Everyone made small sounds of surprise and approval. "Where did that come from?" Stella asked.

Anastasia shook her head. "I don't know. It just kind of came to mind one day. And, well, it is different. It's the middle name we've been struggling with. What do you think of Paul?"

Stella mulled it over in her mind. "Leigh Paul," she said out loud, thoughtfully. "Sounds kind of French, huh?"

"French is good," Anthony said, trying to be helpful.

"I think it's a good name," Anastasia's brother Mario added.

Mario Senior lowered his voice, remembering he was holding a sleeping child. "It's not Italian, but whatever you Americans like is fine with me." He spoke in a gruff voice which everyone knew was for show.

It was settled then. Everyone exchanged glances with the proud parents of Leigh Paul Mattioli.

Spirits were high and the mood in the room was joyous until Anastasia's father came back. He looked upset. It was easy to see he was bringing bad news.

"How's Mom?" Mario asked.

He shook his head. "I didn't get to tell you before, but, well—" He sat down on a chair his son offered. "I hate to give you bad news on a day like today. Her heart stopped." Everyone hushed and listened attentively. "They got it going again, but this is the second time it happened today. They're not so sure she'll wake up this time. They've got her hooked up to some kind of machine that keeps her heart beating." Stella and her brother Mario looked away sadly. Anthony put his arm around Stella as Mark sat on the edge of his wife's bed and patted the blanket over her leg. Mario senior tightened his grip on the baby and tried to fight back his emotions. The room was quiet for several minutes.

Finally, almost as if it was intentionally trying to change the mood of the room, the baby made a small cooing noise. Everyone looked down at the child in Mario's arms. It seemed to be smiling up at its grandfather with arms flailing and outstretched fingers. There arose sounds of sweet approval. Mario was amazed that it seemed to be looking at him. At first, he smiled back. Then, as the infant's eyes seemed to lock on his and focus, his smile faded to a look of alarm. There in his arms lay a child with familiar blue eyes and a haunting expression he remembered well.

CHAPTER 28

Leigh strained to see over his blanket. In all his many lifetimes, this was the first time he was able to witness his own funeral. He could hear a familiar voice, but couldn't quite place it. From the angle his mother had him tilted, he couldn't see the speaker's face. Damn, I wish she'd turn me around, he thought. Then he placed the voice. It was the same priest that had preformed Marilyn and Mario's marriage ceremony. The same had also baptized Mario Jr. How interesting, he thought. But, how did he look now?

Leigh couldn't stand it any longer. He let out a shrill cry, causing his mother to rock him on her lap. He let out another. She laid him on her shoulder. This was even worse. Although, now he had a view of an interesting couple seated in the row behind them. It was Jim with a large woman, or at least someone in a dress with back combed hair and makeup. They both smiled at him. Jim reached a playful finger toward him, annoying Leigh by wiggling it in his face. Unable to pull himself up and away, Leigh waited for him to get close to his face. Then he leaned forward and clamped down on the offending finger as hard as his bare gums would allow.

Jim made a sharp sound. Anastasia turned around to see what the noise was about. Jim smiled at her sheepishly. "That kid's got quit a bite," Julia whispered.

Anastasia smiled with embarrassment. "I think he's teething," she explained over her shoulder. When she had turned back around, Leigh couldn't help by glare at Jim, making him feel uncomfortable. After that, he kept his distance.

Leigh looked around the room as much as he could. There really weren't too many people at the gathering. Then, at the end of the row, he spotted Mario Mattioli, senior. He was sitting with his arms crossed, looking uncomfortable. He was wearing an old suit that no longer fit. He had gained a few pounds over the years, and for the first time Leigh noticed how thin his hair was on top. He was nearly bald, but the thinning strands were still a rich black color, as they had been on the day they met. There was still a fondness. Now their relationship would be almost as strong as it was when they were married, only different. This was interesting.

Mario noticed the infant staring at him. First, it made him uncomfortable. Then, after getting used to those probing eyes, he forced a smile at the child, who smiled back. Slowly, Mario's smile became genuine as well.

When the speech was over, everyone stood for a prayer. Then they lined up to say a last farewell to the corpse. Leigh pulled his neck taught, trying to see over his mother's shoulder. She was at the front of the line. Mark was behind her. Leigh scowled crossly as his father bent down and pushed his face close to kiss him on the forehead. Now his view was blocked again. Leigh shrieked loudly. His mother patted his back. His offended father took a step away. At last he could see the foot of the coffin. There was a large flower arrangement on the floor next to it.

Marilyn was wearing black vinyl, high heeled sandals. The only reason they had put those old shoes on her was because they were so worn and ugly neither of her daughters would want them, Leigh thought crossly. Then the hem of the dress was revealed. It was a long blue— wait! That was Stella's old prom dress. Leigh was enraged. Screwing his face up, he let out a howl.

Mark was watching the whole display with disgust. He just couldn't fathom his infant son's interest in his grandmother's dead body. The fact he showed interest in anything around him was already a curiosity. Their pediatrician kept preparing the couple for a child with an extraordinary IQ, but to Mark, the infant's behavior was just strange. Even so, he was resolved to love his son no matter how strange the kid was.

Anastasia patted the baby's back. Leigh decided he would rather not that she continued, so he stopped with the outburst. His father found it difficult to get close behind the infant, instead keeping a weary eye on him.

Anastasia bent down carefully, pushing on her child's back to keep him from falling forward. She kissed her mother's cold cheek. Then she stood up and turned the baby around to face her mother's body. Leigh looked curiously. He took in as much as he could while he had the chance. The makeup looked good and the hair, well, it was okay.

"Say good-bye to grandma, Leigh Paul." Anastasia whispered softly in the baby's ear, choking up at the end of the sentence. Leigh enjoyed the tickle of his mother's whisper, and smiled. The smile almost turned into a giggle.

Mark looked on in discomfort. To him, the scene looked absolutely ghastly. What was it about his own infant that felt so evil? He swallowed hard and reminded himself the infant was still innocent, and was of his own flesh.

In another corner of the room, Stella and her brother Mario talked softly. Both of them were wearing new clothes. Stella was sipping on a glass of wine. The past few months of their mother living in the hospital had the reverse effect it would've had in another family. Their attitude about life seemed to be refreshed. With her death, a new freedom to do and think whatever they liked had been discovered. Their privacy was no longer being invaded.

"You know, Stella. I just don't know if mother would've liked that dress. It's kind of frilly."

"Oh, I know she wouldn't have liked it." Stella giggled, then looked up at her brother with a devilish grin. "But what's she going to do about it?"

Mario was still apprehensive about laughing at his mother outright. Life long habits were difficult to put away.

"I looked in the basement." Stella stated. Mario's face filled with tension, but curiosity.

"What did you find?" He asked with serious edge to his voice.

Stella shrugged. "Nothing. The cabinet down there was unlocked. But there was nothing in it." She stared for a moment, holding her empty wine glass next to her face. "I know there was something in there. I just wonder what the old witch did with it."

Mario was growing uneasy with the conversation. He began looking around the room spotting their grandparents. "I think I should go talk to grandma and grandpa. They're looking like they might be headed for Anastasia and Mark." He watched them nervously.

"Fine. I'm gonna go find some more of this rot gut. I guess it's better than nothin'." Stella started moving toward a beverage table.

Mario grabbed her arm and turned her around with an irritated look on his face. "Don't you think you've drank enough? This is a funeral, remember?"

Stella pulled away from him with an angry look. "Hey, I'm celebrating, okay?" She looked back at her brother's concerned face. "Come on, Mario." She softened, feeling guilty for the outburst. "You know how much I've been straightening out. This is the first time I've had anything to drink this week."

His first instinct was to remind her that people who weren't alcoholics would go weeks, or even months without a drink, but he stopped himself. He realized that going from an everyday drunk to a weekly drunk was a start. She hadn't gotten this way over night. He reached out and hugged her.

They were still in an embrace when Anthony walked up. Mario looked up at his smiling face. Then he released his sister to him and walked toward his grandparents.

The old man slowly walked Father Roberto to the door of the funeral home. As they neared the exit, he stopped. "Here, Roberto, I have something for you," he said in a whisper. He reached inside his suit jacket and pulled out a bank envelope. Then he looked behind himself before giving it to the priest. He moved his face close to the priest. "Thank you, friend."

The priest looked up at his old friend with sad eyes. He tucked the money inside his own pocket. Now they were the only ones who knew the truth. The secret was safe.

They tried to put the moment behind them by remarking to one another about the weather. They parted with promises to talk next Sunday after church. Then Mario watched though the glass doors as the priest walked away. Saying good-bye to Maria had been more difficult than he thought it would be. Now he felt weak and alone. There was no one to share his grief with since the priest had left.

He turned reluctantly and walked back into the room with her body. People were still milling around, gathering in small groups to talk. There hadn't been too many people. Mario looked around the room and noticed one lone man still sitting in the front row, staring toward the open casket. Slowly, he realized it was Anastasia's father. His heart went out to the man. Maybe he was the only one who had an idea about the sadness he felt himself.

Mario walked toward the man, not really sure of what he was going to say. As he approached, the man continued to stare ahead, just like he had at the hospital. Anyone else would've thought they were being snubbed, but Mario knew there was something else. This man was alone now, too. Mario realized that the man was dealing with his feelings the only way he knew how. He was ignoring them.

"I'm sorry to disturb you," Mario said tenderly. The man responded by changing the object of his hardened gaze. He lowered his eyes to his lap. "I just wanted to tell you how nice the ceremony was. I'm sure your wife would've been proud."

Mario continued to watch the man. He knew he should

get up and leave, but somehow he felt a sad bond with this tragic final husband of Maria. Was this what would have become of him if they had stayed together?

Mario was surprised when he noticed the man swallow and then slowly begin to move his lips. "Thank you." There were tears in the man's eyes, but he never looked up. Mario was filled with compassion. He wanted to do something for this man, this long time victim of his ex-wife. All he could do was look passionately into his face and reach out with one hand to pat the man's arm.

"You know," the man started again weakly. "She told me she was an orphan." Mario silently remembered she had told him the same. "I was an orphan. That's why I kind of felt sorry for her. I thought we had something in common." Mario listened to an all too familiar account, painfully. "She wasn't, though. In fact, her parents are here somewhere." He looked up a moment, then realized tears were running down his cheek, so he quickly angled his face back toward the floor. "I never did know why she lied about that." He shook his head slightly and used the back of his hand to wipe the tears off his face.

Mario was near tears himself. He was leaned forward in his seat, leaving his hand on the man's arm. The man continued. "I just can't imagine why anyone would deny their own parents. I remember my parents." He glanced at Mario with a hurtful look. "They died in a fire when I was seven. I wanted to name my first son after my dad." He looked thoughtfully at Mario. "Byron. Don't you think that's a good name, Byron?"

Mario nodded his head reassuringly. "Very good. Nice, a strong name."

They sat that way for a couple minutes, before Mario broke the silence. "So, tell me. No one has properly introduced us. What is your full name?"

The man looked a bit confused. He glanced up at this wife's dead body. There was almost an angry look on his face. He turned to look Mario in the eyes, almost defiantly. "Sean, Sean Michael MacDouglas." He pronounced each word as if it were new to him. He then held his focus on Mario with a bit of pride.

Mario reached out his hand. "It's nice to meet you, Sean MacDouglas." They exchanged smiles as they shook hands.

"Grandpa!" Mario called from the other side of the room. He was trying to catch his grandparents as they were walking toward his sister and brother-in-law. They both stopped and waited for him to catch up with them. "Have you seen your new grandson yet?"

"Just while he was sleeping. That's what we were about to do now. Get a better look at him." His grandfather looked worn. Losing a child is difficult, even a daughter like Marilyn. His grandmother just smiled sheepishly at her grandson Mario.

"Uh, there's something I should tell you," Mario said softly, looking around to see if anyone was within earshot. They seemed to be alone, but Mario waved them into another room. They both followed in quiet anticipation.

"Remember what you told Stella and I at the kitchen table last fall?"

His grandparents both knew right away. His grandmother looked away uncomfortably. "Yes."

"Well, we never told Anastasia."

His grandfather shook his head in irritation. "It was born with a veil, wasn't it?" He shot Mario a angry look. Mario only nodded his head yes, feeling a wave of guilt and remorse. "Well, I guess it wouldn't do any good to warn her now. She'll be finding out on her own." The elderly couple turned away and headed back to the parlor. They walked directly to a small cluster of people that included Mark and Anastasia, who was holding the baby. Mario walked up behind them.

"So, do I finally get a look at my new great-grandson?" The group of people parted, allowing the grandparents to get closer to Anastasia. She was smiling sweetly and holding the baby away from her so her grandparents could get a better look. No one but Mario could understand their strange expressions. Sarah looked away as soon as the child's eyes became visible. Patrick's face grew hard and cold. Curiously, the baby's eyes locked with its grandfather's in a defiant way. Patrick's jaw tightened. He had an almost angry expression on his face. Mark noticed it. He realized the old man was somehow seeing the same thing he saw when he looked into the infant's face.

Anastasia seemed to be oblivious, or at least chose to be. She continued to smile, drawing the child back to her. "Notice how alert he is? The doctors all think his IQ is off the charts. They've been telling us to prepare for a child prodigy." She said happily, holding the infant to her breast.

Mark watched the old man curiously. The only thing he could tell for sure from the grandfather's reaction was that this wasn't the first unusual birth in the family. He flinched at the thought his mother-in-law may have been born the same way.

He looked over at his wife, feeling someone was listening to his thoughts. He was startled to see the baby staring up at him. He tried to look away from the infant but found himself locked in its gaze. Familiar, blue, knowing eyes. The infant snuggled close to its mother's soft, warm breast and smiled.

AFTERWARD

Despite her grandfather's warning, Stella soon married Anthony and they had three children. Stella became a stay at home mother. She was a fussy, slightly overweight house wife. She cooked, cleaned and even taught herself to can vegetables and jam. They became a couple that was the boring kind of happy that everyone hopes to be. Her family quietly marveled at the change in her, but no one wanted to see her happiness threatened with the truth. Anthony was never to know the details of the old Stella's life. There was no need.

Both Mario and his father never married and continued to share the same house. Mario began making friends and finally achieved recognition for his expertise in deciphering ancient text. He did date, and even convinced his father to double date with him on a few occasions. For the most part, the two men lived together quietly. Life without Marilyn was easier, but they never completely adjusted to the freedom. Thirty years of abuse was something that would always haunt them.

Mark's father, Mario Mattioli, Sr., also remained a bachelor. He lived in the home his wife had shared with him so many years ago. He and father Roberto continued to share meals with one another for holidays and special occasions. They never spoke of Maria again. It was too painful for Mario. He wanted to forget all the bad truth and share only the pleasant lies with his son. That was how he kept his sanity. He loved his grandson. The two of them remained close until his death. Marilyn had succeeded in making him truly happy in his final years.

Jim and Julia moved into a new home together. The death

of his biological mother served as a type of closure for Jim. After her funeral he no longer tormented himself with hopes that someday she would recognize his existence. Sean MacDouglas, his biological father, continued to act aloof, never discussing or admitting to his part in Jim's birth. The happy part was that Jim and Julia were now a permanent fixture in the family. They had standing invitations for holidays and the children's birthday parties. The family ties were so much stronger and laughter much more frequent without Marilyn.

Mark and Anastasia chose not to have any more children. Leigh Paul kept them busy. Mark was always frightened of his son, but Anastasia only saw the gifted infant as the product of a sacred union. Mothers love their children. This beautiful baby was special, conceived in love, nurtured in unconditional affection. This precious infant and Mark's undying love was her happiness.

Leigh Paul grew to be strong and handsome. He even towered over his father. His intelligence as a child was amazing, but despite the love poured over him by all of his family, he had a private side to him that remained cold and distant. He spent most of his time by himself, doing things no one knew. He distanced this private side from everyone, never truly interested in their affairs. From the time he was a young child, he would sneak out at night by himself, hunting with rudimentary weapons he made himself and sleeping outdoors. Curiously, he did beg his mother for one item, which she finally handed over to him when he was five— her mother's gold watch.

Look for the sequel, ***Leigh Paul***, to be published soon.

PHOTO: NICOLE JABLONSKI

The Author and her first born.